Evelyn Ogbebor Iguisi

The Sin
of the
Mother

novum ◢ pro

This book is also
available as
e-book.

www.novum-publishing.co.uk

© 2017 novum publishing

ISBN 978-3-99048-398-5
Editing: Nicola Ratcliff
Cover photo:
Lucian Coman | Dreamstime.com
Cover design, layout & typesetting:
novum publishing

www.novum-publishing.co.uk

DEDICATION

DEBBIE ROOK (1982–2013),
FOR TIRELESSLY DEDICATING YOUR LIFE TO OTHERS
AS WELL AS FOR THE LOVE AND FRIENDSHIP YOU GAVE ME.

CHAPTER 1

'I name her *Iyobosa*,' said Ogidi, at the traditional *Izomo* naming Bini tribe ceremony of mid-western Nigeria. The new-born baby struggled aimlessly and unconsciously for freedom from the two massive hands of the adult male that held her high.

'She will be Iyobo for short, a name meaning "help". She will live out her name. Through her, the entire Ogidi family will shine. She will not die prematurely. She will be great. She will be the best among many. She will be a present help to her parents, brothers and sisters in times of trouble and with her help, our family standing will rise.'

The man held the baby up, showing her off to family and assembled guests. Everyone answered "isẹ" to mean "Amen" at each breath of the prayer made by Ogidi, the child's father.

'I have made my ancestors proud again by producing this twelfth child. I am really happy because the newly arrived is the only daughter amid three sons of my third and last wife,' Ogidi breathed out, taking a shy look at the woman sitting close to him at his left hand side. All the guests laughed and briefly teased Itota, the baby's mother, whom many knew was Ogidi's favourite wife.

The naming ceremony lasted the whole evening. Pieces of kola nuts and carefully chopped coconuts all muddled up in a deep clay bowl was served first. There was plenty of palm wine and "native gin". These fruits and drinks were used to offer special prayers to the god of fertility who had at that point been faithful twelve times in Ogidi's household. Holding up the bowl of fruits with eyes wide open and staring into the heavens, the elder of the group offered prayers to the gods appealing for more fruitfulness both in their homes and their farms.

'May we never know barrenness in our homes and in our farms,' he concluded his prayers to which they all answered "ise".

Men took broken kola nuts while women went for finely chopped coconut, which they all gently and skilfully scraped, using their right thumbnail and gathering tiny pieces in the palm of the same hand. They then scraped the crumbs on the front part of their heads and said a prayer for the baby and then for themselves. This ritual was their part of the blessing. The men drank the alcohol while the women drank Coke and Fanta. Afterwards, pounded yam and *egusi* soup was served to the men and a few of the elderly women. The others ate rice with tomato stew. For this occasion, Ogidi had ordered the slaughter of a goat which was a very rare treat as before he had slaughtered only chicken for naming ceremonies. While eating, they told jokes, laughed and sang, before eventually drifting happily to their own homes. Ogidi hoped that this occasion would not stir up more of the jealousy that already existed among his wives. What was important was that the naming ceremony was complete and baby could now legally bear the name her father called her, Iyobosa.

❖ ❖ ❖

After the ceremony, Itota was filled with mixed feelings. Baby Iyobo was her fourth child and her only girl. Her other three were six, four and two years old. The three boys were named according to their parents' situations at that time. Moses, the oldest, was named after the great biblical leader. The Jehovah's Witnesses who came every week for Bible study spoke most highly of him. Sunday was named so because he was born on a Sunday. For Imaduoyi, it was a response to people's malicious comments when they saw that the first two sons of Itota couldn't walk and were lame on both legs. To these unkind words, Itota responded with "Imaduoyi" meaning, "I have not faulted." She begged Ogidi to please let her third son bear this name and he agreed.

The entire village perceived Itota to be an evil woman. This was because it was believed that her first three children, all boys, were struck by the god called "Esuu" the spirit that devoured limbs, leaving the children unable to walk after being attacked. Moses was struck down when he was two years old, while Sunday suffered at the age of four. Imaduoyi was only a year old when the spirit struck again without warning.

'Why would such evil befall only one individual?' they all asked in the village. Ogidi had been summoned many times to the "Oguedion" the local palace of the traditional ruling council. He was invited to explain to the elders what they thought was a result of a sin committed by his wife, Itota. Ogidi loved his wife too much to even think she had any spiritual problem. The case had been lingering for years.

Before Itota conceived Iyobo, she had visited at least seven native doctors. She had made all the sacrifices required. The only one she found hard to comply with was when the seventh sorcerer asked to have sex with her as a way to effect a permanent cure of the disease. On that day, the mother of three had been seen leaping out of the native doctor's hut like a gazelle being chased by a cheetah. Some girls talked about it while fetching water from the village river, they said that Itota was furious and full of rage. They wondered what must have set her on such an emotional blaze.

Itota knew well that adultery was a crime against *Erimwionwa*, the family god that ensured fidelity to whom she had sworn to at the time of her marriage to Ogidi. She had knelt before this fearsome looking god and vowed fidelity to her husband. If she was unfaithful, she would be provoking the wrath of the god against herself and her children. She refused to tell anyone exactly what the native doctor had demanded of her. Her decision to be quiet was born out of a desire not to be misconstrued rather than fear. Any sloppy move could bring a curse on me and my children even up to a couple of generations to come, she thought.

When she got married, she was eighteen years old. That was the average age for girls to get married in her time. She was slim, tall, beautiful and very light skinned. Her mother, Alice, once told some people she was often referred to as "iyebo", to mean "mother of the white girl". But it was Itota's character which gained her the deepest part of Ogidi's heart. She kept quiet all the time except when she was directly asked a question.

Itota's parents didn't bother to send her to school because they believed that sending a female child to school was a complete waste of time and resources. She was from a polygamous home of about eighteen children borne by five wives to a gentleman who was the most skilful bicycle repairer in the village. Itota's mother was the second wife. She was very hardworking. The piece of farmland allocated to her by her husband was often the best and most cultivated. Bad weeds were hardly seen among the good plants. She planted cassava, maize and yams. She also had a small garden for a continuous supply of vegetables. Her barn of yams was only compared to that of men. None of the women folk could boast of a larger barn than hers. All her children, male and female, were called to the task when it was time to harvest any crop. They barned some for home consumption, saved some seedlings for next planting season and sold the rest. The money they got was used to buy items they couldn't produce, such as palm oil and clothes. Rumour even had it that Alice set traps for animals, an activity traditionally reserved only for the men folk. When confronted about this sacrilege, she justified her action by saying that she had the right to set traps in her farm to prevent invaders. She further added that if there was any animal caught in the process, she would happily take it home. Her husband had warned her several times to stop hunting, although he never refused to eat the food she cooked with the meat.

Alice, Itota's mother and Iyobo's grandmother, raised her five children, three girls and two boys to be very industrious and purposeful. The first wife who was often referred to as her "senior mate" didn't have a male child. This meant her son was the rightful owner of her father's business and other possessions. People often told her she sat on a coal of fire bearing a son when the first wife only had daughters, that is to say that she was in a very difficult position. She must therefore know a couple of strong witch doctors in case anyone was planning to harm her son through diabolical means. She also had to do everything within her power to safeguard her position as the mother of the first son as that was an enviable position to be in.

This made her very powerful, not only in her household, but in the entire village. She wanted her boys to attend school in the city. She was strong enough to do the farming in order to raise the money. Unfortunately, each of the boys impregnated the girls next door and settled in the village to raise families through subsistence farming.

'He! He! Iyobo will be as tall as her grandmother and be as plump as her mother' a couple of experienced mothers said during the ceremony.

'She will be as purposeful and strong willed as her grandmother Alice,' some of them said with a mouthful of laughter.

CHAPTER 2

'How will this girl turn out to be?' Itota often woke up in tears to ask herself.

Sometimes, very early in the morning before anyone woke up, Itota went to the back of the house to face the sky. She took off her blouse except for the wrapper tied around her waist. She knelt down with her two hands smeared with powdered native chalk, lifted to the high heavens. She cried recounting all her sad experiences and all she had been through with her three crippled boys.

'Some people say there is God,' she would say, 'and He lives up there in the sky. Other people say God manifests through the smaller gods. Others say God simply lives in our hearts. I am not even sure. But wherever you are, here are my leaking breasts as evidence that I am a woman who has just gone through the agony of childbirth. Every mother wants to be the mother of a healthy child, whether the child is beautiful or not. This early morning, I see the evidence of your existence through the breeze that freely blows, the river that finely flows and the tree that sweetly sways, all announcing your greatness. I can hear the whistling birds. I can see the evidence of dew by little water droplets formed on the grasses. I can hear the innocent cry of other new-born babies. Though I cannot physically see you, I know you are somewhere. Please let this child walk like a normal child. Give her a good heart to take care of her brothers when I am old or gone to the ancestors. I don't know if these boys will be able to find good-hearted wives to care for them the way I do now, but make this girl the one who will fill my shoes. Bless my husband Ogidi. Bless his other two wives. Prosper all of us. Let my husband continue to love me more and more no matter the jealousy of the others.' She completed her prayer by saying "isẹ".

This wasn't just prayer time, it was one of the few moments when Itota had time for soul deep peace, no interruptions, no accusation. Perhaps the gods weren't listening, but she didn't mind, when the ritual was finished, her burden no longer weighed on her shoulders, she had the strength to carry on for that day.

When she got back inside the house, she poured some alcoholic drink into the different white-painted pots stacked up amidst other pots representing different gods. She then topped up the water in the clay pots which now stank, because of constant topping up instead of totally renewing the water. She then promised the gods that if the children walked, she would come back to sacrifice a goat to them, as if to bribe them. Everywhere went dead silent after her daily prayer, as if the gods themselves decided to be quiet for a while before responding. Yet none of the gods spoke. None of the three boys walked.

For most people in the village, it was difficult to understand the root of Itota's strength and drive to move on in life. 'Living with one crippled child was already a handful but having three of them was a nightmare,' they often gossiped.

❖ ❖ ❖

After her prayer routine, Itota took the long broom, made of bamboo twigs and branches of bamboo trees, bound together with very strong rope, which was often reserved to sweep the outside part of the house. She swept the entire compound, then went to the kitchen which was situated at the back of the main house. Returning to the building behind the main house, she swept off the ashes and charcoal of the day before and polished the entire kitchen building with the thick milky mud which she applied skillfully, via a piece of cloth set aside for that purpose. As Ogidi's third and last wife, this task was hers. There would be complaints at Ogidi's door if it wasn't done. Itota had been doing this in her own home before she got married, so she considered it no great imposition. She loved to see everywhere looking nice and clean.

After the morning cleaning, she put water in the huge cooking pot meant for only boiling water before proceeding to prepare porridge for her baby.

The hardest part of Itota's chores was cleaning up her sons. With no help of any type from anybody, Itota looked for ways to simplify the daily emotional and physical task.

The water in the big family pot was now boiling. Itota poured this into a big bucket, which she mixed with cool water in the big basin outside. Itota found no problem about using this water for other purposes in the house, other than drinking. It was rain water gathered for the purpose of washing dishes and taking one's bath and of course the washing of clothes.

She then boiled some of the water in a clean large cooking pot. She allowed the water to cool, putting a piece of allum in the water to help settle the residues. She then filtered the water with a clean piece of white cloth which she kept for that purpose. This treated water was finally stored in a large round bottom clay pot which sat behind the front door and this water was used for drinking. The lid was a flat aluminium plate on which sat a clean plastic mug which served everybody but was cleaned and replaced every morning.

Itota hated to see her children get up abruptly when they were woken up. To avoid this, while the children still slept, she sang gently without thinking of the meaning of the song:

'Omọmọ n' ukeghede, do ọmọ n' ukeghede, gie era renẹ u ke ghaviẹ, gie iyuẹ renẹ uke gha viẹ, n' u ghẹ kha ghi me mwọn gbuẹ omwinmwẹn oo ọmọmọ ne ukeghede,'

She then sang using each of their names depending on the one whose turn it was to take a bath. If it was Moses' turn, she sang:

'Moses nu keghede, Moses nu keghede. Gie erha rene'

As she sang softly, she took off the clothes of her first born child as if he would break if she didn't use that much gentility. She looked into his sleepy eyes with utmost tenderness. She ran her fingers through his hair, a smile tugged her lips. She had allowed his hair to grow a bit. He declared he would like to keep his hair afro style.

'It seems this is now becoming a bit too hard to comb, my son' Itota said to her son, when she was sure he had opened his eyes.

'Those people who have big afro endure pain when combing their hair but you hate the pain,' she teased him laughing.

'No Mum, I am alright,' said the six year old.

'Moses, my son, you often say you want to be a musician when you grow up. When you start to play your music, I will dance and dance until I get really tired. No, never will I be tired of dancing. I will just keep dancing for as long as you play,' she said to Moses who was now wide awake.

'Yes, Mum. I will play like Victor Uwaifo and I K Dairo and Ebenezer Obey and Osadebe and,' he struggled to continue to name the popular Nigerian artists of the time.

The morning chores for the mother of four continued as she gently pulled her first son out of bed. It was easier when he was much younger. Now, pulling him into the big basin was becoming more and more difficult. Moses had often told his mother to leave him and that he would crawl into the basin by himself. She refused. That was a sight Itota couldn't cope with. Well, not yet. She repeated this task for all three children. However, when Moses got older, she gave in, as she could no longer lift him up. She prayed and wished that one day, she would get an *ikeke uke,* a wooden, specially designed tricycle for the handicapped, which was sold only in the city. She had been told the best ones were brought in from the northern part of the country where there were many cases of the attacks from the wicked god, who shrank the limbs of little children. She would have to stress to Ogidi about the need to buy these tricycles, she concluded within herself.

Itota could not go to farm like the other women because of her children, although she managed a small vegetable garden right at the back of the house. She took delight in clearing the grasses and keeping it clean when the children were playing on their own. She would have loved to go on to full time farming and make some money in order to send her children to school in the city.

The children's clothes were often washed, arranged and finely laid in a big basket made for that purpose. She put all the trousers in one basket and the shirts in another. Some of these hand-me-down clothes were very old and tattered from being passed from one child to the other, as they had been used by many children before reaching Iyobo's.

After washing her children with native intertwined sponge and the local soap known as *Evbakhu'Edo,* she hydrated their skin with *Ediangbon,* a special oil extracted from palm kernels. She combed their hair with the *Oyiyeran* wooden comb. The most painful part was when she had to take them from the courtyard to the main house. As they grew bigger, the clean clothes were all soiled so easily as they struggled, mother and children.

The handicap situation of the boys never prevented them from enjoying a good playtime or games among themselves. Their favourite was the "military game". Moses gave the command to which Sunday and Imaduoyi responded. They all held their limp feet, heads up, chests out, lifting each limb and pushing forward on their bums at the same time. They all chanted in unison, 'left, right, left, right, left, right,' until they got to the destination Moses commanded. It depended on his mood. If he was very happy, he could do it up to half of the harem and on some days, they would do the length and breadth of the whole harem. They all ate and drank together there, with the juice of fruits and oil of food soiling their clothes. When they were tired, their mother picked them up one by one and gave them a good wash before tucking them up into their beds.

CHAPTER 3

The screeching noise of cutlass announced that Ogidi was ready for the day. Ogidi's daily routine was very different from Itota's.

Most of the village men left for the farm as early as 4 am, Ogidi went to farm sometimes at 6 am.

A normal day for the other sons of Ogidi who were of school age was very different from that of Itota's children. For the children of the other two wives, they were at school between 8 am and 2 pm before joining their parents on the farm. After school, they went straight home as soon as they closed from school, to eat. After eating, they took water to top up what their parents took with them to the farm in the morning.

Food was often served at the *Okhogbo,* a hut built on the farm for eating, drinking and resting. Roasted yams, plantains, cocoyams, bush meat and loads of fruits, were just a few appetising meals the children looked forward to when they joined their parents at the farm. The young girls harvested the vegetables, if they were on holiday. If this was a bounteous harvest, they could sell a few baskets in the village market. They then saved the money to make beautiful clothes or to buy themselves sweeties brought to the market from the city.

The early morning rise of Itota had been a major complaint of the other wives. They thought she did all that to win the heart of their husband. They said that Itota disturbed them with her heap of problems. They often reminded her that she did the crime and should quietly do her time, without laying burdens on other people who wanted to get a good sleep. In other words, they were saying that her sin had paralysed her three sons. Their best way of conveying this was through a cliché:

'*Amarukhọ, Aiwukhọ",*,' to say that she deserved the condition she found herself, to which Itota would also reply in a song.

'*Imara maduoyi o, owẹ ni zẹ vbotỌ (2)*
Oreremwẹn ni yeo, owẹ ni zẹ vbotỌ
Owẹ ni zẹ vbotỌ si eghian re o,
owẹ ni zẹ vbotỌ'

With this song, she replied that she had not committed any crime and that people were simply jealous of her. Sometimes, this malicious show down between Ogidi's wives went on for some time until Ogidi shouted, 'Keep quiet! I don't want to hear a word from any of you. Sing your selfish malicious songs to your selves.' Then everyone went dead silent.

Since Itota had started her early Morning Prayer sessions, she stopped this behaviour which she thought was very childish. She decided to ignore all negative comments addressed to her. This would allow her to concentrate more on caring for her children which was uppermost on her mind.

If a problem was too much for her to bear, she turned to her mother, who had answers ready made for her.

'Is that why you are like a wet chicken looking for where to roost?' Alice would say. 'Sit down and eat. Just look at you. You are beautiful, hardworking, the favourite of your husband. Who wouldn't be jealous of that?' she chuckles and then emits a flattering laughter, making mockery of her daughter.

One day when Itota visited her mum, they were both seated, talking about the mockery she'd been experiencing with the other wives.

'Itota!' Alice suddenly stood up and shouted, as if she had not been there all along. 'Listen to me,' as she pulled the lower part of her own right ear, with neck slightly bent and lowered towards her daughter who was sitting down. She then repositioned herself in a form which denoted she was trying to make the most important point of her life. 'Itota, how many times did I call you?'

Itota gazed into her mother's face not saying a word and wondering what she was up to.

'I want to tell you one more time,' she lashed out. 'You are no equal for those women. Their goal is to drive you out of your matrimonial home. Do not accept it. Fight it with all your strength. If you quit your husband, who is the man that will take care of a woman with three handicapped male children? Your patience is indispensable in this matter. Turn super deaf ears to them and live as if they do not exist.' She then breathed out profusely, as if she had just won a fight and then continued, 'Respect them. Kneel and greet them every morning. Help them when they need help. Feed their children if you are in a position to. But, but, do not get weighed down when they try to fight you using songs or actions. I know that one day, justice will prevail. God will hear our prayers. Those who have thrown the arrows that have maimed my three grandsons will have more and sharper arrows thrown back at them.'

'Ise,' whispered her daughter, agreeing to the prayer, while struggling to bring out baby Iyobo who had been sleeping at her mother's back.

'They will not only be lame,' Alice continued, 'they will also carry burdens which they will not be able to bear.' As she said all this, Alice changed her position and this time stood right in front of Itota. Her change of position certainly determined either a recap of what was previously said or a new point was to be made.

The 45 year old grandmother finally took her seat, but this time with her right hand supporting her chin while her little finger made way between the two sets of incisors, as she sobbed like a baby swaying her two limbs right and left.

'What have I done to my enemies?' she exclaimed amidst tears. 'Tell me, what have I done to my enemies? God, you who created the soul, you who made the clouds, the seas, the flora and fauna, you made the god of iron, the god of thunder and all other gods on the surface of the earth. You alone who can see through a man's heart. Let it be fire for fire and lightning for lightning,' she spoke out with a lot of energy, clenching her fist as if in a physical fierce fight with an adversary. She increased the volume of her voice as she said that last and then changed her tone, as if restating an already established fact. 'Children are wealth to mothers.' She then got up abruptly, made her way towards the main door, but suddenly stopped before getting to the door itself, she screamed out, 'Anyone who says my grandchildren will not be healthy, will not have healthy children themselves. My grandchildren will get up and walk because I have hurt no one else's child.'

She walked back to her seat and sat down, swaying her limbs.

She then got up from her seat walked around her finely kept room, hands folded towards her back as in a state of deep reflection. She then sat gently on the mud made bed which was well laid, with a gentle fire glowing at the leg side of the bed, to give some warmth to the otherwise cold room since it was rainy season. This time, she only stared at the burning fire.

To Itota's dismay, one more time, Alice stood up, looked deep into her daughter's eyes and said, 'Go straight home. Remember your husband won't look after the boys the way you would do. Do not worry. One day, justice will prevail. My prayer is now for Iyobo. I pray they do not descend on her with their evil claws, like they did to the other three. They will not succeed.' She then brought out a cup of water, prayed in it, put some in her mouth and spat it out vigorously as if to drown the evil beings with the fountain of water she spilled out of her mouth.

Itota had heard these same words since the calamity of her first born child, her second and then the third.

'God please, do not let this evil repeat itself in the life of my daughter,' she repeated over and over again. On this visit to her mother's, Itota's attention was overtaken by Alice's speech. While her mother still moved around in the room muttering inaudibly, Itota thought about what one of the Witch Doctors she had consulted told her was the cause of her problems. She had been told it was actually a group act to frustrate her out of her matrimonial home.

'The two first wives of Ogidi, your husband have ganged up against you. They have tied both legs of your children to a very high tree in the spiritual world. In short, this was done even before you gave birth to them. If you had come to me before you got pregnant, I would have been able to undo the acts. Right now, it's hard but I will keep trying to see what I can do,' he assured the frustrated mother of three.

'Where to?' Itota said in surprise as she watched her daughter pick up her bag in absolute rage, ready to go.

'Home,' she replied sternly, looking at her mother, as if she was ready to go and fight the devil in his own back yard. She took her sleeping baby, who had been fast asleep on grandmother's bed. She checked if she had wet her nappies made of layers of old pieces of tattered clothes, beneath a plastic pant that hold it all together. She changed the baby, then gently placed her at her back. Grandmum helped to position the baby's head in a way to allow her sit comfortably on her mum's back. She then placed the wrapper very skilfully, with utter gentleness to avoid manhandling the baby in any form. She then applied the *Oza,* a well knitted piece used to secure babies to their mother's backs. She did this with full dexterity leaving a fanciful bow at the front, just below her breasts. She picked up her purse and then the baby's bag which she hung loosely on her left shoulder.

'Ok Mum, bye, I will see you next market day, only if I can get someone to help me look after the children though,' Itota said with a stiff throat, as if forcing herself to release the words from her mouth. 'I am happy Ogidi agreed to stay with them today. Of course, I will pay for it later when the other wives get to know that our husband has been taking care of my children,' she said very slowly as she walked out through the door.

'No problem. You know why I can't come as often as I would like to. I can't bear seeing all those women who have maimed my lovely grandsons,' she said in a stern but defeated tone.

'Sure,' Itota snapped back, though not rudely.

Alice saw her daughter off through the narrow path at the side of her house. They walked together, mother and daughter without saying a word to each other until they reached the road at the end of the path.

'Okay my child, I will now go back home. I feel bad you didn't eat anything. I am sure I blew the whole thing beyond proportion and that was why it was too much for you to carry. Please my daughter, forgive me. Go home and concentrate on your children. God will keep fighting for us.'

'Bye, Mum,' Itota said, forcing a hand up, she waved to her mother as she kept going without looking back.

CHAPTER 4

Iyobo is now twelve years old. She had heard her mother say many times that the gods had been kind to her this time and that it had been her utmost pleasure to watch Iyobo, her only daughter grow up to become a beautiful and intelligent girl.

The day a group of people appeared at the village town hall, all wearing white robes, Iyobo recognised them as doctors sent from Lagos, the capital city. She had been told in school they would be sent to vacinate children in that area against polio.

The only primary school in the area was Agoba primary school with about 200 children, aged 6 to 12. There were eight teachers, comprising of the Headmaster, the Assistant Headmaster and a teacher for each class. There was also the school Administrator, who took care of the office work. All members of staff and pupils had earlier been told about this long awaited visit. They had been told that there'd been an outbreak of a virus called *Poliomyelitis*.

'This is very dangerous and we all need to know about it, how to avoid it and how to cure it.' They were told by the first official who came weeks before to announce how the event would go. Iyobo noticed there was only one woman in a team of twenty who later introduced herself as Mrs Adebayor. Iyobo fixed her eyes on her and noticed that she was small and very dark. She spoke English very slowly so as to allow the Bini male interpreter, introduced as Mr Ogiedo, who came all the way from Lagos with the crew to catch every word she was speaking. He was the only one not wearing a white robe. The group was sent by the Federal Ministry of Health to help villagers learn more about polio in order to prevent children from contracting it. Iyobo learnt, during the presentation, introduced by

Mrs Adebayor, that poliomyelitis or polio is a highly infectious viral disease, which mainly affects young children. The virus is transmitted through contaminated food and water, and multiplies in the intestine, from where it can invade the nervous system. Many infected people have no symptoms, but do excrete the virus in their faeces which could infect other people. According to the speaker, initial symptoms of polio included fever, fatigue, headache, vomiting, stiffness in the neck, and pain in the limbs. In a small proportion of cases, Mrs Adebayor expanded, the disease causes paralysis, which is often permanent. Iyobo also learnt that polio could only be prevented by immunization and that was why they came from Lagos.

'You must therefore feel comfortable and supportive when health officers come from Lagos to vaccinate your children. If you do not cooperate with us or you treat us as enemies, you will continue to have more cases of this disease,' the lady doctor said as she stopped to clear her throat, picking up a paper which she held in front of her before continuing.

'Because of the importance of this campaign, I would like to give a brief history of this disease to help you understand better and to do away with superstitious beliefs. No enemy is causing this problem. No evil people are stealing into your bedrooms and rendering the limbs of your loved ones wasted. Before now, you and I didn't know the cause. People in other countries took time to find out because the same things happening to you now, also happened to them. I will be very brief about this,' she finally paused, adjusting her small pair of glasses hanging loosely on her flatnose.

'In 1789, a British physician called Dr Michael Underwood tried the first known clinical description of polio called "debility of the lower extremities". That was actually the first time the British people recognised the disease. In 1840, in Germany, Dr Jacob von Heine conducted the first systematic investigation of polio and developed the theory that the disease may be contagious. Even though the disease was among them, they weren't sure how it was being transmitted to someone else. It was not until 1894 that the first significant outbreak of the infantile paralysis subsequently identified as polio, was officially documented in the United States of America. You can imagine how long it all took for each level to unfold. In 1907, Swedish paediatrician Dr Ivar Wickman was able to categorise the different clinical types of polio. This certainly was a great advancement. I am sure they congratulated themselves,' the polio expert said, looking into as many eyes as possible to ensure they were paying attention to her before continuing.

'They were able to establish that there were different types of polio. This certainly would make research easier.'

Iyobo noticed that Mrs Adebayor looked up at her audience, heaving a sigh of accomplishment as if she was there when all these discoveries took place. Iyobo looked up to see reactions of the audience made up of men, women and children. The children who attended were ages 10 – 12 from primaries 5 and 6 as directed by the school headteacher. Even though they couldn't quite grasp the meaning of all that was said so far, many of them started to understand that the disease which maimed three boys in one family began very long time ago and the reason why this happened in this magnitude was due to a lack of awareness.

Iyobo was pleased that all the teachers and pupils listened carefully to what was being said, although she realized that she was the only one who came with a pen and a note book to jot down the important points.

❖ ❖ ❖

Iyobo would have been bored had this discussion not affected her personally because of her three brothers, especially when Mrs Adebayor started talking about how in 1908, Austrian physicians Karl Landsteiner and Erwin Popper hypothesised that polio might have been caused by a virus. At this point, to Iyobo's greatest dismay, Ogidi was snoring, a situation which made the speaker stop talking, until people subtly woke him up. The 12 year old wished no one knew he was her father.

'In 1916, a polio epidemic in New York, USA, heightened concern on both sides of the Atlantic and accelerated research into how the disease was spreading.'

This time, Iyobo wished Mrs Adebayor was done as half of the male folks were either sleeping or simply gazing emptily at the interpreter.

'By 1948, Thomas Weller and Frederick Robbins were successful in growing poliovirus in live cells. You may find it hard to understand what this means, but it simply says that the disease was tested on something that was alive so as to find out what danger it might pose to it.'

Iyobo smiled at this and wrote something down.

'Dr Jones Salk developed the first vaccine against polio in 1955. This was an injectable and inactivated polio vaccine. What a breakthrough!' The female speaker announced with great enthusiasm.

'These people refused to give up. The more they searched, the more they discovered. I am sure we have boys and girls sitting in this crowd today who will be like these scientists. You will be the ones to bring light and true knowledge to our towns and villages.'

At this point, even though Iyobo was still taking notes, she wished more than ever before, that the visit of the polio officials would be over soon, especially after the embarrassment she had to suffer when Ogidi was snoring loudly.

'Dear ladies and gentlemen, thank you very much for listening to me. The fact is, that I would like to come to a logical conclusion so that you can fully grasp all we have come to deliver to you. I know that it is most important to deliver to you the cure of the disease, but I know that if you heard and understood how the cure of polio came to be, you would be more involved in dispensing the vaccines. Please bear with me a little longer.'

Iyobo looked round and saw three men yawning. She turned to look at Ogidi. His head was bowed down and so she couldn't tell if he was sleeping or not.

'I know it's past time for some of you to be in your homes relaxing, but please, see this as a sacrifice you are making for life long knowledge, just like those scientists worked to make the world a better place.'

Iyobo sighed and then looked towards Ogidi's direction.

'Dr Albert Sabin then developed a "live" oral vaccine against polio, which rapidly became the vaccine of choice for most national immunization programmes across the world. In 1974, The World Health Assembly passed a resolution to create the Expanded Programme on Immunization to bring vaccines to the world's children and between 1970 and 1980, Lameness surveys demonstrated that polio was widespread in many developing countries, leading to the introduction of routine immunization into almost all national immunization programmes. This was how it was spotted, that there was polio in Nigeria and in many other developing countries. This leads us to conclude that this disease has been all over the world. The first step is to give out vaccines to young people as scientists continue to improve on their research on the polio virus. Eventually, the disease will be cleared off our continent, just like the success story we are beginning to hear about from Europe and America.'

To Iyobo's delight, Mrs Adebayor finally put her scripts down and put her glasses back into an old wooden case which she placed carefully in her handbag that was on the floor at the side of the chair where she stood. Iyobo watched her as she sat down, adjusting herself on the seat.

Iyobo clapped first and saw primary six teacher, Mr Unugboro clapping too. Then everybody clapped.

Iyobo suddenly noticed a woman wiping tears from her eyes with the side of her wrapper at the far end of the hall; she realized it was Itota, her mother. She had looked several times before in that direction but saw her concentrating on the interpreter. Iyobo fixed her eyes on her mother, hoping she would look in her direction but Itota didn't.

Then Iyoba saw another official, Mr Kokobi, who got up to speak about the symptoms of the disease, giving examples of some people in his own area where children had the disease and their thinking that the gods of the land were against them. 'Some even thought it to be the evil work of witches and wizards. You must allow your children take the vaccines which the government has invested millions of naira in.'

Iyobo heard him stress this importance.

A specialist doctor of the poliomyelitis then took to the floor.

'I am Dr Coker, and I work with the Federal Ministry of Health in Lagos. In recent years, a lot has been discovered about the polio virus and we are all doing the best we possibly can to get rid of it. Like many other infectious diseases, polio tends to affect some of the most vulnerable members of the population. These are the very young, pregnant women and people with immune systems that are substantially weakened by other medical conditions. Anyone who has not been immunised against polio is especially susceptible to contracting the infection. That is why it is very important to be immunised. In areas with poor sanitation, the virus easily spreads through the fecal-oral route, via contaminated water or food. That is why it is advisable to always wash your hands with soap after defecating,' he said, puffing out a light laughter from the corner of his mouth. The interpreter smiled while relating this in Bini language.

'There are two vaccines available to fight polio – inactivated poliovirus, the IPV, and oral polio vaccine, OPV. This is a success story everyone must take on board. All hands must be on deck to ensure complete eradication of this disease from Nigeria. We are a big population and we can't afford to play with this important information. Nobody is causing it. You must stop pointing accusing fingers at each other. If there are people who already have it, you must support them. It is a very challenging situation to be in,' Dr Coker finally concluded.

Iyobo noticed her mother adjust herself several times and wondered what she might have been thinking about, after hearing all these facts about polio.

After the explanation from the specialists, Iyobo understood that the plight of her mother being castigated as a witch was the result of pure ignorance. She kept glancing at her mother trying to read her body language. When they had a chance for questions, Iyobo asked the doctor what she needed to do to become a doctor, in order to join the team fighting against the dreary disease.

Dr Coker simply smiled and kept smiling as he admired the courage and sincerity this 12 year old put into that question.

CHAPTER 5

Moses was now 18 and almost a full grown man. His father had suggested Moses learn how to mend shoes, and do so in front of the house since going to work the farm was impossibile because of his disability. Ogidi's inspiration for this was from Chike, an Ibo man from Umuofia, in the eastern part of the country, who had settled in the village almost two decades ago. Chike had a special machine for fixing the shoes right. People with broken shoes came to him and Chike fixed them with ease. His talent had impressed Ogidi and he wanted one of his sons to learn the trade.

Ogidi was disappointed when he learnt that Moses didn't want to become a shoe repairer, his dream was to become a musician like Victor Uwaifo, one of the most famous musicians of their time. Ogidi had records of Victor Uwaifo, who was gifted at playing several instruments, and had seen Moses listen to him over and over again and wish he could just see the man one day.

Ogidi realized that his second child, Sunday, loved to sit in his wooden wheel chair in front of their house, teasing every passer-by, laughing out loud; this he did everyday, except market days, when he wheeled his wooden tricycle to the market place, where he would sit beneath the big iroko tree and beg for alms. When the day was done, he simply pushed himself to the harem. He came out of his chair and went straight into the room he shared with his brothers. Itota had been worried about Sunday, wondering what he could do to avoid begging all his life. Ogidi had been told by family and friends that of the three boys, Imaduoyi, who was now 14, looked most like him in terms of facial features. Ogidi knew that Imaduoyi's dream had been to become a footballer. Ogidi recalled that he had started playing ball at the age of 2 with the neighbours' children and stopped when he got infected by polio at the age of 4. Ogidi also noticed that, like Sunday, Imaduoyi often sat in front of the house wearing sport T-shirts with "Eguavoen" or "Oduah" printed on it. These were bought by his mother from the second hand piled clothes brought to the village market from Benin. These names were football heroes of Bini origin. They were Imaduoyi's people, his stars. He heard about them from city dwellers who visited the village every now and then. Some had even gone to the stadium to watch them play. This was one of Imaduoyi's dreams; to watch professional players play live.

Ogidi however, noticed that Itota's attention was more on Iyobo, as the mother saw the daughter as very intelligent, with potential for achievement at school. Ogidi himself, didn't see it that way, afterall, Iyobo was just a girl. 'A girl could be described as beautiful, hardworking and good material for marriage,' Ogidi often told his wife, 'but no more.' There were, therefore, no plans made for Iyobo's schooling in Ogidi's mind, as he clearly had intentions to marry her off.

CHAPTER 6

Cooking was shared among the three wives. This was done on a weekly basis. The person whose turn it was to cook, also took care of their husband in every other aspect. Itota knew that Ogidi must be enjoying her cooking and her company best, for he often broke with tradition and would sneak into her appartment, though it was not her turn to cook. Once there, he would ask for food and stay to tease, going often to the boys' room to play with them.

Though Ogidi never told her directly, exactly what he liked to eat, she knew he loved pounded yam with water leaf soup, very thick water leaf soup with *bonga fish* or *bush meat*. The other two prepared bitter leaf soup with beef, although he didn't like it, he would not say. He took a pinch and then escaped to Itota's space to fill his stomach.

The point was Ogidi set traps and each time he caught *bush meat* as it is called, he cleaned it up in the bush and brought it home to Itota. This was a simple message which she understood clearly. He expected this to be in the menu. Itota would smile and thank him.

Itota knew how to dry the bush meat on the grill, created in her appartment for that purpose, until there was no longer any threat of the meat getting bad. She would take a good portion each time to make his favourite vegetable soup. When the children were all asleep, they would play like babies and when Ogidi was through with it, he would say sternly but with laughter, 'enough of this tiger romance, you spoilt woman.' Though he would still be holding her close.

'I am spoilt? And who spoilt me?' She said softly revealing her beautiful white teeth and pink gums.

'Now, take good care of my children and goodnight. I hope those other women are already asleep,'

'Are you scared of your wives?'

'No, I am not. I am only scared of how they will deal with you if they find me with you when it's not your turn,' Ogidi teased.

'Okay, good. You don't have to rub it in. Good night and see you tomorrow.'

'Good night,' he said, releasing her hand from his.

❖ ❖ ❖

As time went by, Itota's attention seemed to have been diverted from fully pleasing Ogidi as she used to. She was told by Iyobo's teacher and headmaster that her daughter has become the brightest girl in the whole village. She was the only one who was capable of sitting the Federal Government Common Entrance Examinations in order to qualify to enter the Federal Government College meant for the best pupils in the country. When Itota heard this, she was over the moon and vowed to do her best to support her daughter.

Itota remembered the question Iyobo asked the doctor the day health officials visited their village. She knew she had to do everything possible to help her achieve her dreams. She also understood Ogidi's position in educating girls. She knew this might cause a rift between her and Ogidi.

❖ ❖ ❖

A couple of days before the journey, Itota learnt from the headmaster that they needed Iyobo's birth certificate in order to sit the entrance exam.

'What does that mean?' Itota had asked.

'This is a paper to state when and where the child was born.'

'How can you be asking me for a paper when you know that we all have our children with the village midwife who doesn't write anything on papers?' Iyobo's mum lashed back.

'Ma, when you had your child, you were supposed to inform the local government office. They would have put down her name and issued you a proof that she was born on that day. Those born in hospitals in big cities automatically have this. It's a pity this has not been standardised in our villages. You will have to travel to Benin city where you will have to apply for what is called "declaration of age" before a court official, this which Iyobo would take with her. I fear this might create a problem if you don't comply as those conducting the exam and interview would ask for this document before a child finally gets into a Federal Government College, if they pass the exams.'

The issue of her birth certificate saddened Itota. She didn't tell her daughter about her encounter with her headmaster. Although the headmaster had collected all the birth information and had promised to do something, Itota wondered if this piece of paper was meant to twist the destiny or crumble the dream of her daughter. Itota gathered later that Iyobo would be allowed to write the Federal Government Entrance Exams but wouldn't be allowed to do the interview without her proper proof of birth.

❖ ❖ ❖

On the day of the common entrance exam, Itota woke up earlier than usual to cook her daughter's favourite dish, rice and tomato stew. Iyobo liked the way her mum prepared this with *ehenbemwarie*. This was a special kind of smoked fish which had a very pleasant aroma and a taste Iyobo could not resist. Itota served her daughter some *akara* or bean cake and maize porridge in the morning and advised her to eat the rice and stew during or after her journey to the city.

'I had a meeting with Mr Unugboro yesterday and he said that ...'

Itota held her daughter's hand while she was still talking as if to indicate that she was all ears even though her attention had shifted to two bottles of Fanta she noticed were sticking out of a basket in her own room. She was sure she didn't put the bottles there. Who did? She remembered she hid some bottles of Fanta but certainly not the ones she was seeing now. Eyes fixed on the bottles, Itota noticed Iyobo stopped talking, trying to track the object of her mother's gaze.

'So what did your teacher say?' Itota asked, her eyes still fixed on the bottles, which was making her daughter feel very uncomfortable.

'Okay, come on. You are late. You've got to go,' Itota finally said, after she had partially established that it was Iyobo who put the drinks there. This wasn't the moment for investigations, she convinced herself but planned to find out where her daughter got the money to buy the drinks she hid in her mother's room and most of all, why on earth she hid them from her. Itota was ever so proud of her daughter's openness and honesty, as she was always the first to know if her daughter got a gift from anyone. What Itota didn't know was that Iyobo had bought the drinks from the village market with the 5 naira Itota gave to her when she got the best results three consecutive times in her school and had prayed and wished Itota would not find those two bottles of Fanta she had hidden there for the past two weeks. Itota had also bought four bottles of Coke and Fanta and kept them in the children's basket of clothes under her bed. It was obvious that Itota didn't know that just like her, Iyobo was planning to celebrate with her brothers if she succeeded in the common entrance exam.

'Look you must be very happy my daughter. You know how important today is for every one of us. We love you and are praying for you to come back with good news,' Itota said, wearing a relaxed face she forced herself to maintain.

Itota watched her daughter force a nod in response to her kind words.

Water in a clean bottle, rice and stew in a well covered plastic bowl, a piece of cloth to wipe her hands if she got stained by the oily food. Itota was pleased her daughter had all she needed for the jouney. She smiled admiringly towards her without looking into her eyes. She observed closely her school uniform. It was a plinted pink-check dress. Itota didn't feel it was abnormal that her daughter did not wear shoes since none of the village pupils wore shoes. It had never been a part of their dress code. However, she advised that Iyobo put her shoes in her bag since she was going to the city where more people wore shoes. Her friends in the market place had told her that walking on the hot tarred road in the city would burn feet without shoes.

CHAPTER 7

They all had to meet first at the district headquarters where the five children from the area were to amass before taking a single van directly to the venue of the exam. All the pupils from other villages were to take a Ministry of Education van which would convey them straight to the venue of the exam. In the van, when the other children talked and chatted, Iyobo brought out her book and did revision. She remembered what her Primary 2 teacher told her about timestables.

'A good pupil must know the times table from 1 times to 12 times without looking at the book.'

Iyobo knew it up to 24. She was also confident with fractions, ratios, square roots and cube roots. No mathematical explanation was too complex for her. Her only problem however was English grammar. She knew all her singular and plurals, she was very good with idioms. Her teacher once lent her a 'Student companion' which consisted of a compilation of English idioms. She had enjoyed it. The only time she had to use them was during the lesson when she was asked by the teacher. Even then, because she had read them, she never forgot them.

It was while at the Examination centre that Iyobo realised that students came from all over the country for the exam. It was then she began to understand how important the exam was and how fortunate she was to be counted among those taking the exam. She then opened her bag which, she still clung to, and brought out her pair of plastic shoes.

Iyobo noticed most of the pupils were very well dressed. They had beautiful shoes on, their long hair was well packed to the back with ribbons. The boys wore long socks that went even above the knee. Her attention soon shifted to Mr Uyi, the driver who brought them to Benin City, for the exam.

'Now listen, it is not how you look but what you know' Mr Uyi, said, distracting the 5 young villagers.

'All these children are looking bright because they are children of commissioners, doctors, lawyers etc. Many of them were born in London and America. Don't be intimidated by the way they look or speak. You are the ones to bring light and glory to your villages. Believe in yourselves and excel in this exam, you will then become the commissioners, the doctors, lawyers and presidents of tomorrow. Do you understand me?'

'Yes sir!' they chorused, bowing their knees.

'Yes sir,' they all chorused again.

The exams was in three parts; there was Arithmetic, English and General Knowledge. They were all multiple choice questions. Iyobo and the others were told to remain calm and to make sure they read through the instructions before starting to answer the questions. Each paper was 30 minutes.

Iyobo noticed there was a boy at her right hand side and then a girl to her left. They were both looking very happy and well dressed. It was the girl that attracted Iyobo's attention. The girl had very long hair, plaited in four equal parts. Each stem was done allowing a puff at the end of each thread. The bottom part of the hair was then held by a ribbon and a bead that matched her dress. All of the four hair bulbs had four different colours. Iyobo admired her and wished she had rich parents, or even could she simply become a friend to this fortunate one. She is a delight to look at, Iyobo thought to herself.

Believe in yourselves and excel in this exam, you will then become the commissioners, the doctors, lawyers in your village.

These words were taking root in Iyobo. She then looked down and attempted her first Arithmetic question. It was very easy.

There was hardly a question Iyobo had not seen directly or indirectly in the course of her revision. Her village teacher had taken time out to go through several past question papers with her.

There were times Mr Unugboro even came in with foreign question papers. Anything he laid his hands on was an inspiration for revision. This paid off for Iyobo. She was smiling after the exam. She knew she had passed it.

When they got back to Iyobo's village, Itota was at the school along with Girlie, Iyobo's best friend in the village. Iyobo was first to alight from the bus, which then zoomed off to take the other children home. Iyobo ran into the warm embrace of her mother and started telling her about how beautifully dressed the other kids from the big cities were.

'How were your exams?' Itota finally got an opportunity to ask.

'It was very good, Mum. I am sure I got all correct. They were all things I had been revising with Mr Unugboro,' she concluded.

'I would like to put on brown sandals when I am invited for interview. Almost all other children wore that. If I can pass the exams, then can I wear the shoes, Mum? Please!'

Itota gazed at her daughter for a minute and then said calmly. 'Okay my daughter, if your teacher says it's alright and I manage to sell the basin of garri I have filtered, why not. You must do your best to pass this last part.'

'I promise to do my best Mum.'

'I pray that you pass, my daughter.'

Iyobo's three brothers were also waiting for the result. They'd not been to school. Their father, Ogidi did not see any need to send a physically challenged child to school. The truth was that the school didn't have the infrastructure to cater for their basic needs. Parents with physically challenged children simply hid them away from public until they grew up to be able to beg for alms. Iyobo's dream was to change all that.

◈ ◈ ◈

Their hope increased when the results came a week later, with the results was a letter inviting Iyobo for an interview. Iyobo had achieved a distinction in the exam, having scored 389 out of 400.

The headmaster of Agoba School had been told Iyobo was the best pupil to have taken the exam.

Iyobo's excitement couldn't be contained as she went into the next level of revision for the oral examination with Mr Unugboro. Issues concerning Iyobo's revision and plans to go to the city for the interview were kept from her father, since he was opposed to her taking the Common Entrance Examination in the first place.

CHAPTER 8

Despite Ogidi's positive disposition to life, he had no concrete plans for his three disabled sons. They were not his only children. Imaria his first wife had three children. Her first child was a male who would have taken up the affairs of the dad, unfortunately, he died suddenly at the age of 2 after a strange illness people said was related to the one that struck Itota's three sons. However, the two girls remaining were doing very well. The second wife Tohan was the most educated in the family. She finished her Primary 6 school certificate and even planned to attend a secondary school in the city before she was charmed by Ogidi, who was a good friend to her father. Ogidi's constant visits to Tohan's house and constant showering of gifts on her parents and herself made her give up her future dreams and settled for the position of a second wife. However, she became the mother of the first son. She considered herself very lucky to be the mother to a first son. Tohan was envied by the first wife. Since the arrival of the third wife, Itota, both wives felt utterly threatened, as Ogidi was too much in love with Itota. Her beauty and confidence accompanied by softness and gentility in her ways and voice, wooed everyone who came across her. The two other wives ganged up against this common enemy, leaving Itota often isolated. Ogidi's controlling ability and honour-seeking lifestyle soon silenced the women who were warned by their lord and husband to keep all their thoughts about his third wife to themselves.

'Yu yu yuyu mmmust only be sssseen and not heard,' Ogidi yelled out at them one day in a terrible stutter. 'If you ca-can-can't stand her, pa-paack all your things and gegeget out of my house.

No one is begging you to stay. When yuyuyou gogogo, take your children with you. You will be at pe–apea–peace and I will be at pea pe–peace,' he said sarcastically as he struggled through each word. All his wives knew he was very upset, and when he was in this situation, he meant every word he spoke. They were all quiet.

This however, did not end the bickering and brawls in the household.

CHAPTER 9

It was "Ekẹn" day, a special day of rest for all farmers and market women in the village. The education experts were welcomed in by Ogidi to his "Otọ ẹghodo", a large space used for holding meetings and receiving visitors. There was a bottle of gin on the table. This was only brought out during exceptional visits. The whole of Ogidi's household was present at the meeting because Ogidi wanted everyone to be clear of his stand regarding education of female children.

The teachers were expecting that this kingly reception would amount to good in terms of their lobby for his support to get Iyobo to go to school. After about 15 minutes of chattering among the men, while the women looked on in solemn reverence, Ogidi broke the ice.

'I am very happy for the progress of my daughter at school. It shows that she knows and understands what she is at school to do. However, it is my policy that I will never in my life waste my funds in sending female children to school. My reasons are simple and quite known to most of you looking at me now. Girls end up getting pregnant just when you begin to pour money into their education. When they have a swollen stomach, they can no longer go to school. They sit at home and become liabilities to their family and the entire village. In some cases, you don't even know who impregnated them because they are either too scared to say and prefer to carry the burden alone or they simply don't know in case of multiple partners.'

'Sir,' Mr Unugboro cut in, 'we understand what you are trying to say but your daughter is very different. Everybody in this village knows how responsible and focused she is.'

'Yes, my colleague is right. I have been a teacher myself for more than twenty years before I became the headmaster. I assure you, your daughter is a rare gem from a rare earth. She is inaccessible by all those useless boys looking for girls to spoil. I will personally look after her. Believe me,' the village teacher said beating his chest noisily.

'You are missing the point, my brothers. How do you measure the contents of another man's heart? Every woman is susceptible to this behaviour when under a particular influence. For women who like money, they are lured with money. For women who like fame, they are seduced with fame. Others who like food are enticed by food. Do you know some are even bewitched by knowledge and the intelligence of the men?'

'Sir, you and I know that your daughter is an exceptional girl. I have told my children to emulate her in everything. Anyway, we are here to plead on her behalf. She has done very well in the common entrance and the interview is quite close. Please give her all the support she needs.' The Headmaster casually chirped in, as if expecting Ogidi to consent straight away.

'When my daughter leaves this village to school with big men's children who don't care about small people like us, who would tell her the difference between right and wrong? You find her good and intelligent because we as a family have been watching over her, but by the time she leaves, she will completely be out of touch and I tell you, that's when one boy or even a man of my age will come and confuse her, use her and throw her in the pit to rot.'

'I completely disagree, sir,' Mr Unogboro quickly dove in amidst Ogidi's words.

'Accept it or not, that's where I stand. My decision is made and it is final. Now, you tell me, show me a school where pregnant girls are accepted. Efomo's daughter got pregnant in the city and was forced to come back to her parents in the village. Idemu's daughter got pregnant right before our eyes even though we thought she was a good girl and she was trying to abort the pregnancy which almost killed her. Ewe's daughter died because she was being attended to by a quack doctor. Listen, all the money spent on all these girls' educations was a complete waste of resources. The thing is, that a man who is expecting twins can sit in class and learn and behave as if he did nothing, but not a woman. I think the government should think about special schools where ladies who find themselves in this situation would find help, get proper advice and when their babies arrive, with the help of their families, they could get their lives back again. Good as this sounds, it will not happen with me! I will never accept it in my own home. Even if there is such a school, I will not be a part of it. If any of my daughters gets pregnant without husbands, they and their mother leave my house. It's as simple as that. I think we should end this meeting," Ogidi pronounced in a firm stiff voice, forcing a smile.

'Well, it's your daughter. We can't force anything on you. But please, consider our own side of the story and let her go for the interview. She will come and redeem this village when she studies. She will also be an encouragement to other girls. It is not all the girls who study are put in the family way. Only a handful of them experience what we are talking about.'

'Yes, I know. That handful brings pain and shame to their families. Female children must marry responsibly to bring honour to their fathers. Since there is no assurance of this, my daughters will never go to the city to study. They can learn how to read and write here in the village. Good, I don't pay for that. That's fine. After that, I am out of it,' Ogidi articulated strongly by the gesture of folding his arms tightly across his chest and looking away from his guests.

For the first time, he now noticed the calibre of the audience in the room, made up of the two teachers, his three wives and all his children including Moses, Sunday and Imaduoyi. Ogidi invited all of them first, as a sign of respect for the educationists but most importantly, he wanted to make his point very clear to all of them about how he perceived the education of women. The two daughters of Imaria didn't go to school at all. They were in their early twenties and their mother was worried they still had no suitors.

Ogidi noticed that his second wife cast a glance at him. He remembered she was only sixteen when he began to make advances at her. He promised to buy her beautiful dresses and shoes. They planned to meet on their way to the farm while she went to collect firewood. Ogidi knew he was not alone in this attitude of restraining female children from furthering their education as his father-in-law also had the same mentality. To these men, female children are not good enough to be sent to school. Ogidi remembered that Tohan often reminded her father and himself that she was the life saver in the family, since she alone managed to learn how to read and write before she was married off. Ogidi acknowledged now and again that he had long been enjoying the benefit of this as Tohan was the only person capable of translating to them when they received letters from town. Sometimes, when she was angry, Ogidi heard her say that a time would come when those who didn't know how to read and write would be worse than the blind, the deaf and the lame of society. She often said all these things in anger and frustration and was told to shut up by her husband, who often saw no sense in what she was saying.

At this occasion, Ogidi refused to look at the direction of Tohan, knowing she would not agree with him. He then turned his gaze immediately towards Imaria, his first wife and the least loved. She also looked away. Ogidi was conscious of the fact that Imaria didn't even "carry the slate" as it was often said of stark illiterates. She didn't go to school at all but would like the girls to be sent to school. Ogidi had heard Imaria say that educating one female child is educating a whole community. There is a Bini proverb that says, 'Okhuo suri' which means a woman is worth a thousand people. This means that one educated woman is worth a thousand educated women because she would pass her knowledge down to the generations after her. The education of female children was the only point that brought the three wives of Ogidi together. They all said Ogidi was selfish and out of touch with societal progress. Afterall, he himself never smelt the four walls of a classroom.

'Coming to think about it; now, I spend so much money on a female child, assuming she is really responsible and she completes her studies, she loses my name, marries a man and begins to serve him. Why should I sponsor a woman to go and serve a fellow man like me? I think that's it. No one, I mean nobody in my household has the right to flout my order. That's how it is and let's keep it that way,'

These words from Ogidi brought complete silence to the place as everyone present tried to make sense of his meaning.

'I cannot, I repeat, I cannot bear my own daughter in whom I have invested gold and silver to get married, and begin to serve and worship a man like me she calls her husband. She will cook for him, serve him and do all the things women do for men after I, her father have spent so much money on her. This means the man takes my daughter, takes my money and even in some cases, takes my dignity, when he is through with my daughter and doesn't want her anymore. Now, you tell me the sense in that.'

At this point, there was absolute calmness all around the arena. Women and children kept quiet as their father lashed out the final words, while staring at Itota who was seated close to Iyobo.

'There won't be any need for Iyobo to waste her time, going to the city and taking the exam as this will be a wasted journey,' Ogidi delivered his final words.

Iyobo burst into tears. For the first time in her life, the 12 year old spoke back to her father.

'Father, I am going to be a doctor some day. I want to know why my brothers are the way they are. It's not only my brothers who are like this, there are also other children in the village and mothers who are carrying the burdens my mother has been carrying. This so called sin passed from mother to child has to stop. When those doctors came from the city and addressed all of us, agreed they were mostly men but there was one woman among them. I want to be like her. Please Father,' this time, falling on her knees, rubbing both hands together, eyes blinded with tears, Iyobo continued her plea.

'Please Father, I will not get pregnant. I will be very serious and even if you decide I should not get married, I will obey you but please send me to school. I love school. When I finish, I will build schools and hospitals in this village and I will also make sure-'

'Close your mouth with your two hands,' her father screamed at her at the top of his voice.

Iyobo swallowed her last words. Choked by her own tears; she collapsed in her mother's arms who led her gently out of the meeting.

Iyobo cried the whole day, refusing to eat. It was not until her mother promised to increase the farm production and more sales to raise money for her studies that Iyobo stopped crying. Receiving the backing and support from her mother, Iyobo continued studying for her exams.

CHAPTER 10

Even though Iyobo's father had banned the teacher and headmaster from his house, Mr Unugboro arranged to meet with Iyobo everyday for some time after school. With the headmaster's support, revision went very well. One of their own would be attending the Federal Government College interview very soon.

'Who knows what comes after that?' the teachers wondered.

Since Ogidi was often at work in the farm during school hours, he didn't know that Iyobo went ahead with the interview he so strongly opposed.

Their first lesson started as soon as the final school bell went and other pupils had left the classroom. Iyobo sat timidly at the corner with an exercise book given to her by the headmaster for revision.

'Where is Lake Taganyika?' Mr Unugboro asked expecting Iyobo to fumble, being the first time he was raising this subject.

'It is a Lake in Africa divided among four countries; Tanzania, the Demoncratic Republic of the Congo, Burundi and Zambia. I think it is second largest freshwater lake in the world by volume,' the girl said, as she bamboozled her teacher with a grin.

'You are right but who taught you that?'

'Remember, you gave me a book on lakes in Africa, as soon as my interview was announced, and I memorised many things. I also know names of other lakes like Lake Victoria, Lake Albert and Lake Edward. All these are called the Great Lakes, because they are the only ones that empty into the White Nile.'

'I think you are already quite conversant with the lakes. Let's talk about the montains in Africa.'

'Sir, where is Mount Kilimajaro?' came a surprising question from Iyobo to her teacher.

'In Tanzania,' came a quick answer from Mr Unugboro.

'That is the highest mountain in the whole of Africa,' Iyobo added.

'Sir, What about Mount Everest?'

'Mount Everest was formed about 60 million years ago. Sir George Everest in 1865, the British Surveyor-General of India, was the first person to record the height and location of Mount Everest, this is where the mountain got its name from. Mount Everest is situated at the edge of the Tibetan Plateau, on the border between Nepal and Tibet.' It seemed as if Mr Unugboro was showing off his knowledge of the subject, rather than focusing on conveying it to the one preparing for the interview.

'This is the highest mountain in the world' he finally concluded.

'What about Lake Victoria?' Iyobo subtly cut in, as if to test and protest against the too much use of words she didn't understand when her teacher was answering the last question.

'Now you tell me? Where is Lake Victoria?'

Iyobo laughed.

'Iyobo, I think you are over working yourself for this interview. At the end of the day, it is a secondary school entrance exam and not a Cambridge exam.'

'What's Cambridge?' Iyobo asked, now yawning with her mouth wide open and forgetting to close it with her hands.

There are two top universities in the United Kingdom. They are Oxford and Cambridge. They are called these names because they are situated in these towns in the UK. Outstanding students with extraordinary results from all over the world attend these universities.

'I will like to go to Oxford or Cambridge,' Iyobo said with excitement.

'You are over working yourself for this interview. It won't be as hard as you think.'

Iyobo was silent for a while, as if thinking of what her teacher was saying. 'Yes, you are right. I saw that yesterday. The three countries bordering Lake Victoria are Uganda, Kenya and Tanzania. The lake was named after the United Kingdom's Queen Victoria, by John Hanning Speke, the first European to see the lake'

Mr Unugboro took a pitiful look at his pupil and sighed.

'Iyobosa, it's time to go home and rest.'

'Yes sir, you are right. I must be on my way.' She knelt down to thank her teacher as good kids normally do. 'Thank you sir for all you are doing for me,' she said, carefully putting her revision papers in the clothbag given to her by her mother. She ran home as fast as she could where she met her worried mother at the back of the house getting ready to prepare dinner.

'Where is Dad?' she asked frantically. 'I hope he is not back from the farm.'

'No, not yet. Go change into ordinary clothes to avoid suspicion.'

'Yes, Mum.' They both heard salutations between Ogidi and the neighbours as he returned from the farm.

CHAPTER 11

The reflection from the mirror couldn't be more revealing. The local barber had done a good job. Iyobo's hair was well cut with a parting at the left side of her almost scraped head. Her forehead shone with oil which Itota applied that morning.

Interview day was like the day of the common entrance exam, except that this time, Iyobo had to go alone. This time, the venue was Idia College, Benin City, a very popular Girls school. Iyobo and her teacher, Mr Unugboro got there early. This time, she wore shoes and socks all the way from her village. Iyobo felt quite smart in her brown sandals and school uniform which she had ironed with the charcoal iron sneaked out of Ogidi's room.

'What if they came back from Benin way after school time?' she asked herself.

The way she had agreed with her mother, would be to tell Ogidi that Iyobo went straight to her grandmother's house from school and may not be back until late. This was if Ogidi came at a time when Iyobo was not at home. If he found out about the interview after he had expressed his opposition, Itota would be seen as flouting his orders. This could cost Itota her marriage and Iyobo might end up never going to any school for the rest of her life. It was a serious offence not to obey the law, as Ogidi had spoken and Itota was playing with fire. 'It is worth the risk' the mother of four had said.

❖ ❖ ❖

The interviewers were two white women and a black man. When she went in, the two ladies smiled but the man did not.

After the interview, they expressed their satisfaction with her performance and looked forward to seeing her on first day of term. She came out happily to meet Mr Unugboro, to whom she told all she had experienced, especially the fact that the teachers were waiting to receive her in September.

Results were announced and the British woman among them came round to Iyobo to personally congratulate her for her excellent performance. Everyone looked at Iyobo in admiration. She bowed a knee in response.

'Fantastic,' Mr Unugboro said, embracing her and lifting her up into the air. He dropped her and gave her another hand shake as if they were meeting for the very first time, his smile so wide, he appeared drunk with joy.

'The battle is almost over, my girl,' he said to Iyobo with an air of accomplishment.

Then an order rang out, surprising all of them in its military style.

'If you've been told you have passed the interview, line up here if you have your birth certificate.'

Iyobo still beamed with a smile when she brought out an envelope containing all her documents. With the help of the headmaster, they had typed out a declaration of age bearing the stamp of the school. She lined up with the other successful children. The slim looking woman with a strong English accent recognised Iyobo. 'Oh, dear, you did excellently at interview. Can we take a look at your birth certificate?'

Looking at the piece of paper in Iyobo's hand, she lost her smile. 'A declaration of age is not acceptable, I am afraid.'

The headmaster's secretary had taken almost half an hour to compose that. The woman took another look at the paper, as if wishing it could change to the real one. Iyobo watched the woman, she knew the document explained that she was born on the 21st of February 1963, but as there was no hospital, her birth had not been officially recorded, and that this document should be taken as proof of age.

This document was made when all efforts failed to convince Ogidi to go to town or send someone to go and process a valid declaration of age. According to him it was 'a clear waste of time'. The teachers had no choice but to come up with something and keep their fingers crossed that it worked.

'No, I'm sorry, we have to have proof of when you were born, or you won't be able to come back in September.' She gave the paper back to Iyobo and smiled politely, and moved on to the next candidate.

Iyobo understood what this would cost her. If she did not get in, that would be the end of her dreams as she knew her mother would not be able to pay for the state school. It meant after her primary six school leaving certificate, she would, like her brothers, have to find something else to do before a man from the village came to marry her. In a minute, she thought about all of the possibilities and hated her father. For the first time, Iyobo said to her teacher, 'If my dad dies, I will not cry because he does not love me, because I am just a girl,'

'Stop talking that way,' her teacher quickly responded. 'Your father loves you. He is just reacting to the circumstances of his time. A time will come that we will have female governors and perhaps even a female president. Fathers will feel proud to send their children to school, please my girl, do not be upset, there will surely be other opportunities for you. You are a very smart kid. You will succeed in life if you continue to be good,' Mr Unugboro said. Descretely he pulled a handkerchief from his shirt pocket to catch a tear dropping from his left eye.

Even though Iyobo understood that her father was not the direct cause of her present predicament, her frustration made her see him as the root of all her problems. The fact that the issue of her education had to be hidden away from him disgusted her. If he supported her, both her parents would have looked for another school for her. Her pain increased.

She stepped aside, her chest moving up and down as she struggled with her breathing, followed by tears incessantly rolling down her cheeks.

'Now, these ones at the right hand side, I want you to follow this gentleman into the hall over there. He will speak to you. For the others, I am very sorry, that's the end of the journey. Thank you very much for taking part in all the exams and good luck with your future endeavours.'

While Mr Unugboro was trying to talk to the official about the way Iyobo performed to see if there might be any chance for her, even if she had to wait till next year, Iyobo sneaked behind one of the buildings slumped down, sliding her back down against the wall till she was on bare ground.

With no one watching, she wept aloud slapping her two hands on the ground and rubbing herself on the red soil. She just couldn't believe that the lack of a birth certificate would be such a stumbling block to a move as important as this. This meant her dream to become a doctor was over.

When she finally sat still, questions flooded her mind. First was, 'Where do I go from here?'

She then thought about her best friend in the village, Girlie who teased her for being too full of herself. She wondered if she had been punished by God for the pompous way she had spoken to the boys in her village when they tried to intimidate her. 'What about all the promises I have made to my brothers? Oh no, my brothers must not become beggars all their lives. God, you must help me. I have promised to look after them when I complete my studies.'

Iyobo got up with a start when she felt a gentle touch on her shoulder.

'Oh Iyobo my dear, I have been looking everywhere for you. Stop crying.' Mr Unugboro offered his pupil the same handkerchief with which he wiped his tear. 'We all know you are one of the most talented people on this planet. Do not lose hope. Something else will come up for you,'

Iyobo got up, wiped her already sore eyes with the hem of her dress. She put her papers back into the envelope very slowly and followed her teacher.

Travelling back to the village was a journey to hell. Iyobo tried to imagine how her mother would feel. She thought about Mr Unugboro and all they had done to prepare for the exam and interview. She sat at the back of the cab while her faithful teacher sat in front with the driver. No one spoke.

❖ ❖ ❖

Iyobo ran into the arms of her mother who was confused to see her daughter very upset. Itota looked at her sobbing daughter as she hugged her tightly. She then quietly led her inside before any of the wives could come out to create a scene. Ogidi had no idea what had happened. Iyobo wept to see her dream crash to nothing, her hopes cut off. Itota saw that her daughter was weeping for the loss of her dream and her hopes, but she would not let Iyobo give up as she kept talking about other possibilities.

'There are certainly schools every where in the city but how on earth would I find the money to support you?'

The continous crying and weeping of her only daughter led the heart broken mother of three crippled sons to start looking for a way to send her daughter to the town.

'Even if she doesn't go to a proper school, she could learn a good trade, develop her spoken English and still be useful in future,' Itota convinced herself.

Itota particularly admired the 'salon business'. Sewing, which was referred to as fashion and design was also very lucrative.

'During Christmas season, tailors make a lot of money. A girl who is serious with what she is doing could become a proud owner of a standing machine or even two with other girls working for her as Apprentices,' Itota thought.

This occupied Itota's mind. Her sons were her burdens. They would all become street beggars, she feared. Moses tried mending shoes but didn't focus well enough to get the credibility of customers. They would all be forever stuck relying on the mercy of others.

'I don't believe this is my destiny. God did not create me to carry all these burdens. First, children paralysed and now, the only normal one is being pushed up and down. My daughter is very intelligent and hardworking. How come she has not been accepted into the school? She was rejected because she didn't have a paper of birth. What does that mean? How does that affect her brain?'

Itota wept every night and day and never stopped praying that supernatural help would give her sons and daughter a good future, which would stop other villagers mocking her.

From the day the polio doctors came to the village, Itota decided to stop seeing native doctors. The explanation given by the experts showed that everyone was susceptible to the disease.

Despite her anguish over Iyobo, Itota managed to keep care of her sons. She promised that while she was alive and well, she wouldn't allow her sons to be beggars.

CHAPTER 12

'A typical day in the life of Mrs Osagie is hectic and chaotic. To be honest with you, she would need someone very organized and self disciplined to bring order to her home so that she could go freely doing what she loves best.'

Itota listened carefully to the recommendation of a trader she often stopped to chat with on market day. She had confided in her all that happened to her daughter and this trader told Itota she'd learnt that Mrs Osagie was looking for an *au pair*.

Itota was exceptionally proud of her daughter. After a careful thought and discussion with Iyobo, Itota spoke with Mrs Osagie.

'To be honest with you, my kids are very good and they will not give your daughter any trouble. She would cook simple meals for them and do the normal household chores,' Itota seemed pleased with the city mother of four. She smiled heartily at Mrs Osagie's offer, but this smile disappeared as soon as she mentioned that after a year, she would have taught her dress making, as she had done for her previous housegirl. 'Ah, sure. That is very good and I can see you are very kind but I shall discuss all these details with my daughter and by next market day, I shall let you know what we have decided,' Itota said forcing a smile knowing that Iyobo would not accept, as there was no offer to send her to school.

❖ ❖ ❖

When Itota told Iyobo, Iyobo openly spoke amidst tears that she would prefer to remain in the village if her dream of going to school would not be fulfilled.

'My destiny is not to make dresses. I am created to help others achieve things. Mum, can't you understand? I need to go to school to make things happen. Please Mum.'

Iyobo stopped talking when she noticed her mum's intense gaze which suggested she was getting a bit off hand by the way she was talking.

'I am sorry Mum. It's just that …'

She choked down a sigh using her two hands to close her mouth, preventing any more words from coming out.

❖ ❖ ❖

'She must be a very determined girl to want to go to school. Not all children are so desperate for that. Children like her must be encouraged and all must be done to make sure she goes to school. I will even encourage my children to attend school when they grow up,'

Itota was elated by Mrs Osagie's passionate remark about her daughter. From their discussion, she understood that after a year's faithful service, and if Iyobo stayed with her, undertook the household chores and remained good, Mrs Osagie would pay her school fees. If Iyobo worked hard, it meant at 14, she could be in secondary school. Her dream of being a doctor would live again. The school she would attend might not be as good as the one she missed out on, but Itota was convinced that with hardwork, Iyobo would still be able to be a doctor.

For the first time in many months, Itota saw Iyobo's hopes return. She knew her daughter wanted to be a doctor, preventing every single child from getting polio and if there was a child already immobilised by the disease, there should be a place built for them to raise them like normal children, instead of hiding them in the house as tradition dictated. The mother of four also knew that Iyobo loved her brothers. Sometimes, Itota heard Iyobo say that she imagined they were driving their own cars.

Itota arranged for Iyobo to go to Benin City to live with Mrs Osagie as a house girl. She had gathered that Mrs Osagie was loved by all in the street she lived in. She was the single mother of four. Her children were aged 8, 6, 4 and 3. She was thrown out of her matrimonial home by her mother-in-law, who complained she was too much into money making and never had time to take good care of her husband.

As for Itota, she was ready to do everything to ensure the happiness and success of her daughter.

❖ ❖ ❖

One day, when Ogidi visited her in her apartment, Itota summoned up the courage to say that Iyobo would be going to the city to live with a woman who'd promised to see her through school. Itota knew that might lead to her being expelled from the marriage institution. 'Disobedience is worse than the sin of witchcraft,' the elders drummed into her, before she took the oath of marriage.

'I think it's a good idea our daughter goes to school because she is not only intelligent, she is also willing,' Itota said, even though she knew her words fell on deaf ears.

Itota was however not surprised when Ogidi simply ignored her and walked out without a word. He never returned to Itota's apartment and Itota never tried to talk him into the future of Iyobo.

CHAPTER 13

Fosa was born in Lagos to highly educated parents; his father was an electrical engineer and his mother a Biology teacher at the Federal Government College in Lagos. Mr Odigie, Fosa's father, was respected as a shining example in his federal government service, where he had served for the past fifteen years. He tried to encourage his son to follow in his footsteps by becoming an electrical engineer. He had graduated with first class honours from the University of Ibadan, one of the best universities in the country. He met his wife in Lagos where she was reading for a degree in Biology and Education. When they had both graduated, they had easily gained jobs with the federal government. Soon they got married, settled and had two children. They were interested in sending their son and daughter to Benin City, their home town, as they had been away for many years. They wanted their children to learn more about the Bini culture.

This decision was easily fulfilled when Fosa passed the common entrance exam with flying colours. He was accepted into Edo College, Benin City, one of the best boys only schools available. With this new development, Mr and Mrs Odigie relocated to Benin, their hometown. Their daughter, Joan, was later granted a place at the Federal Government Girls College in Benin. Fosa had long finished the West African School Certificate and was admitted into the Sixth Form in the same school. At the age of 14, he told his parents he wanted to be an Astronaut. He talked constantly and with great admiration about the Russians who were the first to travel into space and since hearing of that, he had made up his mind to be the first African to go to space.

Now 17, Fosa had a one bedroom flat in the boy's quarters detached from the main building of the house. He'd scattered posters and books on space around the flat, his advanced level books less prominent.

He had written several letters to the Russian Gagarin, and the American, Alan Shepard. Fosa was mainly fascinated by the American, because he went to space the day he was born. Fosa was convinced this happened for a reason. He was forever disappointed by the lack of answers to his letters. When he eventually got a reply from Gagarin, he was elated. He had a picture taken with him kissing the letter. He then framed the picture and put it on the wall in his room as if he had just won a Nobel price.

Flying was his passion and he bought loads and loads of magazines on space travel and planes. He understood his career would demand a lot of study and he was prepared for it.

On the day of the federal government college interview, Fosa took her younger sister Joan for the exam. Joan was the girl sitting to the right of Iyobo. Her hair was very well decorated matching her clothes and shoes. Fosa was very sad to learn that the person who scored the highest in the entrance and interview had no place. She had been completely pushed out of the system. He remembered seeing Iyobo during the entrance and the interview when he took his sister, Joan for the exam. He noticed her because of the enthusiasm she displayed. He knew there was something different about her compared to the other girls. She was neatly and very simply dressed. She appeared very clever and was looking at her books seconds before she entered into the exam hall. Months after the interview, Fosa still wanted to meet this village princess, he was captivated by her beauty and convinced of her brains. He felt a strong urge to satisfy this curiosity.

Fosa never stopped wondering why the school hadn't seen fit to take her. He suspected poverty had a role to play and that the case would have been different had Iyobo come from an affluent background. He longed to see this girl, he learnt was the smartest among all the girls who took the common entrance exam in her time.

Iyobo's one year successful service as an *au pair* was celebrated by a visit to the school, Mrs Osagie wanted her to attend. They had been given an appointment by the headmaster and Iyobo liked it, she had to as that was the only offer she could get.

'Here is the list of books and we expect to see her at the start of the school year. All information concerning school fees, rules and regulations about the school are in that official envelope I have just handed to you. You will have to make another appointment with the school's tailor to take her measurements for her school uniform which must be ready before first day at school,' the headmaster said to Mrs Osagie.

'Thank you sir. I am very sure you will be proud of her because she is very enthusiastic about school and also well behaved.'

Iyobo's face glowed with joy as her mistress went with her later in the week to buy her the recommended books. She also had her school fees paid for the year. The excitement was too much for Iyobo to contain, although this joy was dimmed when she got to know after start of school that her present school shared the same fence with the Federal Government College, the school that refused her admission after she passed the exams. She was also not too pleased with the fact that she had to go to school in the evening as she had to care for her Mistress's children during the day. Her discontentment for the evening school stemmed out of the fact that it had a poor reputation. Most of the pupils were either house girls or children of very poor parents who had their children help them sell in the markets, or in the shops during the day. Despite all this, Iyobo still had a reason to be grateful, as she had a chance to be in a school no matter the quality.

Although the Federal Government College shared the same big compound with Iyobo's present evening school, there was no connection whatsoever between the schools. One was for the rich, the famous and the intelligent. The other was for the poor, the unpopular and the less able. At least, that was how society saw them.

The tall fence separating the two schools seemed to represent an unknown force, which imposed a certain destiny on them. Even though one path seemed easier than the other, both were certainly opportunities to shine. Iyobo promised herself never to misuse this opportunity destiny had offered her. She also promised ever to remain grateful to the woman who advised her to stop calling Mrs Osagie by her daughter's name as in "Kate's mum", as is the culture of her people. She now called her "Mother".

CHAPTER 14

Fosa watched the road through the windscreen wipers. It was a very rainy day. The teenage driver drove from home to Federal Government College to see his sister in the boarding house. He was amazed to see a girl whom he thought looked like Iyobo. Bag in hand and an umbrella held above her head, she was walking towards the direction he was going to. He recognised her for the simple reason that he had been thinking so much about her of late and smiled as he considered that nature had an odd way of doing things.

Fosa slowed his blue Volkswagen Beatle to take a better look at Iyobo. Sure enough, it was her. He pulled up in front waiting for her to walk up to the car.

Fosa persisted by pulling forward again and this time, leaning across the passenger's seat and head through the window, he said softly but firmly, 'Iyobo Ogidi' as he watched her slow down her pace giving him a frosty look.

'Iyobo. How are you?' Fosa tried one more time. He realized he was becoming nervous, not knowing what to expect.

Fosa observed that Iyobo finally came to a halt, obviously perplexed by him and what he knew of her. Fosa drove very slowly and parked right beside Iyobo who was now forced to halt gazing at him.

She stared at him, only her lips barely moving 'Good afternoon sir. How can I help you? Do you know me? I don't think I have ever seen you before,'

'I see you now attend Esoba Secondary School.'

'Who are you and what do you want?

What Iyobo didn't know was that Fosa had done his homework by finding out what her surname was from the list of those who succeeded in the Federal Government College interview. Their names were posted on the school notice board.

'My name is Fosa and I am on my way to see my younger sister who attends Federal Government College, the school at the other side of your school fence.'

'I see. I have to go. I am running late for school,' Iyobo interrupted Fosa's trail of thoughts as he was still struggling to figure out what to say for the best. This had happened too suddenly. He just didn't have enough time to rehearse as he would do if he actually set out to speak to her.

'Goodbye.'

The word hit Fosa's eardrums with his head still stuck out in the car.

He took the key from the ignition of the car and stayed there for another five minutes, watching her walk away while he contemplated the features of her face and the grace with which she walked along.

'This girl is just perfect. I want to know more about her.' He thought, as he sped away.

Fosa had the urge to see Iyobo again and again and again as he continued towards his sister's school.

'Joan, Joan, my one and only sister! Come give your big brother a hug. Hey, relax that face if you want me to give you what Mum brought for you.'

'Hey, what have you been doing?'

'Now, I am here. What's up? What do you have to offer me, baby sister?' Fosa said, laughing sarcastically.

'Please give me my provisions and money. You are always doing other things when Mum sends you to bring me things.'

'Eh baby sister. You must be good, otherwise you get nothing. Anyway, don't worry, I'll give you all Mum asked me to give you, but only if you help me find out something. If you play it good, I promise to even add some of my pocket money to yours. You see how generous I can be little sister?'

'What?'

'I need to know about somebody in the school on the other side of the fence. Now listen, I promise to pay for any service. You understand me?' Fosa said, playfully with an American accent.

'Fosa, what are you talking about? What school? That's a very low state school and you want me to go find out what? Who is it by the way and why? There are no boys in that school. What's going on?'

'Joan, you see why I don't like confiding in you. You always blow things out of proportion. There is nothing going on.'

'Why then, do you want to know about someone in that school?' she said, this time a bit quieter to prevent anyone hearing them.

'Bad mouth. No wonder Mum calls you *Elenu shonshon*. You talk without thinking.'

'I am the one thinking here brother.'

'Now, tell me big brother, who exactly are you talking about? I am confused here. Oh, oh, oh... I see. Is it that village girl who took the exam with us? The one who didn't know the hospital she was born in? Oh no, she was not...'

'Stop it Joan. Do not provoke my anger. If you do, I will take all these things back home. Do you know what it is to drive all this way bringing you all these things and here you are, exercising your bad mouth. *Elenu shonshon*. One more word from you, you won't see me again and you know how busy Dad and Mum are. You'd better do big brother right.'

Joan's sarcastic laughter angered Fosa the more.

'Yes. I am looking for someone who attends that school, who probably is in the low income group, but beat you hands down during the common entrance exam to the so called high income group school. Sister, can't you see? She was simply the best.' Fosa got closer to his sister and looked straight into her eyes trying to rub it in. 'The best of the best.'

'I don't know what you are talking about. That village girl who sat at my side during the interview? I remember you didn't stop talking about her, after she was declared the best in the exams. I thought you were just having a crisis because of the situation you claimed was unjust. You simply fail to realise that there are two sides to a coin. Both sides make the coin. It was not only about the brain but also about other things. She couldn't even prove when and where she was born. So, she failed the entrance exam. It's time to get over it brother.'

'What are you talking about my little bourgeoisie?'

'Big bro, I see you have a crush.'

'Do not refer to her as 'that village girl', you must not be rude. Her name is Iyobo Ogidi. I did a little research and I am sure of that. It doesn't hurt to be polite, little sister. Come to look at it, you are also from a village. Dad says we are from Urokuosa village. He grew up there before moving to Lagos. Hello?' Fosa said, walking away to get the stuff from the car.

'Joan, let's be serious. You see, since we both spoke about this girl who scored best and disappeared, I just wanted to see her again. Guess what, I just saw her on my way down here. I can't believe it.' Fosa noticed his sister was not in the least interested in his story. He carried on anyway. 'She said she now attends the school over there. I want to know what's been happening to her. Just that. There are no strings attached. I am an innocent boy just doing the right thing.'

His sister's exaggerated laughter embarrassed him. She already had her provision bags in her hands and was waiting for Fosa to give her the cash from his wallet. She kept looking at his back trouser pocket.

'Look at you. Bad girl. Why ain't you saying anything?'

'Fosa, I still don't understand what you are talking about, jus count me out.'

'Jolossy! Jolossy!,' Fosa said with eyes on his sister's face and smiling most annoyingly, imitating the way the illiterate Binis pronounce the word "jealousy".

When visiting time ended, Fosa was happy to drive back home, deliberately taking the route on which he had seen Iyobo.

Fosa drove quietly into the big compound and parked. He came out of the car, waved a thank you to the gateman. This one, known as 'Maigard', was full of smiles while opening the gate, thinking he might get some cash off his boss's son. He stopped smiling when no money appeared. Fosa made his way straight to the flat they called the boys' quarters, where he lived on his own.

He opened the front door, went to his fridge which was standing against a white wall. After a long drink of water, he went straight to his bed and without taking off his shoes or tie, he jumped into his bed holding one of his pillows in his two hands against his chest, he tossed up and down the eight spring wooden bed, murmuring 'Iyobo, Iyibo, Iyobo,' as he drifted to sleep.

He dreamt he was the pilot of a plane travelling from Nigeria to New York. Iyobo was sitting by his side as if she were a co-pilot. He remembered that landing suddenly became difficult and as he struggled, he woke up and realised he had been dreaming.

He made up his mind to find Iyobo, no matter what. He got up and went in search of his parents, he needed to tell them about his visit to Joan's school.

He realised that for the first time, he was beginning to think about what somebody else might think about his chosen path. He wondered what Iyobo's dreams were and how she must have felt not having been given the position she deserved. He longed to talk to her.

❖ ❖ ❖

Fosa was very proud of his long green trousers and white school uniform. Only the six formers were allowed to wear trousers. The O-level students wore green shorts and white shirts. Even though he did his O-levels at King's College in Lagos, he found it very easy to adapt to sixth form at Edo College. In lower sixth, Fosa had taken Maths, Physics, Chemistry and French. He dropped French when he entered the final exams. He needed straight A's to get into any of the universities he had chosen.

He planned to go straight to the university. He had a choice of going to the Nigerian Civil Aviation Training Centre in Zaria, University of Michigan Aerospace Engineering or the Aeronautic Engineering Department in Glasgow, United Kingdom.

Fosa knew his parents were proud of his career choice, although they had initially wanted him to do medicine. Fosa stayed unmoved in his choice. They have since left him alone and pledged to offer him any support he needed.

CHAPTER 15

When they saw each other for the fifth time, they both knew there was something happening. Fosa dropped by for a few minutes when he finished school hoping to catch her on her way to class. At this point, Iyobo realised she was no longer afraid of what other's would say. One day, she even allowed him to hold her hand for a few seconds and that meant a lot to Fosa. Over a few weeks, this had grown to his putting his arm around her shoulders while gently whispering to her

'Can you visit me?'

'What?'

'You heard me.'

There were two hurdles to cross. How would she convince Mrs Osagie that she was really visiting her best friend Nosa, who lived not too far away from their home? And secondly, who would take care of the children if their mother wasn't back from the market?

The reason Mrs Osagie chose the evening school for her was to take care of the children in the morning and only when Mrs Osagie came back from the village market would she be able to go to school. So far, things had been going very well. Her feelings for Fosa had become too strong for a reason to stop them.

'You can come and pick me on Friday night. I will be under this tree.'

'What about coming to your house?' Fosa puffed out a laughter knowing her reaction.

'Don't you dare. Do you want me to be thrown out?'

'Of course, I don't. I am only joking. Remember you have never given me your house address. I don't know where you live or would you want to give it to me now?' He pulled her a bit closer.

'No, thanks.'

'I will come by taxi, on Friday,' the 18 year old said with a tone of pride.

'Taxi is certainly the best at that time of the day.'

'You will just pass in front there and I will just walk to meet you and then the two of us will just take the taxi together to go to your house?' Iyobo sounded more colloquial than ever, she shivered a little as she accepted the invitation.

Her usual composure deserted her as fear took over. It was hard to guess that it was also Fosa's first time inviting a girl to his house.

❖ ❖ ❖

Friday evening, children in bed, Iyobo finally retired to her room. Mrs Osagie was also in bed as she was very tired after the day's business trip. The love bird snuck out of the house through a back window. She left this window slightly open all afternoon to ensure her getting out and back to her room. During the day, she had purposely planted a small stool close to the wall right below the window to help her get down safely without jumping. She then planned to take a very dark foot path that led to the road where Fosa would join her in the taxi. She felt right about what she was doing but knew that if caught, it could end her dream of finishing school.

Everything well in place, Iyobo looked at the old rusted table clock on her desk. Eight o'clock. Darkness had overwhelmed the city as there was no electric power supply. The national electricity failed again, the third time in one week. Only the car headlamps and fire ants helped passers by to keep their bearings. It was also threatening to rain. The young couple planned to meet at nine.

'Not so good to get there too early. Better that he gets there before me. I don't want to appear too anxious to be with him,' Iyobo muttered as she paced to and fro in her two meter squared room.

❖ ❖ ❖

Fosa had never brought a visitor to the house before, he was not allowed to invite anyone to the boy's quarters. If they were friends from school, they were to stay with him in the general sitting room or simply stay in front of the house and chat together before going home. On this particular evening, Fosa had planned to break all the rules. Just like Iyobo, his reason could not outweigh his emotions. He wondered how he would sneak Iyobo into the boy's quarters without the knowledge of his parents and the gateman.

'Small oga, where u dey go dis night,' the gateman asked when Fosa was trying to open the side gate.

Fosa slipped a 10 naira note into the gateman's crusty looking palm, which was folded in as soon as he got the feel. His lips were pursed.

'Make you go come, small oga,' the gateman bade him farewell, with a permanent smile on his lips.

Would he have to increase this to 20 naira to ensure the secret was kept? He had been taught that men must always be strong and never give in to nerves. Not in front of a woman.

CHAPTER 16

'Have you ever done it'?

'No'

'What about you?'

'Mmmmm, let me see … listen, you never ask a man such a question' Fosa teased touchng her nose with his as they both lay facing each other.

'I am kind of scared about the way I feel. I love you but I also think I am getting too close. I really don't want to be in trouble'

'Ssh!!! Stop it. This is the best thing that can ever happen to the both of us. Don't be afraid. We are doing the right thing. The best thing any two ambitious young couple like us would do.

'What? The right thing? To be honest with you, I know we are not. There is something inside me that tells me I am going to be in a very big problem but I just can't…'

'Stop. One day, I will be rich and famous. You will be a doctor and I will be the first African to travel to space. Wow, what a record! The sun and the moon will bow down to us. Together, we will be an ideal couple. This is what you should be thinking about. I love you and you love me. This is what matters at the moment'

'What if I get pregnant?'

'You sure won't get pregnant!! Why do you think that way? Even if you get pregnant, I will marry you. I will stick with you no matter what,' Fosa said with a sense of pride, pulling her closer. She didn't resist, melting into his outstretched arms. He pulled her closer, whispering, drumming more words of assurance into her ears.

Even though Iyobo saw Fosa as too young to take responsibility of any eventuality, she felt proud and and happy that Fosa accepted to stick to her no matter what. Her heart melted.

'Fosa, I love you. Hold me' she invited him, damning all consequences for that moment.

❖ ❖ ❖

The pair later stared frantically at the blood stained bedsheet after being overcome by emotions.

Iyobo quickly covered up her nakedness that she herself had barely seen before now, when she realized the duvet she had earlier buried herself in had fallen off. She was filled with mixed feelings. It was the first strong feeling for Fosa and then self-loathing. The latter became stronger as the clock clicked on. In utter shame and self-disgust, for succumbing so cheaply to a man she hardly knew, Iyobo burst into tears.

'Why are you crying? Stop it Iyobo. I really love you, we should be celebrating, not crying. Look, you are my first and last love. I will never look elsewhere for any other. Just look, you are a combination of brain and beauty. What else would I look for?'

Iyobo said nothing, only sobs. For the first time, Iyobo looked into Fosa's eyes almost tempted to doubt all he'd been telling her. She fought the unwelcomed feeling and held on to the words she heard. She felt better hanging on, but, again, not for too long.

'What have I done?' she thought aloud in a whisper.

Fosa heard it.

'Come off it Iyobo. You have done the right thing.'

Iyobo couldn't understand what Fosa meant by saying they'd done the right thing. She had an urgent and ardent desire to flee this reality but felt trapped in a mess and somehow, she felt this mess could linger on for a very long time, if her present feelings was anything to go by.

The more she thought about this, the more she hated herself. Her father's words when she first passed the common entrance came to her like a dagger piercing her heart.

'You can't even trust any girl. What if they get pregnant at the middle of their studies? What do you do?'

She went over and over it again, all the fears expressed by her father and the ease with which she fell into the trap. She became more confused.

'Was Dad right? I think so. No he is not. He is a selfish man who thinks only about his own interest. He can't be right. I am not right either,' Iyobo struggled within her tattered emotions without saying a word while Fosa was still holding her very close and soothing her tears.

When Fosa and Iyobo left the Odigie family home, it was midnight. Time had gone so quickly. He took her hand as they crossed the road, and didn't let it go until they got to the kiosk just before the traffic light. The whole Government Reserved Area for the rich and famous in Benin City was quiet and lonely, but it appeared to be the most perfect time for Fosa and Iyobo. The street was deserted as if everyone had gone home so the two could have the whole street to themselves.

An hour ago, the sky seemed to have been angry as it rained cats and dogs but soon mellowed down as if to appease the young lovers. There were still drizzles but it didn't matter.

Between the pair, there was so much to talk about, yet there was no time now. No words, no actions could express what they felt for each other, yet Iyobo was too broken thinking about her circumstances to find anything good about the moment.

It felt normal, yet unbearably scary. For both of them, it had been their first time. Iyobo feared it might be their last time together. She had heard many times of "love'em and leave'em" situations and boasted she would never be a victim. How was she sure this same boy would not want someone else tomorrow? She found that her own questions were too hard for her to answer. Something drummed it continuously in her subconscious that she could be pregnant. She just could not fight this feeling. It was too real and too strong to be ignored. She feared the worst.

As both walked quietly along, glued to each other to catch a taxi for Iyobo, Fosa broke the silence.

'Iyobo, always know that I love you. By the way, I don't like the picture you took away from my album. I would like to give you another one and then wait for you to give me yours when we meet again.'

'I think it's alright. I like the picture.'

'Really?' Fosa held her closer and laughed. He was happy that he was finally talking Iyobo out of her cries and sobs.

'You still haven't given me your address.'

'Are you out of your mind? Do you want me to be sent out of the house because of you?'

'No. It's just that I want to know where you live. We've only met under the tree and that's not enough.'

Iyobo ignored.

'Iyobo, I love you but …'

'Fosa, do you think I do not care for you?' Iyobo giving him a look that was supposed to say so much.

'Of course I know. Then be happy.'

Fosa put an arm around her shoulder. She let him. He then planted another kiss on her cheek and gently pulled her closer as they walked along Gosio Way that headed towards the main road.

'Would you like some sweets?'

'No, thank you,' came a quick sharp reply from a distorted voice, hardly hearing what he asked.

'Come on Iyobo, take something for you or for your little ones at home,' Fosa said as they stood in front of the late night kiosk. 'Please.'

'No, I'll take nothing. I'm fine,' Iyobo retorted rapidly.

'Iyobo, listen. You love me and I love you. We may both be young in the game but we must give it a chance. You are beautiful, intelligent and kind. That's the kind of woman I want for a future wife. Look, darling, this time,' remembering how it was played in the last love film he watched, he continued, 'Iyobo, you have to let this night be very good and memorable for both of us. You are the most beautiful and the most intelligent girl I have ever met in my life. From the first day I set my eyes on you, you have not stopped inspiring me.'

Iyobo raised her head up to look at the face of the person who had been holding and talking to her as if to assess his eligibility.

Even though she sincerely loved him, she felt she had given too much away. She felt cheap and vulnerable. She realised she believed all he said without processing. It all sounded very right because that was exactly what she wanted to hear.

'Can I confide in anyone?' she tried to ask herself. No one on earth came to mind. Once again, she knew that day was her doom's day rather than a special day, like Fosa tried to paint it. For Iyobo, there was nothing good about that day.

As she looked into his eyes, a gallon more tears poured out. It was hard to know what these tears were for. Trapped between love and shame, confusion rose beyond limit. She buried her head in his chest without saying a word. Suddenly, she didn't feel cheap anymore.

Knowing him seemed to be right afterall and a great pleasure and privilege. He had everything she looked for in a future life partner, but her actions tonight had not guaranteed anything, she thought to herself.

'I should have waited and I know, he would have waited too, maybe,' she consoled herself.

Only her heart spoke. Her lips remained sealed. Fosa held her as tight as possible, whispering continuously in her ears.

'I love you, I'll continue to come and look for you,' he was not sure of his next move since he was not allowed to visit Iyobo at her house.

Iyobo still could not move but she knew time was ticking away and any more time she spent there meant more trouble.

'I just pray they are all peacefully sleeping,' she whispered in fear.

They finally crossed the road to catch a taxi. Fosa paid the driver some extra money to ensure safe delivery.

'Fosa, pray that I am not thrown out of the house for getting home this late.'

'I will. I love you. I am going to stay awake praying the whole night,' he whispered into her ears, opening the passenger's seat in front,

He then forcefully planted some money in her hands, for any emergency and then waved as the impatient driver screeched off in his old saloon car. Iyobo waved and Fosa blew a kiss followed by a wave of the hand.

CHAPTER 17

Iyobo got home much later than she had planned. She was scared to death. She thought Mrs Osagie might be all over the place looking for her, but she caught herself in a hypocritical smile as she remembered how much confidence and trust Mrs Osagie had placed on her since she started living with her.

'Other girls would have boyfriends and spoil themselves, but not our Iyobo,' Mrs Osagie told her mother every time they met at their village market.

'Learn from her manners and dedication to her book work,' she lashed out at other girls in the area.

Iyobo snuck back into her room through the back window she had left half open. She was convinced no one knew that she went out, since everything was the way she left it. She quietly undressed and lay on her bed facing the ceiling. The memories of the evening came pouring in like wild fire. She thought of how kind and gentle Fosa was to her but all the good thoughts were short-lived.

'What if I am really pregnant?' she kept asking herself.

She had learnt in the school's sex education lessons that a girl could get pregnant from a single sexual encounter.

'No, it can't be,' she convinced herself. Her last biology lesson rushed through her memory like a tide of the sea. The voice of her teacher added to the agony as she heard in her head.

'One relationship could get you pregnant and if you are not ready, this could change your life forever.'

Iyobo let this class scene run through her mind like wild fire bringing more anguish into her life. She wanted to curse out loud having made such a serious blunder.

'Why have I fallen into this mess?'

Her thoughts shifted to her Bible Knowledge teacher who tenderly and jokingly said to them one day, 'Now that you have become teenagers, it's often time for exploration. Be wise and always look before you leap. There is no emotion that cannot be controlled. Play it smart. Always make a better choice for yourself. If possible, run and run and keep running.' She remembered that speech had earned the teacher the nickname "Miss Keep Running".

The question as to whether she had contracted the AIDS virus was too dark to even imagine. She could not imagine that a girl as intelligent and smart as she thought she was could be lured into bed in a couple of hours.

In a flash, Iyobo saw the possible effects of her actions on her mum that she might have proved her dad's stance of no education for his daughter, may have been proven right.

'What a bitter taste of life this is,' she thought. 'What about my brothers who might die beggars and a community that would continue to drown in ill health, superstition and poverty, just because I have made...' she suddenly stopped as her mind drifted to the man she respected most in the village.

'What about Mr Unugboro? He's waiting to tell the whole world that he tutored me, the first medical doctor from the village. The headmaster will hate me. All the fight, the effort, the tears, the pain, all rendered fruitless by an act that lasted less than an hour.'

'I really love Fosa. I know he loves me but does that give me the audacity to...? What was all that for? Could it be that my father's wives have cast a spell on me? No, no, I am sorry. They even joined in the fight to send me to school. I created this for myself. I am responsible for my action and I must bear the consequences. Many will suffer for what I have done if it turns out that I am pregnant. Now I know ... Now I understand, I have been cursed. My destiny has been twisted. Whenever a solution comes, something counters it. Why? This is indeed more than I can bear. The deed has been done and it is too late to fight back,' she concluded within herself.

Iyobo blamed her father for most of the things happening to her. She couldn't wish more evil on her father. She would be the happiest creature if she heard he was dead and buried. She would only go there shed some crocodile tears and happily move on with her already distorted young life.

'But my father is not the person to blame tonight. My father didn't send me to have sex with a boy within a month of knowing him. How it all hurts. It all really hurts,' she said, considering least her physical body – which literally hurt.

'I didn't even have a chance to resist Fosa. He didn't force me but… he got me so quickly, so easily. I cooperated with him as if I was under a spell, dispelling the pain and all odds. What a mess!'

Fosa was too charming for her to resist, she realised. Her falling so easily, made her feel less intelligent than she had believed she was. If she was smart, she should be able to stand, maintain and control all of her emotions no matter how charming he was.

'Oh no. I want to be a doctor!' she took the lumpy pillow from below her head and threw it to the floor.

'I want to be a doctor. I want to be trained to be able to help my family and my village. That is my dream. That is what I want for my life. That is my destiny. Why am I deviating from what I have been born to do?' she questioned.

'Everything about him seems so perfect to the point that compromising my life and beliefs are the least of the matter. No, this is …' she then turned to face the wall lying on a bed without a pillow and the bedsheet had fallen on the floor of the room.

The potential consequences of her actions continued playing before her eyes as she was drifting off to sleep. Sometimes, she drifted into the tenderness and love with which Fosa treated her. But this little good was too small when compared with the evil the action could bring on her, her mother, her brothers, her village and even all women who dream of going to school. She was the most intelligent girl in her village and if this could happen to her, it could happen to any other girl, the villagers would conclude. Her pain grew worse as she refused to see any reason why she had let herself and everybody else down. She prayed that the ground would open and swallow her up. Her prayers were unanswered.

CHAPTER 18

'I think I should seek help. No, I don't think so. Yes sure, I do,' Iyobo's thoughts swtiched back and forth. She had missed her period the second month running and she was ill most of the time especially in the mornings. Food was her worst enemy and it was the latter that gave her away to her Mistress.

'Even if I have to see a doctor, which one? I think the wisest thing to do is to first go to the chemist and try to talk to him. Oh no, I hate that man. I hate the way the chemist man gazes at me when I pass by and besides, I don't trust him.'

Iyobo was interrupted by the slamming of a door. She jumped up to her feet without realizing it was 2 am. She later realized someone got up to go to toilet. She went back to bed feeling more helpless.

'Who is pregnant? You?' the chemist, who lives along the same street asked Iyobo without raising up his head from doing paper work from the last the customer.

'No, not me,' Iyobo said, relieved that the chemist did not lift up his head to see the expression on her face.

'Ah, Okay. Who then is it? I need to know who the person is to be able to give the right advice.' He finally looked at Iyobo, taking a few glances at her abdomen.

'Ah, it's my friend. She asked me to find out for her,' Iyobo said forcing a smile and clinging to the old cardigan she was wearing as if it was her sole comforter.

'In that case, tell her to come and we will run a test for her. It takes only a few minutes and she will get the result immediately. If she can't come, tell her to see her doctor or go to the hospital.

Sorry for asking if it was you. My mistake,' the chemist finally said, walking away to show he had other things to do.

'Oh, no, it's alright. I quite understand. Bye bye, sir.'

Iyobo left the chemist, her heart heavy with sorrow.

'What kind of life am I leading now? There is a Bini proverb that says that "when you master how to steal, you also master how to lie to defend and protect yourself". The words of our fathers are actually words of wisdom,' she smiled, mocking herself.

She thought about confiding in the Bible Knowledge teacher, whom she felt waös kind and understanding. The day she made up her mind to do it, the teacher was not in school. She was kind of relieved as she was unsure if her secret would be revealed to the whole school.

Iyobo changed her route and continued to go to school. She felt Fosa would be coming this way to see her and wanted to avoid every contact with him. She tried to stop thinking about him and especially about the night she now concluded she got it all wrong.

She had missed two periods and she knew the longer she stayed without doing something about it, the worse things were getting. She felt tired when she walked to and from the school. She slept more often and was beginning to lose sight of the children. She left them alone most of the time and reports started to come to Mrs Osagie who decided to carry out her own investigation.

One Saturday morning, Iyobo was shocked when Mrs Osagie did not go to the village market as she usually did. Iyobo was disappointed. She had planned on that day to visit her friend living not too far away. Since she started living with Mrs Osagie, she visited no friends and no one visited her. She knew where Nosa lived but had never been to her house. On the day she thought she would try to find a solution to her own problem by visiting, Mrs Osagie was not going to the market.

Iyobo got up earlier than usual. She wished her mistress was out so she could do the household chores at her own pace. Her constant sitting and squatting aroused her Mistress's attention. Iyobo didn't realize Mrs Osagie had been watching her through the window for the past ten minutes.

Iyobo didn't know that reports had reached her Mistress about her negligence in taking care of the children.

'Come here. What is wrong with you? I have been watching you for the past two weeks and I have noticed a change in your behaviour.'

'How many times do you want me to ask you? I say what is wrong with you?' she repeated.

'Nothing, Ma. I am just a bit tired because I have been working really hard in school for an upcoming exam. I swear, there is nothing at all. True to God. I swear.'

This aroused Mrs Osagie's suspicion. This is not the Iyobo I know, she thought to herself. Is she sick or what exactly is the problem? I am confused.

'You swear what? When did you start to swear when talking to me?' she asked.

This was the first time Iyobo had heard the low tone and she trembled as she quietly dropped the broom in her hand.

'Iyobo!'

'Ma,' she answered inaudibly.

'Iyobo!'

'Ma,' Iyobo answered a bit louder, this time without confidence in her voice.

'Iyobo,' Mrs Osagie called out, literally shouting. 'How many times did I call you?'

'Three times, Ma.'

'There is something you are hiding from me? I will not waste any more time with you. I will give you the whole of today to think about it and come and tell me what the matter is. For your information, I will not be going to the market today and all my appointments are cancelled. I must get to the bottom of this,' she said very clearly.

Iyobo was more confused than ever. Her body language had given her away. She was convinced Mrs Osagie already knew she was pregnant. She had heard her tell neighbours that if a girl was a week pregnant, she would know only by taking a look at her face and chest.

Iyobo went straight into her room, bolted the wooden door at the back and laid on her bed beside the window. Fosa didn't matter anymore. She even hated thinking about him. She longed to be free. She wanted to be herself again, before she met him. She didn't blame him for what had happened but felt too scared to want to see him again.

'He might feel disgusted by me, thinking I want to stop him from going on to achieve his dreams and he'll hate me,' she concluded. To her, the best thing to do was to stay away and maybe find out how to get rid of the baby. Now, she is carrying the problem all alone. *Yes, Dad said it.*

'It is too late now. I have had sex and conceived and certainly, I can't prevent the pregnancy except I commit the crime of abortion. I will not do that. I will rather suffer shame than take the life of an innocent child,' Iyobo caught herself saying to herself in her native Bini language.

She tasted her tears. She became conscious for the very first time that tears were not bitter but salty. She was expecting this result of such painful and bitter experience to be sour and unpleasant. As if this gave her some hope that something sweet could come out of bitter, she got out of bed, put on her rubber slippers and left the house without telling Mrs Osagie.

She had had her best friend Nosa in mind for a long time but avoided talking to her for fear of it spreading. If she must be helped, she had to take the risk of confiding in somebody. No one knew when she left as she gently closed the door behind her.

CHAPTER 19

Nosa was half asleep when Iyobo opened her door without knocking. It was Saturday morning and Nosa was tired after a long day on Friday, being away with her mum, visiting her grandma.

'Who is it?' Nosa said, drowsy and fearful, needing to confirm the presence of someone in the room.

'It's me,' answered Iyobo sobbing.

She stared at her friend's eyes which had been deepened by too many tears and excessive wiping. The more Iyobo knew she was being looked at, the more tears poured out of her eyes.

'Iyobo, talk to me!' Nosa said very quietly, with eyes full of compassion and ears ready to listen to the sobbing teenager.

Iyobo felt warm arms around her as her friend asked one more time what her problem was.

'Iyobo, what is the problem? Talk to me. Why are you crying? Did you receive bad news from the village? Is anyone sick? Stop crying, sit down and talk to me.' Nosa led her to a low chair close to her bed.

After more than 30 minutes Nosa was still waiting for Iyobo to speak but she only cried.

'Now, you tell me what the problem is and we shall both look for a solution. There is nothing new beneath the sun. What are we friends for? You tell me,'

'Nosa, my dear friend, my life is ruined. My dignity is gone. I am dead. I am so confused. The whole world will laugh at me. I didn't mean to do it. It just happened. Oh, if I had known, I wouldn't have gone. I wouldn't have gone there. I wouldn't have gone there to see him. My world is literally torn apart,' Iyobo sobbed.

'You've been really tired in school of late. Skipping physical education, always making excuses of headache or common cold.' Nosa frowned at her friend. 'You said you were worried for a friend of yours in the village, who told you she had missed her period. She wondered what she could do as she might be pregnant. I told you to tell your friend to stop worrying. A baby is not a curse but a blessing.'

Iyobo couldn't agree, she knew the shame a baby out of wedlock would bring her family, the damage it would do to her future. But Nosa was always such a good friend and in times of trouble, true friends showed themselves to be such.

'Have you told your Madam?' Nosa asked.

'No'

'Why not?'

'I was too scared. She will throw my things in the street and disgrace me the more.'

'I understand.' Nosa was watching her. 'Does he know about it?'

'Who?'

Nosa looked straight into her eyes with her head dropping and eyes now fixed on the tummy area.

Iyobo shook her head to answer.

'Why not?'

'I don't know. He is a good boy. I'm sure he didn't mean to hurt me.'

'Erm, what do you mean?'

'I don't know.'

'You know less about boys than I do! How a boy could put you through this and you call him a good boy? I see. He is a good boy and you are a good girl. How come you both ended up doing something this...' Nosa quickly stopped, realising she was going too far. 'Sorry,' Nosa said, 'you came for comfort and not for a scolding.' Nosa paused. 'Sure, I understand. Things happen but do not cry. There must be a way out and it is certainly not by crying.'

Iyobo nodded. She lay her head on her friends shoulder and started weeping quietly again, wetting Nosa's nightdress with her tears. Nosa kept patting her on the back telling her not to cry.

Ironic, Iyobo thought, Nosa was seen by everyone around as a very flirty girl. She loved to play and tease the boys around and that was where it ended. Sometimes, her mother told her she was rotten and even smelly. No one had seen her with a boyfriend and all they said about her was only speculation. Nosa had told her that Iyobo was used by her own mother as a yardstick to measure her own morals. How shocked she must be to know Iyobo was the one who was pregnant.

'I have more important things to do with my life than to fool myself around,' Iyobo remembered, Nosa often said.

'I will stay here with you. I don't want to go home because my madam seems to know about it already. Today being Saturday, everyone knows it is a special day, traders sell their goods but Mrs Osagie refused to go the market because she was disheartened at the thought that I have put myself in this condition,' she said sadly.

'Nosa, I can't believe I am pregnant. All my dreams have been shattered in the twinkle of an eye. I cannot go to school anymore and I can't even think about what my father will do to my mother and my siblings. My mother sent me to Benin from the village to pursue my education and I end up with this … I am just …'

'Don't worry. Things will be ok. You are a good girl,' Nosa said, this time, unconvincingly. 'I am sure you made a mistake and I assure you, my sister Nekpen will help you to fix it. She understands things better now. You just stop crying,' she finally said firmly to her friend who was now more at ease than when she came in.

'I think you should go home now so that your Madam doesn't start looking everywhere for you as that would complicate matters. Remember our Bini proverb that says: *when the fart has been let out, there is no more need to try to hold it back.*'

Iyobo tried to say that the harm had been done. Village life gave the advantage to the girls to say and interpret proverbs as they heard them from their parents and grandparents.

'Our forefathers say that *what makes the wall crack lives within the wall and it is the rat that lives in the house with you that goes to tell the ones outside that there is food in the house.* You must, therefore, not provoke the wrath of the woman who's been struggling to pay your school fees. Now that you have done this, she might look for every way to paint you black. Besides, you are not her daughter. She loses nothing. Be discreet and be wise. Do you hear me?'

Iyobo had never seen nor heard Nosa like this before. At school, she didn't matter to the teachers because she was seen as a failure. She didn't matter to her mother because she was not as good as Iyobo. Iyobo was the one everyone thought would shine.

'Your madam will be worried. Besides, my mum will soon be up and you know what she is like. If she finds out, you know how she likes to gossip. She would add salt and pepper until she would end up carving her own story out of the one she heard.'

Iyobo didn't budge. She was not ready to go back to a place she now thought of as hell. With constant pressure placed on her to go back home, Iyobo began to doubt if Nosa honestly cared, even though she argued that she did it for Iyobo's own good. As the minutes ticked by, Iyobo became convinced that her battle to try to stay was over. She thanked Nosa and took her leave.

'Please I will come tomorrow evening to see your sister,' she said as she let herself out and waved quietly and timidly at the only friend she was able to confide in. She walked towards home but was frightened about how to face Mrs Osagie.

CHAPTER 20

That night seemed never ending for Iyobo. Mrs Osagie didn't stop talking. Neither she nor Iyobo slept the whole night. She told Iyobo how disappointed she was in her and called her names like "snake" and "fox". She concluded Iyobo must have several sex partners and this was simply the last straw.

'I am quite sure you don't even know who the father of your child is, you useless prostitute,' she hurled at Iyobo. She told her she would never accept anymore housegirls into her house as she had exposed her children to dangers of sleeping around. She ordered her to take off her clothes so she would know how big her tummy was. Iyobo did not comply.

She had sworn to travel to the village first thing Sunday morning to tell her parents what had become of their golden daughter.

'Who would believe you went about sleeping with men instead of going to school,' Mrs Osagie lashed out. 'I have done everything possible to ensure that I did not break the promise I made to your poor mother. I put you in a school as you desired, gave you your own room to make sure you had your own privacy and looked after you as I would my daughter. You have brought me shame and you have also let down your mother.'

'My mother, please do not tell my mother. She will harm herself if you do. I have brought shame to everyone I know but I don't want to you to tell my mother,' she begged as she fell on her knees.

'Shut your mouth, you useless *Ashewo*.'

Iyobo was shocked at the use of this most derogatory word used to describe a prostitute being lashed out mercilessly at her and just when she was processing that, more words came tumbling down at her.

'I can't believe you still have mouth to talk after plunging your entire household into a pool of shame. I am not even talking about the money I have wasted paying your school fees and taking care of you. You shameless dog. No wonder your father vowed never to send female children to school...and you–'

'Stop! Do not talk about my father. I want you to keep him out of this, as this is none of your business. Thank you for taking care of me till now and I will leave if you tell me to. I will not tolerate ...'

'Be quiet! Since when did you start to talk back at me? Ahn? You answer me? You street girl. You whore. When did you start to raise your voice at me? Oh, I understand. Why not? Of course. That's it. I forgot you've started eating the same food like the big girls. You can now talk and shout at me. Huh? Now, get inside, pack all your things and I will take you straight to the village where I found you. I do not want you to ruin my children. You are useless and I do not want anything to do with you,' she said firmly as she entered her room making a cynical noise that often came out from the bottom of her throat.

When Iyobo saw that everything had turned against her and that Mrs Osagie was ready to blow it out of proportion, she knew she had to do something very quickly. She went into her room, picked a few clothes, put them into her bag, came out of the front door and disappeared into the thick dark night.

There was hardly a glimmer of light as Iyobo walked towards Nosa's house but she didn't enter once she reached it.

She just kept walking along the road when she suddenly heard the horn of a car. It was obvious the driver was indicating he was ready to offer a lift. She remembered the first day Fosa trailed behind her in his Volkswagon. At this point in time, it was no longer a pleasant memory, as having any form of relationship was the last thing on her mind.

Her first thought was to walk into the primary school along the road. There was no sign of life and light and she feared she would be attacked.

She carried on walking.

This time she made up her mind not to look back in case Mrs Osagie would change her mind and come after her calling out. She couldn't imagine what shame that would bring to her. She knew Mrs Osagie was a woman of her word. She had said she would create a stir in the village with the news. She knew she would do exactly what she had said. Still lost in her thoughts, Iyobo heard the voice of a man coming out of a car which slowed down behind her.

'Where to young lady?'

Iyobo was desperate to get out of the area she had lived for three years where she had been known to be a good and very studious girl. She called out in desperation, 'Along the road, sir.'

She had heard older girls stop cars with style and say 'along the road', she had never taken time to figure out what made those girls put their lives at risk to ask a ride from a complete stranger. She knew it was wrong and before now, nothing would ever have made her do it.

'Hop in girl and I will drop you wherever you want.'

'Thank you very much, sir.'

'By the way, what's your name? My name is James.'

'Hello Uncle James,' Iyobo greeted, addressing him as younger people often do to responsible older males.

'My name is Rose,' she lied. She also kind of knew the game was played this way.

'Rose, what a lovely name.'

'Thanks, uncle. Your name is also lovely,' she said shyly, looking down, as she adjusted herself properly in the passenger seat of the grey Audi car, with Belgian registration number still hanging on it.

'Please do not call me uncle. Call me James. I am James Obifor. I am a very simple guy. Is that ok, Rose?'

Iyobo didn't respond forgetting she had just declared her name was Rose.

'Rose? Rose?'

'Oh, sorry sir. I thought you were talking to someone else.'

'But we are the only two in the car.'

'Oh yes. You are right. I was just … never mind. What were you saying, sir?'

Iyobo, for the first time took a look at the driver who had been driving the car she had been in for the past five minutes. They had gone past along the road as they had taken at least two more turns since he had picked Iyobo up.

'Sorry sir, Uncle James,' Iyobo said wearily.

'You sound very tired and worried. Is there a problem?'

'I have just been pushed out of the house by my Madam and I have nowhere to go tonight. I would have gone to my friend's house before going to the village tomorrow but my friend's house is full.'

'Oh no. Why would that happen to a lovely girl like you? Such a pretty girl. Let's see how I can help you. Mmmmm Let's see mmm... in that case, let me see,' he chose his words calmly and firmly.

Iyobo started to regret getting in a car with a stranger, fear stole into her heart. Why on earth had she decided to open up to a total stranger who could take advantage of her? It was easy to shrug off the thought as she said to herself that whatever happened to her was what she deserved. Afterall, when Mrs Osagie went to the village and told everyone as she had vowed to do, who would care about her? Maybe Mum would but...

James interrupted her thoughts, 'Do you want to come home with me? I live alone,' came his very low manly deep voice.

'You can sleep at my place tonight and then tomorrow, I will drop you off at your place in the village. What's the name of the village?'

'My village is called Agoba. And it is about thirty kilometres from Benin along Okonba Road,' Iyoba said, squeezing her face with strong determination. She was ready to take a chance.

For the first time, Iyobo thought deeply about her mother and brothers. She then thought about Fosa. She wished he was the one driving instead of James. Things are happening very quickly and there is no way to contact Nosa.

James drove slowly into a house which was fenced round, as were many of the houses in that area, to prevent unwanted intruders. It was 10 P.M.. 'Thank God Nepa didn't take the light,' he whispered under breath.

Iyobo smiled.

The Nigerian Electric Power Authority let them have full power and light as if to celebrate Iyobo's arrival. Even the street lamps were beaming. James smiled. Full power was a rare experience at this time of the day in many areas of Benin City.

Iyobo saw that it was a big house with four small flats. All the other flats were locked and there was no one outside. The whole street was very quiet and deserted. James opened the driver's door, came round to the passenger's door to let out Iyobo.

'Come out, my dear Rose. You are an angel. How wicked it was for your Madam to put you in such danger by driving you out of the house this late at night. Do you have your bag?'

'Yes, sir,' clutching her bag to her side, she walked timidly beside the man she had never met before. The front door was covered by a mosquito net which James shook vigorously to knock out trapped insects, before letting Iyobo in. Iyobo remembered Fosa as soon as she came into the flat. It had one bedroom. It was like Fosa's flat except that this one was not a 'boy's quarter'.

James looked to be in his late twenties or early thirties. He was short and was quite stud, as in hunky and desirable. He wore a pair of glasses that seemed too big for his face, and made him look even shorter. He spoke very quietly as if he was in no hurry for anything. It was hard to know what part of the country he came from, but he didn't sound local. From his surname, he didn't sound, he didn't sound local to Benin, certainly. Iyobo wondered why there was nobody living with him. She didn't ask any questions. She was already too exhausted and desperate to sleep.

'Would you like to take a shower before going to bed?'

'No, sir thanks. I am fine.'

'Please call me James. I am not a school teacher. I am a very simple person who happens to be helping a beautiful young lady in trouble,' James laughed trying to sound as kind as he could possibly be. 'Thank you, sir.'

Iyobo was offered a well made bed in the small bedroom while James slept in the sitting room. She was too tired to think about the credibility of the man she was with. He sounded too honest and too helpful to be bad. Iyobo slept very quickly and easily.

At seven the next morning, breakfast was served on the dining table. Iyobo had never in her life received such an excellent treatment from anybody, not even Fosa. With Fosa, they were always too scared and too held back from anything. This man was certainly heaven sent, Iyobo concluded.

❖ ❖ ❖

Iyobo woke up and got up to go to the toilet when her eyes remained wide opened as she stared endlessly on five passports carelessly placed at the left end of a small table in the bedroom. Three of them were opened and she could easily see pictures of young girls glued in. This sent her wondering and wondering what her host was doing with several passports of young girls. This sent a slight shrill into her spine. It was when she got closer to where the travel documents were laid she heard a loud and firm voice.

'Stop. Don't touch those.'

Iyobo looked behind her, where the voice came from but saw nobody. She concluded James must have seen her through the curtains that seperated the one bedroom and the sitting room although she could not see him.

'Gud morning sir,' Iyobo said out loud with a shaky voice revealing fright.

'Morning Rose. How are you?' Came a creepy voice.

'Fine sir. I need to use the toilet sir.'

'Sure. Door right behind you,' came an uncompromising answer.

Iyobo suddenly realised the foolishness of her request since she had been to that same toilet at least two times before.

Iyobo didn't stop pondering about the passports as she sat on the toilet seat.

CHAPTER 21

'If you like, I could personally sponsor you.' James said at the breakfast table. 'You can send money back to me after working for some time. There is work everywhere in Europe, Belgium is a great country for job opportunities. You can see all the Belgium cars coming into this nation like swarms of fish. You have also seen the way young girls come in here build flats and houses for their families. I don't see why a pretty girl like you will suffer when you've got all it takes to travel abroad,' he continued.

'If you want to carry on suffering and being pushed up and down by women like you, then I will drop you in your village and that will be it. I promise never to look for you again but I can assure you that there are millions of girls dying to get the opportunity I am offering you this morning.' He paused to stir his tea before taking another sip, watching her over the rim. 'I'll give you time to think about it. I just want to help you.'

'Yes, I like the idea. There is nothing to think about. I don't want to miss this chance. I have missed many chances in my life and I must not blow this one,' Iyobo said. 'But I need to tell my mum and my grandmum first, as they would be very worried about me. My brothers also need to know. They certainly would be happy for me that I am going abroad,' Iyobo said innocently.

'Listen Rose.'

The sound of the strange name she had borne for a few hours now scared her to death, as she thought that might reduce her chances of success in this noble cause, so she addressed the issue in full confidence. 'Please I need to correct you on something,' she swallowed. 'I will prefer to be called Iyobo.'

'That's alright. We Africans are used to having two names. One African and the other foreign.'

'Yes, I am Rose. That's my English name but my Bini name is Iyobo and I would prefer to be called by my Bini name,' Iyobo said, as if she had planned this lie before leaving home. Iyobo smiled.

Why not, I could be Rose. That could be my second name. Iyobo Rose Ogidi, she thought and smiled to herself, as if she just won an argument.

'Ok, Ayoba.'

'No, Iyobo.'

'Ok, Iyobo. As we were saying, to me, I think there is no need telling anybody at this point. Experience shows that when a third party is involved, it rarely works out. If you insist, I shall take you to your village but believe me, the whole plan will fail then. You will live to regret having missed this great opportunity. No, consider the trail of events. First it was your Madam who threw you out and now, you throw away a good opportunity. Why Rose? I mean Iyobo. Why would you like to be a loser?'

Iyobo kept her silence as he reminded her of her life till now. She thought about the fact that she had been running on a treadmill of pain and disappointment. She recalled her father's behaviour when she showed an interest to go to school. She remembered the way she was put down by her father the day Mr Unugboro and the Headmaster came to visit. She tried to recollect all the bad words Mrs Osagie used on her when she discovered she was pregnant. As if satisfied after a sufficient compilation of evidence to establish a case, Iyobo realized she had nothing left to lose, but all to gain. She was happy to have another chance.

'Good. I can see you are smiling. That's how to be a good girl who means business, not the former softie I was talking to earlier on.'

Iyobo laughed a bit louder than she'd done since coming here yesterday. As the days went by, she had grown used to James who she would now refer to as 'big brother'.

'Get all your stuff ready. I shall go out to buy you some things you might need, like a few more clothes, shoes and toiletries. Just write down what you need. I will get them for you. Do not be scared. If you have any questions, do not hesitate to ask. I just want help you, nothing else.'

'Thank you. I appreciate all you are doing for me. I shall do my best when I arrive there to pay you back. You are just like my big brother,' she said shyly, putting her head down.

Iyobo stopped thinking about others and focused on her own reality. Everything had been arranged as if they knew she would be coming, passport, new clothes, another pair of shoes, even a wrist watch, which James thought was very important for her journey.

'You know the white people don't believe in African time like us. So, make sure you respect time. Nine o'clock is nine o'clock and not quarter past,' he said jokingly as he gave her the white wrist watch which she found rather fascinating.

For some reason, the tiredness Iyobo felt this past month which had given her away to Mrs Osagie had suddenly stopped. No one suspected she was pregnant. She prayed she would get someone to take care of her in Belgium.

CHAPTER 22

'Look Madam V, this girl is on point. She is young and beautiful. Why would you charge that much money?' James asked sharply on phone.

'Why not? It's what I charge. You are not the one paying, what is it to you? All I ask is that she works and pays me forty-five thousand dollars and when she completes her payment, you get another five thousand. It's as simple as that,' Victoria who was generally known as Madam V had displeased James with her haggle.

'Do you know how much it has cost me to take care of her for the days she spent with me? To even convince her was not easy. I will get six thousand dollars. Besides, just look at her. That girl is a mermaid,' James said, laughing slightly.

'You know me. This is not the first time you and I have done business. If you don't like this deal, you can keep the girl,' she said nonchalantly.

'Okay, Madam V. Madam the madam. Na you dey reign ooo. You be talk na do. Once you say it, you do it. Okay, five grand, deal. From now, she's all yours,' James said in pidgin English.

'That's alright. Deal done. Come with her to my place tomorrow at 3 P.M..'

'Okay,' James said quickly, as if suddenly realizing her young guest might be eavesdropping. He walked quickly into the sitting room. Iyobo was still sitting looking at a magazine.

Madam V was already waiting for James and Iyobo as she heard a knock on the door at 2:58 pm. She didn't wait for a second knock to open the door as her eyes fell on the young naïve girl standing beside her business partner.

'Hello,' Madam V said very kindly as she welcomed them in to her luxurious two bedroom flat she rented in GRA, the most expensive part of town.

'Coke, Fanta, Sprite?' Madam V asked what Iyobo would like to drink?

'Fanta Ma.'

'I know your usual. I have it ready chilled for you. I'll get it.'

Madam V walked quickly towards the kitchen and came back with a bottle of Fanta and a big bottle of stout and glasses all gently laid on a gold plated tray. She got herself a small glass of wine which she sipped as she chatted briefly with James before she focused entirely on Iyobo. At this point, James walked to the other end of the sitting room with his glass of beer.

'Now Iyobo, there are few checks I need to run on you before your journey to Europe is finalised. Do you understand?'

'Yes Ma,' Iyobo said quietly, bending a knee, even though she was very shocked at the sudden change of tone in Madam V's voice.

Iyobo answered all questions intelligently which convinced Madame V that this was a big catch.

'Here is the last question. This is the most important one' Madam V said, 'Are you pregnant?'

This question was a big shock to Iyobo. The stare on Madam V's stern face was extremely intimidating. She quickly recalled when Mrs Osagie asked her this same question just last Saturday and how her body language gave her away. This time, she was more than determined to play the card well.

Head up, shoulders squared and with a wry smile she answered.

'No, I am not pregnant and I wouldn't agree to embark on such a journey if I was,' Iyobo said.

'Listen to me one more time, and listen very well. I have been in this business a long time. Nobody messes with me.' Her voice became harder, stronger, 'I am spending money on you to ensure that you arrive in Europe safe and sound. You do not get work in Europe if you're pregnant. Things are serious over there. I do not want you to get hurt. Declare yourself!'

'What do you want me to declare? What I don't have?'

'Ok, you may travel, but if we find out that you are pregnant once there …' her laughter was dark, suggesting the seriousness of the offence and of the consequences.

This time, Iyobo was intimidated just like with Mrs Osagie to whom she gave in so easily. She pinched herself on the inside and crossed her heart. She twisted her lips to one side of her face, gave a dirty look to Madam V looking at her from her head down to her toe.

'I have said I am not pregnant. What else do you want from me?'

'Do not even dare.'

'Of course not,' Iyobo said, damning all threats.

Madam V noticed that Iyobo turned round to take a cynical look at James who was sat on the richly carpeted floor at the far end of the sitting room. Iyobo's intention was to distract Madam V from her as she was becoming worn out playing the cat and mouse game with the queen of games herself. She walked slowly to James leaving Madam V sitting where she was, while running a check on her. She also sensed James was playing a smart one on her and she felt it was also time for her to run a check on him.

'And, you sir, tell me, who pays for this trip? You or Madam V?'

James raised himself up slightly to get a cigerette from his back pocket before sitting himself down properly. He then leaned forward almost going on his knees to grab a lighter which he had spotted while getting out his cigarette. He put the cigarette carelessly between his overly thick lips which for the first time attracted Iyobo's attention. He took a deep draw from the cigarette and released smoke into the room directing his mouth at the ceiling. The smoke went up in a circus like a whirl wind and returned back to the room and especially to the sender who was taking another big puff.

Iyobo was perturbed yet intrigued at the drama and the sudden change of behaviour. In a split second, he had changed from that caring man into a gruelling monster. *Bouche bée*, Iyobo shifted backwards to avoid the thicker part of the smoke in the room. She only managed to close her mouth when she thought she too might be inhaling so much smoke. He completely ignored the question.

Iyobo came a bit closer again, hands akimbo and eyes fixed on his cigarette rather than him, quietly demanding an answer to her question. He ignored her. Iyobo turned to see Madam V, still at the other end of the room wondering what she was up to, looking on with keen interest.

'Look, I jus wan help you. Wetin,' he lashed out in pidgin English. 'As I see you, you be like good girl dats why I wan help you. Make you listen to Madam V ooo, na she you dey travel with.'

Iyobo noticed that money had changed hands but didn't quite understand how the two adults planned the journey she was about to embark on.

'Do not be insolent with me young lady,' came a feminine voice. Iyobo heard anger in Madam V's voice.

'Am sorry, ma,' Iyobo responded sorrowfully, bending both knees when she noticed the cynical way Madam V stared at her. Even though she succeeded in stopping the talk about being pregnant, she was scared now that she knew that James was more out for what he was getting from the deal rather than her own interest as she had initially thought.

'We are leaving first thing Wednesday morning. Your documents are all ready,' he said to the anxious eyes that peered at his hands. 'Take a quick look to ensure your names are rightly spelt and give them back to me immediately. I don't want you to misplace them.'

'New airport rule is that we must arrive at least two hours before departure. Good thing is that you have no luggage. You will check in some of my things as yours while your luggage is your hand luggage. Is that clear?'

'Yes Ma.'

'Clothes are waiting for you overthere. Be happy, baby girl,' she said, revealing the large gap on her front teeth between her dark thick lips.

Madame V was short, plump and very light skinned. It was obvious she had had a skin bath which left her only with the delicate last layer of her skin. She wore high heeled shoes round the house. It was obvious she had washed her skin with some kind of cream, which gave her an artificially fair look. She looked very sophisticated but not particularly pretty or attractive.

Iyobo saw her as real city woman who travelled abroad and became really big in a professional sense of the word. The young teenager noticed Madam V's makeup was too much, at least for someone like her, who'd never worn any makeup.

Everything was in place and Madam V was spending the rest of the evening talking about how much help she had been giving to Edo girls.

'They are never grateful for all I do for them,' she said in a rather disappointed tone.

Iyobo remained confused as she didn't understand how exactly she was helping. 'If they have to pay her back to the extent that she makes a lot of profit to pay people like James, in what way is she helping them like she is claiming?' she asked herself not venturing to say a word out-loud.

'Even the government cannot boast of helping these girls. Imagine, what the government cannot do, I do it. *Moi*,' she said in distorted French.

However this discussion was going, Iyobo was focused on achieving one thing, ensuring Madam V's eyes and mind were kept from her body so she did not notice the pregnancy.

Sometimes Iyobo felt she was coming too close to the matter. At that time, she simply thought this was happening because she was afraid of being found out.

CHAPTER 23

It was her first time of flying, although she had done this several times in her dreams since she knew she would be travelling abroad. Iyobo tried to imagine how Europe would look. She remembered the white British lady who told her she was not accepted in the Federal Government College because she didn't have a birth certificate and started to feel that the white man's land was probably not the best for her. If she couldn't please them when she was the best, how could she be considered for anything, now that she was up for no good? She resolved she would work hard if given another chance to prove her worth.

'They have been coming to our country for great jobs and have been referred to as Expatriates. I wonder if I would be respected and given the same status in their country if I worked really hard,' she thought. She quickly dismissed this from her mind as she was convinced she was only fooling herself.

Iyobo wondered what life was like outside Africa. She tried to look through the window but only saw clouds. She could not control her thrill although this lasted a short moment before she fell asleep. She dreamt she was in the village helping her mother fetch fire wood. She woke up when there was an announcement that the plane was getting ready to land. Iyobo was surprised to see Madam V walk towards her from the rear of the plane telling her to get out her hand luggage, just when she was beginning to fret, wondering what direction she would go. She was however relieved to see that she was with someone she knew who gave her instructions.

Brussels was sleeping. So were the people when the plane finally touched down. Iyobo quickly took a look around to see what differences there were between what she'd seen and known and what she was now seeing. So far, nothing was different.

❖ ❖ ❖

Iyobo slept on the long settee in the sitting room with her bag as a pillow. Luckily they had bought some food as soon as the taxi dropped them off, which they ate though they were very tired.

The following morning, Madam V woke Iyobo up and reminded her that her work had to start as soon as possible, as work was the reason why she was in Europe. She gave a few lessons while Iyobo was still half awake to a completely new world.

'You must learn that from now on, you must wake up very early in the morning. First take care of your body before anything else. Change your clothes, use the makeup and make yourself beautiful. Do not leave yourself bare like this. I will make sure that your hair receives the necessary attention as soon as possible. You will not attract anybody the way you are now. You must dress and behave like a big girl. Do you understand me? Silly girl. Sleeping when I am talking. Come on, stand up on your feet and listen to me,' as she used a hand gesture ordering her to get up from the settee she was lying on. Iyobo staggered up, rubbing her eyes with strong urge for more sleep.

'Your job is quite demanding and so you do not want to start badly. Stay focused and plan how you want your day to be. You determine how much you make a day and of course how much you can make a month. That's pretty cool, ya?' Madam V said, in a very strong Bini accent.

Iyobo opened her eyes, stood straight but had no clue what Madam V was talking about.

'These are my younger sisters,' Madam V introduced two girls who had come in very early that morning to help settle the newly arrived.

'Good to know you. My name is Iyobo.'

'I'm Belinda.'

'And I'm Gloria.'

After eating, cleaning up, arranging the house with the help of the two girls who were both in their twenties, they now sat down to fill Madam in on what had happened while she was away.

They talked about some girls who had 'fucked up', as they put it, by not bringing in enough money.

'I shall deal with them squarely. Who the fuck do they think they are? Do they know how much it costs me to fly them to Europe? They think they can take me for a fool. This month is their deadline. They must pay me back all my money. I don't care how they do it. Girls I picked from the gutters now want to tell me what to do. Idiots,' she said slapping her hand on the centre table and reaching out for a cigarette.

This scared Iyobo. Putting the discussions together, Iyobo was getting an idea of what sort of business they were in, but wondered if she would be forced into it, since they didn't tell her this before she left home. She became more scared when she remembered she was carrying a child.

Iyobo realized that being led to the window was only likened to leading a sheep to the slaughter as victims like her are often harmless, clueless and of course clothes-less.

'Oh God, what sin did I commit to deserve this? What did I do wrong or what did my mother do wrong for all her children to be cursed like this?'

Flanked by Belinda and Gloria, Iyobo was meant to go to the brothel to observe the other girls. That was her task for the day. She was to take note of their ways of doing things, although she was allowed to bring in her own style if she wanted to.

Iyobo could not believe it when she was stripped against her will. She stood like a statue. It was useless struggling as she had heard all the threats made by Madam V. She looked at herself in the mirror that was placed in front of her, and saw that her stomach was a bit bigger than before. Only she could notice it

'Oh my God, am I going to sell my body with a child in my womb? What do I do now? If I say I am pregnant, I surely would not return home alive. If I pretend, I will be killing myself gently. Both mean the same,' she argued in the silence of her mind.

She still held strong and was waiting for an opportunity to revolt. There wasn't any.

The thought that she would be on sale like one of these girls made her heart quiver and the only thought that crossed her mind was to escape. But how? And to where? These were the only two questions she thought about throughout her tour of the brothel. She was however relieved when she was told she was only out to see but not to start work that day. She went back to Madam V's house untouched for that day.

She had heard too much and just wanted to sleep and prayed if she was lucky, never to wake up. As she lay in the bed offered to her by Madam V, she dropped off in five minutes and dreamt she was in her village. She had been playing hide and seek with Girlie and Nosa. They had both come to visit her in the village and they were all having a good time. She woke up to a new bright and beautiful day, smiling.

When the awareness of where she was dawned on her, sadness replaced joy. When she tried to confirm if there was anybody around, it was a 6 feet 5 inches tall man who greeted her with a grin. He had obviously been watching her while she was sleeping and as soon as her eyes opened, she saw his eyes become fixed on her.

'No wahala, how are you? Are you awake,' came a merciless coarse voice.

'Yes, sir,' replied Iyobo timidly bracing for what shock might come next. The only thing she was avoiding was to be beaten as she had heard happened to some in the course of discussions between Madam and her sisters.

'No wahala at all. My name is Brains. I am just here to chat with you and take you to the spot,' he said, a huge man touching Iyobo slightly on her shoulder.

'Which spot?' Iyobo asked innocently and more timidly.

'Look, do not question me oooo. I am acting according to the order I have received. I am sure you took a tour yesterday with the hope of returning there to start work today.'

'Which work, sir?' she sounded stupid to herself as she got up from the bed and fell on her knees before the giant in front of her.

'A beg you sir. I can't do that. I am very sick and besides, the man who helped me told me I could go to school here and become a doctor to help my three crippled brothers at home.'

A slap across Iyobo's face made her cry out. Suddenly she was aware of just what she had let herself into. She covered her face with her hands, waiting for the pain to subside, blood dripped from her nose. She managed to look up again, this time, to a fierce looking face she would never want to dream about let alone see in real life. She concluded her death was close if she argued with the huge gruesome creature sent to monitor her every move. Iyobo knew she was pregnant and if this man continued to beat her, she would not survive it.

'What? Are you challenging my order?' the man demanded in a deep uncultured voice. 'I think you deserve a good beating. One more word from you and you will be bleeding through your mouth and nose. You little bitch. If you die, we throw you away to the big dogs in Europe to eat you for breakfast, you tiny insignificant mouse. How dare you? I am talking and you are talking, you untamed whore.'

'No sir. I wasn't arguing. I will do exactly what you say sir.' Iyobo got up, feeling dizzy and trying to figure out what to do first.

Iyobo knew it was fruitless even trying to appeal to the heart of this no nonsense man.

'Now, dress up very quickly and follow me. You can put on your clothes first and when you get there you dress for the job. If you don't comply, you will be severely dealt with.'

'Yes sir.'

Scared of being beaten, Iyobo put on her clothes and set out with the unknown man. Iyobo had only one thing in mind. It rang in her mind like a mantra. She wanted to run away and vanish into the streets. It just didn't matter to where.

'If Madam V did this to her own sisters, I stand no chance. Besides, with all I have heard and seen, if she discovers I am pregnant, I know I would be killed and never traced. I must act quickly,' she thought to herself.

'Now get into the car. What did you think you were coming to do when you were coming here? Did you think you were coming to work in the factory your father set up? Or babysit your mother's children? You foolish stupid useless girl. You will soon see what life is about. By the time you work off the fourty-five thousand dollars, your steps will change. You will probably be honest enough to tell others exactly the truth. When your parents sent you to school, you said you wanted to come abroad to make money. Small girl like you. Ok. Come and make the money. Ashewo,' he spoke the remaining words as if murmuring to himself as he noisily closed the passenger's door in front and went round to start the car.

'Do I jump out of this car? Do I scream? What would be the best thing to do now? I will never do that work. Besides, I am pregnant. This is completely not normal. Who can help me? Oh God, help me. Where are you?'

Her thoughts were broken by a very rude voice.

'Come out and walk there. I am still around in case you mess up. You are even older than some of those girls already doing the job. Do you think you are better than them? You are all hopeless fools with no brains. You think you can waste my time. Go and do the job, pay off the money they used in purchasing you and begin to make your own money. One day, you will be a trolley yourself. That is always the story you people have to tell others,' he said sarcastically, as he spat close to Iyobo's feet.

'You too, join them. There you are behaving as if you are better than the other girls,' Brains said.

Iyobo walked towards the windows like a condemned man approaching the gallows. She was greeted by two girls who were probably 19 or 20 years old. They smiled and welcomed her into the fold with a hug. They were scantily dressed. They had dressed for the night job. Rooms were attached to the windows and so, it was easy to dress and undress for the show glass. Iyobo's room was ready.

Iyobo was praying for a chance to run. She was flanked by two girls, Sarah and Tessy and the thought that she was trapped by the giant body guard freaked her out all the more. How would she do it? She took a look around. There was only one door for entrance and exit.

'Can I use the toilet please?' she managed to speak.

'Of course,' said the older girl to her right who was already handing to her, some string clothes for the night.

'Quickly please, there is a customer already waiting. You know you new ones are usually very hot,' one of the girls called.

The second girl laughed very loudly, walking into her room to wait for Iyobo to come out of the toilet while the other followed her.

CHAPTER 24

Escaping through the toilet window was completely impossible as it was made for only air to come in. There was net at the door to prevent insects from coming in. Iyobo guessed this was also to prevent escape. She came out helplessly, head bowed down to meet the broad smile of her hostess.

'Why are you sad? Just accept to do it once and that's it. I have been here for about three years now and I have almost completed my payment. Madam gives me some money from what I make for food and to buy a few bits of makeup. She takes the rest. Once I am free, I will be in my own business. I certainly will not continue with this trade till old age. I will save some money to start an import and export business, send some of my siblings to the university and return home to get married.'

'What if you fall ill? Like get the Aids virus or something? I was told in the school that one could have deadly sicknesses if you slept with several people,' Iyobo managed to ask with shivers in her voice.

'Well, that's the risk in the business. Tell me, is there any business that's a hundred percent safe? No, of course not. I am happy you have spoken at last. Don't worry. I will help you whenever you need help. I know how you feel. I was in my final year of secondary when my boyfriend sold me to my Madam. He used all the sweet words and convinced me life here would be rosy. I even thought the streets here were made of gold. I don't even see the difference between...' as she spoke, there was a knock on her window.

'Sorry Iyobo, duty calls. Speak to you later.'

While Sarah debated the price with the customer, Iyobo knew her moment of escape had come. It was now or never, she thought. She knew it was unsafe but she had nothing to lose, dead or alive, they meant the same. Still dressed in her string pants and bra, she took to her heels towards the shops. She ran into a Pharmacy and was very disappointed when she heard a loud voice 'Pas ici' the man showed her out. She leapt out like a wild cow and kept running, this time without stopping. She had run for at least a quarter of a mile before she finally looked back. She saw no one running after her and took a turn and another turn. It was a bit dark and people were hurrying home rather than taking a look at a stringed whore. She finally went into a telephone shop and pretended she wanted to make a call in a cabin. She took time to rest until a man, she knew would be the shop owner came in and knocked on the cabin door.

'Eh, toi là, qu'est-ce que tu fais là? Dégage! Vite! Salaud!'

Iyobo didn't understand what he said but she saw from his body language that he was telling her to get out of the shop seeing that she was not a customer.

'I am sorry sir. Help me sir. I am being forced to do a job I don't want to do.'

'What, a job? No job here. Go please. My clients don't like to see you like this in my shop. Go out there to look for job. No job. Pas ici. Dégage s'il vous plaît!'

Indicating by his looks how scanty her clothes were, he said in a louder voice 'You must go now. Au revoir, mademoiselle,' he opened the doors and pushed her out.

Frustrated Iyobo started walking along the small road, then she saw a church building. She couldn't read the French sign post but she knew that it was a catholic church from the name 'Catholique'. The door was closed but as she walked towards the back of the building from the side, she saw a woman who, from the way she dressed, must be a nun.

'Bonjour ma fille. Ça va?' the nun said with a smile. 'Je m'appelle Debbie. Debbie Rookas et toi? Comment t'appelles tu ma fille?'

Iyobo stood looking straight into her eyes without uttering a word although she knew she was required to say her own name since she had heard the nun's name. Things happened so quickly she couldn't draw from her French lesson back home.

'Je–je My name is Iyobo. Please help me. I don't want to be a prostitute. I need your help.'

For the first time, Iyobo saw a genuine smile. She walked quickly towards the nun, went on her knees and fell down at the nun's feet.

'Help me. I don't want to be a prostitute. I want to stay with you in the church. Help me. I speak English, please.'

Iyobo guessed Sister Debbie Rookas was probably in her late twenties or very early thirties. She led Iyobo into the Abbey and soon they were both seated face to face in one of the settees in the general lounge made for all the nuns in the convent. Iyobo was relieved when Sister Debbie spoke to her in fluent English. After a short question and answer session, Iyobo saw her get up to go into her room.

❖ ❖ ❖

Sister Debbie came back and gave Iyobo a big hug.

'Welcome home. Here is the house of God. It is your house. Feel free. You are safe by the grace of God. First of all, take off those ridiculous clothes and put them in the bin.' The sister opened her wardrobe and brought out an oversized gown. 'Take this my child. Wear this. First, take a shower, dress and then come to the table to eat.'

Iyobo was served the left over dinner of legumes and some baked potatoes which she ate greedily.

'After food, my child, you can tell me your story and I will see how I can help you. Ça va?'

Iyobo nodded.

'You must say *Oui*, which means yes. OK?'

'Oui,' Iyobo replied remembering her French lessons.

She regretted having hated French while in school as she thought it was a complete waste of time learning any other language other than English. *What if Sister Debbie didn't speak English as most of the others didn't? I wouldn't have been able to get to this point as quickly as I did,* Iyobo thought.

Iyobo had spent a week in the convent and had started getting to know other nuns and some church members before Debbie took a first step into finding her some help. Iyobo was then introduced to a gynaecologist, Dr Maria Ulens, who recommended she stayed in the hospital for some time.

'Eemmm, the sonography would be due next month when foetus is four months, ja?' the female doctor in her late sixties said quietly to Iyobo.

'Ok, ma.'

'Goed,' replied the Flemish doctor.

Dr Ulens had seen cases like this several times in the course of her career. Being a strong catholic, it was against her religion to advise the young mothers to have an abortion. Although, as a mother herself, she was sometimes convinced this was the right thing to do. With uncertainties here and there as to what might happen in the short and long term to the girl, she had preferred to stick to her faith. However, she had vowed to always take good care of any vulnerable person who came her way, even if she had to foot the bill herself. This, she was convinced, was the right and best thing to do, the Christian thing to do.

Iyobo was admitted into the hospital as underaged. The order to send her back to her country was suspended because she was still under 18. Nothing would be said about her immigration status until she gave birth.

For the first time, there was certain longing in the 16 year old to know exactly what was growing inside her. The fact that she was pregnant had occupied her so much that the interest of her baby meant nothing to her. For the first time on her hospital bed while waiting for Dr Ulens to come and do the ultrasound, she began to develop a certain feeling and attachment to the baby in her womb. She felt safe. Other health and social workers came around to say hello. Those who spoke in English asked her why she made a decision to keep the baby. They were however very careful while asking this question because they knew it was a nun who brought her here. Her own answer to that question was easy.

'It's a sin to kill '

'Ah, ça va. Ce n'est pas grave.'

The ultrasound was done.

'Het is een meisje,' annouced the Flemish doctor, in her mother tongue. 'It is a girl,' she repeated in English. 'What do you say?' she asked in a strong Flemish accent, as if Iyobo had a choice.

'I am happy. Thank you, Ma,' Iyobo said very timidly.

'You must find a beautiful name for her. I am sure she will be beautiful, like you,' Dr Ulens said smiling and adjusting her glasses on top of her pointed nose as she moved away to check other patients.

Iyobo remembered her dream to become a doctor. *That is impossible now,* she thought. *If I can't be a doctor, maybe my baby can. Who knows?*

A copy of the scan was given to Iyobo to keep. She was given an album to keep all pictures from the scan up till the sixteenth birthday of the child and give it to the child on her sixteenth birthday. This made Iyobo realise that she too was still a child.

What shall I call the baby? Iyobo thought for the very first time when she was finally alone.

'I think I should call my baby Evbu or Amenze,' she finally whispered aloud after a long silence.

Evbu means Dew and Amenze means Sea water. The first is calm and the second is tulmultuous, she thought.

She then laid her hand on her stomach and said.

'I name you Amenze. Amenze Odigie,' she sighed and then continued, 'I loved your father Fosa Odigie and he loved me too. You will be stronger, better than the two of us,' she said as she continued to lay hands on her tummy.

'You must not have the trouble I had when growing up. Your father is a very intelligent man. I was also often told about how smart I was when I was in school. You shall be very, very smart. You shall be smarter than me and Fosa, your dad. He didn't offend me. I am sure he is looking for me but here I am. Your father wanted to become an emmm, emmm engineer for planes and I wanted to be a doctor. My plans didn't work out. Yours will work out. Your intelligence will surpass mine and your dad's twenty times over. God bless you and protect you. You will grow up with silver spoon in your mouth and nothing will hurt you. I will be a good mother to you. These white people who have helped me will also help you to be great. You will be beautiful like your aunt Joan,' as she continued to pray, she dozed off only to be woken up to have dinner. This was the best life she had lived in years. Sister Debbie Rookas was always by her whispering words of love and support. The teenager was convinced the nun was sent by God to put life back into her. Debbie's permanent smile was proof of that.

CHAPTER 25

'I am happy to have my baby but I am so scared about her future. How would I take care of her?' Iyobo said to Debbie as tears of sadness and joy streamed down her face, as she looked to her new born baby girl.

'Stop crying,' Debbie responded holding Iyobo's hand between her two hands as she sat by her bedside.

Iyobo noticed she took a look at Amenze and then back at her as if considering very intently what to do to help the hopeless teenager. Iyobo noticed a deep pain was beginning to take root in Debbie's face, something she had never seen before with this woman who had been, for her, a source of hope and strength since the day she ran to her. Iyobo remained silent and decided not to talk about her pain until Debbie broke the silence.

'A lot of people give their children away for adoption when they think they can't take care of them. That could be an option for you. Another alternative might be to settle down with her and see how things go. If along the line you find it really hard to cope with, you could consider giving her out to a foster parent. After a few years when you think you would be able to take care of her, you could get her back.'

Iyobo heaved a sigh of relief when she heard there was another alternative to adoption as she dreaded giving her daughter permanently away to a total stranger.

'Okay Sister, I shall think about the two options but I think I will prefer to settle down with her and know her a little bit before deciding to give her away,' Iyobo said, hardly believing the words that came out of her own mouth.

Debbie handed her a packet of tissues one more time as she saw another stream of tears.

'I know. I quite understand what you are going through. There is absolutely no mother who wants to go through the pain of childbirth and give away her child,' Debbie said as if she had gone through the pain herself.

'Even though I haven't gone through that pain, I was with my best friend when she had her baby and had to go through the agony of giving her away because she couldn't keep her because she was helpless, just like you.'

'Really? How old was she?'

Iyobo asked as if the information would make her situation better.

'She was sixteen. She had a dream and that dream was broken. She wanted to become a Nun. She felt she had betrayed the Holy Order and wouldn't forgive herself. Even though she loved that baby, she felt she would forever be reminded of her past.'

'Where is she now?' Iyobo asked.

'I don't know. We soon lost contact.'

Iyobo kept her gaze on Debbie wanting to hear more about this girl whose case was a bit similar to hers, even though they were continents apart.

'She felt really alone. She had a bad childhood, as her parents divorced when she was five years old and she was so scared to bring a child into this world, knowing how much emotional tulmult she had to undergo when growing up. It was actually in an attempt to heal this wound that she opted for the Convent. She didn't want to have an abortion because she was scared and didn't think it was right. I was her only confidant and I too was scared to tell other people because she warned me not to. It was really hard to see her in such an unpleasant situation. She went to her father, wanting to judge how he would react, so she told him that a *friend* of hers was pregnant at sixteen.'

Iyobo clenched her teeth without saying a word. She only replaced one hand supporting her jaw with the other hand. She was staring into Debbie's eyes, hardly blinking, prompting the Nun to continue.

'One thing led to another and my friend's dad got to know her daughter was pregnant. She regretted letting her dad know whom she trusted more than her mum. The only good thing was that she had dated the father of the baby for almost a year on and off, as she later told me and found he was a very good person. Apparently, she hid everything away from me until she was pregnant.' Debbie snapped in with a frown of disappointment.

'According to her, the guy was incredibly supportive and wanted her to do what she thought was best when he learnt she was expecting a baby.'

Iyobo held her breath. In her own case, she decided not to get Fosa involved because she didn't want to mess up his future the way hers was messed up. Besides, she was looking for any way whatsoever to flee the reality she found herself in at the time. Letting Fosa know would make things even worse, as his parents and her parents would get involved to make things even bigger. All this got her scared, she recalled.

For the first time, as she talked with Debbie, she felt her decision was not only stupid but naïve. Iyobo, however, didn't give away any emotion as she wanted to hear the rest of Debbie's story.

'My friend later contacted an adoption agency which she read about in the papers. She met with two of the counselors and discussed how the adoption process would go. I was so scared. I wasn't sure of what to do and what would become of her. She warned me not to tell any of the Reverend Mothers who were waiting anxiously for her to start in September. She said she was dropping out of the process anyway and there was no need scandalizing her name for nothing.

'She made plans with the counsellors from the adoption agency to look through books of families so she could choose one for the baby. The adoption agency supported open adoptions. She picked out a family based on the books. She eventually went into the hospital so she would be induced for labour. The counsellors went with us and stayed with us the whole time. I was the only family she had, although her mother came after the baby was born. Her father, about whom she spoke so passionately, never showed up. He was quite passive about her daughter's decision to give the baby away for adoption.

'She had baby Petula, who was such a tiny baby. She held her for a few minutes and just looked at this wonderful baby that she had somehow brought into this world. She had met the adoptive parents earlier that day before she gave birth. She had the opportunity to ask any questions that she wanted. They told her how excited they were to have a baby. They told my friend how thankful they were to recieve the gift, as they put it. A few weeks later, my friend went to court to finally sign her rights away. That was one of the hardest days in her life. I saw my friend, though completely broken, still kept a smiling face, convinced, that was the best thing to do. You could see and feel that she had so much guilt in her. Even though she knew what she had done was for the best, it still didn't take all of those bad feelings away. She moved without letting me know where she went. I was broken. She often told me it was obvious she didn't regret giving her baby up. She just thought she was missing something. I advised her to join some kind of support group but she wasn't ready for that,' Debbie paused for a while as if to take a deep breath before continuing.

'My friend's parents were very strong catholics and could not tolerate the shame and dishonour their daughter brought to them after they had both signed her in to become a reverend sister.'

Iyobo went limp as the last point hit her. She wasn't prepared for that. She hoped her sudden silence didn't affect Debbie because the Nun suddenly went quiet as she got up to pick up all used tissues, making her way for the bin before returning to her seat.

'Iyobo, if God forgives you, you must also be prepared to forgive yourself. Unfortunately, a lot of people die of guilt or do something bad to themselves, even when God had long forgiven and forgotten.'

'How does God forgive someone who carelessly brings a child to the world and fails to be responsible for his or her care?' Iyobo said with a childish sigh.

'That's why He is God and not man. No sin is too much for Him to forgive, if you follow His advice after you've made the mistake. My friend was told by other Nuns she had been forgiven and that she could rebuild her life again, but her pride wouldn't let her, as she felt she had let herself down and her family was never there for her anyway.'

Iyobo looked at the Nun as if contemplating what next to say to keep the discussion running.

'How does God forgive?'

Iyobo realised Debbie wasn't expecting this question and so was not prepared for it. She noticed the Nun turned towards her, adjusting her glasses and then smiled, thinking of what to say. Iyobo adjusted her pillow and took a long look at baby Amenze who was sleeping away.

'Iyobo, Jesus is the bridge.'

'What?'

The discussion between Iyobo and Debbie was interrupted by a nurse who came to announce that her lunch would soon be ready. While Debbie made her way to the door, Iyobo entered the bathroom and both said goodbye at the door with a kiss on both cheeks.

❖ ❖ ❖

The whole idea of giving up a child for adoption worried Iyobo. Still only sixteen, she had gone through several hurdles in life but this one seemed horrendous. She spent the whole night contemplating Debbie's story, trying to figure out what points she and Debbie matched or didn't. She settled on the bit where she heard the father of the other baby was quite supportive and lamented over the fact that she took such a childish decision of not even trying to tell Fosa she was pregnant. She cried herself to sleep at about 8 P.M. and was only awakened by Amenze's cry at 2 A.M.. It was when she went back to bed after feeding Amenze that she started thinking about the two options for giving a child away she had discussed with Debbie.

CHAPTER 26

Amenze, the daughter of Iyobo was the fourth foster child taken into the home of *Monsieur et Madame* Le Gros in one year. They had two children of their own, a man and a woman who were now grown up and parents themselves. They lived in South Africa. They only visited their parents who were now in their sixties twice a year, at Easter and at Christmas. They often came with their own children. M et Mme Le Gros enjoyed these moments as they loved children running around in their home, an attitude greatly despised by their friends and neighbours. They received criticism for dedicating their last years taking care of children of 'wayward parents'.

Unlike the other foster families, the Gros family didn't ask for any financial help from the government for supporting these children. They did all they did out of love and pleasure. They preferred fostering to adopting as they wanted as many children as possible to benefit from their love.

Amenze, whose name was shortened to Amen, was the youngest of the children presently living in the Le Gros home. She was two and a half years old when she came into this noble family.

'Her mother's name is Iyobo. She could not raise her daughter for lack of appropriate immigration status and the money necessary to cater for a child,' the care assistant explained to the smiling foster couple.

The other child who had stayed with them for the past one year was José son of Mbangala. His father brought him to the foster home because he earned too little to care for his son, whose mother ran away with another richer man.

The Le Gros family home was situated in Uccle, a secluded and well to do area of Brussels, carved out for the international diplomats and the *nouveaux riche*. Their garden was like the Garden of Eden except that there were more people. Their neighbours hardly knew there were people who lived next door, except when the children were out playing in the garden, feeding the animals or throwing water at each other. Their foster children came from all background; African, East European, Indian, West European and Australian.

Monsieur Le Gros grew up in Kinshasa, Congo. His father was there as a missionary for many years. It was there that he met his wife, Helène, a daughter of a white Zimbabwean farmer who was a close friend to the Le Gros family. They got married in their church in Kinshasa and moved to Zimbabwe to settle as farmers. Even though they both saw themselves as Africans, they never forgot their Belgian roots. Madame Lieve Le Gros was Flemish. Her Opa and Oma, as she often referred to her grandparents, came from Antwerp. They encouraged their children to speak Flemish and English. Pierre on the other hand was Wallonie, from the French speaking area in the south of Belgium. His grandparents came from Namur and Liège respectively. They had moved to Brussels in the early 1940s. They encouraged their children and grandchildren to speak only French.

Pierre and Lieve spoke a total of 6 languages; French, Flemish, German, English, Lingala and Swahili. They have recently employed a Spanish teacher because they would like to go to South America on holidays. 'Speaking to indigenes in their own native language is the best thing that could happen to a tourist,' Lieve proudly declared to her teacher on their first day to discuss what exactly she might want to learn.

Although their everyday language was French, Pierre did his best to speak Flemish even though it was often full of grammatical mistakes. The only language Pierre spoke effortlessly was French. The language he spoke the least was English. He only spoke it when absolutely necessary. Even though he assisted Lieve a lot in the fostering activities, he felt a bit disappointed when he learnt that the only language Amen understood was English. Nobody knew why Pierre felt this way towards English. He himself couldn't understand why he was like that. 'English is not very popular in my family,' he defended himself with a very strong French accent.

Lieve often joked that Flemish be spoken on Sundays in their home, because it was a language of love and luck. Early in the morning, in her usual good humour would, as soon as she rose from bed, 'Goede morgen allemal. Vandaag spreken wij Nederlands! Verplicht!' She then turns to Pierre, lifts up his duvet and says very gently in his ears.

'Goede morgen Lieveje. Hoe gaat het? Kusje!' and she kissed him gently on the lips and whispered '*Vandaag spreken wij Nederlands de hele dag. Verplicht!*'

Pierre held her hands and whispered back, not so confident, 'Ja. Naturlich, mijn Lieveve Ik heb, ja, em. Le zeer Lieve,'

Pierre did his best to speak Flemish. Lieve understood why his sentences were made shorter than usual. They were all punctuated with 'Ja' and 'Nee'.

In humility and simplicity of mind, Pierre and Lieve had long adopted and adapted the language of each other.

Lieve in Flemish means love and Pierre means Peter but also a word which the French calls 'stone' in everyday language. They said they were both living their names. Lieve was full of love and compassion. She could give out her last cent and return home with nothing. Her love and commitment to her foster children was a strong conviction of her inner being. It's like she existed for someone else to have a life. Pierre was firm and very hardworking. He was also very calm and quiet. Their life in Africa for decades before they returned home in the 1980s made them fall deeply in love with African children, whom they took in at the first opportunity and treated as their own.

One of the things the Le Gros family tried to bring out in every child they took care of was to find out his or her gift. If they managed to find this out, they played along this line and even brought in the support staff and if possible, a member of the family to ensure the child grew up on the right path. This was very hard to do, especially as the children tended to stay with them for only short periods of time. For this reason, they worked, with experts who help to find out what would be best for the children placed under their roof.

Amenze, unlike her mother, was ebony black and beautiful The black and white which characterised her eyes were distinct, which gave a kind of glow especially when she smiled. She had dimples in both cheeks as she revealed her teeth and muttered a laughter that would make the heart of any mother melt.

While she laughed, there was a drip of saliva that came out of the corner of her lips and it was when Lieve first tried to wipe this liquid that she noticed she had thick and very dark lips that you would think were lined with some dark pencil. Her eye brows were a bit hairy and the length went way beyond the length of the eyes, but were lovely to see. Amenze was the twenty-first child Lieve had taken in since she returned to Belgium. She had never seen such a well moulded, carefully arranged individual like Amenze. She was plump and her head was full of very dark, curly, hair. As soon as Lieve set her eyes on Amen, she felt honoured to be in charge of such a great gift.

❖ ❖ ❖

Shouts of joy, loud callings, violent hugs and crying out inviting customers to buy products marked Matonge, the African shopping area in Brussels. Lieve managed to take her eyes off two men who hugged each other as though they were in for a big fight, only the loud laughter suggested they had not met for a long time. Cassava, plantains, yams, all sorts of vegetables, dried fish and the smell of fermented maize wrapped in special leaves filled the air. Lieve was thankful she knew a short cut to her favourite shop, as she sometimes got lost in the vast area as she tried to locate the shop.

'Can I have my usual soap and cream?' Lieve said to Mama Kinshasa, a Congolese woman who had an African cosmetic shop at Matonge. Lieve could hardly find a place to stand as Blacks from different parts of the world tried to lay hold on what they considered the genuine product that met their needs. Lieve had always known that Matonge was the haven for Africans living far away from home.

Mama Kinshasa was huge in size and often found it difficult to stand up quickly when a customer came into her shop. She therefore used a very long stick to point to the product and the person could help him or herself. She was cheerful and friendly and many middle class black families patronised her shop. She knew all beauty products that were good for the African skin. Madame Le Gros did her research to figure out which one would keep Amenze's skin black, bright and beautiful.

CHAPTER 27

Lieve learnt that at ten months, Amenze spoke her first word which was 'Mama'. She also learnt to say 'Papa' when Iyobo brought out a picture of Fosa, pointed to it and said 'Papa'. It then made people laugh when she said 'Amen' to every child of her age, 'Mama' to every woman, it didn't matter the race and colour and then 'Papa' to any man she saw on photograph. When she was a year old, she was able to associate the male picture she was often shown as papa to every other adult male. She was often caught staring at anything you pointed out to her for some minutes before saying anything. As she grew older, her power of concentration became stronger.

Iyobo had taught her to read the Alphabet from A-Z when she was just a year old. She also knew how to spell her name, "Mama" and "Papa," She even tried to spell, "Tata", "Kaka", "Lala", etc. The word "Kaka" was a Dutch pet word used to say "poo". When she wanted to do "kaka", she would simply babble "K.A.K.A.". It would be followed by her carrying the potty to her mother. She got out of diapers at eight months, which was a great relief to mum Iyobo, who could now stop buying diapers.

Knowing the alphabet at that early age was quite surprising to Lieve as Flemish teachers only taught sounds derived from sylla-bles up to about six years of age. If a child was reading a text in Dutch like: 'Ich heb twee been' (I have two legs) children would be taught to read this according to the smallest sound they could create in form of sylables: 'ik eb twee be en'. They would learn this for even very complex sentences. It is only after this that a child discovered letters for themselves. When Iyobo, who was used to the English system, realised children learnt how to run before walking in Belgium in terms of learning the alphabet, at first, it didn't click. She later realised that the system helped children learn reading faster and better, as they had full grasp of each sound instead of struggling with letters of the alphabet.

It was therefore very easy for Amenze to learn French from Pierre, the new 'Papa' of the house. In no time, it was natural for Amenze to speak Bini, English, French, Flemish, German and Lingala. It was only after Lieve attended a conference which took place at the Eterbeek campus of the 'Vrije Universiteit Brussel' she realised the importance of teaching as many languages as possible to children, as this from early age, stimulated their brain. The theme of the conference was: *Multiligualism in a Multicultural Society* by Machteld Emerechts. This was a joint research of the Linguistics Department and Medecine funded by AZ VUB in Belgium.

Lieve learnt that this was the first time scientists had visual evidence demonstrating differences between monolingual and bilingual brains. Brain scans of about a dozen children between the ages of eight and ten, taken while they solved simple mathematics problems, showed bilingual brains were significantly more active than monolingual brains while executing reasoning tasks, implying that the addition of a language trains the brain to solve cognitive tasks more easily.

In the same way an experienced driver no longer has to 'think' about how to drive a car, bilinguals can automate new tasks, to the point where they make little conscious mental efforts to express themselves. It was after this breakthrough in science that Brussels was encouraged, more than ever, to stick to the 'tweetalig' or 'bilinguisme' system proposed earlier by politics, under the solidarity pact between the Wallonies and the Flemish. Lieve and Pierre learnt early enough that the younger your children were, the better it was to introduce them to different foreign languages. At the age of six, Amen had rudimentary skills in six different languages. She repeated what everyone in the house said and tried to form sentences all by herself, in any of the languages, although she occasionally mixed up some of the languages. Lieve and Pierre made sure the children learnt their mother tongue before French or Flemish. This was how Amenze learnt Lingala from Mbagala, the Congolese.

❖ ❖ ❖

There was hardly a day that passed by without a new discovery about Amenze. The moves fascinated, but also worried the Le Gros family. When Amenze was six years old, Pierre and Lieve made an appointment with Amenze's teacher, Yvette. She was a very tall, lanky lady with a permanent smile on her lips. She was always seen with a camera around her neck like a necklace even during lessons as, according to her 'you never know when a child displays a new skill. You don't only write about it, image evidence is also very vital.'

Yvette revealed to the Gros family that Amenze was displaying the highest level of gifted and talented quality.

'A gifted child would normally develop speech and vocabulary early. Amenze ticked this box because she had a full verbal mastery of French and English languages at age four,' Yvette remarked that some immigrant parents spoke disjointed French and Flemish with their children, in a bid to practise the languages themselves. This completely ruined the child's linguistic foundation, she lamented, adjusting the small camera tied loosely around her long neck.

'Since Amenze's mother spoke Bini, an African language with her daughter right from birth, this has helped her to maintain a firm grip of any other language that might come her way,' she remarked with a broad smile. 'You can see that your foster daughter, Amenze was *meertalig* from a young age.

'Another element of a gifted child is when the child asks so many questions. Although this might be taken as a disturbance, especially when they have several siblings, it is often good to encourage this, as this helps the development of a child. A gifted child is also recognised by early reading and mastery of words in any given language, learning very quickly and effortlessly, having an excellent memory and most importantly, enjoying problem-solving and reasoning,' she continued, looking at the faces of her keen listeners.

Pierre and Lieve listened to Yvette as if their lives depended on every word that came out of the mouth of the primary school teacher.

'That's not all. All I have said so far is to describe a gifted child. What about a talented child? What do you think, as parents, mean a child can be classified talented?'

Pierre was not ready for this. Lieve had a paper where she jotted down all Yvette was saying, but didn't expect a question to be thrown to them.

'Ja, Frau … emm,' she stumbled, not sure if what she would say would be right.

Piere and Lieve had always been very respectful of those who taught their children, they considered teaching a noble profession. But with all the children they had taken care of over the years, this was the first time a teacher had spoken to them of a child being gifted and talented.

'Ja, talented is when a child shows excellence in a practical area such as sport, music or art,' Yvette quickly relieved them.

'In summary, we could say a gifted and talented child is a child who is excellent in academic subjects and practical areas,' she said raising an eyebrow.

Lieve had been given a huge diary in which Iyobo had kept all the records of her baby from four months foetus till two and a half years, when she came to the Le Gros household. This book must also be filled out by the teacher, writing all she noticed that was extraordinary in the 6 year old. Yvette spiced it all up by using pictures to drive home every point she made about Amenze.

Lieve and Pierre finally stood up to go after an hour and a half.

'Dag meneer.'

'Dag mevrouw.'

'Dank u, dag.'

They waved bye to Amenze's teacher with whom they had left the record diary which should be completed by the following week. If recognized as gifted and talented, Amenze would receive a letter from the gifted and talented department of the Ministry of Education, which is located in Arts-loi in Brussels, which would allow her to be moved to a special school to help develop her natural skills.

Two weeks after the visit, Amenze was officially classified as gifted and talented. She was exactly 6 years old. Amenze was moved to a special gifted and talented boarding school in Liège.

CHAPTER 28

It was spring in Brussels. The city had just started enjoying the fragrance of multinationalism and multidynamism which characterised the *va et vient* of daily life. Nationals moaned over the fact that immigrants were flooding into their country. Immigrants moaned that Belgium was not giving them authorisation to live and work in this capital of the European Union which was also the African Caribbean and the Pacific secretariat headquarters.

Emphasis on bilingualism, and in some cases, multilingualism frustrated the *nouveaux arrivés* that were desperate to integrate in their new home.

The politics of the nation was taking a new turn. The language you spoke determined the camp to which you belonged. If you were *Nederlandstalig* or *Nearlandophone* as a foreigner, you would receive all correspondence in Dutch and if you were *Franstalig* or *Francophone*, you would receive your mail in French. Those who spoke French, Flemish and German, which made the three national languages, could notify the authorities as to which language they would like all communications to be conducted in.

Amenze's foster parents had made appointment with Dr Dewulf Vercruysse for a brain scan for Amenze, as this would be stored in their laboratory for scientific research for further development, as they defined it. This was a requirement of the 'Ecole Bruxelloise des talentés' in Liege. This school worked in collaboration with the Ministry of Education. It was felt that such brain scans would help neurolinguistics educational researchers discover why children behaved the way they did.

When Iyobo was informed of the test, she refused, saying she didn't want her daughter to go through that, to establish she was intelligent.

'There would be a brain scan which would take place in ABZ hospital of the Frye Universiteit Brussel. This would be done by Dr Vercruysse who is a specialist in infant brains,' the headteacher of Amenze's new school explained.

'There would also be Dr Marie Perez, who specialised in child speech and education. I am not a doctor, but I think they will use a special machine which could determine how much work a child could do before stress begins to set in. They think overworking a child just because she is intelligent is wrong,' the headteacher of the gifted and talented children's school said, in a Wallonie accent, hardly breathing until he pronounced the last word.

It took the Le Gros family two hours to explain to Iyobo the importance of this test. This was at one of her visits to the house as was agreed by them and the foster agency.

'I don't understand why my daughter has to go through all that to determine something I believe is natural,' the now 23 year old said over a cup of tea, as she visited the Le Gros family home.

'My daughter is smart. That's it. Her father is smart and I am not bad as well. I think it's from the family. It is natural. We don't need a machine,' she said, as she took another sip from her black tea.

'In the school, the teachers are specially trained to give challenges to the children and they must know when to stop. I think it's a good thing,' Lieve said, laying emphasis on each word to ensure that Iyobo was following.

'I also know that your daughter means a lot to you, but you must understand that Amen has a brain which is *extraordinaire* and we all need to *oncurage* her,' Pierre said, this time, in a typical Franco-Belge accent. 'This is a chance she must not miss, believe me.'

Pierre had never felt so passionate about any of his foster children, the way he was with Amenze.

'Her behaviour is exceptional,' he repeated over and over again to Iyobo.

'Lieve and I must see that she's well educated. We love her too. Je t'assure,' Pierre said.

Pierre and Lieve were happy to have Iyobo come and visit Amenze, believing that the bond between mother and child was the most important, even when a mother couldn't take care of the child full time.

One day, while Iyobo was visiting, Pierre turned to his wife as if to reconfirm his fear. There seemed to always be some fear that crept into Pierre when Iyobo came around.

'Chérie,' Pierre turned to his wife, who now stopped with a pot of tea in one hand and an empty cup in the other hand.

'Je suis excité de notre *chouchou,* ce qu'elle va devenir' expressing joy over the future of their foster daughter. He was almost wiping a tear as he rubbed his right eye with four fingers while his head rested on the palm of the other hand, almost not noticing the presence of this African mum.

Iyobo was able to gather from the little French she had learnt, that her daughter, given the opportunity, could change the world.

Iyobo stopped blinking as tears rolled down her cheeks. She remembered Mr Unugboro and her primary school headmaster who went to beg her father to send her to school.

'My teachers saw the same thing in me when I was in the village, like Amenze's teachers see in her today. They did exactly what the teachers here are doing now.' she thought.

She remembered vividly how her father let her down, saying that sending female children to school was a complete waste of money. Was she doing the same to her own daughter, she wondered.

❖ ❖ ❖

What did that oyinbo man say? My own daughter could change the world? But how? Iyobo was lost in her thoughts, as she gazed at the middle of the modestly decorated sitting room, while husband and wife had a chat in the kitchen before joining Iyobo.

'My child, could change the world?' Iyobo whispered under her breath, in her native Bini Language.

'*Osaruese*, thank God,' she whispered, now noticing the arrival of the couple.

'Time flies so quickly. It was like it happened yesterday. Today, people are here convincing me to let go of my daughter to go to a special school for the gifted,' she thought to herself. 'Moi, Iyobosa Ogidigan of Agoba village in Iyokorionmwon. Moi, the rejected girl, moi?'

Iyobo's trail of thought was stopped by Lieve who broke the silence.

'Ça va Madame? Une autre tasse de café?'

'Non, merci, c'est fini,' Iyobo responded very fluently in French, still looking into space. The pair now fixed their eyes on Iyobo.

Iyobo had abandoned her desire for the best and had taken life the way it came. Pushing for excellence was no longer her thing, even though the tendencies were still there.

Everything good about her seemed to have been forcefully taken away from her.

Iyobo got up, slowly closed her eyes. The couple noticed her dark and naturally long eyelashes folded like two wings, as a stream of tears gushed out of her eyes spoiling her foundation.

'Asseyez vous madame,' Pierre offered a seat a second time.

'Merci,'

Amenze was not included in discussions about her. The Le Gros's, however, explained to her all that took place. She was told to come and see her mum after the discussion concluded. When Iyobo knew her daughter was coming to see her, she quickly wiped her tears and sat straight like a good and responsible mother.

Iyobo hugged and kissed her baby and then they played little games.

Oh mon Dieu, she is beautiful, she thought to herself as she continued playing the game of cards with her daughter.

'Oh look, I have a joker,' Amenze screamed in very good English, which she spoke only when Iyobo was there to visit. 'Where do you live Maman?' Amenze innocently asked later, looking at her mother's eyes.

'I live in eme … You tell me … where do you know in Brussels?' Iyobo distracted her daughter with a very wide smile, eyes fixed on another pair of eyes. She managed to dodge the question her daughter asked.

Even the Le Gros family didn't know her real address. She had long left where she was when the papers to foster Amenze were signed. Though she still went there to collect her letters in case there were any urgent messages. Iyobo succeeded in evading this very sensitive question and went on chatting over other things until it was time for her to go.

Amen waved *au revoir* to her mother as the Gros family led her into her room, where she was told to go straight to her piano practice.

CHAPTER 29

The last visit to the Le Gros family home upset Iyobo as she really wanted to be with her daughter without having to say goodbye. She was sick of Madam V sending hired thugs after her time and again and the most recent was too close to sweep under the carpet. The man who was then declared wanted by the state was seen around her home and later confessed he was paid to take Iyobo's life. She knew this was for real. She had been sent anonymous letters asking her 'to pay up her 45,000 dollars or else.'

Apart from that, there had been a letter from her father whom they had also gone to threaten to pay the money or face the consequences. When Ogidi learnt that Iyobo was pregnant, Itota and her three lame sons were kicked out of the house. The three boys would have been allowed to remain while their mother went in search of a new abode, if they were not handicapped and needed their mother's constant attention. This grieved Iyobo's heart. She learnt they had all moved to grandmum Alice's home, which made her even less popular among other wives. There was just too much for Iyobo to take in as letters came pouring in about one negative thing or the other.

Frustrated and not knowing what else to do, Iyobo became a prisoner in the social room where she lodged. She was too sick and tired of the harassment. Loneliness grew into depression. Iyobo, tired of hiding from her sponsor, decided to give herself over to the inevitable.

Iyobo rented a small flat at Molenbeek but was hardly there as she maintained a room at the brothel. She still had a lot to pay to Madam V. Things were really rough as she now also had to send money to look after her brothers and her mother.

She even sent some money to her father who had threatened to report her to the god of iron if she abandoned him as a father. 'You must not look only after your mother,' he threatened his daughter. Iyobo also got letters from her half brothers and sisters who had hardly spoken to her when she was in the village. She pretended she didn't receive some of those letters. The burden was too much for her to carry all by herself.

❖ ❖ ❖

It was first thing one Saturday morning. Pierre was driving, Lieve sat at the back with Amenze to talk about what she might expect and not see in the poor area where Iyobo could afford a place.

'It doesn't matter what I see or don't see. She is my mum. I am very aware of that,' Amen armed herself emotionally. 'I love her,' Amenze whispered to her foster mum with her usual big smile.

'T'as raison mon poussin,' pulling her closer and rubbing her short dark curly hair backwards as if to straighten it. 'You know you are very intelligent,' Lieve managed to say in Flemish as the car pulled in front of a block of flats in an unkempt area of Molenbeek.

For this first time, the visit lasted an hour and a half. The pair had explained to Iyobo that they would prefer she got used to coming to this kind of area bit by bit.

Only those who lived in this part of Molenbeek enjoyed the full joy of communal life, the area was mainly inhabited by immigrants. It was also home to several Africans. These people seemed to find it a lot easier to get along with each other. Africans often found it very hard to find flats to rent in other parts of Brussels.

'Non, pas ici. Pas de place,' characterised responses they received when shopping around for a room. Iyobo remembered the poem *Telephone Conversation* by Wole Soyinka, the Literature Nobel Price Laurel. She couldn't believe she was now the black woman whose voice repulsed the white landlady. She was glad that Brussels in the nineties was more inclusive than the people in that poem.

Iyobo was thankful that the Africans who had moved to Belgium to help build their roads in the 1950s had bought big houses. These *frères et soeurs* were happy to rent out their property to the blacks.

When Iyobo left the social house where she once lived with her baby, she shared a room with a friend in that same area but later got a small flat consisting of a small sitting room, a bedroom, kitchen, a bathroom and a loft. This was when she thought it would be good to have her daughter come over to visit her. Iyobo had planned that the loft would be her daughter's reading room. She had bought a table and chair and children's books in French since Amenze was attending a French school. She put several of the Adventures of Tintin posters on the walls. There was also a collapsible wardrobe close to the door. Iyobo already put some spring and winter clothes which she recently bought.

When the Le Gros's agreed Amenze could visit, she decided to create African as well as European menus.

Money from the brothel served a dual purpose. She first faced her brothers' welfare and then the other part for Madam V after settling her bills. This meant working harder so as to be able to hide so much away from Madam.

Iyobo knew she was ebbing away physically, morally and materially. She looked gorgeous on the outside but on the inside, nothing was working. She felt worse when she realised that everything about her was angled towards material gain, instead of the life of help and charity, she thought she was born to live. The thought of Madam V weighed her down and there didn't seem to be any solution to all her problems.

Iyobo saw herself as a failure as she was unable to fulfil the life purpose she had set for herself. She was now thinking of becoming a 'trolley' herself, being in charge of younger girls after full payment was made to her sponsor. She would be helping to pay the way abroad of other younger ones who would then pay her back.

Although she had toughened up a bit since she moved into the brothel, the thought of Amenze softened her. She hated the idea of sex victims having to be forced to take oaths, threatened and abused to pay up what they had promised. Some refusals had even resulted to death. What's life about afterall? She asked herself. She was convinced that the sex game was risky, both for victims and the 'trolleys' themselves. She had given this a lot of thought. Over the years with all the suffering she had been through, in this trade, feelings had become very secondary in her actions. She was hardly pitied by men who knew she was a prostitute. A prostitute was someone whom society thought was doing the wrong thing. She was always conscious of this. She smoked, she drank any alcoholic drink or anything that would take her out of reality.

Amenze was growing up and she certainly didn't want her daughter to end up like her. Iyobo planned to weigh both to see what she really wanted for her life. Money from the sex trade or resign and look for a cleaning job to take care of her daughter once she left the Le Gros family to live with her.

'I don't want my daughter to be a part of this. Please God, take care of Amenze my daughter. May she not be involved in any sex trade in her life, Amen,' she prayed every single day.

Meeting with her daughter was often glorious and she never wanted the meetings to end. Amen was growing very well and her foster family were angels, as far as Iyobo was concerned. The hard bit was that if she continued to be a prostitute, her daughter would ask her what she did one day and that would discourage her or make her ashamed. If she quit the trade, she would not be able to keep up with the pressure from home. Her father had just left a message on her answering machine that the rains had flooded their compound and they needed a renovation. That would cost at least 300 Euros. This was on top of the usual 200 Euros for feeding for her mum and then her brothers' school fees. Only Moses had been reasonable among his brothers. Iyobo learnt he was now a big time farmer. He now used labourers to farm and this had been very good. He was never hungry. He decided to stay back in the village even though he had built a big house for himself in the city. Since money started coming in, he got a girlfriend who he was planning to marry. Iyobo read in one of the letters from his mother. This pleased Iyobo.

'No one would understand what I go through each day but I've got no choice,' she complained bitterly to herself.

'Life must go on. Amen is still young. I will stop the trade be-fore she is nine.'

As Iyobo continued to float in her thoughts, she heard a knock on the door. It was her friend and business partner, Dorcas.

CHAPTER 30

Dorcas was tall and very beautiful. She had two children back home in Nigeria before coming to Europe to look for a means of supporting them.

'Dorcas, we are all victims you know that well. Even the so-called Madams are victims themselves. Most of them went through harder situations than you and I are going through today. We are victims of a system and situations we were all innocent of. Those meant to protect us have their own hands tied and can't do anything. We all need help from above to deal with our situation.

'Iyobo, you are lucky you do not have a child to look after or take care of back home in Nigeria. Your family would have sapped you and sucked you dry using your child as a bait'

'What about me?' Iyobo continued, 'Can you imagine? I was the smartest girl in my village and now I am a call girl.'

Dorcas struggled to continue with any other conversation as she rose to go to the bathroom wiping tears from her eyes.

Iyobo looked for the remote control and turned on the television. She had learnt over the years to be less sensitive to other people's pain.

Dorcas came out of the bathroom about five minutes later with tissues in her hand, blowing her nose and still sobbing. She sat comfortably in the only settee in the small living room, with her legs folded and a hand pulling down her mini skirt, which had gone up as she tried to sit. With an elbow fully rested on the arm of the settee, she sighed to attract Iyobo's attention.

'Yobo, you see, I think we are all responsible for any decision we make, whether good or bad. Every day, people pass through difficulties. Some decide to be virtuous, face it and keep their self-respect no matter what. Others try to run away from it and in the process meet a bigger challenge.'

'Sure,' Iyobo cut in, turning fully to her. 'Dorcas, I think you are right.'

Dorcas looked pitifully at Iyobo, sat straight on the chair and looked up, as if trying to get some solution from the ceiling. 'Wow! That's hard. Children born here don't think the way we think. They think there is no problem in the world. There is no way you can tell her anything like that now. She is a child. If you do, you know these people, they may even accuse you of child abuse. They will accuse you of traumatising the child.'

'You can say that again,' Iyobo said, laughing. 'I know all that and that's why I am being very careful. I am honestly considering two things. I was just contemplating on these two things when you knocked and came in.'

'What are they?' Dorcas asked impatiently.

'I want to stop this ugly trade.' Iyobo rushed the sentence like it was too dangerous to keep inside.

Dorcas rose up to go, not understanding why in the world she would consider stopping prostitution when they needed it most for survival. Dorcas refused to listen to the second thing Iyobo had in mind. Iyobo was haunted by Dorcas' reaction.

It was now 11 pm and for Dorcas, it was time to go home, freshen up and get ready for the night. That night, Iyobo cried herself to sleep, worried that her daughter would find out she was a whore.

❖ ❖ ❖

Life in the brothel was hard and full of danger. There was no doubt that this type of life was not a life which suited Iyobo's intelligence and seriousness but it was at least putting food on her parents' table and her three brothers no longer needed to beg in the streets, an activity Iyobo hated with every cell of her body though she had often heard from others never to put begging lower than whoring.

Looking back certainly made her dread life more as she had never thought she could face some of the things she faced. Iyobo remembered a night, a very cold winter night. She was to sleep in the client's house that night. She remembered how drunk she was, the drink had been to sure up her courage. Yes. All that mattered then was to impress her customer. She remembered having gone into the house and given him what he paid for until 2 A.M. then all of a sudden, she was told to dress up and to go back. She had just settled in to sleep, thinking she would leave at about 7 A.M. on Saturday morning. When she tried to resist going back to the brothel at that hour, he had screamed and threatened to get rid of her anyway if she didn't do as she was told. She asked for her money to be told 'I'll give it to you on your way home. You just get yourself fucking ready!'

With no form of protection at all, she was frightened so got up and slipped herself into her mini skirt and long boots.

Her tights were thin and did nothing to hold back the dreary cold that savagely attacked her body. Iyobo was still drunk and never thought of any ill that might come to her. She dragged along beside her companion as if he was a trusted old friend. Head on his shoulder, she was pulled along and depended on his movement for hers. When he managed to open the front passenger seat for her, she was happy as she thought she could just sleep until she got home that night. This was a usual night and there was certainly nothing out of the ordinary in what she, they, had done, except that this time, she woke up in a hospital bed.

All she remembered was that she had struggled with a passenger who had tried to push her out from the moving vehicle onto an isolated road frozen with ice. She resisted and that resulted in the car swaying up and down the highway and there would have been a crash if there had been cars coming in the opposite direction. She was soon overpowered and without being paid she was pushed out of the car while the car sped away, with a deafening noise of a revving engine getting off as quickly as possible, while she was left to die. She knew at that point it was fruitless to shout or to cry, as there was no one around. It was only an act of mercy or sheer providence that would keep anybody alive after such an incident.

Thinking about this ugly and inhuman incident took Iyobo's breath away. She wondered what exactly happened to her and how she had come out of it alive.

The Belgian Police prepared all the documents to send her back home after she made a considerable recovery. There was no relative who came forward except for a call she received towards the end of her stay in the hospital which they came to believe was of the woman who helped her come into the country. There was threat in her voice as she thought Iyobo was trying to play her, to get away without paying what she owed. Iyobo later played the voice mail and the tone of her voice, coupled with the unbelievably crude words that came out of her mouth, made Iyobo shriek.

After hospital, came the time in the police cells. Iyobo cried and cried, remembering all over again what made her to leave home in the first place. She had kept quiet all through her interrogation as she had been threatened never to give herself or her employers away if she was ever taken into custody. She didn't know where Madam V lived. She only saw her around the brothel when she came to collect the weekly pay. She certainly heard about this incident and had stopped calling, knowing she could get into serious trouble herself. Iyobo was later told that the Belgian Police identified and arrested her, then sent her home. She was so distraught that she went back to Benin, threatening Iyobo's mum to pay back the remaining money or face the wrath of the gods to which they had sworn fidelity.

Iyobo prayed and hoped that the gods this time would be a bit sensitive and fair enough to know that she herself had been a victim.

The day for her repatriation had come. She was stripped of all her belongings. She was told everything had been set and would be taken back to Nigeria in the flight leaving that day. At this point, the only thing that kept her going was the fact that she was fully convinced that if God kept her alive that awful night, it must be for a purpose. She was also moved into believing that there was no other ugly incident that could rival that one.

Her daughter would forever be taken care of. The thought of Amenze brought a smile to her face. She remembered the night she was rushed to the maternity ward. She was just 16 years old. She knew she now had a double responsibility; looking after the baby and then herself.

In the morning shortly before the female Belgian police officer came in to give her the news about her repatriation, she thought about Amenze, and was overcome with motherly instinct. She got out a paper and a pen and wrote a letter.

My dear daughter Amenze,

I have been told I will be leaving Europe for home, my home town in Benin City, where I came from. I know you are still too young to understand but I write this letter as a sign of gratitude to two women I met in Belgium who are certainly Angels from Heaven. The first one is called Dr Ulens. She resigned from her lucrative medical private practise to set up a social service where she saved lives of young people like me. When you grow up, you must look for her. I think her first name is Mary or Maria. She is Flemish. She was always full of smiles and when I needed anything the government couldn't give to me, she paid for me with her own money. I know you are intelligent and hardworking like your dad. When I was growing up, many people said I was intelligent and ambitious. Please keep yours. If I were a doctor, I would have been like Dr Ulens but there doesn't seem to be light at the end of the tunnel for me. For you, I have hope that you will be all that I ever dreamt to be.

At this point, Iyobo stopped to wipe her eyes. Many tears had soiled the paper she was writing on.

The second people I would like you to be grateful to for me is the Le Gros family. They are now your parents. Please love and respect them. You must never lose your African identity of being a humble and obedient child. Always be good to all your siblings in the foster home where you are. As for me, I will always pray for you. I am happy you are in the right hands, with loving and compassionate foster parents. I hope that one day, you will be able to come to Africa to work for the poor and

needy and especially for those children who are very smart but have no one to plead their case.
I will also be happy to tell you about your biological father whom I loved tenderly. I have his photo which I carry everywhere in my purse in case you grow up and ask me about him. He is tall and handsome. He is very intelligent and when I knew him, he dreamt of being an Astronaut. He said he would lead a crew similar to NASA in the United State. I listened to him but didn't understand what he meant by all that. Most importantly, always know that I love you very much.
Your mother
Iyobo Ogidi.

She had just finished writing the letter when the police came. As the Policewoman instructed Iyobo in the procedure of eviction, her eyes focused on the letter and the pen Iyobo had in her hand. She asked to take a look. She looked assessingly at Iyobo.

'This is really to your daughter is it?'

Shocked, Iyobo nodded.

The woman looked at the letter again, she was frowning.

For the first time, she began to think there could be human side of these hard trained super men and women as Iyobo was made to believe, who risk their lives to maintain peace and other. She was often terrified of them at home and abroad. At home because she knew if a police testified against you or did not like you, you were doomed, especially if you were poor. Then abroad for the simple fact that she could be sent home if she was found with no correct identity as she was facing today. Soft spoken police were only seen in British films. Only the British police would be very polite and respect human rights till proven guilty, at least from what she saw in films.

But today, this police officer was not shouting at Iyobo or telling her how illegal she was. Iyobo couldn't make out what exactly the female police had in mind. She was only left guessing.

This policewoman probably has a child, Iyobo thought to herself. Any mother, whoever, wherever, will understand the pain of seperation from their child.

The Police woman gently folded Iyobo's letter and passed it back, then she got Iyobo an envelope in which Iyobo placed the letter. She got out a diary, from which she copied the address on the envelope.

She then begged the policewoman to please post the letter to her daughter. Iyobo's letter was sent through social services to her daughter an hour before Iyobo's repatriation.

❖ ❖ ❖

A man in a suit walked in, briefcase in hand. Iyobo felt her mouth dry out. He came into the room she was kept, dressed in black. She took that as a bad omen, in her culture she had always been told nothing good had ever came clothed only in black.

'Hello, you are Iyobosa Ogidi, yes?'

'Yes sir,' she heard the quiver in her own voice, 'I am Iyobo,' she felt too dispirited to struggle, certain that his man was to lead her to the plane back to Africa.

'My name is De Wulf,' he extended his hand for a shake.

'What's this about? Ah sure, I see, killing me softly, with your smile,' Iyobo extended her hands with utter suspicion.

'I am your lawyer. I am here to defend you,'

❖ ❖ ❖

'I shall quickly file papers on your behalf, requesting that you be allowed to stay in Belgium on humanitarian grounds.'

'Emmmm?' Iyobo went on her knees, trying to get hold of the lawyer's hand. Pleading tender eyes on her redeemer lawyer, 'Sir, what's happened and what is happening?' Iyobo asked, not quite sure of what she wanted to know at this point.

'I'm here to help, but you will need to be patient a while longer.'

When he left, she sat down and just looked through the window without saying a word. Iyobo was shocked at the sudden twist of destiny. She saw a glimmer of hope. She was not too much of a criminal afterall and to see someone planning to fight her cause was the best feeling she's had in her life. She could stay and be near beloved Amenze.

Barrister De Wulf worked like lightening as unnecessary bureacracy was not popular in Belgian administration. No answering machines were left on during office hours as the workers were all there to take their calls and do the work. A couple of phone calls, emails and faxes overturned the decision to send Iyobo back to Nigeria. While the case was still open, a social assistant was assigned to her and she moved from the little cell where she was being held to a room where she shared facilities with other young girls from different countries.

It was in this house that Iyobo found out that she was not alone. What happened to her in her country had also happened to other young girls in other countries. Everyone of those girls was brought into the country by a human trafficker.

CHAPTER 31

Maimu was from Senegal. She came through an Agency who said they recruited young girls for white families abroad. She and her mother and her two-year old daughter shared a room where she tried her hand at everything to bring food home. Life was hard as the father of her daughter travelled to another country without telling her.

When Maimu was told she was coming to serve a rich family abroad, she jumped at it, little did she know she would be handed over to a woman who promised to pay all her expenses and take good care of her so long as she did all she was told. She started working in prostitution but was very unhappy. She planned an escape and a rescue agency came to her help.

Life in the social house was dull and boring for Maimu who grew up in the streets of the bustling city. In Senegal, she did what she liked and didn't listen to her parents who did all possible to send her to school. She became out of control and often ran away from school. After drinking, she would beat up her mother. Out of frustration, depression set into her father's life. He eventually died. Maimu remembered the last time she spoke to her dad. She cried when she told it to Iyobo. 'He asked me to fetch him a chair,' Maimu explained. 'I gave him some cheek about not being a housegirl, and he said he asked because I was his daughter and he had been sick. He said please.' She wiped her eyes. 'I then walked into the house, got dressed and went out with my boyfriend to have a drink. I came home at midnight to see people gathered in front of my house. Dad was dead.'

'What? Just like that?'

She nodded. 'It was said that I'd killed him. That was the rumour that goes on among my family members. I can't forgive myself to this today. If I was a good girl, listened to my parents, Dad would have been alive and I wouldn't be here,' she said, shaking her head regretfully.

'Bad as I was, I was all Mum had. We shared a room and I turned my hands at everything before Rene came into my life. After the birth of my baby, I didn't see him anymore,' clapping both hands as if to wake Iyobo up, who was lost in her story.

'There is a proverb in my country that says: "Those who have bums do not appreciate using them to sit down." You had parents who loved and cared for you but never appreciated them. This is the repercussion.' The girl sighed. 'Eh, tais-toi là. Just be quiet. What about you? If you were obedient, why are you here?'

'It's true we all have our own stories. Mine is certainly different from yours.'

Iyobo remembered the day her friend Girlie told her she was praying to meet a driver in the city who would take her from the village. Iyobo remembered how disgusted she felt. She recalled for a moment, the laughter and the way Girlie ran after her raining abuse until she entered her mother's apartment. Then, she was full of hope. She worked hard and dreamt of a bright future. Talking with Maimu was quite different.

'Iyobo. Why are you not talking?'

Iyobo forced a smile.

'Oh, I'm fine. Let's buy some chewing gum in the Moroccan shop at the corner of that road.'

❖ ❖ ❖

Maimu hated the life in the social house. They both had temporary stay permit. Life was slow and boring. Maimu attended a Netherlands school while Iyobo attended a French school. They had no future plans whatsoever.

'If our concern was to pay off those debts, why in hell are we spending valuable time in school and not on our backs getting paid so we could pay off our debts?' Maimu angrily breathed out to Iyobo.

CHAPTER 32

The stench of spermatozoa filled the air. Threat letters from sponsors' broke hearts. High competition for customers made the whores appear more ruthless than ever. The only stories that were exchanged in the brothel were brokenness, pain, disappointment and fear.

For their madams and sponsors, money was all that mattered. They had spent so much and risked a lot bringing in these vulnerable young girls, that the aftermath of their disobedience meant nothing to them. Iyobo still had 30,000 American dollars left to pay. Staying in the social house was a waste of time and a prolonging of her misery. It was Maimu's suggestion to go and settle in the red light district, according to her, to make a 'better' life for themselves. Iyobo's near death experience made her reluctant, but the money had to be paid or the debt would get worse.

Gar de Knor in Brussels was still bustling with business and girls of all shapes and sizes stood in and out of the windows.

At this point Iyobo, now more conscious about her beauty than ever before, decided to ascend to a new level in this business.

'I have all it takes: just look at me, beauty, brains and bravery. I will give it all or nothing to get to the highest pinnacle,' she boasted to Maimu one day, as they sat on her bed in her room in the brothel having a chat.

'It's simple, I will be a lot more expensive than before. Anyone coming my way must be well loaded It's either I get all I want or go back to the ghetto where I came from,' she said, as she laughed getting up and play dancing in front of Maimu.

'Just look at you Iyobo. Once a whore, always a whore. Bad girl.'
Iyobo rolled her eyes.

'If you want to eat a toad, you must eat the fattest and the juiciest one. Ah? Oui ou non?'

Every girl in the knocking shop had a story. Most already had children. Children out of wedlock seemed to be a major cause of their vulnerability. Some were ostracized while others simply looked for a means of escape. Once abroad, their status changed. They transform from being problems in the family to being problem solvers of the family. They even forgot about themselves and concentrated on solving problems of other members of the family, including distant relatives, sometimes, the entire village. It was often the only way to cope with the way they were forced to live. Some of them had been called a few times to help build roads leading to their family farms or market places.

Every call they received was about one relative or the other who needed money for something. Mothers were the greatest beneficiaries. They carried a bulk of the blame when these girls were driven out of the house. With daughters in Europe, mothers now lived relatively luxurious lives while daughters suffered pain and distress in the country where they are forced to hustle. This was the life Iyobo found herself in.

CHAPTER 33

Scott saw Iyobo and walked in. His face seemed different from those of other customers who patronised the brothel. He looked clean but worried. He held a paper in his right hand and a brief case in the other. He appeared lost and needed help. Iyobo had made up her mind to completely ignore him if he was in for anything other than what she was there for. Her *madam* had come a day before and had taken every last cent she made, leaving her with nothing to live on. Even though she was standing there at the window, she was thinking about her life and how she thought she had made a fool of herself from the day she met Fosa till this day. Her anger was especially against her father. She wished she would hear the news that he was dead and buried among the wicked. The saddest thing was that her father, even now, threatened her with dangerous gods who he said 'punish children who neglect their fathers', in order to extract money from her. She'd long since bought him a car, his house in the village had been transformed from thatched roof to zinc. All these went through Iyobo's mind. As Scott knocked and walked in, Iyobo didn't quite see the physique of this stranger.

'Bonjour mademoiselle,' the man said with an unfamiliar accent.

Oh, he speaks French. I wonder where he comes from. Am not in the mood for extra linguistic stress, she thought and remained where she stood without moving.

'Hello,' came the same voice, still waiting for Iyobo to respond.

Iyobo sensed he needed some help, like directions of some sort, but the girl at the window is not there to give street descriptions, she thought.

Iyobo opened her eyes and looked straight into his.

'Hello,' Iyobo replied hardly opening her mouth.

'Please I am not here as a client but looking for someone to speak with,' came a voice that sounded very honest.

This man had an accent she had heard before. He sounded like the woman who interviewed her for the Federal government college entrance examination in Benin City, Nigeria.

'Pardon?'

This accent immediately brought mixed feelings to Iyobo while she remained standing, not attending to the man.

'Please I need company. I am bored in my hotel room and I am not a club kind of person. I don't know why I have come to you in particular, but ... emmm ... emmmm ... Can you please dress properly and ... em ... let's go somewhere else for a chat,' he had a deep husky voice.

Iyobo looked intensely at this man who seemed to be coming back from work but dropped by to look for a companion.

'How much?'

'We will talk about it when we are out of here,' fidgeting with the handle of his suitcase, which suggested to Iyobo that he was kind of embarrassed being in that environment.

'Sorry, no. My time is valuable. I have to earn a living.' Iyobo said looking away, as if not paying too much attention to him.

'Well, I'll promise you this. You'll like my offer. I only want someone to talk to and that's it.'

Iyobo laughed loudly. He stood waiting for further reaction from Iyobo.

'It's alright. I'll be right back.' Iyobo finally consented, walking away to get dressed in the room. Iyobo walked out into the street with Scott by her side. Scott let her into the front seat of his brand new red Chevrolet car. The car drove away to a country hotel about twenty miles from the brothel. They finally settled down in a bar to chat and have a few drinks. Iyobo brought out her packet of Malbourough, offered Scott one. He shook his head, adjusting a seat for his guest.

'We didn't quite agree on a price you know. I don't normally do that.'

'Is that so? Thanks for the trust,' Scott said sarcastically.

'So, how much are you paying for the night?'

'The night? I am not keeping you for the night.'

'Why am I here then?'

'Have a wee chat and then drop you off.'

'You pay same amount anyway.'

'Ok. I'll pay.'

'Ten thousand Belgian Franc.'

Scott paused.

Iyobo realised he was converting it to pound, it was under two hundred, though she wasn't sure of the exact amount.

'Okay.'

Iyobo wondered if she should have charged more, and felt it was time to keep her mouth shut and waited patiently for Scott to speak.

'So tell me, where do you come from and how did a beautiful girl like you end up working as you do?'

Iyobo was surprised by the question. It was however her policy never to discuss her personal life with customers. Her outing with Scott was purely business and she would keep it that way.

'I don't talk about myself to my customers.'

'Customer? What am I buying from you?'

'My time.' Iyobo took a puff of the cigarette, blowing it aimlessly in the air.

'What about you? Where do you come from and what do you do?'

'I come from Scotland, I'm an Investment Banker.'

'What's that?'

Scott laughed.

Iyobo was shocked to know the calibre of man who came for her once Scott had explained in simple language what he did for a living.

'What? You are all that? I am just a whore.'

Iyobo said, lifting up her glass of beer with one hand, a cigarette burning endlessly in the other. She sipped her drink slowly, minding her lipstick and later took a quick glance at her customer, to read a reaction from his face. Scott gave nothing away. He maintained a small smile.

'I didn't used to be that,' she said. 'I was pushed into it. I am praying that one day, I will get out of it and become a woman of my own, with my own will in my own home.' 'You sound very intelligent to me. You sound to me like someone doing a degree in the university,' Scott said.

'Ha, I didn't even finish secondary school,' Iyobo said, taking a sip of her beer.

'I want to help you. But you must promise me one thing.'

'What? Sure, that's my job. Give the customer what he wants. It doesn't matter to me anymore.'

'No, that's not what I mean. You must promise to quit the trade.'

'Quit what trade?'

'I mean you must quit prostitution.'

Iyobo couldn't believe what she was hearing.

'I don't know what you are talking about. I am out to make money to pay my debts and then to build a better future for me and my daughter.'

'You have a daughter?'

Iyobo nodded her head, eyes fixed in her drink.

'All the more reason you should quit and look for another way to make money.'

'Well, I am sorry. I know you picked me from the brothel but that does not give you the right to look down on me. Is that clear. I must go. It's either you take me into your hotel room or you let me go.'

'I never had any intention of taking you to any hotel room. I am not looking down on you. I needed company but having spent time with you, I just want to get you out of the brothel if you let me.'

'And how do you think you can help, if I may ask?'

Scott laughed while Iyobo got up, insisting she wanted to leave.

Scott took Iyobo back to the brothel pinning into her hand double the amount she had asked for. This made her have a re-think about Scott. Iyobo later thought of it as history repeating itself again and decided to let go.

CHAPTER 34

It was Sunday morning. Iyobo, Maimu, Florence and Justina, friends from the red light district, were all looking at an invitation card. Justina had brought the card in from a family friend she knew while in Ghana. Ajua, the new mum, was married and had a baby girl. She was now dedicating her 4 month old baby in a church at the Christ for All Community Church situated along Avenue Louise, an affluent area in Brussels. It was predominantly French but an interpreter often helped English speaking people to understand the sermon.

Ajua had been in this church for five years and had come to accept it as her home church. She liked Pastor Jean-Paul who was young, dynamic and humble. Ajua still struggled to speak French but that was not a problem as Stefan, the interpreter made things very easy for her. Stefan was originally from Holland and so spoke Dutch as his first language. He also spoke French and English fluently. He was really talented with languages and according to him, he loved to use his talent for the glory of God.

On this special Sunday, Pastor Jean-Paul, a very humble and God fearing man, stood at the Church door. Along with the ushers, he welcomed everybody in.

Church affairs were kept out of brothel life. To many of these young girls, talking about church was like driving guilt mercilessly into their spines. These four went to church without talking too much about it.

These four, without thinking about it, all wore scanty clothes. That was their world. As they walked into the church, many stepped back as they noticed Pastor Jean-Paul managing to maintain a permanent, slightly embarrassed smile.

After Iyobo's experience with Sister Debbie Rookas, church for her was a place for help and rest. It was a place where God brought some power down to deliver vulnerable people from those too strong for them. She attended masses with the nuns while living with them but her focus was only on what they had to offer her. One thing was certain in her mind, these nuns who opened their arms wide to receive her when the world was collapsing on her, made her think there might actually be God.

Iyobo didn't know what to expect from these church people. She had heard a lot about church, both good and bad. She decided to stay neutral and also to pray for God to help her accomplish her life's goals, especially to be able to pay off her Madam so she could move on with her life.

Florence was the first to shake the Pastor's hand, humbly bowing a knee, a gesture she was used to, Maimu followed and did not bow a knee, simply smiled. Iyobo was third while Justina was last, each giving a slight bow.

The congregation turned one by one, distracted from the silence that hit the church before worship started. Justina wore a mini skirt with a blouse revealing most of her upper body. Her legs were well covered with long boots up to her thigh level. Even though this was normal dress for her, it was unacceptable in this rather conservative community church. Since the inception of the church, 95 years ago, no one had dressed so outrageously to attend the house of God. To this community, the four girls' manner of dress was too revealing for a spiritual environment, but they were very happy to be in the house of God, a bold distraction from their everyday life activities. They took their seats at exactly 9:59 A.M.. Worship started at 10:00.

CHAPTER 35

The ceremony was made up of singing from booklets, they were given at the door by the ushers. The four kept close to the program, singing and praying when they were asked to. At the front, near the altar, the choir sang and musicians played the piano and the drums. It was a solemn time for the four.

For most members of the congregation, their eyes did not leave the guests who they considered whores, women who should not be on holy ground. Only the pastor felt at peace with their presence. Once at the altar, he never took a second look at the girls.

It was a guest speaker who took to the floor after the worship period. This new pastor, probably in his fifties, mounted the podium with a big fat smile on his slim face.

'Hello, my name is Pastor Greg. I come from Sydney in Australia. Can you all say hello to one another,' he said, waiting for the interpreter to convey the message to the congregation in French.

'Leave your seats; do not be afraid to greet people you have not met before. Give a hug and a kiss in the name of the Lord.'

'On se dit bonjour,' the interpreter said with lesser enthusiasm than the preacher. This was not indepth enough for the ambiance Pastor Greg was longing to build, as he saw members barely stretching hands to those around them.

'Bonjour' and 'Bonjour' filled the air but the atmosphere remained cold as about fifty worshippers finally sat down, focusing on the speaker.

The coldness of the church made Iyobo and cohorts stick together apart from Pasteur Jean-Paul and Pastor Greg who came down from the podium to give them a hug. The four felt very welcomed when this happened. They were now more comfortable to listen to what the men had to say.

'God is good,' shouted Pastor Greg.

'All the time,' thundered the congregation, except the four, who were watching to see how things were done. Ajua's voice was heard as she screamed it more than every other person in the congregation. Baby in hand, she stood up, waved a white kerchief and shouted an extra "AMEN!" before sitting down. The four looked at her and smiled. Iyobo noticed there was no man by her side. She wondered why she came alone for a baby dedication. She whispered this to Justina, who whispered back, 'Her husband is in Africa. He only comes to make the babies and goes back.'

The pair chuckled.

'Ah, that's cruel.'

'No, it's normal.'

'They could both be unfaithful to each other.'

'Oh, he's got a wife over there. That one was first before he knew Ajua. At first, the one over there didn't know but since she found out that her husband might get a stay permit which could be tranferred to her own children or even herself, she calmed down.'

'Ah, men are the same everywhere.'

'But Ajua doesn't mind.'

'What?'

'She's got her kids and she is now a wife of somebody. This makes her feel very responsible, unlike us who are irresponsible. Who will marry us?'

They both laughed almost distracting two members sitting very close to them.

'You can't always have everything. The one at home gets the man while you get... em, well; she gets what she is happy about. The children,' said Justina.

'The children have the right to their father,' Iyobo said as she thought about Amenze and Fosa. She then shut her mouth and tried to focus on the preacher. He had been preaching for the past ten minutes. The church was a bit noisy, the result of simultaneous interpretation, which gave the two girls opportunity to chat. However, Florence and Maimu were listening but their minds were far away until they all got captured by a sudden question posed by the Australian Pastor.

'How many of you here love to please those you really love?'

Half of the church put their hands up, including three out of the four, as Maimu didn't want to physically participate much in what they were doing, even though she was listening intently.

'Good. Well done. Here is another question,' said the Preacher. 'How many of you have worn shoes just because you wanted to please somebody else, gone through pains because those shoes that look good don't really fit. You wore them all the same because you felt they looked good on you?'

To Iyobo, this getting so informal while talking to people in church was not what she expected. She's never really paid attention to churches but her imagination of the pastor-congregation relationship was that of piety and that words should be carefully chosen to please God and to please the holy people of God. This so called man of God was getting way too liberal for her. She felt he was going too far. The church she attended with Debbie was much more formal. There was no playing about with too many words. Everything was well written out and recited in a very pious manner. That, to Iyobo, was how church should be. People should know the difference between their sitting rooms and church.

To make matters worse, Pastor Greg at one point, came down from the podium and faced individuals in the congregation as he carried on talking.

'This was way too informal,' she convinced herself.

Iyobo looked round one more time to be sure she was in a church and nowhere else. The pastor's words came thundering back into her ear as if they were some kind of continuation of her thoughts.

'Sure, you are in the church and the best place to commit sin is in the church because when you do, you are ready to be forgiven. Sinners must come to the church the way they are. When you are washed, you no longer need to be cleansed.'

'What? No, what am I hearing? The pastor is wrong. The church is certainly not for sinners like me. It's for those who have repented and are faithfully following God.'

Iyobo struggled with her thoughts. She took a slight glance at the other girls and saw they were all staring at the pastor who was now talking about his wife and children as he carried on with the message.

'Many of you think it is absurd to talk about committing sin in the church because it is a place for good people.'

'Why does this pastor always know my thoughts,' Iyobo questioned and became suspicious. Could he be using a form of voodoo?'

'You even get shocked when you hear that people in the church have made mistakes because they are expected to be good. Consider this: The person who suffers from a heart attack is better off having it in the hospital so that he could get medical help right away. How many of you agree?'

Many raised their hands up but this time, Iyobo didn't.

'Help is always in church for anybody who is struggling with one thing or the other,' he shouted out, as if losing his voice at this point. 'The title of my message is "Pleasing God".'

Iyobo remembered that was when she was chatting with Florence about Ajua.

'I know how to please my wife and it is sometimes crazy to think about all I did to please my wife especially when we were courting,' he chuckled, facing the floor as if shy.

'This man must be very in love with his wife. I would really like my husband to be in love with me. This pastor's wife is really lucky,'

'Shut up, Maimu.'

'I don't think I will ever experience love, not after all I have done to my parents. Love doesn't come to bad people like me,' Maimu muttered and continued listening.

'I can remember she wore dustbin bags to go out for jogging in order to sweat more, so as to lose more weight just to please me.'

'What? No way. I wouldn't do that for a man,' thought Florence.

'It is very nice to think that someone would go to that extent to please another person,' the Pastor said, this time, pensively.

He then kept silent as he gazed at the congregation, as if waiting for some form of response. Sporadic claps crept across the room.

The girls sat still and were now feeling more at home than when they came in. People in the brothel were strongly advised not to listen to too much gospel as they would be encouraged to stop working and paying their Madams.

Maimu was a non-practising Muslim and so coming to the church was strictly non-religious. None of those words were to be taken for real. To her, the Pastor was doing what he was paid to do. She however, found what was happening quite entertaining. Life in the brothel could be boring.

'I remember having gone out of my way to please my wife sometime ago,' the pastor continued.

'I was sure she was already in bed. Normally, she would read a book before finally falling to sleep. I was in the sitting room. I tip-toed out of the house with my car keys and I drove several kilometres, unknown to her, to buy her favourite ice cream,' the pastor paused.

'Enough of this love galore. I am getting sick of it,' moaned Maimu.

'When I brought it, I didn't walk straight into the bed room with the icecream. I stood at the door and saw that the light was still on. I quietly opened the door, and stretched my hand with the ice cream into the room through the slightly opened door. I made a bit of noise to attract her attention. She looked and saw her favourite ice cream popping out of the door,' the pastor paused, walking closer to the congregation, as if waiting to be assured of their utmost attention. 'The appreciation, gratitude and love on her face was unbelievable,' Pastor Greg finally revealed, waiting for the Interpreter to convey the message.

'Now listen, God reacts in the same manner,' he said very quietly and slowly bending towards the fifty pairs of eyes staring at him.

'If you go out of your way to please God, you will be amazed at what you will get back in return. If there is something you are looking for and you don't know what to do to get it, just please God first and you will be amazed!' Pastor Greg screamed out. He turned to the girls for a second and looked straight ahead at the whole congregation.

'Let's go to Ecclesiastes chapter 2 verse 26,' he said quietly.

'For, to the person who pleases Him, God gives wisdom and knowledge and joy; but to the sinner, he gives the work of gathering and heaping up that he may give to one who pleases God.' He closed his Bible, put his right hand on it and turned sternly to the congregation.

'I am talking about doing something to please God, not out of compulsion but out of the relationship we have with Him. It is impossible to please God if He doesn't love us. This kind of love is not possible if he just commands it and expects us to comply like robots. Look in Ephesians chapter 1 verse 5–6.

'Because of His love, God had decided to make us His own children through Jesus Christ. That was what He wanted and what pleased Him and it brings praise to Him because of His wonderful grace. God gave that grace to us freely, in Christ, the one He loves.'

❖ ❖ ❖

Florence still thought about how the Pastor pleased his wife with her favourite ice cream hardly hearing the second scriptural reading. Her mind wouldn't come off the fact that the pastor drove kilometres to please his wife!

'That sounds really sweet. I wouldn't mind a man doing that for me. Not only buying my favourite ice cream but also my favourite clothes, shoes, car and house. But after all I have experienced with men, no man will feel true love from me. Never. Fire on Pastor, I am with you,' Florence finally laid the thought to rest.

❖ ❖ ❖

Iyobo brushed it all under the carpet.

Anything that didn't have some mental exercise or some nut cracking; in terms of intellectual analysis was not her cup of tea. The world is hard. You can't just get what you want without a struggle. Something as good as this Pastor claims cannot come in such a simple manner, Iyobo concluded.

Iyobo had read the Bible while she was in school. Bible Knowledge was certainly not her favourite subject. She loved Maths and Science. Right from her very early age, she never allowed her belief about anything, to cloud her reasoning. She loved the stories she was told by Fosa about space. They sounded real and scientific. She dreamt of growing up and getting married to the first African astronaut while she went about her medical aspirations. All these ideas had fallen to ash and all dreams have been broken.

'But why? If God so loved me as the pastor claimed, why did I have to go through all that pain in the first place?' Iyobo demanded.

'Hearing words today about a God who we should please because He selflessly loves us has no relevance at all to my miserable life,'Iyobo thought.

Her immediate problem was to pay Madam V and then set up her own trade route of human trafficking, do that for some time and come out clean, to be what she would then decide to be. This is the dream of most prostitutes but deep down in Iyobo's mind, she knew that no human trafficker will ever be 'clean' as that is a road to self destruction and, in ecclesiastical terms, hell. Advocating this sort of behaviour as 'good', as a way for Africans to benefit, when it is only the top dog who will benefit, everyone else is a victim, even the money grabbers, was not good in any way. She knew deep down that she was not the kind of person to attract sympaty as she would forever be seen as dangerous and deadly. Human trafficking was not the way to go if she was to access the path of prosperity and progress. These thoughts streamed out of her innermost being, sounding too true to undermine. She suddenly realised she was in church.

'This will be my very last time in church. It puts me on the spot and brings old tormenting memories to me. I am so filled with guilt and condemnation. This is it. This is it,' she almost spoke aloud, but to herself.

While she was thinking about the frivolity with which the sermon was being delivered, like in a single sweep of thought, Iyobo remembered Debbie Rookas. Her mind lingered on the past a moment. The time she spent with those nuns was the most special time in her life, she accepted. She then went on to think about Dr Ulens who was also a devout Catholic who didn't know her but loved her unconditionally without judging her.

'These are white people and I am black,' she almost shouted out without knowing why.

Or were all these people pleasing God when they showed me uncondi-tional love? She thought about Mr Unugboro and the headmaster. She remembered the determination with which they pleaded for her to go to school. These were not church people but they were good people. She tried to draw a line between these two sets of people. She got more confused, especially when she thought you could be good without going to church. Or as Pastor Greg said, be bad and go to church.

She considered her father, Madame V and James. She wondered what these ones were made of. She quickly pushed them from her thoughts.

'Do not be stuck with your past. Many are stuck with things God has forgiven and forgotten,' Pastor Greg called out.

These words fell on Iyobo's ears like a bomb and as she struggled to marry this with what she was just thinking about, she found she could now look at the pastor's mouth. She sensed she was now being spoken to directly. It was becoming too much. These words didn't sound intelligent to her but they simply sounded true.

'The religious system was all bad news. The mindset was about what you can do and can't do. They were using fear to make people follow God. They threatened people with the word "judgement" to get people to repent. Do not be ashamed to accept the news that Jesus died for you to set you free from your sins and the consequences of it. He has given you a brand new life. It is done. It has been paid for already. You have nothing else to do than to accept it as a gift.'

Pastor Greg walked up and down the aisle lowering down his microphone, as if recharging his battery. The interpreter trailed behind him faithfully.

'The problem is that people tried to make religion out of faith and this created confusion and misunderstanding, as the lifestyle of the carriers of religion did not match the message they preached. Many either backed out or did not follow at all,' he wiped the sweat that settled on his forehead and then continued.

'How much do you think you are worth? You can't do enough for Jesus to earn His love. You don't need to seek His approval because He already approves of you. All God wants from you is to rest in what he's done for you. So, stop looking at your obedience and just accept His offer of love to you,' the pastor continued.

'If you don't allow accusation, guilt and condemnation to come your way, the devil can't do anything. When you hold fast to the fact that your freedom depends on the finished work of redemption, you become unmoveable.' Now Pastor Greg was back on the podium. He dropped the microphone as if he was done. The interpreter looked helplessly on, unsure of what he was doing. He then paced up and down the stage, went back to take the microphone. He came to the edge of the podium and stood. This time, he was standing right in front of the congregation. He made sure everyone was listening and said very clearly.

'The moment you believe, God does not leave you. He responds.'

Iyobo finally picked up courage to look at the other three. Maimu was sleeping. Iyobo woke her up. The other two looked at Iyobo and they all smiled. When people were invited forward to come and accept Jesus as their personal Lord and Saviour, no church member came out. Three of the four did. The Pastor prayed a prayer of thanksgiving saying they were lost but now are found, just like the prodigal son.

❖ ❖ ❖

The four girls returned to the brothel at about two in the afternoon. They had thought they could be back at about noon. That evening, Justina sent her customers away, making up her mind not to accept customers on Sundays. To her, that was her way of pleasing God.

The moment you believe, God does not leave you. He responds.

The words of the minister haunted and taunted Iyobo like a ghost.

'The moment you believe, God does not leave you. He responds,' Iyobo muttered several times in a row to herself. She began to imagine how God would respond to someone like her. Surely, she had done too much evil for a holy God to respond to her.

'I have made my home in a citadel of sin. I can't even think about all I have been through from the village up to now. All I see is darkness and hopelessness,' she thought aloud when no one was watching.

'But God is holy. I am not holy. I am sinful. Despised by my dad, haunted by the so called sin of my mother. How else would I interpret all that had been happening to me? Got pregnant at sixteen. Broke a family dream. Disappointed my parents. Gave out my only daughter while I settled in a brothel. In the course of my job, I live a constant lie, stealing and all sorts of things. I abuse my body with alcohol and drugs,' Iyobo tried to hold back the tears rolling down her cheeks.

'The Pastor tells me that someone called Jesus has paid for all that. It just doesn't make sense. I commit an offence and someone else pays for it? There is no sense in that. I have committed an offence. I must serve the punishment. Yes, this one makes sense,' Iyobo choked and coughed. She kept crying, locked up in her room all by herself.

'If God would really respond to me according to the word of the pastor, I will believe,' she quietly whispered.

'I can't just believe such illogical things said by the Pastor. If all he said was true, let me get a sign or a proof,' Iyobo said sobbing noisily.

As Iyobo rolled these thoughts over in her mind, those same words drove through her as if every cell in her body was responding to every letter that made up the sentence. This time, it became personal.

Iyobo, the moment you believe, God does not leave you. He responds.

The tone that spoke those words became too powerful to be ignored.

At this moment, Iyobo fell on her knees and began to sob uncontrollably. It started very quietly then increased but this time with words which sounded like prayers, if prayer be defined as communication between man and God. This communication felt very personal. It felt like knowing a very good and kind person for the first time to whom you wanted to go to again and again. This felt awesome.

'Forgive me Lord, I believe,' were the only words that came out of her. These were the only prayers she finally caught herself uttering.

When Iyobo came out of her servile demeanour, demented, so it seemed, she took a look around like a crazy young thing who felt ashamed after she had suddenly been restored to some form of sanity. Her own sanity this time was that of purity, forgiveness, assurance in God and hope. She only knew she was there but didn't quite get what was happening to her.

'If any man be in Christ, he is a new creation, old things are passed away and everything has become new.' She remembered these words from the pastor in church. They were now resounding in her spirit as if she just heard them in her room.

Iyobo had an electrifying feeling of excitement and thrill followed by a certain feeling of total freedom and serenity. Disgraceful behaviour and guilt gave way to pure, righteous and saintly composure.

For the first time in her whole life, Iyobo felt highly valued. She felt accepted by her own self. She loved herself.

'If God accepts me, I don't care what people say about me,' she whispered to herself. Realising she was sitting on the floor, she got up, wiped her face with a tissue and made way for the bathroom. Her heart was filled with so much joy that she wanted to tell someone, of the strange but Godly experience she had just had. Then, it suddenly occurred to her that she was in a brothel.

CHAPTER 36

It was 9 A.M.. The cathouse has become home to about fifty whores, of various nationalities. Every now and then, new girls arrived, most of them, against their will. You could tell by their naïve attitude and first time, they often refused to comply with house rules. This was often followed by an older one calling the newly arrived into her room for a so called sisterly session.

'If you want to become someone great and independent, you must follow the rules,' a sister said maintaining a deadly look.

'It is not the end of the world. We have all been there. Just look at me, very soon, I will pay all my money and be free to start any business I want to do. I admit I have an incurable disease but that is part of the business.'

The first time Iyobo heard these words, her innocent look-ing eyes shone with terror, as she tried to understand why this girl was being a braggart over an activity that brings a killer dis-ease into her life.

'If you begin with this attitude, first you are not doing your-self a favour and secondly, you are putting yourself in grave dan-ger. Remember the gods you swore to before boarding the plane, they are always around and will not fail to strike at any iota of be-trayal. You better get this into your head and be obedient to your madam. She is your goddess in this Europe.'

Iyobo could not understand what her so called *counsellor* was saying to her. All she could get at that instant was that she should accept what was deadly and inhuman. In all she heard, what wor-ried Iyobo most was the ease and the natural way her interlocutor passed the message to her. This just showed that she, herself, had fully accepted the rules of the game, without pausing for a second to consider what the end result might be. As she spoke, fear soon gave way to faith and then strength to do the unpleasant and unpalatable gradually set in. To survive, it was often said among the whores that you must have faith in the trade and in the *god-sent* man or woman who made this possible for them.

Iyobo was there. At first, she felt belittled, then time, money and the hope that one day, the agony would be over, gave her enough strength to carry on. She wished and wished she could go back to school. She felt she was wasting her time but she was too tied down to even try to imagine a way out of this dungeon which stank of sweat, sex and seminal fluid. Besides, it was becoming over-crowded which made it more unhealthy. Those at the top of the game cared only for the quick money they made and for the victims, they had to sort themselves out. They risked their health, liberty and also their lives if payments and promises are not kept.

The worst was when some men came in refusing to use condoms. They insist on the 'skin to skin' thing and that is very dangerous in passing on deadly viruses.

'Who cares' was the slogan that kept most of them going. They would say it stylishly, hitting their bums with one hand. Then they would laugh and laugh. Making all sorts of jokes lightened the burden of the inhabitants of this pleasure house. If one person said 'who cares?' as a way of saying hello, the other person replied 'who cares' with the normal expected gesture.

Iyobo, Justina, Maimu and Florence gathered in Florence's room as usual. They often did this before they got dressed for their daily activities. Florence was older than the others. They all respected her and looked up to her as a big sister. The church experience didn't seem to nag at her. To her it was business as usual. They were used to greeting each other with the two magical words that seemed to not only put them in the mood of the business but also spur them on to pave the way for greater accomplishment, which was wooing as many customers as possible. They all had dreams but their dreams had now changed.

Justina had an experience similar to Iyobo's after the church visit but she suppressed it and let it go. If she succumbed to this compelling voice that seemed to be telling her to quit this trade, she asked, what would she do? To whom would she go? There were too many questions. She pondered over this over and over again, prayed a simple prayer and slept.

Unlike Iyobo, Florence was a daughter of a known preacher. Unknown to her parents, she sneaked along with a couple of her friends to Europe through a 'lady trolley'. She wasn't really poor but she wanted to make a life of her own and thought it was greener at the other side of the sea. They travelled night and day across the desert to make this happen. She loved the big cars and big houses as people in this business came home to display to other young people. When she arrived, she thought she could work with her hands and earn good money. Life in Europe was certainly not like that because it was even harder for their people to get good jobs. 'Aprapra' or a cleaning job was too slow for people on the fast lane. She was soon advised by a friend to change course. She then made the hard choice. She had come too far to want to look back. While in church, some guilt came over her and she really wanted to repent but fear of the unknown kept her bound to complete her vision. She crossed her heart as she had often done; backed out as she forced herself over and over again to overturn every word she had taken in from the pastor. In no time, she was herself again.

When the pastor invited those who had been touched by the message to come out, Florence was among those who went. She had come out like this several times before but always went back. Florence had two bibles in her room. There was one she had kept preciously in her briefcase and the other, she kept on her dressing mirror table. Iyobo had seen it before with her when she tried to read some books of psalm after a scary dream. Today, Iyobo wished she could ask her for a Bible. She was hungry for the word of God and just didn't know how to ask this preacher's daughter turned prostitute.

On this day, Justina was first to come out of her room with a cup of tea in one hand and a cigarette in the other, shouting as loud as she possibly could 'who cares?' Maimu joined her, chanting the phrase.

Iyobo came out gracefully with a big smile and a form of inexplicable confidence. She entered the room and while the other three laughed and made a joke of everything they saw, including people they met in the church, Iyobo sat down at the edge of the bed, hand on jaw, silently watching as the other talked. When they had all had their turn and fell quiet, Iyobo turned to them as she spoke as confidently as she ever could.

'The moment you believe, God does not leave you. He responds.'

Everyone laughed as loud as they could, thinking Iyobo was making fun of Pastor Greg.

'Sure, I remember that.'

'He was handsome though. It's just that his jacket was out-dated. Preachers these days are more fashionable than that. What was his name again?' muttered Florence as she opened a packet of chewing gum.

'No, stop it,' shouted Iyobo firmly. 'He is a man of God. You must not talk about him like that. We all heard the truth yesterday and must change our ways. We must accept Jesus as our Lord and Saviour and become children of God. God is true. God is real,' she struggled to continue.

They laughed and jeered.

'I can't believe what I am seeing. Iyobo, the church you went to yesterday has changed you so soon?' said Florence.

'Look at me; I am a Pastor's daughter. I have two Bibles in my room as I am talking. I still have to control myself because this money, I must catcham. Do not spoil show for yourself ooo! Why are you behaving like a bush girl? At least God knows that things are hard,' Justina said in pidgin English, drawing another pull of the cigarette placed firmly between two fingers of her left hand, while she adjusted herself on the bed where she sat.

Iyobo knew she had no written facts in her head, neither had she experienced enough or even heard enough to defend this worthy cause but her inner conviction and last night's experience with God who promised and did what he promised overwhelmed her. She then began to speak passionately about the God she now knew as her Father. Her audience of three listened with utmost and intense shock.

'Iyobo, you of all people. Please be quiet and be real.'

'I am real but I will not be quiet. I am a new person. I am changed on the inside. I can't explain what happened to me,' Iyobo tried to convince her listeners.

'Oh, don't worry. Things like that happen. You'll get over it. I never knew you were such a softie,' Maimu added.

None of the words Iyobo said seemed to make any impact on the girls. Justina though, became a bit sober later and it was this that made Iyobo feel free enough to ask her for a Bible which she happily gave up.

'Thanks. I will buy one today when I go to town. I need to quickly check a few things and I will give it back to you.'

'Oh no, don't worry. I've got two. There's been one lying under my suitcase.'

'You've got two Bibles and you never told us about the love of God. You've been keeping it all to yourself. By the way, how did you get to buy two Bibles at once?'

'Buy? No, I didn't buy any of them. My dad is a pastor and I just took them from the house.'

'Please lend me a Bible'

'Sure. You have this one, I can use the one in my suitcase.'

'It's really kind of you.'

The whole day, Iyobo locked herself in the room without dressing to come out and there was no knock on her window throughout that day. She voraciously devoured the pages of the Bible where she opened. The first chapter she set her eyes on was Isaiah 46.

This chapter made her understand the ignorance and possible danger in worshiping idols. She thought about the first time she was initiated into pagan worship. She was just three years old. She was made to dance to a form of god. However, her mother promised this god could be upgraded if she continued to be a good girl. The new god would be a carved doll. She would have beautiful long blond hair. She couldn't get this doll before the mishap of her unwanted pregnancy and consequent escape to a new country.

The Bible now assured her that old things were passed away and all had become new. This meant she now had a brand new life in Christ Jesus.

At a point, she gazed at the ceiling of her room and said, 'I am not ready to soil this new relationship. Wherever God tells me to go, I will go and whatever God tells me to do, I will do. If I have to go back home, I am confident He will take care of me. If I knew God just a tiny bit, all these years like I know Him now in just these past 24 hours, things would have been different in my life,' she said aloud in her room.

Iyobo read the Bible at random. After Isaiah 46, she then went to Isaiah 53. She couldn't understand most parts of Isaiah. She went further to read the gospels. This was much easier. The more she read the Bible, the more her confidence grew in the things of God. She read John, chapter 1 three times. When she got to verse 12 and 13, she wished the Bible was hers. *So, I am born of God because I believe in the Lord Jesus Christ,* she repeated over and over again. She would have underlined the verses. Instead, she memorised them. Verse 14 made her chill. *So, Jesus we all hear about is the word of God. He became a human being and lived with other humans.*

When she returned the Bible to Florence, the other girl told her she could keep it, as a gift.

'Thanks Florence. To be honest, I just couldn't get how you kept this precious book in your closet for such a long time without reading it. Do you even read it?'

'Sure, when I have strange dreams of course. I read a couple of psalms but that's it really. As you know, I am a very busy person.'

'Well, thanks for giving me the Bible, talk to you later,' Iyobo said with so many unanswered questions on her mind about Florence.

'Who cares what man says about me,' Iyobo screamed allowed one day after a reading of Romans chapter 8 verse 31. 'If God be for me, who can be against me?'

'Madam V is here. Iyobo, I hope you are ready for her. It's either you rain money from heaven for her or you preach to her,' said one of the girls one day, teasing the newly born again.

Iyobo was calm and said nothing. She had heard of all the rantings of Madam V threatening to deal with her if she played a fast one using religion as a cover. Iyobo had received warning notes reminding her of all the oaths and papers she had signed and taken. She had also been reminded about how dangerous this could be to her in all aspects. Iyobo's calmness and especially her unwillingness to move away from the brothel despite the threats confused Madam V and the entire sex team. Her boldness gave strength to other girls who also decided to forsake the trade.

The following Sunday, Iyobo was first to arrive at church. She was alone. She invited the other three; they all shunned her, telling her she was out of her mind. She had bought another Bible which fitted in her bag. She also bought a small exercise book, where she jotted Bible passages that touched her personally. She remembered what Florence said about arriving at church in time. 'Being late to church is very rude. I do not want to be rude in God's house,' she promised herself.

Iyobo wore a pair of cropped trousers with a short sleeve pink flowery blouse. It was summer, so this was ideal. Iyobo now had a purpose for going to church: to serve God.

When worship started, the new convert didn't quite know what to do except to follow the crowd. She sang when they sang, clapped hands when they did and then when it was time to hear the word of God, she realised she was very happy and wanted it to come quickly. She got out her pen and exercise book. She jotted down what was said and went back to brothel to go through it all again.

CHAPTER 37

With Iyobo in front, all other 49 call girls, of different races and nationalities, walked into the church late. They sat at the empty seats at the back of the church so as not to disturb a service that had already started. Pastor Jean-Paul froze as he gazed from the altar at the non stop influx of scantily dressed whores flocking together like a group of meerkats in their most unnatural habitat. Their clothes left very little to the imagination.

Iyobo saw Pastor Jean-Paul pause as he watched the women enter. They had spoken the week before and she had said, the physician is not for the healthy but for the sick. After a moment of thought he had asked who was he to determine who and how people should come and know their God? His job was simply to say, 'welcome home'. Despite the brief break, he began preaching again and Iyobo was comfortable that she hadn't upset him too greatly.

Since Iyobo's first experience with the Christian God, she had been fasting and praying for the salvation of every girl in the brothel. Her constant burden was to pray for them, to which she yielded without complaint. The more she prayed and preached to them in the brothel, the more they came to church but one thing Iyobo didn't do, she didn't lecture them on how to dress or how to behave in the house of God. Those who attended church kept their own fashion but it was easy to know they were responding to the gospel by the hunger they had for the word of God. Most of all, they were faithful at church. The girls kept coming Sunday after Sunday. Some even came for the midweek Bible study and prayer meeting. The funny thing about this group of girls was that they all flocked together with Iyobo at the front. On Sunday, they all walked to church. The message of the Bible had spread so much that windows in the brothel were shut on Sundays, to open again Monday morning.

On this particular Sunday, the pastor preached a message titled 'Grace for all'. After the service, Pastor Jean-Paul asked to speak with Iyobo while the other girls waited.

'How did you find the message?' Pastor Jean asked passionately.

'Great, sir. The interpreter was excellent, so everything was really good. All my friends are also blessed. I am very glad. All our lives are changing bit by bit. Please continue to pray for us. I can't even believe what I am seeing among us. I am very happy Pastor.'

'Hallellujah! My sister!' Pastor Jean-Paul spoke in French for the first time to Iyobo.

'Do you know that, while preaching today, the calling was very strong on me, that for the first time in my life and in the history of this church and this community, I spoke in tongues? I have read this in the Bible and I have even preached it, but I never knew I could experience it. What about you? Do you know what speaking in tongues means?' the Pastor asked with excitement, as he had started having confidence in Iyobo's astute spirituality.

'Oh, yes sir. While praying one day in my room in the brothel, I received the baptism of the Holy Spirit.

Pastor Jean-Paul sighed. 'I wonder why such a holy experience should occur in a brothel, and yet I am reminded that Mary Magdalene was herself a prostitute. If Jesus would work with such a woman, who am I to question where or how God reaches people?'

'And two other girls also spoke in tongues a few days later during one of our prayer meetings. God is not partial. This makes me respect God more. He manifests Himself to anyone who surrenders all to Him. It doesn't matter what your social or religious status is. God sees the heart, but humans look at the flesh,' Iyobo said piously.

'Yes but you must know that speaking in tongues is unacceptable in this church. This will drive people away. The thing is, I am never going to stop speaking in tongues. When you come to church next week and see no one here, know that it will not be about you or your girls, but about some great things God is doing. I am ready to ride with Him,' the pastor said, with a huge smile.

Iyobo stood before the pastor not knowing what to say. She simply smiled and smiled.

'God's little secret,' Iyobo whispered, walking away.

'Yes, God's little secrets,' the Pastor whispered back as he also turned to go.

'Merci, Pasteur,' Iyobo managed to say.

Iyobo and the girls went back to the house of ill repute. At their place of dwelling, things had changed. Many now attended the Tuesday Bible study Iyobo organised in her room. They brought extra chairs from their rooms, sometimes overflowing to the corridor. Customers that came at this time were ignored.

Iyobo learnt that Madame V vowed to rain down thunder and brimstone upon all culprits. She was mainly disturbed with known customers who had to go elsewhere. If this continued, she feared she would soon be bankrupt. Iyobo heard of the threat and intensified prayers.

Wednesday, Iyobo turned up for weekly activity in church but to her greatest dismay, no church member turned up for Bible study. The Pastor had guessed right.

At first, Iyobo thought she came on the wrong day until she saw Pastor Jean-Paul sitting all by himself, reading the Bible. Mariam, his wife was arranging the flowers at a corner of the church. She didn't notice when Iyobo came in.

The three were expecting this would happen because of the presence of a band of whores in the Church last Sunday, coupled by the Pastor behaving strangely and speaking in some unknown language. They thought they were losing their church to some unholy hookers who were no good. For the first time, Iyobo had the opportunity to tell the first family in the house of God a bit of her story. They listened, jaws slack in surprise at the tale.

'You see why I can't look back,' Iyobo told the pair listening to her. 'There is nothing to look back to. The Bible says, old things are passed away and all have become new. This simply means, I no longer have a past. I am new. Jesus has made something beautiful out of my ugly life,' Iyobo said laughing slightly, with tears rolling down her cheeks.

Mariam took over the issue of grace the Pastor started off last Sunday. 'I think the more we preach about grace and unmerited favour of God, the more God sees our helplessness and comes down to bless us with His divine presence. It's every one of us who has sinned. Not a few. The Bible says all have sinned and come short of the glory of God. All means the whole world. It doesn't matter where you come from, how you were raised, whether rich or poor. We all have inherited sin from our first parents, Adam and Eve. It is only when we recognise that Jesus paid the price for us on the cross and that He rose again from the dead for us that we are saved. Even if you are the richest in this world and don't have Jesus in your life, you are poor.'

Iyobo had never seen Mariam like this before. She was always in the children's area taking care of the children. Earlier, she was told by one of the ushers that Jean-Paul and Mariam got married last year and both of them had decided to stay serving God without thinking of having children for the next three years at least. They were both young and ready to please God at all times.

For the first time since losing Fosa, Iyobo wished and prayed quietly that God would give her a man of her own who would cherish her the way Jean-Paul cherished Mariam. She yearned to serve God with humility like Mariam.

The three shared experiences and prayed before going home. Iyobo discovered that Jean-Paul broke the silence when he decided to make a few calls. First to the deacons and then to the workers. They all said the same thing. They couldn't be in the same church with hookers. The church is a place of sanctity and sanity not a brothel or a haven for outlaws. 'We all must say "no" to anything unholy and strive towards what is pleasing to God,' one of the elders stated forcefully.

CHAPTER 38

There were two items always on Iyobo's prayer list. The first was the salvation of all her friends in the red light district and the second was to have Amenze live permanently with her. She was now coming to the house she rented, more frequently than before and the bond between mother and daughter was growing stronger by the day. She hated to be in the brothel while keeping a flat in town to deceive her daughter. She longed to be a responsible mother. Since committing her life to God through Jesus Christ, Iyobo stopped receiving customers though she remained in her room in the brothel. Iyobo noticed Madam V had come more frequently than before, since she couldn't keep up with payments. The sex baroness had openly threatened to get rid of her if she didn't effect the full payment on the date they agreed. What Madam V didn't know was that Iyobo had just gone on three days fasting and prayer for her salvation. She felt that if Madam V could be saved, many whores would be set free from sex slavery.

Iyobo's growth in spiritual matters had been so rapid that she quickly learnt to cast all her burdens on the Lord, convinced that, after all, He cared very much for her.

Iyobo couldn't keep what she called 'the good news' to herself. She started a revolutionary mission in the brothel. Midweek fellowship started off in the room of the ex-hooker. Iyobo told her old colleagues that salvation was simple and free for all; not even a fool should get lost.

'If you had a child who got lost and you had a choice to tell the child how to get home, would you give a complex explanation or would you use simple language to direct her home? Well that was what God did. He chose to make it simple. Only believe in Jesus who He sent to die for you and salvation is yours. Believe in your heart and confess with your mouth. He travelled all the way from Heaven for this and He is happy to see you free and happy with no form of guilt in your life. My dear sisters, all things are possible if you only believe. Read the Bible and find out what happened to all the prostitutes who believed. They were rewarded for their faith in God. You may not see it now, but it will definitely come, not only for you but also for your children and their children,' Iyobo finally said, looking at the ladies randomly, as if trying to verify which of them would join her in the new fight she had started.

That day, all the girls smiled, walked out slowly after prayer without saying a word. On another day, she invited many other girls to a meal with the last money she had, without knowing where her next meal would come from. She had a chance to talk to them again. This time, she made them to understand that now that they were in this deplorable state, where some people laugh at them and others exploit them, Jesus had died for them.

'Why then can't you love Him back by accepting this free gift He has given to you? I know why. Fear of the unknown. Fear of what others will say at home. You have given all the impression that you are making money and you don't want to fail. I understand. You must not fail to understand that without God, there is no life for you and if you die today, life will go on without you. Your parents, brothers and sisters will carry on living without you.'

Iyobo at this point dissolved into tears, allowing others to reflect on what she had said.

'Just look at us. In winter, we must dress to appeal to customers at the expense of our own lives. We can't put on warm clothes because the more we give away, the more customers we get. Jesus wants us to come to Him and He will give us a better life. Do not refuse Him,' she finally said, amidst sobs.

On this day, some of the girls resolved to start going to church and not accept customers on Sundays. They thought they could start with that. They managed to squeeze out some money from the Monday to Friday earnings to pay their madam and some to be sent to families at home. Wednesdays were meant for prayer meetings with Iyobo and so had to be kept holy. This was gradually moved to Saturdays when Iyobo saw that most of the girls were getting more involved with the word of God. To most of the girls the fun of the whore game was doomed as the real deal was on Saturdays and Sundays. They survived on the barest minimum. On top of that, guilt flooded their weary souls as they battled within themselves, if God would accept the tithes and offerings they gave in church. They felt the money was unclean and so a holy God would not accept that. Iyobo's answer was subtle but to the point.

'You have received Jesus Christ into your life. Let the Holy Spirit speak to you. Let the word God has given you guide you to the truth. In all things, reflect on the fact that God is more interested in your giving your whole self to Him than anything else you can possibly give.'

Iyobo had a huge problem helping the new converts to wear appropriate clothes when in or outside the house. This was made apparent the day they had their annual thanksgiving in the church. Iyobo invited all of them. Fifteen girls turned up at church with skirts up to their hips. On this occasion, Pastor Jean-Paul struggled to get the full attention of worshippers.

For the first time, the pastor considered speaking to Iyobo to help advise her friends to dress appropriately for church. He reminded her that it was a community church and so even the elderly were all born and raised there and he would not like to spoil the tradition and the good works others had put in.

Iyobo apologised but couldn't keep some words back from the man of God.

'But how will they change if they don't hear the gospel. How can they dress up in the way you want them to dress up if they do not know how much God loves them? Theirs is to impress and nothing else gives them worth than their looks. We have all come a long way Pastor. You have no idea. One thing you must know is that I was once like that. Remember the first day I walked into this church? I was worse. Today, I am changed because I have seen the light. I can't see myself going back to that world because the Bible says old things are passed away, behold, all things have become new. Pastor, you probably were not like one of them but there was certainly something you did, God saved you from. Do this with love and compassion. Remember when prostitutes came to Jesus? What did He do? Pushed them away? Or do you think all those prostitutes were all well behaved before Jesus met them? It was an ex-hooker who saw Jesus first when He rose from the dead. Check out the genealogy of Jesus. Rahab was a whore. It shows that God loves us all equally,' Iyobo made the last statement looking straight into the Pastor's eyes.

'I understand totally what you are talking about but the point is that it is not about me. It's about the sheep I have been called to guide. They are upset because each time you come with your group, they are all dressed inappropriately. This is dividing my church and upsetting my ministry.'

These words entered into Iyobo's ears almost convincing her.

'Pastor, I am one of your sheep. When the other hookers come to the church and give their lives to Christ, they also become your sheep. If you like, call them dirty sheep. You need to roll up your beautiful sleeves, wash them by teaching them God's word and talk good of them all the time, like I do with them. Remember Jesus already paid the price for their sins. Just like my eyes were opened to see this life giving light of Christ, so they will see. Please, pastor, help us,' Iyobo pleaded.

Two days later, Pastor Jean-Paul got a letter from the General Overseer asking him to honourably resign and look for somewhere else to preach. This news was not shocking to Jean-Paul, neither was it something he was fully prepared for.

CHAPTER 39

On one fateful day, Scott reappeared at Iyobo's door.

He noticed she was not among the girls standing at the window and decided to make his way to her room with the help of one of the girls. He took a critical look at the transformed girl standing in front of him and noticed she was beaming with smiles. Scott's eyes swept round the room and finally returned his attention to his hostess from whom he accepted a chair close to the door which was wide open, covered only by a transparent silk curtain.

'Wow, something about you has changed. You seem happier. What's been going on?'

'Something very good has been happening to me. You are welcome to my room. Believe it or not, I am still here in the brothel but I am no more part of the happenings. I am now a Christian, born again. I am a new creation. I am holy, unblamable, irreproachable in His sight.'

'In whose sight?'

'In God's sight, because Jesus paid the price for me. I have believed and received Him into my life according to the word in John 3:16.'

'I am really sorry I couldn't come back to see you as promised.'

'Don't worry. Am fine. God has been taking good care of me. I promised God, after I had promised you that I would quit the trade and I did. I did it by the power of God who now lives in me. Since then, God has been taking care of me. My Pastor and his wife and some other brothers and sisters in Christ have been really good to me. My job here now is to help those who want to quit the trade, like me. I encourage them by holding prayer meetings and Bible studies with them. You must have seen there are only a few girls left. I fast and pray all the time that they all get saved like me. I believe God has a future for me like He has for them. It takes boldness and faith to face this future you know nothing about. I used to be scared of my madam, of the trade, I wasn't even sure if I would come out of the trade alive. But now, greater is He that lives in me than that which lives in the world.'

'Can you please come out with me to a bar or something where we could chat for a bit longer?' Scott quickly said.

'Oh no. I am really sorry. I belong to God now. The Bible says my body is the temple of the Living God and to be honest, I do not even want to be seen with a man who is not my husband. Your being here is bad enough,' Scott watched Iyobo stand up from her bed where she had been sitting and walked towards the door.

'What would you like to drink? I have apple and orange drink.'

'No, thanks. I had enough drink before coming here,' he lied, a bit confused at the present scenery he was forced to be a part of.

He stayed in her room, talking with her and left without giving her any money. After that, Scott visited Iyobo almost every other week and was able to understand the extent of her transformation. He was happy for her.

What amused Scott the most was that each time he got there, he was bombarded with Bible Scriptures. 'Does she know where she is or to say the least, does she know what she has been? A prostitute talking to me about God?' Scott laughed and wouldn't stop laughing when he got to his lonely flat. The thought of it all killed the boredom that sent him to look for company in the brothel. 'I just wanted to help her. She is a good girl though', Scott encouraged himself.

In less than a week, Scott had convinced Iyobo to move out of the brothel, promising to pay off her sponsor as an act of charity.

❖ ❖ ❖

When Iyobo heard she would receive help to pay off Madam V, she didn't pray to know that this was a gift from God. She was sick of living in the whorehouse. She was convinced that God had finally heard her prayers. She also knew she was not moving in to live with any man. She immediately thought about Amenze. She dreamt of living in the same house with her daughter who was now at boarding school, an institution for gifted and talented girls. Iyobo was filled with joy and hope, and for the first time in her life, Iyobo began to dream. She thought about going back to school.

The debt to Madam V was 45,000 dollars and she had paid more than half of the amount. She was grateful to God that she was alive, although threats never stopped coming at her. Scott finally helped to pay off the remaining amount. Iyobo was finally officially released from her debt.

'How could I ever thank Scott for saving my life?' she often asked herself. Who was he after all? She'd heard stories about angels and how they came to save people from bad situations. Was he an angel just pretending to be human? If really, he was sent by God, why does he not believe in God? 'God's little secrets' was the phrase that came to her mind.

Since Iyobo became a Christian, she had met several other dedicated Christians who had encouraged her in her Christian faith, among whom was Christine, a British lady who came with her husband Pastor Ken Lane to set up a community church in a suburb of Brussels. Iyobo met Christine at the *Grande Place* in Brussels where she was sharing leaflets containing extracts from the Bible. Christine spoke fluent French and Flemish, with flawless accents, but switched easily to her native English if her conversation partner required it. This was what she did when she met Iyobo.

Christine had preached to several young girls who thought they were in Europe to pick gold from the streets. She and her husband had opened their home to many victims of human trafficking, especially those from Eastern Europe.

'Many have now come to know Jesus as their personal Lord and Saviour,' Christine once testified to Iyobo.

'I was born to share the good news because this is all I have known in my entire life,' she told Iyobo on her first visit to her home in Tervuren. Christine and Ken became Iyobo's spiritual parents in Belgium. She grew stronger in her faith and her life style changed for good. The stronger she became, the more convinced Iyobo was to pray for all her friends in the brothel. She wanted all of them to see the light that she had seen.

'Jesus, who saved me, forgave my every sin and has become my light and hope, is able to save all the others. We were in it together and I believe we shall all come out of it together,' she prayed every day.

CHAPTER 40

When Iyobo woke up on Monday morning in her rented flat, her first thought was to make an advert in the local newspaper for an "aprapra" job. The word was explained to Iyobo by Ajua. It means cleaning in many places in Ghana language. "Apra" as a word means "clean" but when it doubles up as in "aprapra", this is to show it is being done in multiple places to make a living.

The Nigerian community in Belgium was quite small at the time and so getting an "aprapra" job was not too difficult as not many immigrants were there except for the purpose of studying before returning home. Whatever had been the case, the obvious fact was that it was a challenge for Iyobo. How could she now become a cleaner? If she wanted to get another job, she would have to speak fluent French and Flemish. Her inability to communicate fluently in either language was a hindrance to her progress.

While attending night school, Iyobo started working in old people's homes as a cleaning lady. She was so good that she beat most of the Polish and Philipino cleaners who were known to charge less than the Ghanaians and the Nigerians.

She smiled while at work and on some occasions shared her new faith with her employers and their families. They loved her overall countenance. She was recommended by her employers to other homes and in no time, Iyobo got enough cleaning jobs to sustain her. Though she considered these earnings peanuts compared to what she made from the sextrade, she said she had more peace and most importantly, she was making her daughter proud. She had also learnt to tell her family at home that she didn't have enough money to send like before.

This latest development made her mother furious. 'Come back home if you are not ready to send us as much money as before,' she shouted at Iyobo one day on the phone.

'My lifestyle has changed and I can't go back to my old life. Your brothers are all doing well now but they can't meet up with my expenses.'

❖ ❖ ❖

Iyobo promised the girls at the Brothel God would sort them out in His own way and time but appealed to them to take a leap of faith and quit the trade. All they needed to do was to give their lives to Christ. However, Iyobo thought about the case of Florence, the Preacher's daughter, which she considered pure hypocrisy. You must first be clean before serving God. She was not too much into this God thing, as she would put it, because she was not done yet with her work.

Iyobo had totally quit prostitution but went to the brothel to see her friends and to continue with the weekly Bible study. Most importantly, she had begged God, she wanted all her friends saved. She had received threat letters but she had only prayed and shown the letters to Jean-Paul and Marian, with whom she still had contact after they had left their old church. These two supported her financially as well as prayed with her. Since she had decided to serve God, at least ten girls had totally stopped whoring and their families or some form of organisation had paid off their debts.

While coming from her cleaning jobs, Iyobo came across some of her old acquaintances in business that lived in other places in town. Some of them asked her if she was crazy quitting the job when she still owed. Iyobo only smiled. Others longed to have the peace and serenity she was now enjoying. Most of them said they couldn't quit the business because they'd got debts to pay. 'If only I would get someone to pay this debt for me, I would be out the next day,' most of them said.

'If we don't pay, there will be people after us. Besides, we swore before some very fierce gods that we would pay back. You can see we've got loads of things on our hands. As for you, enjoy your freedom and good luck.'

'If you trust God to fight for you, He will,' Iyobo said firmly.

CHAPTER 41

Iyobo was able to convince the foster service that she had stability in her situation. The Le Gros family was contacted and Amenze was allowed to move back to live with her mother at weekends and in school holidays. Iyobo was granted full custody of Amenze, although she could go to the Le Gros anytime she wished. Although Amenze was happy to reunite with her biological mother, leaving the Le Gros family was heart rending, both for Amenze and the Belgian family, whom Amenze continued to call Mama and Papa.

❖ ❖ ❖

Reuniting with her daughter was the best thing that happened in Iyobo's life. It was easy for her to tell Amenze that she was a cleaning lady when she came visiting for a week during the Christmas holiday after which Amenze went with the Le Gros family for another one week to Paris. Now that she'd come to stay, she knew she had to be clear with what she was telling her.

Iyobo also had an opportunity to learn some Dutch from Amenze, who spoke English, French and Flemish with ease. Iyobo was happy to give Bini lessons to her daughter who was eager and happy to learn as many languages as possible.

Amenze had learnt a lot of Bini before as a child with her mum but the gap in communication meant they had to start again from the scratch.

Amenze told Iyobo how much she loved and respected her and promised to work very hard at school so that one day, she too would be able to buy a house in Uccle just like Mama and Papa Le Gros.

She said her biggest dream would be to go to Nigeria, the giant country of Africa, as she had learnt in geography. She wanted to see her grandmother but never mentioned wanting to see Iyobo's father. 'I would also like to see your brothers. One day, I will be a big woman working in Nigeria and stopping bad things from happening. This is what I am being taught at school. I will be a good leader taking care of other people.'

'Ok, my daughter. I am really proud of you. Keep up what you are doing and always remember to pray. This must be the first thing.'

'Ok, Mum. Thanks.'

❖ ❖ ❖

Amenze was now 10 years old, she was thin and a bit tall for her age. Amenze's teeth, like her mother's, always caught attention. They were sparkling white. She was now a bit lighter skinned than what she was when she had been very little.

Aside from the academic achievements, Amenze also knew how to play the keyboard, the recorder and the violin. She loved to run commentary on football games. She preferred to do this in French. Her favourite team was *Anderlecht FC*. She hated naming players as her favourite because according to her, if they all play well, having a favourite player would be subjective. Reading was her passion. She read anything and everything. She brought some French books for Iyobo to read.

'My daughter, how I loved to read when I was your age.'

'Mum, reading has nothing to do with age. You can still continue to read. This will make you a better mum,' she said with a smile, peering through her glasses at her mum's tired face.

'Ok. Put them there. I will read my Bible first and then I will come and read those books.'

Both of their eyes met and Iyobo pulled her daughter closer, hugging and cuddling her.

'Amenze, you are a very beautiful, intelligent girl. When I was your age, I was also told I was beautiful. I had dreams like you. I wanted to grow up to be a doctor, so as to help my brothers and especially my mother who was doing everything to support me and my brothers. I did all I could do until something happened that changed my life forever.'

'Ah, what was that? We have been taught at school that true life experiences help us to be better people.'

'Now, you are too young to understand. When you become eighteen, I shall tell you the details of what happened. I shall hide nothing from you.'

'Ça va maman. Will you also talk to me about my papa? I know his name is Fosa. He was very intelligent with very rich parents but you had very poor parents. But Mum, why would some people be very poor and others very rich? If I become a leader, nobody should be really poor. Do you want to tell me now more about my dad and about my country of origin, Nigeria?'

This question hit Iyobo like a rubber bullet. She was not expecting it at all. Iyobo often told her that her dad was fine and that one day, she would tell her the whole story. She didn't want to spoil this night. 'Sure, I will, but you must wait until you are eighteen.'

'No Mum,' came a childish but stern voice. 'I will not wait until I am eighteen to hear this. Tell me where he is and you can reserve the other story for later. I think I have the right to know where my dad is. All my friends in school talk about their dads and I don't even know anything about mine. Please Mum, I will not judge you. I know I am still young but I will understand. I know many women go through very hard times. We've learnt some of that at school. If you tell me, I shall feel much better within myself. I will not ask you again until you want to talk about it. For now, I feel I am in the dark.'

Iyobo feared each time a discussion like this ensued. She had a picture of Fosa which she took from his album. In that picture, he was leaning against a mango tree with one leg folded backward and the other straight. His two hands were folded. This picture was taken in the massive garden of their home in Benin City. He was wearing jeans and a striped t-shirt. He wore a beret which looked like what the military wear with a pair of sun shades. Iyobo took it and hid it in her bag when he went to get some drinks from the main house during her one and only visit to Fosa's family home. This was the only momento she had of him.

This picture which Iyobo carried everywhere in her purse was certainly not enough to tell the story about a father to a daughter, but at least it was a proof of his existence.

'Mum, where is Dad?' came the question again.

Iyobo kept quiet for a couple of minutes, not knowing what to say.

'Ok Mum. It's alright. I really can't wait till I am eighteen. But what about sixteen, Mum? I am sure I will be ready at that age,' she said, with her head slightly bent to the right.

'Eighteen,' came a firm but polite answer.

'Tell me about Benin Kingdom. Did you say that the Oba of Benin owned all the properties in Benin?'

'This is figurative. This means he is the father of all of us. Just like the Queen of England.'

'Mum, I have read a bit about Benin massacre. Can you give me the gist one more time? How did the British come to Benin? What exactly was the influence of the British on Benin kingdom?'

Iyobo loved talking with Amenze. She realized that Amenze enjoyed hearing the stories about her roots especially her life back home in Africa. Iyobo was always very careful about the stories she told Amenze as there were so many things she was not ready to unveil. There was only one thing she felt her daughter had been unhappy about, her not letting her know more about her dad. Iyobo did not at all plan to tell her daughter this part of her life. She had promised it would only be between her and her God until she had enough courage to let Amenze know. She said she would do this to protect her daughter's credibility in future.

'I have been forgiven by God but why rub it on an innocent girl?' she concluded within herself.

Iyobo was grateful the subject had been changed.

'Now, my baby. I am going to tell you a bit about the great kingdom of Benin before the white man visited us. It is very important that you know your history,' Iyobo said very proudly.

'I am all ears, Mum.'

❖ ❖ ❖

The sun was now peering sparingly into the room and very light breeze picked up the thin silky curtains attached loosely on the very high window.

'But Mum, if Benin is such a place of honour, why did you leave to come to Brussels? Was it for studies or were you sent by your country? We have been told people emigrate from Africa for different reasons.'

Iyobo pretended this light breeze picking up the curtains took her attention. She stared at it, avoiding giving an answer to her daughter's question. She wasn't ready to upset this mother–daughter funtime.

'I am sure you are hungry, my dear. Oh, I forgot to buy some fish from the shop yesterday to prepare your favourite fish stew.' Since becoming a Christian, Iyobo had become more confident, but she was still struggling with many things. Telling her daughter all about her life was still too hard.

The only thing Iyobo was determined to achieve in life, was to ensure that her daughter went to school and had an excellent education. She was sure her daughter had all it took to be great. As she thought briefly about this, fear closed in on her for the first time.

'What if my daughter gets hooked to a boy she hardly knows and gets pregnant, just like me? I was intelligent, so many people said, I was ambitious.'

She quickly and quietly allowed this thought dissolve out of her system. She remembered the Le Gros family and offered up a quick prayer for them. Stretching her right hand calmly and slowly to reach her daughter who was sitting close to her on the same settee, Iyobo pulled her gently to her side.

'Amenze, you are still too young to understand so much. Please, my dear daughter, concentrate on your studies and I promise to do all I can possibly do to support you through school. I thank God for the Belgian government who found out your skill and are sponsoring you. I thank God for the Le Gros family who took you in when it was absolutely impossible for me to look after you. Most of all, I thank God I am now a child of God. I now have a new mindset. I will always be praying for you. Amenze, my daughter, make me proud again. I used to be proud when I came top of the class. My mother would buy me beautiful clothes from the local village market. It didn't matter if they were second hand, what mattered was that they were beautiful. Then the sky was my limit. I wanted to save the world. I probably went a bit too far,' Iyobo burst into tears.

'Oh Mum, it will be alright. Ça va?'

'Oui, ça va mon bébé,' Iyobo replied, holding her very close with a big smile. She then dried her tears.

When Iyobo released her daughter from her firm grip, the 10 year old girl got up, made her way to her room and got out a book to read, when suddenly she heard mum's voice calling out from the kitchen.

'Amenze, let's cook dinner. I have put the onions and the red pepper here.'

'Yes, Mum'

CHAPTER 42

Iyobo and Amenze finally settled at the community church where Ken and Christine were ministers. Iyobo had time to take part in many church activities when Amenze was at school. She would be in the boarding school till the end of primary school. Iyobo became part of the welcoming team in church and was also in the evangelism team. She enjoyed going out with Christine and the rest, to the towns and villages around Brussels to share extracts of the Bible in Flemish and French.

Iyobo invited Scott to one of the services. She had tried to invite him several times earlier, but he always gave one reason or the other for not wanting to come. To Iyobo's delight, that Sunday, he accepted. Pastor Ken had just arrived from a special training programme for community churches' Pastors which took place in Nigeria. He preached a message titled 'Sins and Sons'. When the pastor made an altar call, seven people came out to surrender their lives to Christ. Scott was one of the seven. Scott's acceptance of the gospel was a shock and a delight to Iyobo.

Scott joined the church and served in the technical team since he was quite good in that area. This meant seeing Iyobo every Sunday in church.

'Congratulations Brother,' Iyobo said to him one day.

'Hello, sister. Thanks,' he replied with a beaming smile.

Three months after Scott gave his life to Christ, he disappeared into thin air and no one knew where he went. Every attempt to call him to find out how he was doing failed.

❖ ❖ ❖

Iyobo was a very busy person. Language school coupled with her evangelical work gave her little or no time for other things.

Six months went by and she heard nothing from Scott. One day on a winter Wednesday night, Iyobo was returning home from Bible study when she saw a man standing in front of her door, his back was to her and she didn't recognise him. She looked at the time. It was 9 P.M.. 'Who would be looking for me at this hour?' she asked herself.

'Hello sir. How can I help you?' Iyobo asked in French.

The outside light shone brightly and the man turned at the sound of her voice.

'Hello,' came the voice of Scott.

Iyobo stood for a few seconds staring at this unexpected guest. She then went a bit closer to him to acknowledge his presence after she was sure it was Scott.

'Where have you been? You suddenly disappeared and no one knew where you were!' Iyobo cried out, as she came closer to open the door.

Scott moved back allowing Iyobo open the door.

'Please come in and sit down. It's quite late. How are you?'

Scott ignored her comment.

'Good to see you Iyobo.'

'Good to see you, Scott. Please sit down. Tea or coffee? Where have you been?'

'Iyobo how are you?' Scott asked with genuine concern, as he took a seat in the small sitting area of Iyobo's flat.

'I am well. And you?'

'I am very well and you know what, God has been very good to me.'

'Oh yea?'

'Sure. Tell me, how is Amenze?'

'She is well.

'That's really good,' Scott smiled, giving Iyobo a sly look.

'You look more beautiful than the last time I saw you. What has been happening to you?'

Iyobo laughed half heartedly. 'Where have you been?' Iyobo tried to keep the conversation flowing.

When Iyobo finally brought two cups of tea to the centre table, she sat right in front of the man she believed God used to take her out of the brothel.

'I am happy to see you again. I hope everyone in church is well. I do hope they will forgive me for the abrupt way I left without telling them.'

'Sure they will. They love you and have been asking if I'd heard from you.'

Iyobo was delighted to see Scott but wondered why the sudden brief appearance. She waited for an explanation but got nothing along that line from Scott who got up to leave after thirty minutes.

The following day, Scott was at the door at exactly 7 P.M., just ten minutes after she arrived home.

'Oh, hello Scott ça va?'

'Oui, ça va. Et toi?'

Iyobo kissed Scott on the cheek as she welcomed him to sit at a chair right opposite her.

'Tea or coffee?'

'Tea is fine, thanks. It's quite cold tonight. Now Iyobo, we have to talk,' said an anxious male voice when they were both settled with their cups of tea.

'I am sure you wondered where I was all this time. To be honest with you Iyobo, you've been on my mind all the while. I have been in Brussels and have been attending a small French church not too far away from my house. It's about twenty members. Those Christians have helped me to grow in the things of God.'

'Oh, very good. I am quite happy to hear that. I even worried you might have left the faith. I am happy you've been busy with the Lord all this while.'

'One of the reasons I left the church without telling anybody was to clear my mind about something that was troubling me. I realised I was fighting a certain feeling concerning you.'

'Concerning me? How do you mean? Did I do anything wrong?'

'Far from that. To be honest with you, the first time I met you at er...'

'You mean at the brothel.'

'Yes. There. That was the first day I came into Brussels to resume my job. I wanted to talk to someone that night and that was it. Nothing more than that. But when I saw you at the window,' Scott pronounced the last word a bit slowly showing slight embarrassment. Iyobo stared into an empty space and there was silence for a few seconds.

'Sorry, I mean, I saw you were someone very different who needed help. I offered to help but you didn't seem to have believed me. I disappeared because I didn't want to be seen around the brothel.'

'Of course, I understand,' Iyobo said nodding her head.

'I was very happy for you and I thought that was it.' Scott paused, gathering his thoughts.

'Iyobo, I must say that your behaviour has been a balm to me. You have made me see the practicality of the Christian faith. You have shown genuine love to the people around you and the way you carry yourself, since you met the Lord is enough proof that God is real. I must thank you for helping me discover Jesus. If not for you, I wouldn't have known the goodness of God.'

'Thanks Scott. You are really kind. I feel very humbled by all you have said. I must confess that I have been enjoying life since I have come to know the Lord, especially compared to the way I lived before. You were the angel God used to deliver me fully. Since the day I gave my life to Christ, I prayed that God would deliver me but I didn't know how until you appeared.'

'No one understands the ways of God. His word says He will never leave us nor forsake us. Just imagine. You are from Nigeria and I am from Scotland. We both see and feel the goodness of God in our individual lives,' Scott said, in a stronger Scottish accent than Iyobo had ever heard.

'Iyobo, I have come to make a request. I would like us to become good friends.'

'Of course, we are stronger than just friends. We are brother and sister already, knowing that we both have Jesus as our personal Lord and Saviour. We are one in Christ.'

'Ok. Thanks. I would like you to give me the freedom to visit a bit more frequently and I could learn a lot from you in spiritual matters,' shyly smiling and looking into Iyobo's eyes.

Iyobo remained quiet. Scott got up to go. He took Iyobo's two hands, looked into her eyes and said very quietly

'I really care about you, Iyobo.'

Iyobo found herself in an awkward situation and didn't know what to say. She did not want this kind of discussion to come up between her and someone who once knew her as a whore. She struggled to say something but just couldn't say anything.

'Say something,' Scott said pulling her a bit closer to him.

Iyobo resisted.

'Don't you care about me? I love you and I want to marry you.'

These words hit Iyobo like a ton of bricks. She held herself pretending to be in control.

'Scott, I care about you but it's all happening too fast and I need to put myself together to think about what you are saying.'

Scott then let go of her hands and went for the door.

'Good night,' Scott finally muttered as he stood at the doorstep.

'Good night,' Iyobo responded, still in shock.

Iyobo was bewildered by not only what was happening but the pace at which it was all happening. Iyobo was convinced she had a lot of explaining to do when Amenze came home especially as she had never seen Scott. Iyobo prayed fervently that she got things right. She wasn't ready to say yes to Scott until she was sure he was fully born again. She'd seen the other side of life and she wasn't ready for anyone who would mess up her present walk with God.

CHAPTER 43

'Iyobo, I am waiting for an answer to my proposal,' Scott said in his usual quiet manner in the car, while coming to drop her off at home after church service.

'No, I can't. Look Scott, you are being unreasonable here. I am just trying to rebuild my life. Thanks to you, I am free from debt and I can now serve God the way I longed to. How then do I just go with you not really knowing whom you are or what you are up to? I know you picked me up from the brothel but God cleaned me up before you came. I need to honour Him. Sorry Scott. I can't make any commitment to you. I must wait for as long as it takes to see if it is of God or not'.

'Iyobo,' Scott smiled, 'now I love you even more. I promise to wait for as long as you want. But please have me in mind and make sure you do not run after any Nigerian man. I know there are quite a lot of them with lush looks around,' Scott said laughing and teasing Iyobo.

Iyobo ignored, maintaining a slight frown.

'When is Amenze coming back on holidays?'

'In two weeks,' Iyobo replied quickly, looking elsewhere as the car finally pulled into a free parking space just before they reached Iyobo's block of flats.

'Iyobo, please give me at least a word to keep me going.'

'I think I'd better go. I am expecting a cousin of mine tonight and I promised we'd eat dinner together.'

'Am I invited?'

'Scott,' Iyobo whispered out, as if calling him to order.

'Ok, my Nigerian princess, you pray about my proposal while I also pray. Good we both have the same heavenly father. On a serious note, I love you and I want to spend the rest of my life with you,' Scot rushed these last words as if the answer he longed to get from Iyobo depended on them.

'Have a good evening, brother Scott,' Iyobo said cynically alighting from the car.

'Bye sister Iyobo,' Scott replied slowly with hands off the steering, although the engine was still on, as he watched Iyobo march off towards her home.

At home, Iyobo sat down to think about each word Scott had spoken in the car. She decided she was not going to think about any proposal because she had too many things to put in order. Besides, going out with a man who brought her out of the brothel was absolutely not a good idea as he would continually remind her of her past. Even if she was going to consider the proposal, she would not be hastened into it as she would like to pray about it for as long as she wanted. Iyobo did all she could do to discourage any contact or meeting with Scott.

❖ ❖ ❖

The meeting Iyobo had with Scott sent her adrenaline running towards the prospect of settling down one day whether it be with Scott or somebody else. Iyobo remembered she first had the desire for that kind of life after she met Jean-Pierre and his wife. She thought about them and made up her mind she would want nothing less for herself especially now that she had learnt to place value on herself being a child of God.

❖ ❖ ❖

Two weeks had gone by very quickly. She had told Scott to stop dropping by for visits since she wanted more time to pray. Scott had adhered to this, saying as he too was praying. Fasting and prayer in the first week was almost unachievable as thoughts bombarded her instead of prayers and meditation. It was only the second week she settled down to read her Bible and to find out what exactly marriage meant for God and then for her as a child of God. The issue as to who to marry was still out of the question. In the Bible, Iyobo read.

"Wives, be subject (be submissive and adapt yourselves) to your own husbands as [a service] to the Lord. For the husband is head of the wife as Christ is the Head of the church, Himself the Savior of the [His] body. As the church is subject to Christ, so let wives also be subject in everything to their own husbands."

Iyobo wondered if all married Christian women have actually read this part of the Bible before making commitment to the men. She struggled with the phrases "as a service to the Lord" and then "be submissive and adapt yourselves". If the essence of marriage is to reflect the character of Jesus and the church, the formal union between a man and a woman must be very vital in the heart of God. Since she had vowed to please God all her life, she must be ready to submit and adapt to her husband as a service to God.

"[…] and let the wife see that she respects and reverences her husband [that she notices him, regards him, venerates, and esteems him]; and that she defers to him, praises him and loves and admires him exceedingly."

Iyobo wondered why so many couples made vows to serve and please God in this way and then fell out along the way. To her, it would be better to stay single than get married and displease God. Iyobo began to reflect on marriage as not only for human pleasure but mainly for fellowship with the father through Jesus Christ.

CHAPTER 44

What Scot found out was shocking. He had read it several times before in the Bible but they now jumped out as if hitting him personally;

"Husbands, love your wives, as Christ loved the church and gave himself up for her, so that He might sanctify her, having cleansed her by the washing of water with the Word, that He might present the church to Himself in glorious splendor without spot or wrinkle or any such things [that she might be holy and faultless]. Even so husbands should love their wives as [being in a sense] their own bodies. He who loves his own wife loves himself. For no man ever hated his own flesh, but nourishes and carefully protects and cherishes it, as Christ does the church because we are members (parts) of His body. For this reason, a man shall leave his father and his mother and shall be joined to his wife, and the two shall become one flesh. This mystery is very great, but I speak concerning [the relation of] Christ and the Church. However, let each man of you [without exception] love his wife as [being in a sense] his very own self."

Scott did more research and saw this;

"I say to you: whoever dismisses (repudiates, divorces) his wife, except for unchastity, and marries another commits adultery, and he who marries a divorced woman commits adultery."

'What does this mean? I don't understand this bit.' Scott frowned and re-read the passage. 'If loving Iyobo was a way to please the Lord, I would do it ten times more,' he prayed.

Since Scott's road to Damascus experience, he had totally forgotten the state in which he met Iyobo. Everything changed completely and to him, Iyobo would be his virgin as the Bible puts it. The more he prayed, the more he wanted to be with her.

❖ ❖ ❖

'Iyobo, we need to talk after service,' Scott whispered in her ear as he brushed past her at the church entrance where Iyobo stood welcoming people into the church the following Sunday morning. Iyobo smiled, mainly because of people who were around, she thought might be watching, rather than for expression of any emotion towards Scott.

Scott didn't wait for a second more after the end of the service to make his way towards the person he was convinced would be his bride.

'We can't talk here. I am busy and people are watching us. Scott, can't you understand? Do you want people to start saying negative things about me?'

'So what? I am going to scream it out now. I love you and I want the whole world to know. I have prayed and the more I pray, the more I want to be with you. Iyobo, why are you doing this to me?'

'Look, Scott, the pastor's wife is looking towards this direction. I must go at once.'

'No you can't. I can't go through another week without an answer from you. I am ready to go and see the pastor and the wife and talk to them if that's what you want. I thought we could talk first as …'

'Scott, stop. What about my feelings? Like I have said, I cannot talk to you right now.'

'In that case, I will come to your house tomorrow. I need an answer.'

'No, you can't. My daughter arrives tonight and I need to give her all my attention.' They started to get suspicious gazes from other church members.

'Iyobo, I can see you don't have any feelings for me. I thought you did, that was why I came back knocking at your door. Why have you hardened your heart? I have never loved a woman before Iyobo. It's my first time. Do not destroy it. I shall come and see you tomorrow after work. I shall spend time with you and Amenze and please prepare diner for all of us. Here is some money to help with the shopping,' Scott dropped an envelope inside Iyobo's shirt pocket while he mouthed 'I love you'.

Iyobo displayed no emotion. She stood stupefied and remained still as she watched Scott walk away without looking back.

CHAPTER 45

Iyobo had received a letter from Amenze saying she would like to visit the Le Gros family as soon as the school broke up on Friday. She wrote she would spend the Saturday and a part of Sunday with the Le Gros family, who would drop her off at Iyobo's house later that evening. Iyobo had tidied up her daughter's room and was ready for a splendid one week holiday. For this reason, Iyobo had taken a week off work to spend more time with her daughter. She hoped Scott would not be a hindrance to her plan.

Iyobo's journey back from church was quick as she avoided even eye contact with those she used to hang out with after services. Even though her past life was not an issue among her Christian brothers and sisters, she didn't want to stir anything that would arouse any form of suspicion. Most of them knew she was an ex-hooker saved by grace. They loved and respected her, especially for her zeal in the things of God. She talked openly with all brothers and sisters and that was it. She was gutted by the sudden appearance of Scott into her life as if to marr this positive image she had taken time to build for herself. Worse of it was that Scott didn't even care. Iyobo re-ran the whole experience in her head and then held her breath when she remembered Scott saying he was ready to go to the pastor and his wife. The last section of her journey home was a ten minutes walk from the metro station. She must have done that in three minutes.

Iyobo went straight to her room and fell on her bed without removing her shoes. She was happy Amenze was coming much later in the evening. She would have time to play around the Scott story with her daughter before tomorrow. She wasn't sure what she would tell either of them. Her confusion rose as she finally decided to go on her knees to pray.

'Dear Lord, thank you for today's church service. We were all blessed. Please Lord, I am very confused. I really love you Lord and I honestly want to serve you the rest of my life. You have done so much for me. Despite my flaws, you love me and you bless me all the time. I have a beautiful daughter you helped me to care for through a family you chose for her when I was still deep in sin. You sent someone to pay off Madam V so as to set me free from the debt I owed her. My life has taken a good turn. I have found a good church with very good people.

'Lord, now, I am kind of confused about Scott. I know what I have passed through in my life and I don't need a marriage that will please me alone because I know that such a union can fade because it is based on my emotions and selfish desire. If I have to get married, I would like it to be the one that meets your requirements as you spelt out in your Word. I find this really hard on my own and so, I have decided to stay on my own, serving you. You are too special Lord for me to let down. I don't trust myself enough to have such a marriage.' Iyobo wept loud and uncontrollably.

She then sat on the floor of her bedroom with her head laid on the bed, contemplating what she would tell Amenze later today and then Scott tomorrow. She drifted off to sleep and woke up half an hour later. She felt more refreshed and she realized the confusion had died down. She went to the kitchen to prepare dinner for her and her daughter.

When she finally heard the door bell ring, she was elated. She ran to the door and could hardly see Lieve's hand waving at her as she zoomed off in her car while mother and daughter returned to the flat with Iyobo carrying two bags.

'How are you?'

'Fine thanks and how have you been, Mum?'

'How is Pierre? I saw only Lieve in the car.'

'He was busy. He couldn't come with us.'

Iyobo looked closely at her daughter and realised she had grown taller than she was the last time she came home.

'You've grown taller. Just look at you, you're almost as tall as me,' she declared. 'Come on! Your room is nice and tidy. You can arrange a few of your things before dinner is ready. The remote control is on the shelf in the sitting room,' Iyobo screamed the last bit while she was already in the kitchen.

'Okay mum,' came the faintly heard answer.

'Oh you've made my favourite!' Amen said when she saw dinner. 'I love jolof rice and chicken. It's delicious.'

'Thank you, my daughter. Please eat. I made this much because of you,' Iyobo said as she poured water into two glasses while they kept chatting.

'I am sure you are very tired and would like to rest. You sit down and rest in the sitting room while I clean the dishes.'

'No Mum, I'll do it.

'Don't worry. You will start to do chores from tomorrow.'

Amenze soon dozed off on the couch she was sitting on while Iyobo was filled with thoughts about Scott.

CHAPTER 46

Iyobo knew quite well that the prospect of marriage or remarriage makes some children worry that their mother would not have enough time for them. Often, they're concerned that a step-parent will take over and start telling them what to do. Knowing how much liberty Amenze enjoyed when she was home on holidays, Iyobo worried about how her decision to get married might affect Amenze. Unfortunately, the fairy tale myth of the evil step-parent persisted, and many kids believed it. Would it be the case with Amenze?

❖ ❖ ❖

Amenze finally woke up and went to the bathroom to freshen up before coming back to the sitting room in her night gown to watch the news.

'Amenze, you have been a very good girl not letting me down at all in any aspect of life. The Le Gros family and myself are very proud of you,' she said as she lowered herself down, sitting by her daughter's side.

'Thanks Mum'

'Now, I would like to speak to you about some adult things.'

Amenze's eyeballs burst opened as she couldn't wait to hear what her mother had to say. She thought she had to be eighteen to gain her mum's audience for anything since that was all she heard from her on adult issues, some she already knew about.

'What would you say if I told you I wanted to move on in life?'

Amenze didn't get exactly what her mum was saying. She faced her mother, opening her eyes instigating her to explain what she meant by that,

'I would like to know how you feel about my possibly getting married.'

Amenze wasn't ready for this. She lowered her head, a bit shy and mostly embarrassed, as this was the first time her mum had talked to her about anything intimate.

'Mum, I don't know. Are you planning to get married? To whom? Is my dad going to come back here and …?'

'Amenze, my darling, I am not getting married. I am thinking that a time would come when I would start thinking about something like that. Is it something you would like or would you prefer me to stay on my own? Afterall, I've got you.'

'Mum, you haven't told me about my dad. Do you still talk with him or are you divorced?'

'We were never married. We were just friends. I was sixteen and he was eighteen when …' At this point, Iyobo turned her face away from her daughter as if wanting her to understand less of what she was going to say.

'I mean when I got pregnant with you.'

'Really? Why then didn't he come with you to Belgium? Why did you have to bear all the burden alone? Did he not like it that I was being born?'

It's just that…' Iyobo went dead silent.

Amenze got more confused. She thought about her relationship with the Le Gros family. She felt they saw her as a big girl and spoke openly to her about almost everything except when they thought it would not help her in anyway. Amenze couldn't understand why her mother talked to her most of the time in riddles making what she was saying hard to comprehend.

'Mum, tell me about my dad. I have the right to know.'

'Mum, I need to go to bed now. I need to finish reading a book before sleeping.'

'Okay my daughter. I know you are tired. It's been a long day for you. We shall continue with our discussion tomorrow.'

Amenze got up from the settee and made her way to her bedroom while Iyobo sat still, feeling more dejected than she was before she asked to speak to her daughter.

CHAPTER 47

The following day, there was an uncomfortable silence between mother and daughter. The excitement of yesterday marking Amenze's arrival was gone. While Iyobo was trying to be careful so as not to upset her daughter, Amenze did her best to avoid her mother by staying in her room as soon as she finished her usual morning chores. Iyobo wondered why on earth she started last night's discussion in the first place. To make matters worse, Scott would be coming tonight and they were all expected to have dinner together. To Iyobo, this was a total mess and she was to be blamed for everything.

She summoned up the courage and invited her daughter to go to the supermarket with her, saying that she might have too much to carry.

'Okay,' came a rather sharp response, a tone Iyobo felt was disrespectful. Iyobo pretended it was alright as she waited patiently for Amenze. In the supermarket, Iyobo did most of the talking while Amenze simply obeyed all instructions until they got home. This distance was now getting to Iyobo and she thought she should do something about her daughter's attitude but this was not the right time. Scott would be coming tonight and she wanted everybody to be happy. At this point, there was only one thing she thought of doing; to go to her room before doing anything else. After praying, she felt more at peace and started singing songs while she cooked and arranged the house.

'Mum, may I help? You have been doing all the work alone.'

'Oh my daughter, of course, you can help me. Now, help to arrange that table and put the flower vase at the side because we will be having diner with someone you've met only once. It's possible you can't even remember you once saw him.'

Nothing seemed to surprise Amenze about her mother's way of communicating with her.

'Right. Who is coming for diner? What's his name?'

'His name is Scott. Scott Macdonald.'

'From the name, he is certainly not African.'

'No, he is Scottish.'

Amenze paused for a second and took a look at her mother. Iyobo sighed but said nothing.

'Who is he?'

'A Christian brother.'

'Right. Okay. I'll give this table the best shot because I was told by one of my friends who's half Scottish that Scots are very homely people. They like their things clean and tidy,' Amenze said. 'Is it the first time he has had diner here?'

'Yes,' Iyobo felt a bit awkward answering that question since she wasn't sure why her daughter asked.

'Right. In that case, first impressions are quite vital,' Amenze muttered to herself. 'Mum, do we have ribbons?'

'There are some in the cupboard in my room.'

Iyobo had decided to prepare jolof rice, chicken and some salad. After setting and decorating the table, Amenze joined her mother in the kitchen to help with the salad. She boasted to her mother that she had learnt so many things from the Le Gros family, as each child had their tasks during holiday, whether it was cleaning the house or doing the cooking.

Iyobo smiled. Mother and daughter soon found themselves chatting away and Amenze wasn't tired of talking about all the teachers in their school. Iyobo paused, danced, jumped, hugged and sometimes sat while listening to her daughter. The cooking was complete, table set as they both waited for their Scottish guest.

Mother and daughter didn't know what the evening would bring but they were both joyful and, hoped for the best.

When they eventually heard the door bell ring, Amenze made way for the door while Iyobo stood watching both of them as they greeted, with Scott first introducing himself.

'You must be our genius,' he said.

Amenze smiled.

'Come tell me all about your school. I have been dying to hear from you since I learnt you were attending the school for talented pupils,' Scott said.

'Mmmmm,' Amenze grinned leading him to where Iyobo was waiting.

'Hello Iyobo,' he said making eye contact with her at last. 'You look stunning tonight.'

'Thanks Scott. How are you?'

'I am fine, thanks and how are you.'

'As you can see, I am very well, especially with Amenze keeping me company,' Iyobo said, mildly responding to a kiss on the cheek.

'Have a seat. Would you like a drink?'

'Nothing for now. Amenze and I were in the middle of something. She was just about to tell me about her school,' Scott said, facing the ten year old who was sitting observing her mother and Scott.

Amenze soon got comfortable as they talked about different subjects from the culture of the Scottish people to the Napoleonic invasion of Belgium. They spoke about their favourite food and their least favourite colours. Iyobo listened and chuckled with slight laughter.

'Can we all now move to the table?' she said after she had made sure all was in place at the table.

'Iyobo, you have to bless the food.'

'Oh mum, you do it.'

'You do it! Don't be shy.'

'Common Amenze, bless our food.'

'Father, thank you for this precious gift. We pray that you bless and sanctify it in Jesus' name.'

'Amen', the other two responded.

The table was filled with laughter as they ate and teased each other. At the end of the evening, Scott was like an old pal to Amenze. Scott left mother and daughter kissing both on the cheek and telling Iyobo he would see them again on Wednesday at Bible study.

❖ ❖ ❖

'Mum,' Amenze said once they were alone, 'that man was really nice.'

'Really?' Iyobo was happy to hear it.

'I like him,' Amenze confirmed. 'Was my dad that nice?'

'Yes he was.'

'Nicer or less nice?'

'Amenze, you have started again,' Iyobo said, laughing picking up a cushion to throw lightly at her daughter.

'Okay, sit down and let's talk.'

'Scott attends my church. I knew him long ago.'

'Really? Where did you know him? I thought you met him at the church?'

'Not really,' Iyobo said, followed by a long pause.

'Right,' Amenze finally broke the silence, trying to get used to how to hold conversation with her mother.

'Anyway, he was in the church and then vanished. I didn't see him for a long time and then he came back not too long ago.'

'Fair enough,' Amenze tried to keep the conversation as interactive as possible. She smiled at her mum, waiting to hear what she would say next.

'He's now asking me to marry him and I have told him no.'

Amenze went stiff as that was not in the least what she was expecting. She wanted to hear about her dad, and now it's about someone whom she met somewhere, wherever that place was, then in church and now marriage. She was forced to see her mother differently. Her smile turned into a slight frown. The ten year old got up, adjusted her trousers and walked straight into her room and didn't come out until morning when she had to do her own morning chores of making sure all plates and cups were in place and everywhere in the kitchen was clean before making herself a cup of tea. She got lost in her thoughts as she sipped her tea when she heard the phone ring.

'Bonjour.'

'Is that Amenze?' said the voice at the other side of the line.

'Yes it is. Who's on the line please?'

'It's Scott. How are you?'

Amenze paused not knowing how to reply after the discussion she had with her mum.

'Amenze, are you alright? You are a bit quiet. Are you upset about something my angel?'

'Not really.'

'Make sure you come for the Bible study on Wednesday so we could have a wee chat before I drop you guys off at home. Will that be alright?'

'Okay, I'll let my mum know. She's still in bed,' Amenze said a bit wearily.

'Okay then, my regards to your mum. Ah! Tell me, what's your favourite chocolate?'

Scott had touched on Amenze's soft spot. This brought a mild glow to her face.

'Emm, wait a minute. Are you planning to bring me some chocolate?'

'Of course. You've been working really hard in school and you deserve the best. You just name it and you'll have it,' came a happy voice from the other end of the line.

'Emm, let me see,' she said very slowly

'Cote d'or is my favourite.'

'Okay then. I'll see you on Wednesday and my regards to your mum.'

'Thank you very much'

CHAPTER 48

Dear Iyobo,
Thank you for the sumptuous meal. It was great spending time with you and especially getting to know Amenze who I find very interesting. I hope you will give me the chance to become someone closer than just a friend to your beautiful daughter. True we haven't had time to talk but I am still waiting for you to get back to me. I love you and I want to marry you. I can't see anyone else in my life. I don't want to come over to your house too soon. This means we can only meet in church on Sunday. I am still waiting as I am more than convinced we are meant for each other. Have a lovely night and please dream of me, just try.
Je t'aime fort,
Scott.

Iyobo read Scott's note with mixed feelings. She had been fighting her feelings for him as she didn't want to be seen around with any man for fear it would remind people of her old life, no matter how she had reformed. Besides, she knew she would find it hard to convince Amenze as the issue about her dad had not be properly dealt with. Finally, she wanted to be sure she was not saying yes to Scott out of obligation, afterall, he rescued her from the brothel. All these things played on her mind and sometimes, she wished she didn't have to be in this situation. She felt very comfortable with Scott and she noticed how happy he was each time they were together chatting.

The only thing she could think to do was to speak with the pastor and his wife. She couldn't carry this all by herself anymore. She was most disappointed because she couldn't give Amenze the warm welcome she deserved now that she was on holidays. She prayed her daughter would not go back to school with negative feelings, as that might affect her studies. She had fasted and prayed about Scott. The more she prayed, the more she got confused. Iyobo folded the letter and kept it back in her bag. Amenze avoided talking to her and went straight to her room, taking her packet of chocolate with her. Iyobo went straight for the phone when she was sure Amenze had shut her door.

'Hello Christine.'

'Hello Iyobo, how are you?'

'Are you alright? We just left church?'

'Yes, you're right.'

'How can we help you then?'

'I need to see you and the pastor tomorrow'

'Alright. Are you coming with Amenze?'

'I think so as I wouldn't like to leave her alone at home.'

'That's fine. Amenze could stay in the lounge watching TV while we talk in Ken's office. Will that be alright?'

'Yes. Thanks Christine.'

CHAPTER 49

'Dear Lord, I thank you very much for making me your child through Jesus Christ. I have read your Word and have seen that you support marriage. Your purpose for marriage is a good one. I love Iyobo and I want her to be my wife. Please soften her heart towards me. I am happy being in her company and I know we will be happy together. I promise to be a good father to Amenze whom I cherish just as I would my own daughter. Thank you Lord. I need to see Iyobo but I don't know how. She is not responding to me. Let your will be done in all this. Thank you Lord for your kindness towards us all. All this I ask in Jesus' name. Amen.'

Scott was more restless than he'd ever been as he lay on his bed thinking about all that went on during the day. The Bible study was about Jesus. The pastor had stressed that there was need for them to understand who Jesus really was so as to appreciate His ministry. According to the pastor, Paul thought Jesus was an ordinary man and went about persecuting the Christians. He received the shock of his life when on the way to Damascus, he heard a voice in the middle of nowhere saying, 'I am Jesus,' This was the same person he thought was dead and buried like all other fake prophets, the pastor stressed. Paul later thanked God, he was given a second chance to repent, the pastor concluded. Scott thought there were people in our world today who still undermine the personality of Jesus. They would all be in for a shock, at some point.

Scott preferred to meditate on the word of God than think about Iyobo who didn't seem to care for him. After meditating he fell asleep in no time.

Following his morning prayers, Scott was filled with the desire to speak with Iyobo. This was so strong that he didn't care what anyone would think. He decided to drive to her house first thing in the morning before going to the office. *Even if I don't see her, I will be happier knowing that I went to her house.*

Scott received the shock of his life when he found no one was at home. Fear gripped his heart and he wondered where mother and daughter had gone to so early in the morning. If there was anything wrong, why hadn't she spoken to him yesterday? He wondered.

I think this is too much for me. It's better I talk with the pastor so that I lay all to rest. It seems I am pursuing shadows and I really don't want to continue my life this way.

He decided to call the Pastor'Is that Ken?'

'Yes please,' came the surprised voice. It was the first time he had recieved a phone call from Scott.

'Will it be ok if I came to see you after work today?'

'Of course, Scott. I'll be delighted. How are you?'

'I am fine, thanks.'

'If it's that urgent, why don't you drop by at my house for a few minutes? I will be leaving for the office a bit late since I shall be talking to another church member.'

'Okay then, I am on my way.'

❖ ❖ ❖

As Iyobo reached for the Pastor's doorbell, Amenze pulled her hand away from her mothers, and watched the car pull into the Pastor's drive. Iyobo looked around too, her anxiety level increasing as she recognised Scott and waited for him to get out of the car. Amenze seemed not to share her mother's worries, and instead went to Scott, holding his hand as they returned to the woman who had yet to actually press the doorbell. 'Hello gorgeous.' Scott smiled.

'Good morning Scott.'

'What are you doing here? You should be at work.'

'What are you doing here?'

Scott's eyes were now fixed on Iyobo's and she could read all the questions in his eyes. Amenze looked away, standing between both of them, her hand loosely in Scott's. Confused, Iyobo finally pressed the doorbell.

Christine came to the door and saw the three of them.

'Come in. Please make yourselves comfortable. Ken will be here in a bit.'

'Hello Amenze. Not so good that Mum had to wake you up so early this morning, huh?'

Amenze laughed lightly.

'You come over here to play on the computer while the adults talk. Is that alright my dear?'

'Yes, thank you.'

'Did you come together?'

'No, we met at the door.'

'Hello Scott.

How are you Iyobo? Lovely to see you both.

'Hello Ken' said Scott.

Hello Pastor Ken, Amenze said.

'How is Amenze?'

'She is fine. She is right there playing on the computer' Christine cut in, pointing in the direction of the room where Amenze was.

'Did both of you come together?

'No sir. We met at the door' Iyobo quickly replied, as if to clear the air of any possible illicit relationship.

'Ah. Good.'

'Iyobo. Why don't you join your daughter for a moment since Scott will have to go to work?'

'Of course.' Iyobo said as she went in the direction led by Christine to join Amenze.

'Now tell me, how can I be of help to you?'

'To be honest, I don't know what to say. I am just confused. There is someone I have met and I want to marry her but I honestly don't know what she thinks about it. She won't even give me the chance to talk to her.'

'Is she in our congregation?'

'Yes.'

'In that case, I will have to see you after work so we could talk more about that. Is that alright?'

'Sure,' Scott answered quickly not knowing how much harm he'd done by talking to the Pastor without detail. He made his way to the door and then his car without another word. Ken waved a hand and headed towards the room where Amenze and the women were. After a brief chat with Amenze, he then asked to speak with Iyobo, who then followed him into the lounge.

'So tell me. How are you?' Pastor Ken said, leaning back in his couch opposite Iyobo. 'How can we help you?'

'Please, I think, I'll have to reschedule this meeting as I am too confused to say anything,' Iyobo said quietly, bowing her head down.

'Okay, in that case, come to my office tonight.'

'Is that alright?'

'Yes pastor Ken'

Pastor Ken reflected a little bit and just then, what Scott told him struck him but he refused to process what was going on in his head.

'Let us pray before you go'

❖ ❖ ❖

When Iyobo came face to face with Scott for the second time in one day in the church's office, she went straight to him before Amenze even noticed he was there.

'Why am I seeing you everywhere today?' Amenze said, jokingly

'I was wondering why *I'm* seeing you everywhere *I* go, my gorgeous,' Scott said very softly, giving her a gentle peck on the cheek. 'Perhaps it's a sign from God.'

'Are you okay? Why do you want to see the Pastor?'

'To tell him I love you and would like to marry you.'

'You must be joking. 'How can you do such a thing behind my back?'

'How is that behind your back when you are right here?'

'Iyobo, you are not treating me right. Look into my eyes and tell me how you feel. I will understand if you say you do not care about me but do not leave me without an answer.'

'Scott, we are on church premises.'

'I have told God I love you. I can say it anywhere. What do you want Iyobo?'

'Scott, I care about you. But I am scared. There are so many issues to be settled before...' Iyobo quickly caught a tear from her eye.

Scott stood in front of her helpless, not knowing what to do to help her.

The pastor came out to join them and ushered them into his office.

'Where is Amenze?'

'She's with Christine.'

'Alright. So tell me, what is happening?'

Scott and Iyobo sat down without saying a word.

'Okay. I can guess. Scott, was it Iyobo, you spoke to me about this morning, yes?'

Scott nodded. Iyobo looked at him from the corner of an eye.

'In that case, I will give you both time to talk'.

As soon as the Pastor left the office, Scott stood up and sat beside Iyobo, patting her back.

'Iyobo, we are meant for each other. This is from God. Can't you see? I love you and your daughter very much and I promise to look after her as I would my own daughter.'

For the first time, Iyobo looked into Scott's eyes with deep affection.

'Oh Scott, thank you. I love you very much. I don't know what to say. All I'll say is that the love of God is for anyone who turns to him. I turned to the Lord and he turned my life around.'

Scott pulled her up and embraced her, kissing her strongly on her cheek. They sat back down when they heard the Pastor coming.

'So, have you resolved some things now?'

'Yes pastor,' they said in unison, sharing a quick glance and smile.

'Good. Now, Scott, what is happening?'

'I love Iyobo and I want to marry her'

'Have you prayed about it?'

'Yes,' again they spoke together. They looked at each other and laughed. Scott's heart leapt for joy. Iyobo felt relieved.

'Good. In that case, I shall be speaking with both of you individually and then we take it from there.

'Does Amenze know?'

'No.'

Iyobo heard the sorrow in Scott's voice.

'Iyobo has only just accepted that she cares for me. A few minutes ago in fact, here, in your office.' Scott said laughing at this last.

'Ah, it's quite recent then. You two must be gentle with Amenze. The way you act can help her or hurt her. We shall go through all that later. Okay. Christine and I shall pray for you all. If you genuinely love each other, the Lord will guide you through the power of His word since you are both born again.

'It's getting a bit late. Christine is waiting for me and I am sure Amenze is hungry. It's good she gets back home soon,' Pastor Ken said in his usual quiet manner as he got up to reach out for his coat hanging on the hook behind the door.

Scott took Iyobo's hand and mouthed 'Thanks' with a very wide smile and Iyobo returned the same gesture. They all left the office with smiles and laughter to join Christine and Amenze on the other side of the building.

CHAPTER 50

Iyobo's marriage to Scott took many by surprise. The church celebrated it in a very quiet way, although Iyobo planned she would go to her village for a proper native law ceremony where her parents and family members could take part. With excitement, she had written loads of letters to her family about her wedding to Scott but the response she received was so shocking that she decided she might forget about taking Scott to her village for any native wedding. She knew how much value families placed on this kind of wedding as it was a way to honour them. Her family didn't seem to see it that way.

The most excruciating of it all was the response she got from her mother. She made sure she hid the letter away from Scott as she feared she might lose face.

In the letter, Itota expressed disappointment about her daughter's plans to get married. She reminded her of all the problems yet to be solved at home and that marriage at this point was a mere distraction. She reminded her she already had a child and she should be satisfied with that. Her daughter would certainly be a good companion to her. She drew her attention to the fact that other girls who travelled out came back setting up businesses for their parents and siblings and marriage was the last thing they had on their mind.

Her brothers were very rude when they questioned her asking what on earth gave her the ugly thought of marriage. Iyobo had spent sleepless nights trying to figure out what changed her mother from that caring and gentle mum, to such a greedy woman who didn't even care a bit about the happiness of her daughter. Could this be as a result of what her mother had to suffer because of her own actions, things like losing the love of her husband and being kicked out of her matrimonial home? Iyobo sometimes thought, trying to justify her mother's actions.

With the support of her church, Iyobo went ahead and married Scott in the church where Ken and Christine were ministers and ever since, she'd experienced the joy of a good family life, especially with Scott taking the role of father for Amenze, a role he did with all the fear and love of God as he had been advised by their Pastor and his wife.

CHAPTER 51

Amenze completed her primary education successfully at the école pour des filles talentées. Her results were outstanding. Her language skills stood out. She communicated fluently in Bini, French, Flemish, English and German. She even spoke a bit of Yoruba. She had been learning this on her own through the internet. She had planned to perfect Yoruba, Hausa and Ibo after she found out that they were the three major languages in Nigeria.

According to her, 'speaking my own language, Bini, is true proof of my identity but speaking other languages is a good proof of what I am worth.'

The Le Gros family had thought that going into the European school in Uccle for secondary education would be the best idea as she would get a chance to continue with her languages as well getting a good secondary education. Iyobo and Scott MacDonald didn't need to show up during interview although, Mr Black the Scottish year 6 teacher would have longed to speak with Scott after he found out Amenze's stepfather was also Scottish.

'There seems to be a special bond between you people,' Iyobo teased Scott when Amenze told them the story.

'Sure. We are a very peculiar and interesting race,' Scott answered proudly.

'Hang on, Scott. Now, if you committed a crime and a Scottish man was the judge, do you reckon you might have a lesser sentence?'

'Iyobo, stop it. We are very honest people. No Scottish judge will give a lesser sentence for a crime because you are a Scot,' Scott said firmly, pressing his index finger on the table in front of him.

'Ok, I am just kidding. It's just that this idea of nationalism can be portrayed as …'

'Oh, not us. We are honest people,' Scott squashed what Iyobo wanted to say.

Iyobo knew it was time for her to stop. Scott was way too passionate about his heritage and she understood why.

Scott only smiled and carried on with the ironing avoiding looking up at Iyobo, who was convinced it was absolutely time to stop.

❖ ❖ ❖

Scott suggested moving to the UK but Iyobo thought it would be better to let her daughter complete all her studies in Belgium.

'Going to the UK would mean knowing English in a more detailed form than Amenze knows it now. That would be extra work for her,' Iyobo explained to Scott.

Besides, Iyobo was now settled and had taken a permanent position as a Mentor in the Maison de la femme in Brussels. It was a special institution for women who wanted to learn new skills for economic and social development.

Iyobo was one of five women teaching various skills such as French Language, tailoring, cooking, beauty therapy, and business management and entrepreneurial skills. She therefore found the idea of going to the UK rather unsettling.

As they debated the best place for Amenze to continue her studies, Scott received notification that he was being transferred to London. Iyobo could no longer insist on staying in Brussels, particularly as they were planning to have another baby.

CHAPTER 52

Big Ben, West Minister Abbey, the Millenium Dome, the awkward looking double-decker buses were quite attractive to Amenze, and all these confirmed what she had read in the books about London. The multicultural life was not too different from her experience in Brussels except that Londoners mostly all spoke one language which kind of made life easier for everyone she thought. Amenze was happy her mother didn't have to carry the French-Flemish dictionary in her handbag for fear of getting stuck in a conversation with someone.

Amenze realised Iyobo had different feelings about London. Although she felt a sense of freedom, in terms of immigrant relationships, which was absent in Brussels, she loved a quiet life and pleaded with Scott to move to a more peaceful area. She had read many books and found out a lot about England and so, decided to explore the Essex area.

'You can take the train to work in London and that's cool,' she tried to convince him, but suprised her husband more by her choice of language.

'Ok. Iyobo, find out what area you might like best in Essex.'

'I've already researched it. Brentwood, I think, is good. What do you think?

'Why Brentwood? Why not Basildon, Westcliff? Wickford? Southend-on-sea?'

'All those places are too far from London. I took a train to all these areas and Brentwood particularly caught my attention. It's all green and serene. I had a chat with some people there and they sounded friendly.'

'Ok.'

Amenze got into King Edward Grammar school in Chelmsford while they settled in Brentwood as a family. Scott and Iyobo agreed that it would be better to put Amenze in the boarding school for maximum concentration on her studies. Amenze loved this as she was used to boarding since primary.

The Macdonald family quickly settled in Barnett Lane Community Church where they met Pastor Joseph and Sister Mary, his wife. It was very easy for them to settle in at this church, as there was little difference between this ministry and the one in Brussels, except that this one was more involved with community work. They fed the community and even helped the police in the area. Iyobo was fascinated by the church police group and became part of it. She was pleased to work hand in hand with law enforcement to ensure peace and tranquility in the area. Youth Pastors, Regis and Anne, saw faithfully to the spiritual welfare of all young people in the church. Many were added daily to the church through school evangelism and house to house witnessing. Iyobo encouraged Amenze to be part of this group but this fell on deaf ears as Amenze made up her mind to be focused instead on her studies.

'It's a mere distraction and I will not be pulled away from my studies,' she said to convince her mother.

❖ ❖ ❖

'Do you know how much God wants you to pass your exams?' Regis said one day to Amenze, during one of her school holidays.

'Of course, I know.'

'How then do you think He will prevent you from focusing on your studies when you should?' He flattened his lips waiting for the hesitant Amenze to give an answer.

Amenze kept quiet.

'Hello Amenze,' Anne said, as she walked in to whisper something to Regis.

'That reminds me, there is a trip to Normandy where all the kids will have a chance to be together by themselves. There will be guest speakers and several interesting activities. Please register your name if you would like …'

'Oh, no thanks, Anne,' Amenze said sharply hardly allowing Anne to complete the invitation.

This became a subject of discussion when Amenze got home as Scott and Iyobo explained to Amenze the importance of being a part of youth group in the church. Amenze soon started attending the normal Saturday night meeting.

❖ ❖ ❖

Barnett Community Church gave Amenze, now 14 years old, a new perspective on life as she gradually quit leaning on her own understanding and relying more and more on the spiritual guidance she had resisted. Her favourite passage in the Bible was Joshua chapter 1 verses 8 and 9. Amenze thought often on this passage *'This book of the Law shall not depart out of your mouth, but you shall meditate on it day and night, that you observe and do according to all that is written in it. For then you shall make your way prosperous, and then you shall deal wisely and have good success. Have not I commanded you? Be strong, vigorous, and very courageous. Be not afraid, neither be dismayed, for the Lord your God is with you wherever you go.'*

Amenze read her Bible every day and every night according to the dictate of these verses, which she quoted time and again. One day, she put a poster of these verses in her room. She read it over and over again and then prayed on her knees by her bed.

'I know I will succeed in all I do. I do not rely on myself because I am human. No matter how smart I am, I have limitations but you are without boundaries. I know that as I rely on you, I shall pass all my exams and receive favour everywhere I go. I will have good success because I meditate on your word. Amen.'

Amenze finally laid down, facing the ceiling thinking of what the future might hold for her, as she saw no restriction to her upward journey. She prayed for her parents. She also prayed for her father Fosa, wherever in the world he was, she prayed that God would bring peace to the world. As she prayed, she spoke some previously unknown language, a sure sign of having received the baptism of the Holy Spirit, the evidence of speaking in tongues. Amenze found this a pleasant experience.

That night, Amenze dreamt she flew a plane all by herself to Nigeria. She was welcomed by the president and his wife. She was given a medal and was advised to keep it preciously. She humbly accepted it and kept it in her school bag. The pair prayed for her and wished her the best in life. As she got up to leave, she was woken up by her alarm clock.

When she told her mum the dream, Iyobo smiled, 'My daughter, I sense you are destined for some great adventure in life although I don't know what it is. Whatever you do and wherever you go, always take the word of God with you.'

CHAPTER 33

When Dr Poola told Iyobo that she was expecting a baby, she had never been so happy in her life. She decided to break the news to Scott and Amenze in a very special way. Amenze would be coming home for the half term holiday in two weeks so that meant keeping this golden secret for a fortnight. It was the hardest thing Iyobo could do, as she kept talking around the subject sometimes almost letting the secret out.

She was delighted when, on the evening she had been waiting for, Scott went to pick up Amenze from school. She had prepared the family's favourite meal, fried rice with plenty of vegetables and prawns for Amenze. For Scott, it was a lot more complex, but Iyobo was ready to have a go. Every year, Scott took the family out to a restaurant to eat Haggis. He often complained that there was no one in the area who prepared the Scottish national dish as well as his mum. He talked about growing up in Glasgow with his parents and their celebrating Burns Night. At the table, they were served full flavoured Haggis.

Iyobo had long contacted the local butcher about her plan to make an authentic version of Haggis for her husband for a special day.

'Ah, would that be your wedding anniversary?' asked the curious butcher.

'No, but please make sure you have all the parts for me.'

'It can't be much, ma'am. Haggis is largely offal, and we are not allowed to sell some of the traditional ingredients anymore.'

'Ok. It doesn't matter. But get me what you can.'

When she finally got the ingredients, she realised they were much more expensive than she had expected.

When cooking this delicacy, she remembered Pastor Greg and the story he told of travelling many kilometres to buy his wife her favourite ice cream while she was already in bed.

She smiled as she served the food for her husband and daughter.

Scott couldn't think of a more sacrificial and loving way to announce the coming of a new baby. Hugs, kisses, gifts followed, to show that he actually cared for the mother and the baby.

As Iyobo's stomach grew bigger, the debate about the sex of the baby grew stronger. Amenze hoped it was a girl. There had been so much talk about the sex of the baby that all three had agreed that the sex of the baby should be a surprise, although Amenze would have been happier knowing. There had been speculations and guesses to checking out the size of Iyobo's stomach.

"Some people believe that you can tell using a simple sum to predict gender; add your age to the number of the month you conceived in, if the number is odd, it's a girl and if it's even, it's a boy", said Scott as he read out from a book.

"In that case, let me see, that will be emmmm, then it's a girl"

"You may be right dad", Amenze said firmly, wishing Scott's finding was correct, although it didn't make any sense to her.

"No, that's not the best way to find out shouted Iyobo at the pair. There is a well known theory that suggests that if you are craving sweet foods, you are expecting a baby girl, if you fancy a savoury snack, it's a boy"

"In that case, it is em, not a boy" affirmed Scott.

"It is not a girl either" Amenze said under her breath.

"Oh you two, forget it. All I want is a heathy baby. It doesn't matter if it's a boy or a girl. They all laughed, leaving Iyobo alone in the corner of the living room she loves to sit and rest.

❖ ❖ ❖

The day baby Paul was born, Amenze was on a school trip to Rome. She returned three days later. Scott had gone to pick her from school and took a camera with him hoping to video her reaction on the news of her new baby brother. Iyobo and Scott decided to let her know on her arrival from her one week trip to Rome.

"Yippee!!! Oh dad! Really, it's a boy! Ah, I thought it would be a girl. In that case, his name is Paul, I was hoping it would be Paula" All these, Amenze said as she tried to get into the car while Scott filmed on.

"Oh, come on dad. Let's go home. I can't wait to see the baby. Who does he look like? Me or mum or you? I think a bit fron all of us. Is he big or is he like, little? Oh dad, drive on I am now a big sister … Yippeeeee!"

All through Easter and long holidays, Amenze never let baby Paul out of her sight. She looked after him when Iyobo was out in the shops or when she simply wanted to take a rest. Baby Paul was a source of joy for all three although for Amenze, a baby girl would be important in the family in order to balance the equation.

CHAPTER 54

When Amenze got the offer to read English Law and French Law at Oxford, the first person she told was Iyobo and then Scott.

"Hey, big sister Amenze is off to uni", Amenze whispered in Paul's ears in the sitting room, taking him away from his play and holding him close as she made her way to the kitchen to show her mother the admission letter. The two year old didn't look at her as he struggled his way out of her grip to continue with his play on block construction.

As Amenze handed the admission letter to her mum, who was heavily pregnant with a third child, she looked into her eyes and said, 'Mum, I am going to read Law and when I finish, I shall go back to Nigeria, our country to attend law school there, followed by the National Youth Service Corps,' she announced with ardent passion. She had previously had extensive discussions with Scott about various options after graduation. Amen watched her mother struggle down from the high stool she was sitting on while slicing the vegetables, paper in hand with a big smile on her face. She was filled with relief and gratitude as she listened to her daughter talk about going to Nigeria after her studies. That meant a lot to Iyobo.

'I will make sure with the last drop of my blood that no female child would be forced to do things against her will.'

Iyobo was happy but couldn't understand how her daughter had become so assertive about defending the right of women. Amenze had confronted her mum about this issue. Though she didn't tell the full story to her daughter about her life in the brothel, whom she thought was still too young, Amenze did not judge her, neither did she let her mother understand how she was dealing with that idea that she was the daughter of an ex-whore. Her behaviour to her parents did not change. She appeared to be very proud of them.

'Mum, at that age and from what you have told me, you had no choice. As for me, I have a choice and I will help others have a choice.'

Amenze had viewed every stage of her mum's life not as a plot staged by destiny to curse her as Iyobo believed, but as a tale of adversity through circumstances. Her case was simply borne out of ignorance, first from her dad, Ogidi, then her own misfortune of becoming pregnant when she was not ready to bear the consequences.

Amen's anger was more against a system that failed to do something after recognizing the intelligence in a little girl. 'How do you build a nation if everything was based on only paper qualifications and documents,' she didn't stop wondering.

Amen was grateful however that there were still people like Mr Unugboro and Mr Atita, the headmaster. Those two stood for the teachers but they needed a fairer system to operate by. They couldn't effect any policy.

'As for me, Mum,' Amen finally walked away from her mum towards the refrigerator, 'as for me,' she repeated as if to lay stronger emphasis on what she was saying, 'I will fight for the cause of young girls and will leave no stone unturned. We have often been told that knowledge is power and the only reason women are being deprived of knowledge is to prevent them from having power. I am on my way to Oxford Mum, and I know I will win this fight.' She finally summoned up courage to look at her Mum, who stood gazing at empty space, the admission letter from Oxford in hand.

They were both silent for half an hour. Amenze finally sat down and poured herself some apple juice.

'Mum, now I am eighteen. I want to visit Nigeria before my course starts. Would you take me there or do I go on my own?' Amenze hoped Scott and Iyobo would be able to help her.

Amenze looked at her mum from the corner of her eye as she turned swiftly to look quizzically at her. Amenze smiled, took another sip of juice, put down her glass and smiled again.

'Ah, I need to call Papa and Mama Le Gros right now,' Amen announced standing up from her seat.

CHAPTER 55

Before Amenze travelled to Nigeria, she was under the impression from the newspapers and television reports that any trip to Africa was certain to show her the depths of poverty and crime, that she could expect to be robbed, raped or murdered.

Of course, just like any country, Nigeria had its issues and there were always places in every city that were best avoided, but the truth was, that was not something that she had spent even one minute thinking about. She was looking forward to an intensely rewarding experience that would amaze and impress her, with every new activity, sight and interaction. She was out to experience firsthand anything that would create a bond between her and the people of her country of origin.

On her journey from London to Lagos, where she spent a night with Efe, her mother's friend, she had really encountered nothing but genuine hospitality in every location; from the airport to the house. Everybody she met in Iyobo's friend's house was introduced to her as a relative of some sort. The person was either a brother, a sister, uncle, aunty, Mum or Dad. She didn't stop smiling as all of these people did one thing or the other to make her feel welcome.

In fact, far from having to constantly worry about her safety, the biggest thing she had to worry about was the noise in the streets as every car seemed to drive with horns constantly on. This soon stopped when she was ushered into her room for the night and was told she could stay as long as she wanted to, although she politely turned the offer down.

Amenze's journey from Lagos to Benin City by bus was more eventful. The pot holed roads made her dream even bigger as to how to bring about a change when she had a chance to have a say. This unpleasant road experience soon gave way to laughter from passengers who made the best of every minute on the bus. Since she dressed in African clothes, no one knew where she came from or who she was. She was treated and teased like every other passenger.

However, one thing saddened Amenze. As they journeyed from Lagos to Benin, she began to feel a wave of depravation and the hustling and bustling of Lagos soon gave way to very pathetic views of people who needed help urgently. She found that the quality of life depreciated as they moved into the interior. Peasants living in thatched houses, children were hardly dressed, which suggested lower quality of life. As she watched each person and house through the bus window, she was more determined to be the saviour that could bring a change to the society.

At the same time, Amenze didn't want to ruin the moment as passengers screamed jokes across the passenger filled bus. Even the gallops brought laughter as a messenger would suddenly come out with "eheee", "eheee" "eheee", a rhythm everyone follow creating laughter. The sight of an accident with casualties gasping for help and other vehicles flying past not wanting to be involved, suddenly deadened the laughter as passengers looked to see exactly what had happened. This became the point of discussion for the rest of the journey.

Amenze, at this point listened attentively to each comment wanting to know how they felt. The conclusion she came to was that the people had resolved to put up with what could not be changed.

The bus went quiet after they had exhausted their pains and plights. Amenze watched others fall asleep. She wondered how people could possibly sleep after such a horrendous scene. She noticed the journey became smooth again as they progressed towards Benin until the sleeping passengers were vigorously awakened by noisy and desperate roadside traders who literally stuck their goods against the bus windows. If there was a passenger who wanted any of the goods and couldn't reach it, it was thrown to them while the seller ran after the bus which was now moving very slowly to park. Amenze gathered from the sign post that this place was called Ore.

The town of Ore provided eating and toilet facilities and a bit of last minute shopping before they reached Benin city. Amenze came down from the bus looking for a toilet. Other passengers went to local restaurants and small shops scattered all over the place. It was obvious that some of the passengers already had fixed places where they ate their favourite menu like bush meat, isi-ewu or goat head pepper soup and other delicacies. Amenze saw that everyone was in top form again and returned back in a light mood as when they had started the journey.

Amenze enjoyed the journey to Benin City where one of her cousins was waiting for her with her name on a placard and her picture in hand. He drove her straight to GRA where Itota now lived.

Her meeting with her family was eventful and a turning point in her life as she saw for the first time, what life was like in Africa. Cries, sobs, stories both good and bad filled her ears. Her grandmother, Itota whose room she shared didn't stop crying as she thanked God for what Amenze turned out to be.

Amenze heard some exciting stories about how brilliant and well behaved Iyobo was when she was very young. Grandmother, uncles and distant relatives who knew that Amenze was in town, visited and all rallied round to make her stay comfortable, although she was later informed that her grandfather, Ogidi expressed disappointment because she didn't come to see him in the village. Itota sent a message back to him saying he had no right to be rude to her granddaughter living in her house.

CHAPTER 56

Amenze kept her distance from all family squabbles and concentrated on the reason why she was there.

'Uncle,' Amenze said to Moses who had come one evening to be with his niece, 'I am very interested in politics and I need your advice on the matter.'

'Let me see', Moses breathed out as he adjusted himself in the chair he was sitting in.

'My dear, politics in this country is not like what you have abroad and I don't know whether to encourage you to think along that line or not but emmm…'

'Right.' Amenze would not be deterred. 'The point is that I have made up my mind on the matter. I have been following a lot of stories in the news since I arrived. I can see some things are not as straight forward as I would have expected, but I think this is because I am used to a very different culture.'

'In that case, go for it. It would be lovely to see my niece at the top of government one day. That will change our family forever. We will become famous.' Moses said amid laughter.

Amenze had learnt from her mother that her three uncles had all gone to night schools for their Ordinary and Advanced Level certificates and that Moses was already at the University while the other two would get in soon. She knew it was time to close the discussion, as her uncle was thinking already of personal gain rather than asking what difference she might be bringing to the country if she succeeded. Amenze didn't hide her feelings, as she immediately tried to subtly change the subject.

'Uncle, which of the universities do you attend and how are you coping with family,' Amenze chirped in wryly.

'I attend the University of Benin. It's not easy at all, especially the financial part of it. It's good, I have a car adapted to my condition, thanks to your parents, but it's still hard doing many things.'

Amenze smiled and wanted to end the discussion, as she so desperately wanted to talk to someone who would contribute positively to her political ambition.

'I know quite a number of people in politics and I can find out a lot of things for you if you like,' Moses quickly added when Amenze went quiet. 'I think the first step to take is to register as a legitimate voter since you are already eighteen years old.'

'And how do we do that?'

'That should be done at the INEC office, which is the Independent National Electoral Commission at Akenzua Street.'

'In that case, I'll go there tomorrow morning.'

'I can see you are really interested. I shall introduce you to a very good friend of mine who should be able to help as he was once in politics but stepped out because he felt they were not meeting up to his expectations. He used to be in Holland but wanted to be a member of house of Assembly in our state as a way to kick off'

'When can I see him?' Amenze didn't let his uncle complete his last sentence as what she needed now were no words of discouragement.

'I'll invite him here tomorrow, you can meet him when you come back from INEC.'

'Ok uncle. That's really kind of you,' Amenze smiled.

❖ ❖ ❖

'I think the first thing you must do is to determine at what point you would like to begin. Politics is quite hard, more difficult than people think, and so focus is very important. I have heard a lot about you and I know you are brilliant but for a woman, there might be some major challenges, though we need women in politics. I think women do very well when encouraged,' Mr Izebu said, hardly breathing between the sentences. He seemed to have a lot to say and was glad to find someone who would listen, especially someone who had lived outside Nigeria.

Mr Izebu's words pleased Amenze who was left wondering why he had to quit politics, despite such a positive disposition. Amenze looked at him, a middle aged man wearing a grey suit despite the scorching heat. The air conditioner in the sitting room kept him cool for that moment, but there was no guarantee how long that would last.

'That's quite kind of you sir. I have resolved to always look at the positive side of things,' Amenze said very confidently.

'That's the right attitude,' Mr Izebu said with a light laugh.

'I will advise you to go straight for your dream. If you want to be a governor, start working towards it and if you want to be a senator, find out what it takes. All the parties have their branches in all the states. Take time to research what their manifestos are and see if they suit your ideology. Once you have identified a party you like, start your ground work.'

'What does that mean?'

'You must search yourself to see what you would be bringing into the party. If you are sound and they see you talk well and are able to convey good information fluently to the public, you will see different party representatives at your doorstep wanting to buy you over. If you are slothful and shabby, you will only appear at the general rally of the party. Let me tell you, young lady, there are some parties who are honestly looking for young, intelligent, vibrant and genuine people to promote their parties and it's all for the benefit of the nation at the end of the day. I see that in you. I will introduce you to some people when the time comes. Maybe I can advise you until you no longer need me,' he laughed, this time, in an exaggerated manner.

Amenze smiled. 'Thank you sir. You are really kind. I have read about Nigerian politics and though I will be starting uni this September, I hope to do my final project on Nigerian law and politics.'

'Your uncle told me you got into Oxford.'

'Yes sir.'

'Wow, you are really smart. You are certainly the kind of person we need for a breath of fresh air in this nation, humble and intelligent.'

'That's kind of you sir. I have just one last question.'

Mr Izebu met her gaze, but Amenze could see he had no idea what she was going to ask.

'Why exactly did you quit politics? Mr Izebu laughed, looking away as if recollecting exactly what happened.

'To be honest with you, I think I behaved like a wimp when I decided to quit politics. It had to do with fear of the unknown,' Mr Izebu paused.

Amenze waited patiently.

'I indicated I wanted to go into the house of Assembly as encouraged and applauded by friends and family, but what I didn't know was that I was stepping on the toes of the elder statesmen who were in the business before me. The Chairman supported me based on my experience and my ability to drive the party forward, but many thought I didn't deserve the attention I was getting since I just came back from abroad and even though they knew my coming made a lot of difference, they felt threatened by my presence.'

Amenze tried to guess what he was driving at but decided to be patient to hear the end of the story.

'One day, I was shocked when a man and a woman, who I recognized as members of my party, came into my home asking to see me. This was 6 am. I was still in my pyjamas. After exchanging greetings, the woman told me she came that early in the morning for my own interest. She began to relate what evil had befallen people who just came into politics without understanding the rules of the game. I realised the man was quiet. He didn't say a word. She said many things but it was what she finally said that made me quit.'

Amenze said nothing and gave no reaction but listened, prompting him by her looks to continue.

'You can't imagine being told that. It was barbaric and I fell for it. She asked what my reactions would be if I woke up one morning and found a corpse at my door. To be honest, as soon as she said that, I knew I was done with politics. I know people could go as far as digging out other people's past to castigate them but talking about such a criminal act was way more than I could take. The following day, without discussing the issue with anyone apart from my family, I handed in my resignation. Guess what, the man who came with the woman who spoke with me took up my position immediately. That was when I knew that they had planned it to scare me away.'

Amenze smiled but was appalled by the story. She quickly ran a check on herself, wondering what an opponent might say against her once she decided to go in for any position. So far she had done nothing wrong, she had nothing to fear.

'Do not get scared by my story. We all have our own destiny. For me, it was not meant to be. I promise to always be here for you.'

'Thank you very much.' Amenze said, smiling.

The visit to Nigeria opened Amenze's eyes to one thing that separated both cultures. African people were the kindest, warmest people she had ever met and she hadn't really understood that until she was on the same soil as them. If there was any rift among them, the problem might possibly be coming from outside, she thought.

Amenze was however happy to be back to her two brothers, Paul and Peter. Her desire for a baby sister was finally put to rest when Iyobo told her that she was through with childbearing. She found that her mother's hands were full and did all she could to help around the house, although she was often reminded to focus more on her studies.

CHAPTER 57

It was during a Edo Youth socialising event in London. All Nigerian parents of Edo origin from Midwestern Nigeria were encouraged to invite their children to the function. Amenze, Paul and Peter went with their parents, Iyobo and Scott. In this gathering, they met the Omogiate family, and shared a table. Iyobo and Scott felt some relief when they were informed younger children had a place of their own where they were being supervised; although Amenze was happy to be with Paul and Peter, the couple felt she too should socialise with other people of her age. Through conversation, Amenze got to know Silver Omogiate, he was a final year student at the London School of Economics. His father was a lecturer at the University of Ibadan in Nigeria but he came to London to see his family every summer. Amenze found it really interesting that Silver's mother had attended Oxford University. She read law and was now working at the law firm Clifford Chance in London.

Amenze noticed that Silver soon started talking to Scott about his ambition to make a difference in the banking industry in Nigeria. While Iyobo listened to all of them, she contributed only if what they were saying had to do with family life. Amenze and Mrs Omogiate talked half of the time about schooling and graduating from Oxford University.

Amenze realized that Silver was often staring at her, even though he was talking with Scott. Before now, Amenze had given no thought to boys or relationships. Knowing what Iyobo's experience had been, she had pushed that side of life away to concentrate on her studies. As far as she was concerned, relationship and marriage was not for her, at least, not at the moment.

"Hey."

"Hey." replied Amenze, they were serving themselves from the buffet as the party progressed. When they returned to their seats, Amenze watched as Silver took his mother's seat when she had gone to take her own food. Now next to him, Amenze had no option but to chat with Silver.

'Have you been told what your name means?' he asked.

Amenze laughed, knowing that was an African thing for names to always be linked with parents' life and experiences.

'Yes, of course. It means "sea water". It's a very long story. Amen looked at him and smiled. She quickly looked away when she noticed Silver kept staring at her without saying a word.

'So, how is Oxford?'

Amenze tried to avoid Silver's eyes while she answered his questions as briefly as possible. She gave him her contact number when he asked but specified, she would prefer he contacted her by email, which she also gave him.

'Yes I liked every bit of the evening' Amenze told her mother after the event. 'It was quite different from all I've been to before.'

'I found the young man at our table quite interesting.'

'I didn't. I found him really boring' Amenze snapped from the back of the car, where she was sandwiched between two sleeping children, as Scott drove them home.

'Why not?'

'Dad, the guy just kept staring at me. I didn't like that. I mean, we were out there to socialize and talk to people and all that, but all he did was stare at me. What was all that about?'

'Oh Amenze, that's what young men do when they start to like a lady. You are a beautiful young girl and guys are bound to look at you a bit more, when they meet you.' Scott told her excitedly.

'I felt that way when I met your mum. She was beautiful back then and I just couldn't take my eyes off her, or get her out of my mind.'

'I am still beautiful, Scott,' Iyobo spoke out, a bit louder than father and daughter.

'Of course you are my darling,' replied Scott, as the three laughed.

'Did you exchange contact details?' Scott said, refusing to let go of the topic.

'He took mine.'

'OK. Now, listen, that doesn't mean anything. You can just become friends and share ideas. You don't have to get involved with him if you don't want to.'

'Oh Dad, leave me alone. I've got a lot on my mind. My priorities are my studies and then politics in Nigeria. You know what I mean. Don't you Dad?' Amenze said slowly, drifting sleepily away.

'Of course I do, my darling.'

'Truth is, I've got no time for anything more than what I already have. My time's full.'

'When you get there, you'll have time.'

'Ok then,' Amenze said hardly hearing what Scott said.

Amenze slept while they drove home.

❖ ❖ ❖

'Hello Amenze, this is Silver.'

'Hi, how are you doing?' Amenze responded, as she held her mobile phone to her ear and picked up her bag to join the rest of the family on their way to church Sunday morning.

'I am on my way to church and just decided to say hello and to thank you for being such good company last night,' Silver said. 'Sure. Thank you too. I'm on my way to church. It was all very good.'

'Are you driving?'

'No, I'm with my family.'

'I just wanted to know if I could drop by one of these days to see you in school.'

'I'd rather you contact me by email.'

'Oh sorry, I forgot you told me this before.'

'It's alright.'

'Any special reasons for that?'

'I get really busy in university, so I don't want anyone to think I'm snubbing them, but I can respond to an email at any time of day, and I always answer emails."

'Fair enough.'

'Ok then, we'll chat later – by email.'

'Ok, bye,' she said, hardly hearing his last sentence.

'Who was that?' Iyobo asked, as soon as she felt Amenze was fully settled in the car and had stopped talking.

'Silver, the guy I was talking to yesterday during the party.'

'What? This early in the morning? What did he want?' Iyobo asked firmly but quietly, leaning a bit backwards to get answers from Amenze, who was sitting right behind her at the back of the car.

'I don't know, to say hello I suppose. He said he was on his way to church and …'

'Ah, what church?'

'I don't know.'

'Darling, they just met last night. She wouldn't know,' Scott pointed out.

'Please be careful my daughter. Men are quite funny creatures. When women see them, they see them from their hearts. When men look at women, they want something else.'

'It's not always like that. Christian men don't do that,' Scott defended.

'If they are born again Scott. That's what I mean by telling her to be careful. These days, it's hard to know who's born again and who's not.'

'Just ask God.'

'You are right Scott. Just ask God. Amenze, I hope you have taken that in. Since you don't know who's real and who's not, spend time in prayer and ask God.' Iyobo said lightly but firmly.

'Mum, I don't know what you guys are talking about. I ask God for light in my studies and political career. That's all I know.'

'You pray concerning everything in life. No man is allowed to jump on you or force things on you. You are still very young,' Iyobo spoke almost bitterly.

Amenze and Scott remained quiet when they noticed that Paul and Peter were completely being cut out of the discussion, despite their quests for attention through pointing out things through the car window and words they threw at each other. They were however, glad to jump out of the car as they hurried to join their friends who came out from other cars in the church car park.

❖ ❖ ❖

Back to campus meant work, work and more work for Amenze. Studying at Oxford is stressful enough and maintaining links with her political party in Nigeria gave her little breathing space. She also didn't want to miss out on church activities. Regis and Anne called her from time to time if she wanted to be part of youth camps, which she responded positively to. Amenze knew a passage in the Bible which she read every day. It was Psalm 127 verses 1 and 2:

"Unless the Lord builds the house, its builders labour in vain. Unless the Lord watches over the city, the watchman stands guard in vain. In vain you rise early and stay up late, toiling for food to eat – for He grants sleep to those he loves". This reminded her that all she was planning, doing and executing was subject to the Creator of all, God Almighty.

❖ ❖ ❖

Despite all that Amenze had in mind for herself and her career, she couldn't totally ignore all the emails she received from Silver. She was grateful that he had avoided calling her phone but wrote regularly by email as she had insisted. The messages were short and he didn't seem to be pushing anything, as her mother had led her to suspect. She understood her mother's point of view, even her suspicion of young men, but she enjoyed listening more to Scott who saw love, as he often put it, as something God created to be enjoyed by us to His glory and honour. For this, Amenze was glad she didn't grow up with her mum alone as she suspected fear for men would have dominated all her life. Amenze had promised she didn't want to live under the shadow of her mother's experiences, past or present. So far, she'd been blessed with the Le Gros family and then with Scott who had been a good father to her since he had married her mother. What else could she ask for in life?

Finally, at age 20, Amenze decided to accept Silver's invitation to his church's annual thanksgiving service. Amenze had not seen Silver since the day they met at the Nigerian party. Despite all their emails, she couldn't entirely remember what he looked like. She felt excited at the prospect of finding out again. The journey from Oxford to London by train took about an hour and a half.

What struck her first was his cream three piece suit with a Cambridge blue tie and a handkerchief of the same colour in the breast pocket. He was really tall and thin. He had dark and well kept hair. Amenze got caught in his beaming smile as their eyes met across the barriers. As soon as she was free, he embraced her with a rather heavy peck on her cheek, which suggested a long held desire to see her. Amenze's heart leapt, was her mother right after all? But she showed nothing out loud.

'Hi.'

'Hi.'

'Let's go. My car is around the corner,' said Silver, rather anxiously.

'Right' Amenze breathed out, maintaining a smile as they walked along.

'You are beautiful, Amenze.'

'You are tall,' replied Amenze. She smiled and suddenly both were laughing.

❖ ❖ ❖

Amenze's final year at Oxford was tough. She knew other Nigerians like Yusuf from Sokoto and Baday from Oshogbo with whom she had various political debates about Africa, especially Nigeria. Baday planned to go for the Legal Practitioner Course to qualify her for the post of solicitor while Yusuf and Amenze planned to go to Nigeria for law school and Youth Service. Amenze benefitted more from Yusuf since he had lived a bit in Nigeria, before coming to the UK while Baday was born in Liverpool, the most northern edge of the midlands in England, although she went to Nigeria every year with her parents on holiday.

Amenze's thesis was titled: *The Effect of Law and Order On Political Stabilisation In Nigeria.* Her research took her from Sakpoba, a village in the midwestern part of Nigeria to Sokoto, a city in the extreme north west of the nation. She left no stone unturned. She searched for ways to establish, maintain and sustain a firm political structure. Her work got the attention of the Oxford community after she bagged a first class degree. She was contacted straight away by her department to continue a PhD programme which she turned down, saying she was going back to Nigeria to set her people free, a statement most of the political tutors considered overly ambitious.

Despite Amenze's ambitions in the political arena, she made time to see Silver. It was on her 21st birthday that he finally summoned up the courage to propose to her.

CHAPTER 58

Silver was disappointed when Amenze said she would only consider marriage after her first term in office as the President of the Federal Republic of Nigeria. She had told him over and over again that her destiny was to rise and create a change in the nation, and he supported that. He planned to support her through the process, but doubted he would be able to wait for her all these years without getting married.

Over the course of time, Silver had come to appreciate Amenze for her intelligence, her hard work and her Christian character. He appreciated every moment they spent together, as they both made the best out of their circumstances. Silver felt humbled when Amenze told him the full story of her mother. The only thing that worried him was why Amenze was so reluctant to take their relationship to another level. He'd got to know Iyobo and Scott and had seen that they genuinely loved one another and wished Amenze would be like her mother in terms of building a happy home, but was scared Amenze's high political ambition might ruin their love and future life. He was confident he was the right man for Amenze, he thought he ticked all the boxes for the kind of person a woman of Amenze's calibre would want. Despite his attachment and devotion to her, the woman he loved and admired, to his pain, held back everything from him. She never gave him any indication that she was in love with him. He had made up his mind to propose but just couldn't figure out how. He asked his father for advice, but found him too out of touch with modern life. He tried to squeeze a tip out of Scott but his experience with Iyobo was miles away from his with Amenze. He decided to follow his own heart.

It was Amenze's 21st birthday and he'd booked a table for two in an exclusive restaurant in London's West End. Silver had given Amenze a beautiful bouquet of rose flower. They were carried away talking about politics, Amenze's favourite subject when all of a sudden, she got distracted by a stranger handing a parcel to her.

'What's this?' Amenze asked, looking into the eyes of the bell boy, a young man all dressed in red, offering her the parcel in his hand.

She stared at the brown envelope.

'Silver, look. Who knew I would be here? Someone is sending me this.'

'You open it. Could it be past question papers or something,' Silver said, pulling his face to a corner while Amenze was busy trying to figure out who would send such parcel here.

'Silver, who did you tell we would be coming here?'

'Nobody of course. I didn't tell anyone I was coming here with you, except my parents.'

Silver's heart pounded not knowing what to expect from Amenze after she found out that he sent her the pack.

'It's possible. Just open it and see,' Silver breathed out, trying to play it down as much as possible.

After careful examination, Amen opened the parcel. She took a quick look at the colourful letter now open in her hands. This letter was written on an A3 paper which served as a wrapping paper for a pink coloured Bible. Silver watched Amenze lay the Bible on a corner of the table while she read through the letter.

'Amenze, I must tell you the truth. You mean all the world to me, there is no one else who's walked on this earth that takes my breath away like you do. You are the most beautiful girl in the world and the most special thing that has ever happened to me. The greatest thing about us is that Jesus Christ is the foundation of our relationship. That is why we have vowed not to defile our marital bed during our courtship. On this I promise to wait until our wedding night, since my mission is to bring glory to God. This promise to wait until our wedding night was made to God, who's kept me holy since the day I said 'Yes' to Jesus Christ. Amenze, I want to love you as Christ asks me to love you. He asks me to love you like he loves the church. I see you as bone of my bone and flesh of my flesh. Amenze, please marry me.'

As Amenze looked up, she found Silver on one knee, looking passionately into her twinkling eyes.

'Oh, Silver, why?' she whispered, laughing as if to cover up some embarrassment.

'Why, what honey? Why I am asking the only woman I love to marry me?'

'No, it's not that. It's just that …'

'That you are not ready because of a political career?' Silver said very slowly but apologetically, wishing he never had to speak to her like that while proposing to her. There were so many things he would like to talk to her about but her body language always prevented him

Amenze felt slightly embarrassed as they had started attracting the attention of other customers to their corner table.

'I love you Silver. I will marry you but…'

'You don't need to go any further. I am blessed and pleased with those words. Let's celebrate and then talk about the 'but' later,' Silver said.

'Silver, we will talk about the 'but' straight away,' Amenze said like a school teacher to a naughty pupil.

'I'm as excited as you are by this, but we express ourselves differently.'

'Now listen, I know you might see this as selfish, but I…e.'

Amenze paused and stretched her hands across the table to take her Silver's hands in hers. Looking into his eyes, she whispered, 'I love you Silver but I need to fulfill a calling, a destiny.'

'Then let's marry now, then you can be –'

'No Silver,' maintaining a calm that was borne of years of meditation.

'I will have you with me forever but I will not have the political opportunities I have now forever. Can't you understand?'

'What are you saying?'

Amenze went quiet, picked up the bottle on the table and emptied the last bit of water into a glass in front of her. She dropped the bottle back noisily on the table and then pushed the glass away from her, as she put down her head as if she didn't want her sole audience to hear all she wanted to say. Looking up again in a manner to portray she had gathered momentum, she said, 'I don't want to get married now. Let's get engaged and leave marriage for much later.'

The words Silver dreaded most tumbled in his ears. He looked into her eyes to find compassion, but they were closed. He looked down into his glass of wine they had popped open for the birthday celebration.

'That's not fulfilling God's plan,' Silver managed to say.

'Paul remained unmarried to fulfill God's plan,' Silver heard Amenze defend herself.

'I should have known better. This is about us, not about Paul,' Silver said burying his head in his hands.

'Silver, I've got to go. I have so much to do tomorrow. Sorry. Thanks for the beautiful outing and ...'

'Amenze, we can't leave it like this, please. Tell me something that will keep me going tonight. I can wait for as long as you want if ...'

Amenze picked up her handbag and the envelope. She put the Bible in her bag and with a nod, insisted she had to leave. Silver got out his wallet and put some notes on top of the bill that had been placed at the corner of the table. He didn't stop to think how much change would be left. Saying nothing more, he took her hand and helped her up. They came out of the restaurant in complete silence. For the first time, Silver doubted if he was doing the right thing being with Amenze, as she was again putting her career her dreams before his.

Amenze had told Silver many times she was going into full time politics. As a result, Silver's dream drifted from being a stockbroker in London into creating an agency that would serve as a power house to move the banking industry in Nigeria forward.

Amenze finally convinced Silver she would marry him after her four year tenure of office if she managed to win presidency.

'How could you think of a thing like that in this society?'

'Why not? I need every second to focus.'

'Amenze, you seem to put only your interest forward in our relationship. What about us? I am ready to support you all the way but you must also know that we both have a life to live, before and after any tenure of office.'

After Amenze discussed the possible marriage with Scott and Iyobo, they encouraged her to marry sooner rather than later.

'Ah, Mum, I know you and Dad want grandchildren. I don't want that now. I have a career to fulfill. That is my calling. Every fibre of my body vibrates for this and a marriage would, especially if it doesn't go well, deter my plans. Can't you understand?'

'Of course, that will be between you and him. It has nothing to do with us,' Iyobo laughed, adjusting her glasses wishing quietly that her daughter would consider marriage before her career.

CHAPTER 59

Amenze had joined Power to All People's Party (PAPP), on her first visit to Nigeria aged 18. She was welcomed with full support to the party and ever since had been kept updated about happenings in the party.

Amenze had noticed during the short period she spent with Alhaji Suleiman, the Party Chairman, during meetings that he was a very good listener. According to him, 'listening helps you to make good judgement'. Qualified in Politics to a masters level, Suleiman had been a political activist since his university days and had always been considered as a *kingmaker* by his school mates.

When Suleiman saw Amenze for the first time during a rally in Lagos, he was intrigued by the powerful yet passionate way she spoke despite her still young age. He had told Dr Uche, his deputy, that it was time to start investing in the right people from an early age. He recognised that Amenze was capable of moving the nation forward, so told Uche it was the right thing to do to keep close links with her. Dr Uche agreed and ever since, minutes of every meeting were emailed to Amenze.

When Amenze graduated from Oxford, she was offered placements in two top commercial law firms in the UK. She chose Clifford Chance and was happy to be assigned to a separate branch from Silver's mother. She wanted a taste of work before going to attend Law School in Nigeria. Now three years later, Suleiman was still in the party, though he was no longer the party chairman. That position had been taken by Professor Ibru.

Amenze had followed the recent debate about the minimum age for presidency in the country to have been moved from 40 to

35 years as the people longed to have the younger generation with more energy to serve their nation. She knew however, that at the age of thirty, one could only be a Representative in Parliament.

Coming from the UK where anyone over the age of 18 could enter Parliament, Amenze felt appalled that age was such an issue, as it was clear Party members were not really considering what she had to offer. While she recognised this, she realised that she would have to wait until she was 35 to gain acceptance in her ambitions. The theory was, that at this age, any adult was at their best in maturity and experience and so should be able to manage a country. Amenze accepted this but was not convinced by the arguement.

Amenze had read about all the great politicians in the world and what made them great. She concentrated on Magaret Thatcher. There was only one thing she wanted to do differently. Amenze would like more women to be in the parliament, as this would give them more confidence to join in decision making. She was happy to have visited the Aso Rock, the presidential villa, during the previous government. She noticed that the wife of the president had put everything in place to ensure that women got to the top in politics.

The day she was given the go ahead to vie for a position in the House of Representative, Amenze was over the moon as she saw this as the most effective avenue to get her voice heard among the people. The party allowed her to go ahead based on her general input to the party which she had not only served as a legal adviser but also as campaign manager. If voted into the House of Representatives, she planned to serve two terms and then indicate her desire to stand for President.

The campaign to get Amenze into the House of Representatives went well, but faced criticism and threats, not only from opposing parties, but even internally, from jealous older statesmen who felt Amenze was too young to be trusted with such responsibility.

'This is not Oxford,' they sometimes said to her. Amenze remained tactful as she pressed forward. She kept the story of Mr Izebu, with whom she still chatted to from time to time, close at heart.

She had spoken with Scott and Iyobo as well as the Le Gros family about her desire to run for presidency. Each had a very different reaction.

'My daughter, you must be more prayerful than ever because it's not child's play to be the first female president. The only reason why I am not afraid for you is because I believe the Lord is on your side.'

Amenze listened to her mother on phone.

'Oh my precious gift, I knew it from the first moment you came into our home that you were a talented person. I hope your people will recognize your skill and hard work and join you to build the nation,' Lieve said with her Flemish accent while Pierre simply shouted 'Très bien' from the back ground.

Of all the comments, it was Scott's advice that helped Amenze most.

'Amenze, you are still young. The reason why you have achieved so much is because your people value you. You must value them too, no matter their age status or background. Make sure everybody you talk to feels your loyalty to them and then to the nation. What people want to see and feel is love. Love is tangible and has a great deal of impact. The look on your face, the graceful words you use, your zeal and genuiness to accomplish what you have said, will make people have confidence in you. Even if you forget everything else, one thing you must never forget is, to love and respect people, and do not make promises you won't strive to keep.'

CHAPTER 60

It was during a campaign towards the end of a two year tenure in the House of Representative at Abuja, that Amenze first made a speech that received nationwide attention.

'I start by saying that there is neither a PPP Nigeria nor a GCPP Nigeria. We do not even have a PPA Nigeria. We have only one nation which remains undivided by parties.

'Let me express my deep gratitude for the privilege of addressing this convention. Today is the most important day of my life pushing into second place, the day when I received a letter to Oxford University in the United Kingdom to study law. I feel a bit uncomfortable standing on this podium to address you, as I think of my circumstances in life which have not in the least deterred my dreams of becoming the best I could possibly be because of my determination to never give up no matter what.

'This is a character every parent should inculcate in his or her child.

'I was a product of what many people would refer to as a dysfunctional home before I was given out to foster parents. I may have been a product of a parental mistake but the good news is that I am not a product of divine error, as I have a lot to offer the world.

'My parents were eighteen and sixteen when I was conceived, both still in school. My mother carried the whole burden of having me and making sure I was raised to the point of being capable of addressing you noble people this day.'

'My mother was scared to death of her father, a man who was so shortsighted he would not send daughters to school, so she ran away, to make a better life for herself and for the baby in her womb. Too late she found out the angel she thought was delivering her, was a human trafficker. Unknown to her, she had been traded for a large sum of money which she had to pay back by getting on her back.'

The crowd remained sober and most were pensive. No one cheered. They seemed anxious to know what next Amenze would say.

'It was a question of life and death.' Amenze said, breathing out loudly.

'Confused, as any seventeen year old mother would be, she tried to find the best possible alternative for her baby. That was how I was given up to foster parents, people who my mother still calls angels. Yes, they were angels. They did everything possible to find out what I did best. They invested in me by sending me to special school for gifted and talented children. There I had the best six years a child could possibly have. I came out with the best results.

'I learned from my mother that my good results reflected hers at the same age, when she was a pupil at Agoba primary, Agoba in the Orhionmwon Local Government Area. She worked hard and was privileged to get the best results of the year at the common entrance and interview to get into the Federal Government College in her time. She was denied that opportunity because she didn't have a birth certificate. She was born at home in Agoba and her parents were ignorant of such official documentation. No provision was made for people who were academically capable but didn't have the right proof of birth. Her father was more than happy because he loathed the idea of sending female children to school. Despite everything she went through, my mother had big dreams for me. The question was, how would she achieve this dream with a sex trafficker on her back, in a land where she hardly understood the language?

'The best thing that ever happened to my mother, as she is proud to say wherever she goes, is that she met Jesus Christ. While still in the brothel, she and some of her co-workers were invited to church and the journey of her life started. The pastor there didn't know he was addressing four prostitutes who were broken and in great need of help and guidance. My mother got saved and didn't stop there. She didn't stop praying for all her old colleagues who were determined to stay in order to pay off their debt. Long story short, God sent help in different ways and my mother got out of the brothel and started leading a good Christian life. A couple of years later, she married Scott, a Scottish man who is now my step-father and of whom I am so proud. When he took my family back to the United Kingdom, he ensured I went to the best Grammer School.

'I would like to deviate a little bit. This is in order to talk a little about my foster parents. They are Belgians and I wasn't the only child they fostered. They took care of disadvantaged children from anywhere around the globe but they said there was always something about me that kept them wanting to maximize my potentials. They knew I was not Belgian. They knew I was Nigerian. They knew that whatever they did was not only for the individual but for the development of the whole world. They often said that all they did for me was a contribution to the world. Now, this is how I reason. I do not think ME. I think US.

'My foster parents shared not only an improbable love; they shared an abiding faith in the possibilities of nations where their foster children came from. They kept my African name, Amenze. They also kept my biological father's name Odigie as that was my mother's wish. They went to African shops even when it wasn't convenient for them to buy me beauty products to keep me the best African I could possibly be. No wonder mum calls them Angels.

'They imagined me going to the best schools in the land, even though I wasn't their blood relation, because they believed that everybody who showed ability was worthy of achievement. Whether I am in Belgium or in Nigeria, I am still a part of the global village. Their salute to diversity in such an intensity is my driving force to embrace such a beautiful nation with the beauty that diversity offers

'I stand here today grateful for the diversity of my heritage, aware that my mother's dreams live on. A dream which she got from her own mother, who did all she could to send her to school despite her husband's wish.

'I stand here knowing that my story is part of the larger Nigerian story, that I owe a debt to all of those who came before me and have in one way or the other made it possible for me to be here today.'

'Today, we gather to affirm the greatness of our nation centred on a very simple map. This can be summed up by our most common needs of food, shelter and raiment. This is based on the simple fact that we are all created equal and that our basic needs are the same. Added to this simple premise is security. A secure nation is a blessed nation. The latter comes naturally when the former is properly addressed.

'My dream for this nation is an insistence on the most important things of life for example, to be able to send our children to bed at night knowing that they are fed, clothed and safe from harm. My dream is to see that we have freedom of speech; that we can say what we think without being molested by authorities; we can write what we think without arrests, that we can have an idea without being shut down by impossible circumstances, starting a business or going about our private activities without paying bribes to those who should be protecting us, that we can participate in the political process without guilt or fear and that everybody from the age of eighteen will come out to vote and their votes will be counted knowing that each vote stands for a legitimate voice.

'And, fellow Nigerians, I must say to you, today, that we have so much work to do and we must not give up.

'I may be young and may not yet have seen as many years as many of you here, but I certainly have confidence in collaborative work as this will never fail. This is when the older ones pass their experiences and the younger receive and implement with utmost humility. Our great nation has to first come to terms with the fact that a woman is capable of ruling.'

There was huge applause mainly from the women folk after which Amenze continued.

'There have been very many success stories of female ministers and directors. Results have shown their sensitivity to these simple issues which are indeed very important when piled up which the men folk often underscore. Having said that, it will be vital to state categorically that this is not gender race. It is like a relay race where we all are part of a team, with people being positioned where they perform best, all heading to the same direction.

'We have more work to do to eradicate corruption. It is possible. If children are taught from very early age what is acceptable, show them practical examples of consequences, they will grow up to know they shouldn't do it. It's as easy as that. In this regard, we would have to underline the consequences and follow it up more seriously knowing that the value of a nation is at stake. No one is bigger than the nation. We will tackle job issues with tact. No one expects this to be done overnight. You don't expect a government to solve all of the problems at once. People know they have to work hard to get ahead. And of course, they want to.

'Go into market places, offices and restaurants in and outside Abuja, people will tell you they are fully aware that government alone can't teach kids to learn. Parents are ready to help educate their children to meet the standard of a great nation.' People clapped their hands but not so loud.

'They know that parents have to teach that children can't achieve unless we raise their expectations and turn off the television sets and eradicate the slander that says to hide something from an African, better write it in a book. Or, to say the least, "Africans are only good in their football and nothing more". This is a slap in our face. Having said that, we cannot build a nation without sports but all sports must come into play because this is the way we shine among nations. We also want to shine in science and technology, in literature, etc.

'People don't expect Governments to solve all their problems. But they sense, deep in their bones, that with just a slight change in priorities, we can make sure that every child in Nigeria has a decent shot at life and that the doors of opportunity remain open to all. They know we can do better. And they want that choice. This will prevent pointing accusing fingers at one another.

'In this election, we offer that choice. Our party has chosen a woman to lead us who embodies the best this country has to offer and I promise I will leave no stone unturned for the sake of national progress.

'I am a Christian and my faith has helped me in making the choice of today. There is a portion in the Bible, Joshua chapter 1, verse 8. God recognising how big and challenging the task of leading the Israelites out of the desert would be, said to Joshua: "be strong and courageous". There is another quote in the Bible that says "I can do all things through Christ who strengthens me".

'This God-given strength also helps me understand the ideals of community, faith and service because they've defined my life from when I lived a few months with my mother in a social house to when I went to the Le Gros' affluent home and back to my mother and Scott, being a family of two continents. All these experiences have made me tougher, brighter and better.'

The cheer became very loud and it took time to calm down the crowd.

'I believe in a country where hard work is rewarded. I believe in a nation where all Nigerians can afford the same health facilities just like those flying abroad at first sight of any symptom.

'I believe we need electricity to make our dreams happen. Concrete plans must be in place to make this happen.

'Like the last government, I believe in energy independence. We produce enough to take care of ourselves and to sell. We should therefore not be held hostage to saboteurs who take delight in hoarding oil for personal gain. Again, it is about accountability.

'I believe in the constitutional freedoms that have made our country the envy of the world. Our nation allows dual nationality for the purpose of encouraging citizens to bring the skills they acquired from other nations. This in turn should not give way to crime increase that would jeopardise our reputation at home and abroad.

'I believe in one Nigeria. And I know that it's not enough for just some of us to prosper while others languish in poverty. Alongside our famous individualism, clans and tribes separated by different religious belief, there's another ingredient in the Nigeria saga, a belief that we are all connected as one people. This means that if there's a child in North Western Nigeria who can't read, that matters to me, even if it's not my biological child.

'If there's an old person somewhere who needs financial help, that makes my life poorer, even if they are not my family members.

'It is the fundamental belief that I am my brother's keeper or I am my sister's keeper that makes a country work. These are the simple things I was talking about. All these help us to pursue our individual dreams but still come together as a nation to tackle national issues.

'Now even as we speak, there are those who are preparing to divide us; those who want politics only for personal gain. This should not be encouraged. What they must know is that we are no more divided by parties, clans, tribes, religions and cultures. We have all been united by a single purpose of progress. It is the Nigerian factor.

'In planning to achieve all these basic elements on a large scale, we recognise that these needs will not all be met at the snap of two fingers. I am talking about hope in the midst of difficulty and uncertainty. Hope in this context is a mere belief that things will be better.

'I believe we can afford good roads for those who work hard to keep this nation going. We can equip schools for children we are counting on to carry forward our big dreams. We can encourage our workers after a period of hard work to take a fully deserved holiday by rewarding them adequately.

'As you all can see, the things we all need are quite basic and achievable and if you all feel the way I do, our country will soon become a haven of rest.

'Thanks for listening to me.'

CHAPTER 61

Amenze stood by her hotel window and looked out over Aso Rock, the 400 meter monolith left by water erosion. Abuja, Nigeria's capital city, was dominated and shaped by the rock. Much of the city extended to the south, including the Supreme Court, the National Assembly, and, holding more interest for Amenze, was the Presidential Complex. Her aspiration to settle there for eight years being two terms of services occupied her mind more than ever before.

'Your credentials are strong enough to rescue a nation,' Yusuf, Amenze's old Oxford classmate, teased.

'Thanks, Yus,' she said turning away from the window and smiling at her supportive friend.

Since graduating, Yusuf had set up his own law firm which he was dedicated to fighting for the rights of children in Sokoto state. 'There may not be too much money coming in, but I feel satisfied that I am doing what I love, putting people on the right track and helping them to discover how powerful they can be when they put their heart and soul into doing anything,' Yusuf often said in his usual quiet voice.

This was the man Amenze longed to make her deputy, when the time was right to vie for the position of the President of the Federal Republic of Nigeria.

Yusuf was a man of the people, an icon and a seasoned lawyer. Before returning to Nigeria, he had worked at the Human Rights Tribunal in The Hague as a support staff to a senior judge. His input to the tribunal as an organisation was phenomenal.

His hobby was watching and listening to cases. The 1994 OJ Simpson murder case was his particular interest. He had watched the DVD of this case so much that he could recite every word the lawyers, the Judge and the jury members said during court proceedings. He got close to this case out of disgust he maintained against celebrity trials.

He downplayed the display of civility trivialised as race became a focal point when a murder case was at stake in the OJ case. Yusuf was grateful those in developing countries didn't have their cases dealt with publicly, although there were more serious factors that could mar judgment in this part of the world.

OJ's Defence Lawyer, Cochran was his hero.

'The guy is a black lawyer who knows what he wants right from the start and he goes for it. During the OJ case Cochran dictated his own music and danced, while others simply watched in admiration,' Yusuf said with excitement.

'To be honest, I love it when fun is brought into cases, that are indeed perceived as very serious as this brings another dimension to how the case is seen,' he said almost laughing but holding it back to show the seriousness of what he was saying.

At this point, Amenze was beginning to pull back in the discussion, as she reminisced over Yusuf's last sentence.

"Yusuf, lots of people were watching in horror and thought this was a clown performance to distract from the fact that OJ was guilty. You must also remember that in 1997, a civil court awarded a judgment against Simpson for causing the wrongful deaths of his wife and Goldman; and a $33.5 million fine as judgment. A lot of people think this proves he is a murderer and the cases for kidnap, etc that came later didn't exactly mitigate in his favour anyway. Did you ever think about that?"

'What I am saying is that lawyers at some point should devise a fun way of displaying evidence while holding strongly to the root of the case,' he added when he saw the grin on his listener's face.

'Humour during court proceedings, could be a way to energise evidence but you must not forget we are dealing with human lives. Fun in serious cases? This suggests murder is something to laugh about, whereas surely – the taking of a life is no joke. Do you not have a concept of the importance of your own role as a lawyer? Do you not believe in the sanctity of God given life as a human being? Yus, let's look at this very closely; this is the worst kind of human betrayal, this is allowing the Devil to take control when we trivialise important cases like this. I disagree with people who uphold the motion that a lawyer has no clear sense of right or good. Not for me Yus. I do have a clear sense of wrong and right in the dispensation of my duties as a laywer and most importantly, as a head of state, Amenze said, with a broad smile directly in Yusuf's face who returned the smile.

'Look Yusuf, if I am told to deal with a case, I make sure I explore all evidence,' Amenze said very quietly but firmly, as if to drum those few words into the ears of her listener.

'Amen, this is nothing personal. I will give you an example of what I am talking about. Can you remember the humour created when OJ wore the gloves he was accused of wearing when the crime was committed and they wouldn't fit? That was funny,' The Sokoto born lawyer asserted, with a slight Hausa accent mixed with English speech mannerism. People who watched wondered why there was a case anyway if the gloves would not fit but the sight of it was funny, even though we all knew this was a very important matter to be attended in a more focused manner.

'Really? Funny? A lot of people viewed it as nothing more than showmanship, OJ being an actor as well as a sports player,' Amenze slotted in.

'Amenze, OJ didn't create the gloves. If you can well remember, the grin on the accused's face, created by this scenario, was of someone who was already half way through his ordeal. Having said that,' Yusuf continued, hardly allowing Amenze to say a word, 'one thing that worries me is the fragility of the term "truth" in the legal profession. It worries me when the term "truth" becomes open and versatile, especially when dealing with a high profile case. It becomes heart rending when the word is replaced with "proof" and when these two become synonymous. I think it's easier to get to truth with the less priviledged,' he finally said, pausing to take his glass of orange juice on the side table while Amenze kept quiet to ponder about all they had been saying.

'You are right, Yus. Though law is a noble profession and law-yers are often respected worldwide, there seems to be this loop-hole that sometimes leaves laymen open mouthed with surprise. Something that we all seem to wonder about but never seem to find solutions to, that the innocent are sometimes convicted and the guilty set free,'

'Exactly,' Yusuf said, nodding his head continuously and then looking away and then turning back to Amenze. 'I dream of pro-moting the civil court in my village as this allows for a lower bur-den of proof than the criminal courts and should cost the people less. When cases are subject to too much scrutiny and scrupulous analysis, things often go wrong and that's not what we want,' Yusuf said confidently.

'Amenze, watching cases in The Hague changed my life. When you hear and see what people do and go through in the name of law, all I want is to stay away from bogus cases and focus on the ones I am most sure about. Look at this,' Yusuf raised his voice, drumming his index finger into the arm of the settee he was sit-ting on, 'every child needs justice and that's what I stand for,' he said and kept quiet.

'You're playing it safe, Yus. Be honest,'

'No I am not. This is what I feel comfortable doing. My heart breaks when people who deserve justice don't get it. Why fight a cause I am not sure of when there are millions of genuine cases I can get honest justice for?' he declared, leaning back, taking an-other sip from the glass of orange juice in his right hand, show-ing off a thick gold bracelet with the inscription "for men only".

He sipped the orange and carefully placed back the glass on the table, looking straight into Amen's eyes when he spoke.

'You can't be serious about this, your political bouhaha. Do you think it is the same as what you had abroad? Look, things are different over here and you might not find it as smooth going as you are expecting. Be real,' he whispered gently. 'First you are a woman. Who votes for women in our country? Secondly, you studied abroad. You do not understand the culture of the people, even though they are your people. Finally and most importantly, you are way too young for the Nigerian politics. You've got to have grey in your hair, wrinkles on your face,' Yusuf said, sarcastically, laughing enough to upset Amenze.

'I can't believe you are talking like this Yusuf,' Amenze said controlling the upset in her voice.

'First of all you must understand that a nation needs the young and the old to function. If I become a leader, I shall create a special institution for the former heads of government. They would serve as special advisers. I would make them special because they are and whatever good suggestions they made would be highly rewarded. If you drop them like a piece of cloth, that's when they want to come back and then back again.

'As for me being too young, I can't believe you of all people would say that Yusuf. We were taught to be leaders at Oxford, not just professionals. We were taught to know how to excel in any field we chose. We were taught to excel by pulling others along with us. I don't see my ambitions as unachievable but rather as challenging,' she affirmed as she adjusted herself on the seat, this time, sitting at the very edge and leaning forward with her glass of water in her hands.

'Yusuf, the satisfaction you get working among your people is indeed better than your pay cheque from The Hague. To me, that's what working for a good cause is all about. Now listen, egg head,' Amenze uttered with a grin, 'in the same vein, my passion is the entire nation. This nation is a great nation and leaders seem to come in, get a taste of the goodies then back out. To some extent, we are both fighting the same cause. I follow my path of passion by opting to lead the people selflessly, with dedication and without thinking of what I get back. Yusuf, talking about being born and bred abroad,' Amenze continued, adjusting her glasses with her left index finger,'maichi da uwa ba shi kuka'n soodi.' The Hausa language she had been taking private lessons in.

'Wow, you speak Hausa. I am impressed. Now, tell me, what does that proverb mean, my fair lady,' Yusuf asked sounding very British.

'He who eats with his mother will not have to ask for the soodi, the leftovers, as she will naturally give it to him.'

'Good girl,' Yusuf smiled.

'What I'm saying is, that I'm already in the country, doing all I am supposed to be doing. I am no longer a forigner, but now a bonifide Nigerian. I will be accorded my due when the time comes. So, chill, brother,' Amenze said laughing.

'Amen, don't get it twisted. I know you and know what you are capable of doing. We watch TV each day and we see the way the politicians argue about nothing and achieve less. Politics would be so demotivating for me,' he spoke as if those were the last words he would say on the topic, for all he knew that wouldn't stop Amenze.

They had both achieved first class honours at Oxford so he knew what Amenze was capable of.

'Don't see things that way. Haven't you watched parliaments in the so called developed world? They argue, maybe not about the same things as our country but that's because we are different. People argue to agree. Why are you a lawyer if you avoid cases and arguments?

'Yus, what I need is the right person. A person who combines skill and selflessness, one who's a step ahead of the people in the way of rendering a helping hand. A person who is committed, zealous and open. A person who is able to create an atmosphere conducive to accountability and motivation for everyone from the highest ranked worker and the lowest. Yus, when people see they are important, that their input, no matter how small, is valued, they become selfless and highly motivated themselves.

'*Ba afafi giandumma ran taffia*. We must not leave this till the last minute before we start to prepare,' Amen affirmed in Hausa and English.

'*Yowa*,' Yusuf agreed. 'The big question is who will lead the charge? Who will selflessly serve the nation to the point of bringing about the redemption you speak of?'

Amenze heaved a sigh of relief as they had finally got to the point she wanted to make

'I will, Yusuf, and you know what? You will come along with me and together, we will not only give justice to the children, we will deliver justice to the whole nation. Come on Yusuf, *Yawa shi Kan Sa zarre ya ja duchi*.'

'Of course, unity is strength,' Yusuf interpreted. And then paused for a while as he hadn't expected this. 'I am flattered,' he said looking at Amenze, their eyes met without blinking for some seconds.

'*Rama ba muta ba,*' Yusuf said with all seriousness but didn't get the same effect with Amenze as she burst out into laughter. Yusuf knew at once that Amenze took the words of wisdom literally, 'being thin is not dying'.

'Sorry about that, Yus. Some of these proverbs really make me laugh. Now let's get serious. What you are implying, I suppose, is that our nation has hope and potential and the fact that we are like this today does not mean that there is no hope for tomorrow.'

'Yowa.'

'In that case, are you agreeing to join me?'

❖ ❖ ❖

'Instincts are sometimes stronger than actions. If you feel it, it's half done. Let us follow our hearts. It doesn't matter what we both believe now, when the time comes, things will be in place,' Amenze stated as if delivering a speech to her singular audience. She then sat on the floor making sure both her legs were hidden beneath her flowing skirt. With her glass still in hand, she hastily took a long drink of water.

'Yusuf, you will be my eyes and ears in your part of the country. I know you have not been there since your childhood, but they are still your people. They'll listen to you. The same applies to me in around Benin City. That is how we can now bring our skills into play. Yusuf, I want you to be my honourable vice president when the time comes.'

'Are you sure I have the right qualities?'

'A bad axe of your own is better than one you have to wait for until the owner has finished with it,' Amenze translated a popular Hausa proverb into English.

Yusuf laughed unconvincingly, got up from his seat, went to the table, looking for a way to change the subject. It was becoming too cold for comfort. He picked up his car keys.

'Amen, don't worry. I'll call you when I get back to Sokoto. I'm travelling back first thing tomorrow morning. Thanks for a lovely evening.'

'Ok Yus. It was a lovely evening, but do think about my proposal. I shall be waiting for your call.'

'Sure, bye.'

Amenze stood still at the door where she waved *au revoir* to the man she strongly believed would be her Vice. She had left no stone unturned before deciding to woo Yusuf into the game of politics.

It paid off.

Time went by so quickly. So many meetings, campaigns, more meetings, other campaigns. Amenze Ogidi and Yusuf Abubahari worked together day and night along with other senior members of the party. No reference was made to Amenze being a whore's daughter and a whore herself. She had a chance to explain to senior colleagues the real situation and they all supported her. One thing was always on Amenze's mind, her opponents could pull a surprise at any time. No matter what happened, she was ready to take it and congratulate whosoever won the election. That was the right thing to do. If she didn't get the presidency, she figured she could go for a doctorate and become a lecturer.

Three weeks before the election, despite all the hard work, for the first time, Amenze wondered if she was on the right path. Things she heard and saw happening didn't seem to be playing in her favour. All her strategies had been employed. She remembered Anne and Regis in Brentwood. They had been praying with her, through the heat of the campaign and the tension that never stopped rising. She decided to do one last thing proposed by Regis.

'Just keep praising Him. Whatever be the outcome, God remains your Father. He promises never to leave you nor forsake you.'

Amenze adhered to Regis's advice and stopped worrying.

CHAPTER 62

"WHORE'S DAUGHTER FOR PRESIDENT"
PPAP ENDORSES DAUGHTER OF
EX-HOOKER AS PRESIDENT"

Amenze's eyes ran through the captions on three national news-papers placed on her table, with her heart pounding.

They all carried the story of her mother being an ex-whore with phrases in her last speech relating to her mother underlined.

'Do you think this is Europe where people are so open to talk about their lives? Why should you mention what your mother did in Europe? Everybody knows such things go on but you don't have to rub yourself with it. Permit me to say that, on this occasion, you have done a stupid thing.'

Amenze watched Emma speak with tears in her eyes, stamping her feet to the ground several times.

'I told you yesterday. Look, you can do that in America, in the United Kingdom, in Holland or even in India. People will listen, be sympathetic or learn from your mistakes. If you try it here, it is to your own detriment. If I had seen the speech before you mounted the podium, I would have told you to delete some parts. Who announces their mother was a prostitute? She went abroad and did business or worked as a shopkeeper or something like that. Who will investigate?'

'Emma, thanks for your concern,' Amenze finally gathered strength to speak. 'But I know my opponents, the truth was out there and they were preparing to use it. Only by being the first to speak of it could I head off their assault. I have done what I have done and I did it in the belief that it was for the best. Seeing this, my only concerns are for my family, I see now how hurt they will be by all this. I had not thought it through quite enough.'

A tear dropped from Amenze's eye and Emma reached out for tissue and put it in her friend's hand.

Amenze asked for three days off political activities and the Party Chairman was happy to let her go; although the Presidential candidate heard later that day from Emma that the same chairman had planned to set up an inner committee to investigate how much damage this might bring to the party. If it was too much, Amenze's candidature would be withdrawn.

CHAPTER 63

From being a prostitute's daughter to being a country's president couldn't be harder for Amen. Her CV was in place, but talk of her mum's ugly past was everywhere.

In fact, as time went by, more gossip there was that Iyobo pimped out her daughter, that Amenze herself was also a prostitute. She was sickened reading all about her mother who they said left the village to go to town to cover up some shame and later went to Europe for big time whoredom. Most of what Amenze read was news to her even though she was convinced her mother never hid anything from her. She had confronted her mother time and again with some of these issues but always found her burst into tears saying 'Amenze, my daughter,' as African women would call out when making a strong truthful point, 'those are all lies but I can't deny it now. But please forgive me for the pain and shame I have brought to you and your future ambition. I also had ambition. I used to be considered as intelligent and at one point the most intelligent in my village. Lust made me lose my way and I traded my destiny for something less. I have forgiven myself. God has forgiven me. I believe my people will also forgave me. How would I have ever known that what I took part in thousands of kilometres away from home would turn out later to haunt my daughter in future? It is impossible to see the future,' Iyobo said, wiping a stream of tears from her sore and hurting eyes.

❖ ❖ ❖

Amenze could not imagine the serenity and peace Iyobo had achieved since she was born again. While she worried all night about issues, her mother and Scott simply slept after they put all things in God's hands.

For now, the only goal Amenze had was to fight her way through the primaries. The presidential election was just ten months away. She seemed to have control over everything that came her way, except convincing people she was morally suitable for the office she'd always wanted.

While she still lived in Brussels, Amenze had heard Dorcas, Iyobo's friend say, 'my journey from Benin to Brussels through the bush needed some brains. The undetermined gave up even before they embarked on the journey. What kept people alive were their dreams. The day the dream falls out of your hand, that's when you begin to sink.'

Amenze also recalled a Bible story. Peter admired the master, Jesus for walking on top of the sea. He wanted to do the same and he did. He did the impossible, which only Jesus could do. Peter, a mere man, defied the laws of gravity and walked on water but something happened when he strayed a bit in his thoughts and started wondering, questioning and doubting the reality of what he was doing. As soon as he doubted, he started to sink. He was immediately rescued by Jesus.

Amenze picked up strength from all these stories and became more determined than ever to continue with the presidential race.

'If she's not emotionally ready for the hard truths and adversarial nature of politics, then she isn't ready or worthy of being a president.'

Amenze heard from the secretary of the Party Chairman, allegedly boss had said it in Amenze's absence at a meeting. The secretary advised Amenze to be bold and strong as no softie would survive Nigerian politics.

Emotionally, Amen was not ready for the naming and shaming, he had not realised what it would cost her, but she had to carry on, she was not a quitter. In school, she was taught that every problem in life had a solution. Some solutions are there, easily identified, while others had to be worked out or even created. Some solutions could come through past experiences or from a third party. Most often, a person has to look inside, and there inside is a wealth of possibilities to resolve all that life can throw at a person. Iyobo often told Amenze that if every road to solution seems closed, then it's about time God showed some power.

Amenze called Anne and Regis in Brentwood to always remember her in their prayers. The pair prayed for her daily but also advised her to look in the Bible to see what made great kings and what made weak kings. If she found out, Regis said, then she must follow suit as God is always the same. This advice gladdened Amen's heart. She prayed night and day and read her Bible. She made a list of all the kings in the Bible, finding for what made some good and others bad. She underlined the fact that none of the kings lived without challenges. She also highlighted what they did in face of difficulties. She kept her Bible study book preciously as she reflected daily on what she read.

While she did this, Professor Lukido, her political opponent, breathed fire. Professor Lukido, a PhD in Law and retired Professor from one of the nation's most prestigious universities threatened to oust the prostitute's daughter. He vowed to let the world know that Amenze was an outlaw and not the holy angel she claimed to be, that she brought down the nation by her race to the presidency.

During an open air rally near, where Itota resided, Professor Lukido sighed as he bowed down his head, as if reading each word from a paper. He then looked up in the sky, as if seeking some permission before lashing out at his female opponent. He spoke like a man full of wisdom, whose stock in trade was to give out advice. He picked his words very slowly, as if purposely rubbing them into the hearts of his listeners.

'The mother of the presidential aspirant was once a first class whore and also a breeder of other hookers both at home and abroad.'

His listeners, made up of his party members erupted in laughter, clapping their hands and chanting a song of victory. The presidential aspirant then beckoned for a long time before he managed to get enough quiet to continue his speech.

'News even reached me that as an escort, Iyobo, Amenze's mother, even charged more than the normal rate deceiving men through "sweet and intelligent talk" telling them she was not in the same social class as the other hookers. In other words, Mum must have passed the wrong moral values to her daughter. This makes my opponent unfit to become a head of state no matter how much she has the nation at heart.'

The people cheered and booed. Journalists took notes and a few people from Amenze's camp had their hands on their jaws listening and saying nothing.

'This country has gone too far to look back. Inexperienced selfish prostitutes should not, I repeat, should not be allowed to come close to the golden door of legislation. Before we know it, prostitution will be legalised and our daughters dragged down into that degrading trade. My opponent is intelligent and hard working. She has extended arms of love to the people and has even started to buy the people to her side. Unfortunately, those hands are polluted. We must not be bought by western ideologies, to bring down our most cherished culture and tradition. It is clear that Miss Amenze Odigie is the daughter of a prostitute. She lived with her mother and witnessed the horror of that trade. I was reliably told she participated and it was with the money they made that she attended the most expensive school in England. Today, she seems to have all we need but lacks the moral backing. We should say "no" to her and send her back to where she came from.'

❖ ❖ ❖

'What Professor Lukido doesn't understand about present day Nigerian politics is that people have moved on. It's now about what people have in plan to eradicate poverty, crime and unemployment. Concentrating on the sin of the mother of a presidential aspirant shows the banality of his mindset and only a fool will put a penny on their words,' Emma responded to a political analyst who visited the office the day after they learnt Amenze had gone on a three day leave of absence.

CHAPTER 64

'Honey, why are you crying again? Since you started following the Nigerian News on Televison and newspapaers, you have become rather depressed.'

'Scott, you will not understand unless you are in the situation yourself.'

'Iyobo, I *am* in the situation. I'm your husband. I told you to be patient. It all happens but it dies always, so quickly. I believe our daughter will win the election because she's the right candidate to lead the nation. After winning-'

'Winning what? What are you talking about? She's got no chance.' Iyobo cut in like a hawk diving for a prey in the long grass.

'I know my country. It's not always about what you can bring in. It's first and foremost about who you are.'

'Good then,' Scott affirmed. 'Amenze is an Oxford graduate with a first class degree in law. She is also-'

'The daughter of an ex-hooker Scott. Don't you understand? Can't you see why I can't rest while my daughter swallows up all the spitum of sadness lowered on her by some political pressure?'

'Iyobo, I have warned you several times to stop referring to yourself like that. You are my wife and I deserve some respect too. Don't you see that?'

'Scott, you know I love and cherish you. It's just that, I can't take it any longer, what's happening to Amenze.'

'Now listen to me. I speak to you from the bottom of my heart. The next time you speak like that about yourself, I shall be very cross with you and I promise-'

'Stop it Scott. Do not make this personal,' Iyobo said, turning fully to Scott who got up from the chair. Iyobo got up and followed Scott into the room, wiping her tears and sobbing at the same time. Scott closed the door to make sure the children didn't hear while he talked to Iyobo.

'Scott, I am sorry. I didn't mean to be rude.'

'I know. We've been married now for two decades and this is the way you refer to yourself? Each time something hard comes on you.'

'Scott, those were the exact words I read in the papers this morning. I followed the news. It is very hard to bear. If the rock was tumbling on me and me alone, I would understand and bear the pain, the outcome.'

'Amenze is fighting back. She's not a baby. She has a huge political party behind her. They want her to represent them because they knew she's equal to the task. They would fight it tooth and nail to get her out of any.' Scott slotted in.

'Get her out of any what? And this isn't the way political parties work, they'd drop her like a hot potato and never look back',' Iyobo said still sobbing.

Scott held his wife close, leaving a half loose tie around his neck. Iyobo finished it off and they both got hooked looking at each other without a word. Putting his arms around his wife, Scott held Iyobo close. She leaned into him, the support they had shared over the last twenty years still strong. Silently, she turned to look up at him. He looked down, meeting her gaze with one that was serious and full of love, the love they shared between themselves, their family and their God.

'Iyobo, Jesus loves you the way you are. The day you confessed Jesus as your Lord and personal Saviour, you were made a new person, old things were passed away, all things become new. Can't you understand that?'

'I know. I am renewed. But you know, even if God forgives all, the world never let's go. At least, not in Nigerian politics,' Iyobo tried to force a smile. 'Scott, I have a plan. I can't remain here reading all that rubbish in the newspapers and pretend I didn't see them.'

'What do you want to do, my love?' Scott said in a playful voice doing his best to lighten the mood.

Iyobo looked deeply into her husband's eyes, held him close and whispered, 'I need you to support me.'

❖ ❖ ❖

The family meeting was scheduled for 5 P.M.. Iyobo and Scott had talked it over and over, they both agreed what should be done to help their daughter regain her rightful place in the popular consciousness as well as establish the facts behind all that happened before she was born.

When Iyobo called Amenze, she was relieved at how excited her daughter was by the plan. Iyobo couldn't wait to see her daughter's relief, as she was looking forward to being officially introduced to her biological father and also to meet other members of her wider family. Iyobo had contacted all parties involved. Iyobo thought the time and effort invested in gathering all these people was not wasted, not compared to the gain she hoped to receive.

The venue was in Benin City and all invited were to arrive for the meeting to start at 5:00 P.M. on the dot. Fosa and a group of four women arrived at four. They sat at the extreme end of the hall. Scott and Iyobo had been there since five to. Moses, Sunday and Imaduoyi glided in on their wheelchairs around quarter past. They came with their mother Itota and their wives. The three men were ushered in to special places where their chairs were comfortably fixed.

Tension was high in the hall. None of the guests knew exactly who Iyobo had invited. They all sat very calmly no one spoke, though several harsh looks were thrown around as they came in.

Mr Unugboro and his wife were the next. Iyobo couldn't hold herself back from running towards her old teacher. She fell on her knees and said 'Miguo sir', Mr Unugboro was from the Urhobo tribe in Nigeria and this way of greeting was the greatest respect you could ascribe to an elder statesman of that tribe.

'You still made it. Even more than I dreamed, my daughter. A genius will always produce a genius. I wasn't shocked when I heard one of our presidential candidates was your daughter. Iyobo, my dear, no one can predict tomorrow.'

Iyobo smiled and turned to his wife, bending a knee. They exchanged greetings and they all quietly moved to their seats.

Amenze had been in Benin since two with Silver. They were in the Hotel Plaza while she had to attend a local PPAP meeting which was scheduled for that day knowing that she would be in town. She eventually got to the meeting at exactly 4:26 P.M.. She came in with her fiancé and his parents. She also had a team of body guards who remained outside during the meeting.

Mrs Osagie came in at quarter to five and sat not too far away from where Amenze sat with her personal body guard. Mrs Osagie had never seen a presidential candidate live before, let alone been able to sit so close to one, and to think that this one's mother had been her house girl, it made her blood boil. Amenze didn't know her but smiled at everyone that came her way.

Itota would love them to start this meeting without Ogidi who had still not arrived there ten minutes before five. She knew he would like to come in when the meeting had started so that he would get some attention. Itota had whispered this in Iyobo's ears, who asked Amenze to wait till 5.02 P.M. for the sake of family. Amenze concurred.

Iyobo had mentioned by phone to the Le Gros family about a family meeting but didn't go deeply into what it was meant to achieve. They were presently visiting Ghana and the Congo, while waiting to support Amenze in any way she needed them to, during her presidential campaign. Iyobo had received a call from Lieve just that morning saying that she would like to attend the meeting but wasn't quite sure since Pierre was a little unwell.

When Iyobo then heard that they would be attending the meeting, she was thrown into uncertainty. She was disgusted at the kind of life she lived in Belgium and didn't want this noble family to know the details. At the same time, so many things had happened and a lot was water under the bridge of forgetfulness. She still felt she owed this family a heartfelt thank you. By involving them in her family matters, would prove to them that their labour was not in vain. The Le Gros couple walked in soon after Amenze.

Iyobo was delighted to see the Le Gros's as she watched Amenze quickly get up from her seat to hug Mama Lieve and Papa Pierre.

The Le Gros family took another look at their foster child. They looked at each other and smiled while they sat down in their own place, taking a glance at every opportunity.

'How are you my darling? Lieve asked in Dutch.

'Oh my baby, are you ok?' Pierre spoke in French.

'I am well and happy to see you both.' Amenze replied in fluent Dutch. They both smiled.

Ogidi had still not arrived. Iyobo decided to start the meeting since her daughter had schedules to keep to.

Iyobo got up and left Scott by himself towards the front, close to where Amenze was. Behind Amenze, stood a female aide de corps who moved at any tinniest movement Amenze made. When Iyobo moved to the front, the Aide de corps moved, ready to hold back anything that might come close to the presidential aspirant. She maintained a straight face as she was trained to be cold and calculating in her protection duties.

Iyobo was careful when she moved close to her daughter, taking nothing for granted. Cameras were kept outside the hall. Everything seemed to be set and all that were invited were settled except Ogidi.

'I, in consent with Amenze Odigie, my daughter, have called for this rather rare and special meeting which will enable us to crack the nut that had proven so stubborn for so long. A lot of rumours have been spread and many things have been believed.'

Ogidi finally arrived at the gate at 5.30 P.M., dragging his feet as he walked in, along with two personal bodyguards he hired from the village. He had told people he was in danger since he was the grandfather of a presidential aspirant and so he needed security. He paid them by himself. Unfortunately, the two men were turned back at the gate by a couple of army men that came with Amenze. Ogidi came into the meeting furious but nobody looked to him. Itota pretended to be looking through the window opposite the door he came in through. Others were focused on Iyobo's speech.

Ogidi walked into the hall in very quick steps, stopped, looked right and left and when he saw no one gave him any attention, he waved his left hand to his daughter who had to stop reading because of her father's interruption. Ogidi was dressed in traditional Bini attire with his neck and both hands decorated with beads which made a lot of distracting noise while he walked and when he waved. In his right hand was an *ezuzu* a large hand fan made of leather and cow tail which he waved creating an awkward scene.

Iyobo waited for a minute for him to sit down without making any eye contact with him. She simply stared at her paper and tried not to show how appalled she was at her father's bahaviour. Ogidi waved his *ezuzu* at everybody focusing on those sitting at the front around his granddaughter. In a normal situation, a wave of that nature by a prominent personality would demand a response like 'long may you live'. On this occasion, Ogidi was ignored by his family and dignitaries.

Since no one was giving him attention, he sat down quietly close to the door from where he came in.

Ogidi later raised up his head, looked at Iyobo who sighed a bit, pretending to clean her face while she waited for her father to settle down.

A minute later, when Iyobo looked in his direction after she resumed her speech, she saw that her father sat quietly with his *ezuzu* leaning against the wall. He was looking through the window, Iyobo almost laughed. She reserved that for later when she could be alone with Scott.

'My daughter is almost losing the presidential race because of speculation in the newspapers that her mother was a prostitute in Europe.' Iyobo paused to wipe her tears. 'Yes, I was a prostitute. But you must listen to my side of the story before you judge me. God knows I will not be speaking only for myself, but also for all the innocent girls that are carried out of this nation day in, day out, to be forced into a trade they loathe with all their guts.'

Scott kept smiling at his wife who at last seemed to be very proud of her strength in overcoming all the challenges that had come her way. Iyobo looked around her. Amenze did not give away her emotions. Mr Unogboro scratched his nose and held his wife more closely. A tear fell from Fosa's eyes as he adjusted his sitting position. Ogidi buried his face in his hands and then unconsciously lifted up his ezuzu and then laid it on the bare floor as if to demonstrate how disgusted he felt when Iyobo confirmed she was a prostitute.

There was stiffness in the air. Nobody seemed to dare even blink as they all wanted to hear what followed. The Le Gros family were not overly surprised, as they knew how young foreign girls could be taken in and used up in European cities. They had wished they could help in that area before they got into fostering but they preferred to go into helping younger children. Mrs Osagie feigned shock, then scowled, muttering 'she was sleeping around before she travelled abroad.'

As far as she was concerned, she only made it international. Her bringing home a white husband was a proof of her promiscuity.

Too many others there, they were like people who dreamed. The mother of the president openly admitting having been a whore was painful to hear. Iyobo's three brothers were numb. This bit felt like a nightmare revelation.

Iyobo had talked about it for hours with Scott and he had advised that she knew Nigerians better than he did, so she should do what she believed would bring stability to their daughter's life.

'Please can my old teacher, Mr Unugboro come forward?' Iyobo called out to a further surprise of all her guests.

'Point of correction, please. I am now Dr Unugboro,' he said.

'I am sorry sir,' Iyobo said, forcing a smile. Iyobo recalled she heard from her brothers that Mr Unugboro had resigned as soon as he heard what happened to Iyobo and left the village as a way of protesting against parents who didn't allow their daughters to go to school. With the support of his wife, he went back to school to do a Teachers' Graduate Two Certificate at Esigie College, Abudu, before proceeding to the College of Education, Abraka, his home town. After that, he worked for two years before going to the University of Ibadan for a degree and a Masters degree in Child Psychology. He had been teaching at the college of education in Warri and at the same time doing a part time PhD degree at the University of Lagos. Just this year, he earned a doctorate degree specialising in Child Education.

'I am very sorry sir. I didn't know you were now a doctor. We haven't had time to chat. I am very proud of you, sir.'

'It's alright. I'm happy to see you again.'

Iyobo ignored and continued with her speech, taking a random look at a paper she held in her hand.

'Dr Unugboro, who was then my primary six teacher along with my headmaster at the time, who, I was told passed away a few years ago, went to my father to beg him to send me to school. I had passed the Federal Government College for Girls and was the best in the common entrance and interview. This did not encourage my father. His mind was made up saying education was not meant for females. He argued that when they got pregnant, they ended up in the man's house and that was all the money wasted. I was determined to go to school. I begged my mother to speak to a female friend of hers at the time to take me as a house girl.'

Mrs Osagie moved her legs and adjusted her big "Buba" blouse.

'She was quite kind to me and she helped me to satisfy my ambition of getting into a secondary school,' Iyobo continued. Mrs Osagie heaved a sigh and then focused on her with four folded fingers against her chin, waiting for the worst to come.

'She took me in but didn't quite know what I was doing when she wasn't there. She was a normal trader who had no time to do anything else except to go from one village market to the other selling and buying goods. I was very good to her children though,' Iyobo remembered.

'Unfortunately, she didn't know me. She thought I was promiscuous because I got pregnant, something she told my parents.

'I am not here to defend myself, I can assure you,' she affirmed as she took time to look at the points she jotted on the paper in front of her.

'I thank her because she gave me a chance to taste school life when I was very hungry for it. I got to class four in the secondary school and was looking forward to completing my secondary education when the unexpected happened,' Iyobo continued.

'One night, I sneaked out of the house to visit a young boy whose sister I had met during the common entrance exam. I was so fascinated by the way this girl was dressed that I begged my mother to buy me beautiful clothes so as to dress up like her. We couldn't afford that kind of life but Mum bought me a pair of plastic shoes which I wore for the interview.'

Everybody in the room forced laughter.

'Two years later, I saw a young boy who I recognised to be the brother of this same girl I had so admired. According to him, he had been looking for me because he was swept off his feet by the outstanding results I got at the interview. He had learnt from the teachers I was the best in the entrance and the interview and felt bad that I couldn't get into school while those who performed worse had got in. This young man was as ambitious as I was.'

For the first time since they all assembled in the room, Iyobo looked in the direction of Fosa and burst out crying uncontrollably. She saw the sudden frown on Fosa's face and his uncomfortable shifting on his seat, which suggested to her that he was very confused. Scott quickly got up, walked towards his wife and held her tight, whispering in her ears words of assurance and wiping her tears. Fosa held a handkerchief and was also crying uncontrollably, flanked by people Iyobo believed were his mother, his sister and his wife. She wasn't sure who the other woman was but guessed it might be her mother's sister since they appeared to be similar in age. She concluded the youngest one who probably was in her twenties was Fosa's daughter. She recognised Fosa as soon as he walked in. She also recognised his sister. She didn't know his mother as she never had a chance to meet her when it all happened.

'I was only sixteen years old and Fosa was eighteen at the time. He was very kind and passionate. He spoke to me in a way no one else had spoken to me before. Even though we were both young, I sensed he respected me as a person despite the difference in social class. He came from an affluent family and had big dreams of becoming an astronaut. I was a village girl who had dreams of becoming a doctor but wasn't sure how to achieve those dreams.'

Iyobo took another look at Fosa and then at his sister. She wiped her tears again and looked at Amenze.

'My dear daughter Amenze, I am sorry I didn't go into details with you. I didn't want to upset the beautiful life the Le Gros family were moulding for you.'

Iyobo saw Amenze, from the corner of her eyes as she looked down but wasn't crying. She knew her daughter had been taught in school that leaders must always read the mood of the public and respond accordingly. She had heard all that over and over again from her daughter. On this occasion, a second glance at Amenze made her believe she was in utter confusion. Iyobo tried to read her daughter's mind. Could it be that she wanted this to be done in a more private manner, most probably just mother, daughter and biological father present? Iyobo knew her daughter would have flung herself on the floor and cried, hugged and kissed them both. She couldn't do that here. At this point, Iyobo looked towards Fosa. She tried to imagine what he would be thinking about. Would he be thinking of coming forward to hug Amenze and then, herself? She realised he was wiping tears from his face.

'The sad thing was that Fosa didn't know I was pregnant,' Iyobo continued.

'I didn't want him to know because I knew how committed he was to achieving his goals, and I didn't want to destroy that for him. Aside from that, I just didn't know what to do. I kept everything hidden from him and changed my route to the school to make it more difficult for him to find me.'

Iyobo heard the noise from Fosa blowing his nose. This was so loudly done that everyone turned to look at him. Iyobo gave him an obvious stare. Their eyes met, Iyobo looked away, blinking three times, her eyes resting on an elderly woman she was convinced was Fosa's mother. Iyobo wondered how all these things happened without his mother's knowledge. She then briefly remembered Musa, the gateman and the money Fosa gave to him to silence him the night she came to their house.

'What I did with Fosa was a one off. I didn't know much about reproduction. I was simply carried away, as my father had prophesied. When Mrs Osagie found out I was pregnant, she did what most African women would do in such a situation. I was threatened to be disgraced. She said she would go back to the village to proclaim it in the village market that I was a disgrace to the family and the entire community. I left that night. In my desperate search for help and a place to sleep, I was picked up by a human trafficker.'

Itota got up and cried aloud. Nobody comforted her. Her three sons looked at their only sister and wept quietly.

'That was the beginning of my woes. You must not forget that I was pregnant. If I had told them I was pregnant, I would have been killed. They took me to a house where they had forced me to stay to be part of the sex trade. When my captors were not looking, I escaped into a country whose language I did not speak. I ran to a catholic church where I met a reverend sister. Fortunately for me, Sister Debbie spoke English and so I could communicate with her. I fell on my knees to beg her to help me. She did. I was taken to hospital. I was also given a room in the convent. The Belgian government allowed me stay in Belgium on humanitarian grounds since I was a minor. That was where Amenze was born. I took care of her until she was two and half years old. I knew the traffickers were serious, as I had seen what had happened to stubborn girls. When they found me again, I had no choice. I had given up everything but didn't want my daughter to go through what I had gone through. There was a time I was told I could register in an office where good families could help me by fostering Amenze.'

Iyobo looked in the direction of her daughter.

'If Amenze had lived with me, she wouldn't have been what she turned out to be. She lived with some very special people. Please, I would like all of you here to stand and with respect, clap. It was Pierre and Lieve Le Gros who did everything possible to raise Amenze till she was ten years old. While with them, after they had noticed that she was very intelligent, they ensured she attended a school for the gifted and talented in Brussels.'

The Le Gros family remained pensive. All others in the room including Amenze stood up and clapped. Ogidi remained seated, leaning his chin on his beaded right hand.

'While in the shared accommodation I was given to care for my daughter, I received threat letters from the Madam I had been sold to. Basically, the man who picked me up from the street pretended to be a good Samaritan while in essence, he was out most nights picking up girls who he then sold out to trolleys. These women paid heavily hoping to get their money back by forcing the girls into prostitution. Apparently, they were threatening my family with all sorts of things. I was horrified. One day, I saw a heavily-built man in my room, not knowing how he got there. I tried to scream but he warned me to be quiet. Something I didn't understand prevented him from hurting me,' Iyobo was tense, laying emphasis on each word, as she watched Itota stand up and raise her two hands to the sky shouting 'Praise the Lord,' then she sat down.

'He told me he had been paid to kill me but he would not do that because he had a sister who he loved so much and wouldn't want anyone to hurt her. He looked at me closely and as he was walking out, he was picked by the police. He went to jail. I don't know what happened afterwards.'

'After that, I was convinced by one of my flat mates to go back to the brothel as I would be safer there. I did. That was when I became a prostitute. The trade was deadly. I was once beaten and left for dead. I was exposed to all types of hazards and dangers. I continued becuase I had to pay my Madam as well as get my brothers off the streets where they were becoming beggars. I took care of my mother who was thrown out by my father because of what I had done. I was afraid, ashamed and constantly felt guilty,' she dared to look up but made no eye contact with anyone.

'But I was rescued,' Iyobo smiled as she spoke.

'I was invited to a church by someone who lived in the same brothel. I received Jesus into my life as my personal Lord and Saviour. He did many things for me. I was forgiven for my sins and through me, all the other prostitutes in that house, except one, quit the trade and followed Jesus. God sorted them out one by one, as they all came to love and trust Him. Help came to me through a pastor and his wife I met while I was sharing the gospel. Bless them. They became my parents.

'For the first time in my entire life, I was happy. God sent a man in the most extraordinary way to deliver me. Scott, my husband here, was the man who delivered me. He paid off the money I owed the Madam and rented a small apartment for me. He didn't propose marriage to me then, according to him, he was just helping me.'

Scott held Iyobo very tight and whispered his love and support in her ear.

'He also gave his life to Christ. He was happy, served the church but soon disappeared. No one heard from him as he told no one where he was going. I didn't know where he lived and so I couldn't look for him. He didn't give me his telephone number because he didn't want any contact with me apart from the help he had been offering. I understood.'

A tear dropped from one of Iyobo's eyes and Scott caught it with a tissue he had.

'He reappeared several months later and proposed to me. Since then, he has looked after Amenze as his own daughter. He has been her father. She went to the best schools and achieved great results because Scott and I continued what the Le Gros family had started,' Iyobo stopped for a minute. Only the clock was heard ticking. She spoke again only when she was ready. 'This is a good time. Please let us reconcile and forget about the past. I pray that no other person would go through all I went through.'

'Amen,' they all shouted.

For the first time, Iyobo looked directly to Ogidi, her father, who was now leaning heavily on a walking stick.

'Dad, I am sure you are proud of your granddaughter today. You can now see that what a man can do, a woman can also do. I do not blame you at all. That was all you knew at the time,' Iyobo paused.

Ogidi struggled to stand up and came forward.

'My daughter, Iyobo. I gave you that name. I gave you that name because I wanted you to come and be the helper of your brothers.

I wanted you to come and relieve your mother of all her troubles. But I see that I did things wrongly. I am openly asking you and the entire family including these Europeans who have helped and rescued you and your daughter from wicked people. Please all of you must forgive me as I didn't know any better,' Ogidi stopped and faced Itota who was looking elsewhere when he stood up to talk.

'I especially apologise to you, Itota for all the troubles I caused when I heard Iyobo was pregnant in an irresponsible manner. It's not that I didn't love you both but that was the only way I could prove to the community that I –' Ogidi choked on his tears. He remembered a Bini saying that says that 'a man never cries; only his eyes get red'. He pursed his lips and looked aimlessly on the ground.

'That's ok. Am happy it's over now,' said Iyobo.

Fosa and his family quickly joined Amenze despite the forbidding face of the aide de corps. Father and daughter spoke for the first time.

'My daughter.'

'Hello, sir,' Amenze said, courteously bending a knee as she had been taught by Iyobo. Fosa took no notice of that. He hugged her, crying while Iyobo stood motionless fighting a storm of emotions.

Fosa introduced his mother, his wife and his daughter to the presidential candidate who formally greeted them. She promised she would visit them very soon. Fosa now went to the Le Gros family, hugged and thanked them. He also went to Iyobo's mum bowing down. He finally went to Scott and Iyobo who remained glued to each other. As soon as Scott saw Fosa coming towards them, he let his wife go. Fosa shook hands with Scott and thanked him for having been a good father.

'She is still very beautiful,' he thought, hugging her and letting her go almost immediately while Scott looked very closely on.

'You went through all that? I looked everywhere for you. I didn't know you were pregnant.'

'How then did you know about Amenze's aspiration?

'I followed the stories in the papers'

'By the way, where is your father? And where is Musa?' asked Iyobo.

'Dad passed away last year and Musa went back home to Kano state,' Fosa stammered to explain, as he was taken out of his train of thoughts.

'Ok, honey, you need to rest now. Remember Paul and Peter are all by themselves in the hotel,' Scott said with a strange Scottish accent as if not wanting the retired General to understand what he was saying.

'Sure honey. Just a minute,' Iyobo said softly to Scott, with a wink that made Scott smile a bit sheepishly.

'Oh you have other children?'

'Yes. Two boys.'

'I have one daughter,' pointing to the youngest of the four that came with him.

'Yes, I can see she looks like you. Amenze kind of looks like her.'

'Yes, well they are sisters,' he said smiling.

Scott pretended not to be listening to their conversation. However, he stayed very close until Iyobo said goodbye to Fosa.

The meeting was finally dismissed with a prayer led by Scott. That night, Amen and Silver, along with her aides, travelled back to Abuja. Amenze was happy that the controversial issue about her birth and upbringing had been finally brought to a close. She had an election to concentrate on and was fully armed to do so.

CHAPTER 65

Amen's mind was made up to give the talk tonight. There was no turning back. Everything seemed to be playing against her. First, she was a woman, second, she was a single woman. And worst of all, a single woman who aspired to break the glass ceiling and become the first female president was a prostitute's daughter, who didn't know her father. Worse yet, the man she called "father" was a white man. All these factors raised controversy.

'This was the one who picked her up from the gutters, while her mum went about her trade,' she was surprised to read in one of the tabloids.

After the family meeting, she was more armed than ever to fight the good fight of politics.

As Amen reflected on every word that was meant to frustrate her out of the presidential race, she remembered the words of a preacher she listened to when she and her mother were invited by a friend to a church called the *Heilbron Kerk van die Herr* in Holland. The Pastor said something Amenze recalled for the first time.

'Yes. Yes. That's it,' she finally heaved a sigh of relief, 'that is the solution to all the whimpering that's been going on around me.' she whispered victoriously to herself. She wondered why she hadn't seen it before now.

Pastor Klass Hollander said that the way to dispel an evil report in the minds of the people is to shout it out by yourself. After shouting out what they accuse you of, you condemn it at once and then ask for forgiveness if you are guilty. In her case, she doesn't feel guilty but she was ready to do exactly as the Dutch Pastor said.

The stage was set on the exact same spot where Professor Luki-do had delivered his speech sometime ago. Emma, her best friend and close political adviser quickly slotted in her own piece, 'Listen, Amen, people have seen your good works and sympathy towards them. They will think twice and certainly vote for you. Professor Luke is looking for dignity but you are offering food, medicine and shelter to the people. They will certainly prefer your package no matter how filthy your outstretched arms are, what matters is the heart. The heart never fails. People may see the hands, but they feel heart,' she said sounding a bit philosophical, unsure of what Amen had in mind to say to the people, whose minds had been clouded by the venomous speaches of Professor Lukido.

Amenze took to the podium. Without a preambule, she started.

'Yes, my mother was a prostitute. She was a prostitute who had a dream.' As soon as Amen saw the ideas pouring in cease-lessly, she knew this was the right time to get rid of her Goliath, once and for all.

She then got a pink book, a special diary where she kept very important speeches, opened it and continued, 'A prostitute who needed to save people, my people. Your people. They were sick, in pain, hungry. Mum had a choice. Stay with them which could shorten the life of their overburdened mother and then watch her brothers become street beggars as is often the case for the poor handicapped people in our midst. The alternative was to go to school so as to be able to change their situation. Mum chose the latter but unfortunately, things didn't work out according to her plans. We condemn them as soon as they are born. No effective shelter, no money for healthy meals, no appropriate clothing. We send them on to the streets to beg. People look down on them before offering them a coin,' Amenze looked up to see if she was gaining momentum among the crowded listeners. She noticed their gaze was glued to her mouth.

'No government of this great nation has brought about a permanent solution to the plight of beggars. I mean beggars who are forced into the streets because they have nowhere else to turn. You turn the destitute into beggars. My mother felt it in her bones. She escaped the horror of what she was to see her brothers become. Denied education simply because she was a girl, denied of a place in a federal government school because of the circumstance of her birth, denied human dignity because she was poor and sent to a home in the town thinking she could get an education, she was turned into a slave. Her hunger to study and fear for a decaying future turned her towards those she felt could encourage her. You turn the destitute into beggars and children into slaves because you do not know what they go through. You are satisfied with what you inherited from your parents and grandparents. You turn away those who inherit nothing. They become your slaves and clap for you. You dance and dance and think you are the best. No, you are not. You are just not the best.

'Where were you when a beautiful ambitious little 16 year old left the country instead of being in the classroom? Did you notice this or report it to the police? What did the police do? Nothing. Like you, they stand idly by while your beautiful intelligent young girls are turned into prostitutes. You turned my beautiful lovely intelligent and innocent mother into a detestable whore because you have nothing to lose. Yes you have. I am the product of what you set up. Take me for what I am. Fortunately, I was not a victim of such a circumstance. My mother made sure that I had a better life than she did. I was not the whore I have been accused of being, I grew up with the love and care of a foster family who cared enough to let me know my mother. A woman who found the strength to move away from the situation life had pushed on her, she found love, she married and she gave me everything, all the opportunities she was denied. Now, I have come to rescue those of you who have been caged by your political ignorance.

'Think about that. You ask, how have I done this? By your policies! Your manifestos have no standing, no base, no content. It's all watery wash. Lies to cover the fact that my opponents cannot meet or beat me in a fair fight of policies.

'I am not here to defend a prostitute; I am here to oppose prostitution. I am here to say to young women, put on your clothes and let us fight for what is rightfully ours! Our forefathers fought for it and we have a right to it, in full measure. We've been the toy for too long. We can be soiled no longer. Now, it's time to do it right. If you are being pushed into prostitution against your will, then say so. We've pointed fingers enough at each other. It's time to identify the real criminals.

'I am 35 years old and my mum is 51. Think about that. What I am today was her dream. Even as a prostitute, her dream did not die. She quit prostitution as soon as she could. She did not allow what you did to her to consume her. She forgave her father and built him a house in the village. She made sure her three brothers got an education and today, the three of them are independent, leading better lives. She has forgiven the society who did not look after her the way she deserved, by sending me to you to rescue those who might be heading towards the direction she was forced to take.'

As Amenze spoke, tears rolled down her cheeks. Emma handed her a handkerchief, which she quickly took as her face was already blinded by the outpouring. She was now able to take a good look at her audience. She suddenly realised they were all quiet and seemed to be meditating on her every word. Some were wiping their faces. She was beginning to feel very uncomfortable under the *gele* tied tightly around her head, she had only started to wear one for the sake of politics rather than convenience. The inconvenience of her clothes was nothing compared to the chunk of words that suffocated her chest. She had lots to share, but had to be careful. She was taught in school to release ideas based on reactions from an audience. She would, bit by bit, but she didn't want to say things that would push them into gossiping rather than thinking of the motives behind those words. She coughed three times, intentionally. It was to attract the attention of her audience.

'Just think about this,' she continued, 'a 12 year old girl was the best pupil in a village of about three hundred children of her age. She hid from her dad with the help of her teacher to study. She took an exam in the big city and was the best. The best were those who attended federal government college. She couldn't go. Her father vowed she would never go to school because girls often brought shame to their families in the villages if they went to town. Yet, there was no school to attend in the village. She accepted being a house girl to a woman who paid her nothing just for the promise of being sent to school.

'Like many young girls, she fell for a young boy who seemed to possess all she had spent her life dreaming about. Her fantasy for him landed her into trouble. She got pregnant and that threatened to take her life. An opportunity came up to run away from the situation, as well as try to save others who would in future be in her painful position. She didn't know what was going to happen in Europe, but she dealt with it when it did happen.

'How I hated to be tagged the daughter of a prostitute. This has been the ugliest time of my life. I would have preferred it be buried in the oblivion of the past. My opponent went all out to uncover my history. He failed to mention that I attended a school for the gifted and talented. Only the best attended that school. The best there did not necessarily mean the richest or the most privileged so, I was able to get in despite the 'flaws' my opponent would have you believe in. I also studied in Oxford and maintained my dignity. My mum supported me all the way. She cleaned and scrubbed night and day to see me through. I owe it all to her.' Amenze wiped another tear.

'In her eyes, I see love, I see tenderness and compassion. I see the willingness of a woman who planned and dreamt of doing so much, but felt she did nothing. For me, I have long known all that she has done for me. First, she did not throw me away when I was the worst burden to her. She felt responsible for the upkeep of her three lame brothers and her mum and even her dad who made things much harder for her in the years of her struggle. She found the most civilized way to take care of me. She sent me to a foster home where I was treated like a princess.

'Mum didn't want to become a prostitute, she wanted to become a medical doctor. She wanted to help others. Her quest and strong drive to succeed, was haunted by the disregard of an awkward father that drove her into what she is condemned for today. I love my mother from the bottom of my heart and no one can change that,' she paused.

'Mum once told me our case was like that of David and Solomon in the Bible, except that she felt less loved by God when she was growing up, whereas David was anointed to be king from a very young age. God loved David so very much that He even called him the apple of his eye. Despite this strong relationship David had with God, he was not allowed to build God's temple. God told him his hands were full of blood. However, Solomon the young lad born through murder and adultery was qualified according to God's standard to build the temple. Solomon had very special traits that other children didn't have. "God," mum told me, "has chosen you to do what I would have done,"' Amenze said, holding back tears.

'I would like to conclude my speech by saying this, do not cast your vote because of the circumstance of my birth but rather because of the contents of my heart. I have heard my opponent also say that I should not be allowed to contest for the post of president since I was not born in this country. I do have a dual nationality and Nigeria is certainly my country of origin. There is nothing in the Nigerian constitution to suggest my illegibility to be President. I love my country so much that I deserted the comfort of a good job and a safe home in the UK. I came to this country for the first time aged eighteen. It was the best birthday gift mum ever gave to me. I knew I would be back as soon as I finished my studies and I did that despite wonderful job offers in the most prestigious law firms in the world.

'I know it is rather unusual to see a woman on a podium like this vying for the position of president. Do not be deceived. If you believe I can deliver the package, then give me your vote. You will be shocked at what you will see. One thing I have promised is to see Nigeria included as a first world country. This seems impossible. Today, many of you will begin with me a journey of belief but I assure you, a new day of hope will emerge.

'First get the truth into your heads by learning about what is right and wrong, then get it into your heart by actually believing and responding to it as being right and wrong and, finally, you need your hands to live out what you have learnt and believed.'

The crowd responded to Amen's speech with a great shout raining and pouring without stopping.

CHAPTER 66

'I do solemnly swear by the Federal Republic of Nigeria to be loyal and faithful to this great nation. I shall speak the truth and nothing but the truth, so help me God.'

With the new vice president, Yusuf, standing by her right hand side and the new defence minister Air Marshal Admiral Adejo Magaji at her left hand side, Amenze was sworn in.

It was a day to remember in the history of the nation. There was so much to be done. So many things had happened. The world seemed to have turned upside down.

'Who would have thought that a black man would be the president of the most powerful nation in the world? In the same way, who would have thought that a woman, would become a president in Nigeria?' said Alhaji Umar, one of the senior political advisers to President Amenze.

'The bottom line is that the present world is very active and people are becoming more aware of the fact that the one who is able to do it should do it. It's called meritocracy, the ideal that isn't seen much in the real world. This is the right politics,' Yusuf said.

Pierre and Lieve Le Gros and Scott and Iyobo MacDonald were there watching. Paul and Peter sat right in front of their parents on the special seats reserved for family and close friends. There were many Oxford graduates who attended. Amenze was shocked when Anne William called from Brentwood to say that she would be attending. She was the church youth leader when she was attending grammar school in Brentwood, England. Amenze just couldn't understand how all these people she knew and met at different points of her life, built her up to have the confidence and strength she needed to become the leader of a great nation. Silver had mixed feelings at the proclamation of his fiance as President of Nigeria. He was worried about the fact that he would have to wait yet another four years before they could eventually get married. He had given Amenze his word and there was no going back. Silver, being an only child had been under immense pressure to settle down and raise children. He had told his parents he would wait to marry the woman he loved. Silver had heard his mother, who at the beginning got along well with Amenze, now calling her names, such as selfish, and at one point, read aloud to her son what the papers were writing about Iyobo. Silver was already sick of his mother calculating how old Amenze would be when they got married, how she would be beyond the best childbearing age.

Silver refused to give in to any form of blackmail from his mother. On the other hand, he saw his dad as more composed and understanding. Each time Silver dropped by to say hello, he simply whispered 'I am praying for you my son.'

These few words stuck more to Silver's heart than the million words spoken by his mother.

Quite recently, Silver went to functions Amenze invited him to, with his parents. This was another time Silver's mother wanted to be close again to Amenze whom she started referring to as her daughter-in-law-to-be. Now that Silver had become the most important person in the country after his fiancée, it was easy to win every member of the family to himself as they all saw this as an opportunity not to be missed to be a part of the ruling class.

❖ ❖ ❖

The first challenge was to bring a reliable electricity supply to the nation as that would bring in many more business opportunities to individuals and companies. The president and the vice saw this as a major challenge.

Day in day out, they examined why other presidents had failed even though they were honestly working hard to bring about constant power. They went to the 1959 plan which was laid out by the colonial masters up till the last regime. They saw that there was possibility for the country to have a reliable flow of power if they were all committed and free from corruption.

President Amenze and Vice President Yusuf put their heads together to figure out a long lasting solution for the power problem in the nation. They soon identified three of their Oxford friends who were now electrical engineers.

'That's the advantage of attending a good school. You come across the best of the best,' Yusuf breathed out.

'You can say that again,' Amenze hailed back.

While at Oxford, the three Greek students and friends of Amenze were sent from Athens on full scholarship. They were the brains behind their nation's power success for years. They went to Oxford for their PhDs. These guys were electrical wizards. They had long gone back to their country to continue to work.

Amen invited Philemon Herodotus, Pierro Laestrygones and Julius Damaskenos to Abuja. They all sat with the Greek engineers trying to work out a solution to the country's number one problem. Their follow up on the matter was tremendous. Abuja was the first to receive a steady electrical supply. This slowly went to other states. Once this started, even the rural communities received electricity. As this took hold, the economy grew astronomically. However, what sustained this new revolution was the elimination of all forms of corruption.

Amen's second focus was to tackle corruption from grassroots level. To achieve this, she was instrumental in drawing up a plan whereby secondary school children would be taught that bad practices and consequences of corruption were poison to the nation. She said it was important for kids from a very early age to know what this meant to a nation, as a whole. A sweet given to a child on the play ground to beat up another kid was a way to explain manipulation to them at an early age, she explained.

If there was no corruption, people could concentrate more on their own bit of the work and do it effectively. The constitution on corruption was reviewed and stronger penalties introduced.

CHAPTER 67

"Who gives this woman to be married to this man?" said Bishop Kayode looking in the direction of Scott and Amenze.

Scott and Pierre Le Gros stepped out, according to the wishes of Amenze.

"I do!" came a very loud distressed voice. With a sudden intake of breath, all the guests turned to see who put a halt to proceedings. A man walked in wearing the uniform of a General in the Air Force. He was followed by an elderly woman and another woman that was probably a couple of years younger.

'I am the father of the bride. My name is General Fosa Odigie. I am the biological ...'

'True enough,' said Scott, 'then come here and join us. We have all played one role or the other in Amenze's life."

'Mais Ben,' Pierre said, shrugging his shoulders, raising a hand to shake Fosa.

'You have both done all I should have done by raising my daughter a lot better than I could have. I will remain grateful to you all the days of my life,' Fosa said, giving a strong military salute to the two white men. Scott's eyes met Pierre's and they both sighed, as they turned to Amenze and Silver. Amenze looked down while Silver watched the General with a concealed smile. There were sporadic claps around the room with guests looking and trying to understand what exactly was going on. There was then a sudden silence in the whole room until Scott broke the silence:

'Come on, Mr Odigie, let's get on. We will talk later."

'Who gives this woman to be married to this man??' Bishop Kayode raised his voice above the whispers of the men. He looked at the three fathers and one daughter in front of him. The three men chorused,

'We do.'

Amenze looked at all the men through her veil, one after the other. She smiled at Pierre and then at Scott and they both happily smiled back. When she got to Fosa, her smile made way for a slight frown. Fosa's head dropped as Amenze took a short step closer to Silver, clinging to him.

'I Silver, take you Amenze to be my wedded wife. To have and to hold, from this day forward, for better, for worse, for richer, for poorer, in sickness or in health, to love and to cherish, till death do us part. And hereto I pledge you my faithfulness.

'I Amenze, take you Silver to be my wedded husband. To have and to hold, from this day forward, for better, for worse, for richer, for poorer, in sickness or in health, to love and to cherish till death do us part. And hereto I pledge you my faithfulness.

'Mr Silver Omogiate and Miss Amenze Odigie-Macdonald today are hereby joined together in holy matrimony.'

Bishop Kayode announced to the congregation.

Amenze noticed Fosa's face lightened up at the mention of Odigie, his family name. It didn't matter that the same name had been used all through presidency, as he was never close to any of the ceremonies. Amenze was happy she kept that name, thanks to the Le Gros family, who took delight in keeping the true identity of the children they fostered. It didn't matter the position the name appeared, it gave her an indication of where exactly she came from, at least it helped in her presidential campaign when her opponents argued she was European. For the first time, it dawned fully on Amenze she was taking up another identity as a married woman. She would drop her double surnames to take one.

Amenze was excited as it was the name of a man who'd waited in patience and love for her to be ready for this day for more than twenty years. Even though most people saw it as selfishness on her part, she saw it as victory. She saw it as victory of accomplishment and dignity. And as for children, she had resolved to do what she had learnt to do all the years amidst turbulence, that was to pray and believe that God was ever smiling on her. 'I think God is very proud of me today and of course, He will give me any gift I ask of Him' Amenze lightly thought.

'Now, let us welcome Mr and Mrs Omogiate to the house!'

Amenze smiled deeply and she fixed her eyes on Silver's as he took away her transparent veil, both smiling and gazing at each other's eyes. When they both looked around, the three men were gone.

Amenze later looked at the congregation and saw that her three fathers were sitting with her two mothers in the congregation. Madame Le Gros and Iyobo were dressed in the same African attire as were Pierre and Scott. Even though Fosa later sat with them along with his wife, daughter and mother, Amenze noticed he didn't really fit in as a full part of the family. Amenze noticed that Iyobo was the happiest among them as she got up at the slightest opportunity with a broad smile and gestures to show she was in charge.

After the procession, Amenze was picked up by Silver. Locked up in his arms, they made way for pictures outside. Laughter and cheers filled the air while the choir sang.

CHAPTER 68

Iyobo and Scott stayed behind in Benin to have a meeting with Bishop and Pastor Madeleine Dosa, who were Pastors of the Church of God, they were to share ideas on how to assist pregnant young girls and their children. The MacDonald's had gone to seek spiritual advice from these people of faith they had been hearing about for a long time.

This meeting led to the *Yobo Foundation* which was commissioned a year later. The Dosas were there to bless and pray for the project which they believed was worth every effort put in it. Several dignitaries were there and a branch of this foundation was inaugurated in every corner of the country. President Amenze was supportive of everything which the foundation stood for, the defence of women and children's right.

At the meeting with the Dosa family, Scott also discussed possibility of setting up a branch of the Church of God in Stirling, his home town. He planned to resign from his bank job and become a full time minister. Pastor Madeleine Dosa travelled all the way to Scotland to grace the occasion. The Pastors of Church of God, Glasgow and Edinburgh were also very supportive. This church worked hand in hand with the Baptist church in Stirling.

Scott and Iyobo both became full time Pastors of the Gospel under the Church of God, whose headquarter was in Benin City, Nigeria. Their church thrived. Their Church became known as the Restoration Centre focused on winning over people from the red light districts in big cities to Christ. They travelled to many capital cities in the world, from Amsterdam through Mumbai to Warsaw and then to Zurich. It was shocking to find that most stories Iyobo heard from the women were so like hers. It didn't matter the colour or nationalities. During these crusades, several people across the nations visited by the McDonalds surrendered their lives to Jesus Christ, who they believed forgave all sins, no matter the magnitude.

It was most rewarding for the McDonalds to learn of all the changes that had taken place in the lives of the people they had had contact with.

Madam V, Iyobo's ex-Madam, who suffered a strange and incurable disease, gave her life to Christ during a healing crusade in Brussels where she was miraculously cured. She received Jesus into her life and had been looking for Iyobo to testify. She heard that Iyobo was in town and decided to go and look for her. Iyobo was contacted by Itota that the "ex-trolley" was looking for her.

Iyobo left the hotel room to wait for Madam V at her mum's house. Scott stayed away to take care of the boys. Itota left her house when she knew Madam V was coming, saying she didn't want to set her eyes on the woman ever again.

Madam V confessed that when she later learnt that at the time Iyobo was being trafficked, she was pregnant of the present president, she felt worse than a monster. She bent down on her knees before her victim and wept sorely.

'That baby that was in my womb is now the president of our great nation,' Iyobo rubbed it in.

Madame V could not look at Iyobo's face for a full five minutes. She only wept, head down, sitting on the floor.

'I was a murderer. I can see this is what we deprive humanity of when we embark on such an inhuman trade. I am grateful I came soon enough to Jesus not to die in my sins and go to hell to continue with my punishment,' the sixty-five year old said amid tears of joy and sadness.

'There is hope for everyone. Somehow, there lies a second chance for everybody and only the wise quickly grab the opportunity like you and I did.'

Iyobo looked at her overly bleached face now turned green despite the layers of make-up meant to disguise it.

'Sister Victoria, get up please. Sit on the sofa. Sit here with me. I love you very much,' Iyobo finally invited.

'Thank you, my dear,' Victoria said, wiping tears from her face.

Iyobo watched her take her seat and suddenly remembered the hired assassin this woman had sent to take her life. If he had succeeded, they wouldn't have been celebrating life today. 'All because Jesus cared for me,' she thought, her lips echoing the words.

'Yes, you are right. All because Jesus cared for me too,' sister Victoria picked up without knowing what had just gone through Iyobo's mind.

'I love you very much, Sister Victoria. I want to see many trolleys come to Jesus as you did. They must know there is salvation through the blood of the Son of God. He forgives all sins and gives us a new beginning and provides for us in a more dignified way if we honestly surrender to Him.'

'Tell me that again. Who would have thought that I, despite all I have done, would be left to die by my family in a specialist hospital after building mansions and buying expensive cars for them. I sponsored my younger siblings for expensive shopping sprees for their weddings and paid their children's school fees in expensive private schools, anywhere they chose in the world. Look at me today. I am sixty-five years old. No child of my own. You won't believe that my mother, I mean my own mother confessed that she did some voodoo to prevent me from getting married so as to keep me pouring money on her and my sibblings. That was how far it went,' Sister Victoria stated.

Iyobo remembered how much her own mother tried to dissuade her from marrying Scott. She then continued to listen to Sister Victoria.

'It was a friend who "stole" me at night to attend a Christian crusade that was held at a school compound down somewhere around Mission Road. Iyobo, this man carried me like a baby. I was already wasted and there was no life left in me. My family members stopped coming to see me and they were enjoying all that I spent my useless years labouring for,' Sister Victoria stopped for a while. She wiped her face with a part of the wrapper she was tying around her waist and then continued.

'Iyobo, my darling. Life is not what we see now. It's about what we become later. If you do things with the love of God, even if you are poor, you are respected by God and man. Do you know I only started getting better when I listened to the message of Jesus? The Pastor did not even call anybody out to be prayed for. I can still remember the scripture he quoted from the platform. Even though I was too weak to get up, I heard it. It was first John chapter five verse four,' Sister Victoria quickly got a Bible from her handbag. She went for her glasses and opened up the passage. It was obvious she had been spending a lot of time exploring the book she carried with her everywhere.

'For whatsoever is born of God overcomes the world and this is the victory that overcomes the world, even our faith,' she read pronoucung each word clearly. She closed the Bible and laid it aside on the centre table right in front of them.

'After repeating the sinners' prayer led by the pastor, he assured us we were born again and qualified to receive anything from God. We were given free Bibles and a daily devotional. When I was taken back to the hospital, I was still weak in my body but I was strong on the inside. Right on my bed, I managed to open the scripture that sank into my spirit and started praying everyday to God, repeating the same scripture. I read the daily devotional and prayed, regretting all the bad I had done until peace fully came to me. I called the names of all the girls I had trafficked, one by one. There were some, I couldn't remember their names and I told God I didn't remember their names. I started to pray for them to be set free wherever they were. I knew God forgave me because I had absolute peace. The sort of peace mentioned in em eem Ephesians chapter four verse six. That sort of peace could only come from God. A week after I attended the crusade, I was shocked, I was getting better and better. I could sit to eat and the doctors and nurses were shocked at the sudden progress. Look Iyobo, I couldn't believe what was happening to me. I kept confessing God's word. I only spoke the word of God they advised me to speak. I read it all out aloud until I could say some without looking at the Bible. If the doctor spoke to me, I replied with the word. If the nurses asked me any question, I replied with the word. Rumour got home that I was getting better and my sister dropped by one day to check. As I am talking now, all my brothers and sisters are born again. My doctor and a few of the nurses also gave their lives to Christ. Only Jesus can save.'

'Oh, Sister Victoria, I can see you went through a lot. Thank God we all came out of the wicked way the Devil mapped out for us. Today, we are free to live and free to love.

'If I may ask, where is Uncle James now? Remember the man who sold me to you?'

'Oh yes, I know who you mean. To be honest, I sincerely believe that someone must have been praying for all of us. You knew the Lord before us. I believe God answered your prayers concerning us. James was arrested and given a ten year sentence. He was actually my boyfriend then. He was in charge of shopping around for any vulnerable girl and connecting them to me. Whatever profit came out of it, I gave him a certain percentage. Around that time, something came over me and I wasn't giving him his real share of the money. He was planning how to eliminate me since I was breaking the deal we had made. He was caught right in the very act. The jury also found him guilty for other trafficking offenses. The miracle was that while in jail, James came across a girl in the female side of the prison during their monthly joint fellowship programme. Her name was Marleen. She was sentenced to five years imprisonment for bank fraud. The truth was that she was innocent of the offence. She happened to have signed a cheque without properly looking at it. This girl kind of knew God a bit before going to the prison. While there, she read the Bible most of the time and became really strong in the things of God. The authorities kind of trusted her and allowed her and a few other ladies to go to the men's side alongside the Church of God Prison Minister who came regularly to preach and to pray for them. James received the word and was born again. He became the leader of the Male Bible study group. Marleen soon came out and set up a church called the Truth Ministry.

'Marleen and James still kept in contact even though James was still in prison. He came out five years after Marleen and they got married. You can't believe they both tour the world now, preaching the gospel. They have two children,' Sister Victoria finally concluded. 'I don't know how to explain the things of God. I think what matters is that people should be honest when they come to Him. He will bless them as if they never sinned. The problem is that people find it hard to believe this truth you and I are witnesses to. Some may even think we made up all the stories. Who will be eating from a dustbin when you are convinced you are a child of the king. Nobody. This is the crux of the matter. Getting people to know the truth about what and how the Almighty God feels about us is hard. Only the Holy Spirit can do it.'

'What a story of victory. You are right,' Iyobo agreed. 'I was earnestly praying for all of you. Of all the hookers in the brothel at the time, only one person did not come to the Lord. Maimu was the last to surrender her life to Christ. First, she was amazed at my transformation and saw no more good in being a hooker. She then sought God herself and according to her, discovered Jesus is the way, the truth and the life. She still sometimes visits me in Stirling. We now talk about how to make the world a better place. Her daughter and her mother have long joined her in Belgium. The person who didn't fully come to the Lord was Florence. She was actually the daughter of a pastor who didn't listen to her parents. She enjoyed following us to church and seemed to find all we did as normal. Nothing really moved her like it moved the rest of us. Most of us had never had the opportunity to hear the gospel and she was born in it. I thought she didn't quite value what she had. I was shocked when I heard her name on the news. She had been arrested in Asia for drug trafficking. She is now pleading against the death penalty. Scott and I have spent time praying for her.'

'I still can't believe she was a pastor's daughter. She was recruited by one of my friends who loved her so much because she was very faithful in paying her money back. By the way, I heard that, my friend, who brought Florence died of the very disease I was cured of,' Sister Victoria quickly added.

'Who are we to judge others when we ourselves barely escaped? Come on sister, let us break bread and celebrate. We are blessed. We are alive and we are well,' Iyobo said jumping up off her seat.

'I vow to pray for as many people as possible who were in my business. Just as God heard your prayers and brought me out, He will hear my prayers and bring them out so that we can live in a world free from slavery and human trafficking.'

'Amen, in Jesus' name,' Sister Victoria said with hands lifted up high and eyes closed.

As the two women spoke and praised God, the phone rang.

'Mum, it's me Amenze.'

'Oh glory to God. I was telling your father today I had not heard from you for a long time.'

'Which of my fathers mum?' Amenze started an annoying laughter.

'This is not funny. Amenze. How are you?'

'I am doing very well. It's good to be at home for family life. I only attend party meetings and I come back home. That's not why I am calling.' Amenze hesitated.

'Are you alright my daughter?'

'Mum, I am pregnant with twins. We decided not to tell anybody before now because we wanted to be sure. It's actually four months now.'

Iyobo congratulated her daughter and when she put the handset back down, she ran towards the kitchen, unsure of what to do next. She danced round the house while her ex Madam joined in. She quickly called Scott who was in Ghana on an evangelical trip. Iyobo also called Paul and Peter who were in the boarding school at Eton grammar school in the United Kingdom. Iyobo spoke with Peter who ran to tell Paul that they would soon become uncles.

Iyobo called her daughter back.

'Hello?'

'Mum, their names are Pierre and Lieve, I have been talking with the Le Gros family and they said they would be here to take care of their grandchildren when they are born. You know what mum, the Bible says all things are possible to those who believe.'

'That's right,' Iyobo said, nodding her head. 'Say it to your children when they are born and do not forget to tell them to also pass it on to their own children,' Iyobo said with a heartfelt laughter as she reacted to the laughter she heard from the other side of the line.

THE END

HERZ FÜR AUTOREN A HEART FOR AUTHORS À L'ÉCOUTE DES AUTEURS MIA ΚΑΡΔΙΑ ΓΙΑ ΣΥΓΓΡ
ΡΤΑ FÖR FÖRFATTARE UN CORAZÓN POR LOS AUTORES YAZARLARIMIZA GÖNÜL VERELIM SZÍ
RE PER AUTORI ET HJERTE FOR FORFATTERE EEN HART VOOR SCHRIJVERS TEMOS OS AUTO
ZÖINKÉRT SERCE DLA AUTORÓW EIN HERZ FÜR AUTOREN A HEART FOR AUTHORS À L'ÉCOU
ACÃO ВСЕЙ ДУШОЙ К АВТОРАМ ETT HJÄRTA FÖR FÖRFATTARE Á LA ESCUCHA DE LOS AUTOI
AUTEURS MIA ΚΑΡΔΙΑ ΓΙΑ ΣΥΓΓΡΑΦΕΙΣ UN CUORE PER AUTORI ET HJERTE FOR FORFATTERE EEN
ARLARIMIZA GÖ ZÖINKÉRT SERCE DLA AUTORÓW EIN HERZ FÜF
OR SCHRIJ ACÃO ВСЕЙ ДУШОЙ К АВТОРАМ ETT HJÄRTA FÖ

The author

Evelyn Ogbebor Iguisi was born in Benin City, Nigeria. While lecturing at the University of Benin, Nigeria, she met her husband who was a Research Fellow at the Institute for Research on Intercultural Cooperation at the University of Maastricht, Holland. She became a young mother while studying for a Ph.D. degree in Belgium at the University of Brussels. She later became the publisher of AFRIFAME magazine, published in English and French.

Having relocated to the United Kingdom, she went to the University of Nottingham for a post graduate certificate in Education. She has been teaching French and German in a Language College in Essex, England. The Sin of the Mother is based on information Evelyn has gathered over a long period of time and says "She has depended entirely on the master teacher of all, The Holy Spirit who is polishing her every day on her art of telling stories."

The publisher

He who stops being better stops being good.

This is the motto of novum publishing, and our focus is on finding new manuscripts, publishing them and offering long-term support to the authors.
Our publishing house was founded in 1997, and since then it has become THE expert for new authors and has won numerous awards.

Our editorial team will peruse each manuscript within a few weeks free of charge and without obligation.

You will find more information about novum publishing and our books on the internet:

www.novum-publishing.co.uk